ON *MISTRESS IN TH...*

"I recommend...*Mistress In The Making* to anyone who enjoys **electric passion, witty humor, and a beautiful love story!**"
Reading Rebel Reviews

"...**funny and well written** and I can't wait to read more of this author's books. **Highly recommended reads and definitely keepers!**"
Five-Star UK Reviewer

"Sweet and Spicy!!! **Such a gem!** I fell in love with Daniel and Thea – when it came to the end, I wanted more! I've found **with every story Mrs. Lyons writes, I'm left with a smile.**"
Krysta Reviews, on *Seductive Silence*

"Mostly Epistolary, **All Wicked Delight.** I absolutely **adore this author's writing style,** as she imbues it with so much humor that it is **a sheer delight to read...**"
Five Star Reviewer Jamie, on *Lusty Letters*

"A beautiful ending. **This book completed the series in such a lovely way.** I have other books by Larissa Lyons and **I love her style of writing. This is a series I highly recommend.**"
Crystal, a Vine Voice Five-Star Review on *Daring Declarations*

ON LARISSA'S OTHER FUN AND SEXY
REGENCIES...

"**Witty, Enchanting and Roaring Hot!**
I think I've found a new author to binge! I would definitely
recommend it as a good gateway book to shape-shifters or to
lovers of historical romance."
Five-Star Review on *Ensnared by Innocence*

"I love the fact this is **shifter and regency** all rolled into one...
I was amazed by the storyline and couldn't help how
addictive I found this text...**I loved the originality of this**
book and thought it really stood out for many reasons...
A true talent for writing..."
Five-Star Review on *Ensnared by Innocence*

Miss Isabella Thaws a Frosty Lord named first in The Romance
Bloke's list of **Best Historical Romance Novels** to read in
2021.

Lady Scandal awarded the Golden Nib! "I can't praise this
book enough. Regency fans, if you like gorgeous wit in with
your devilishly superb, well written, sexy reading matter,
Lady Scandal should be on your 'Must Read' list."
Natalie, Miz Love & Crew Love's Books

Top Pick from ARe Café: "[*Lady Scandal*] is the most
flirtatious, sensual, and delectable treat." *Lady Rhyleigh, ARe*
Café ~ Selected as a **Recommended Read!**

MISTRESS IN THE MAKING

FUN AND STEAMY REGENCY ROMANCE

LARISSA LYONS

LARISSA'S BOOKLIST

Historicals by Larissa Lyons

ROARING ROGUES REGENCY SHIFTERS

Ensnared by Innocence

Deceived by Desire (2022)

Tamed by Temptation (TBA)

MISTRESS IN THE MAKING series (Complete)

Seductive Silence

Lusty Letters

Daring Declarations

FUN & SEXY REGENCY ROMANCE

Lady Scandal

A SWEETLY SPICY REGENCY

Miss Isabella Thaws a Frosty Lord

CONTENTS

Proofread by Judy Zweifel at Judy's Proofreading; Copy edits by ELF at elewkfl@yahoo.com; Edited by Elizabeth St. John; Cover by Literary Madness

At Literary Madness, our goal is to create a book free of typos. If you notice anything amiss, we're happy to fix it. litmadness@yahoo.com

This series is dedicated to anyone who has difficulty speaking up for themselves. May you find a way to be heard.

And for my dear Mr. Lyons who's always requesting another Regency; here you go, you spectacular man. (Sorry I don't enjoy housework and cleaning the kitchen as much as I do escaping to 1815.)

I

SEDUCTIVE SILENCE

He listened in perfect silence. She wished him to speak, but he would not.

— JANE AUSTEN, *EMMA*

1

THE MISTRESS CONUNDRUM

My mistress' eyes are nothing like the sun;
If hairs be wires, black wires grow on her head.
I have seen roses damask, red and white,
But no such roses see I in her cheeks;
And in some perfumes is there more delight
Than in the breath that from my mistress reeks.

William Shakespeare, "Sonnet CXXX"

———————◦∞◦———————

LONDON, 1815

"'THAN IN THE b-breath that from my mistress reeks.'" Daniel Holbrook, the fourth Marquis of Tremayne, repeated the last few words with a grim smile.

"Reeks is right," he muttered beneath his breath (breath that most assuredly did *not* reek of onions as that of his former mistress often had). He crumpled the topmost page off the stack he'd liberated from a desk drawer and tossed it over his shoulder.

When it bounced against the window coverings and crinkled to the floor, a curious sort of satisfaction threatened to dissipate his gloom. With great zeal, he balled up more of the filled pages that had been languishing in his desk ever since her ill-fated demand.

Poems. Stupid poems.

Said *former* mistress had begged him to memorize and recite poetic verse to her. Though he'd—wisely—refrained from succumbing to her urging, Shakespeare's 130 had been the only sonnet to remotely tempt him into performing.

Thinking of her likely response to his stumbling recital, assuming she perceived the intended slight and took affront, a real laugh emerged. Cy huffed a surprised bark at the sound, the first Daniel had heard from his faithful, snoozing companion since the damnable rain had caused man and beast to retreat to the safety of his study. Now, with drapes drawn and fire roaring, he sought to forget the downpour lashing the house and the dark memories apt to drown him.

He'd only taken to cleaning *out* his desk in order to avoid what resided *on* it—an advertisement he'd saved and Penry's unanswered note: *Are you still planning to attend the festivities this eve? Lest you forget, you already agreed.*

Ahhh, the "festivities". Amorous festivities, no doubt.

Was he going to attend?

Daniel didn't rightly know. He fingered his bruised jaw, working it from side to side. The swelling had gone down to the point he didn't think he'd terrify a potential inamorata with his battered visage. But what if he did?

Mayhap 'twould be a good thing—scare off any candidates *before* he opened his mouth.

Was replacing the reeking Louise really something that had to be done tonight?

Just to hear the potentially uplifting crackle, he hefted several bunched-up poetic missiles overhead into the burgundy drapes. Cy gave a curious sniff, his languid gaze following one paper ball when it rolled drunkenly toward him.

Louise. Sometimes he'd thought marbles resided in her upper garret. But he'd tolerated her less-than-desirable qualities in exchange for the ones he did like. Most notably, her mouth.

Fact was, despite her off-putting fondness for onions, he'd often found her mouth worthy of appreciation (if not its very own sonnet), for she typically kept it open and active, chattering about everything yet saying nothing. He could spend two nights a week in her company and only be called upon to utter a handful of sentences per fortnight.

Add her lack of expectation for meaningful conversation to her lusty fervor for lovemaking and was it any wonder he'd made her his mistress a decade ago at the absurd age of twenty-one?

His long nap complete, Cy stretched and sauntered over, placing his ugly mug on the desk until he received the expected scratch behind his ears, then thanking his master with a sloppy bark. Daniel blotted the ever-present drool with the handkerchief he kept at the ready. He'd rescued the one-eyed mangy mongrel, now plump on doggie pudding and old age, when he'd caught the scarecrow of a pup being whipped for making off with the baker's meat pasties. A coin flipped in his direction persuaded the baker to turn over the dog. A meat pasty in Daniel's outstretched hand persuaded the frightened animal to follow.

It might have taken several years and several hundred hours to win the canine's trust, but Daniel had accomplished the deed, and gladly. He had no use for those who beat others, whether they had four legs or two.

Cyclops gave a hearty whine and pushed past Daniel to nuzzle the drapes aside where he promptly pressed his nose to the windowpane, the unrelenting storm on the other side making a hash of the view.

Daniel frowned at the grey sky. *I know, mate. I detest this weather too.*

But he detested more the dance necessary to find a new mistress. Waltzing the pretty and paying glib compliments to secure a warm and willing body in his bed might prove to be his undoing. Of a certainty, contemplating it posed significantly more pain than Penry's lightning jab, else he would have seen the task done before now.

Gad. Ten weeks.

His head clunked forward into his waiting hands. Ten blighted weeks equating to seventy long nights he'd palmed his staff rather than find another ladybird to do the job for him.

He scrubbed at his hair as though the friction would lessen the growing tension centered in his groin. Blast. If he chuffed his pipe any more frequently, he'd likely yank the thing off.

The momentary ease such release brought was just that— a few seconds' respite from urges growing ever more insistent. A surging morning erection growing ever more persistent. "I need a woman."

"Well, aren't you the fortunate one?" A decidedly feminine voice jerked his head upright. "Just as you call out to the universe, I present myself in all my wilted glory."

Raking his hair into some semblance of order, Daniel skewered his sister with a glare. He hated being caught unawares.

Beyond the glass panes Cy had revealed, rain drizzled

freely and her fashionable attire did the same. The once pristine walking dress, made of the palest cream French cambric and complete with intricately fringed hem, was topped off with a fur-trimmed spencer in what was supposed to be a coordinating spring green. Wet, it looked more like something Cyclops had cast up after emptying one of Daniel's snuff boxes.

What a decline for the costly toggery (he should know; he'd paid enough for it when she'd spied the plate in *Ackermann's* and pleaded with him to have it made up). Evaluating it now, he doubted the finely woven cambric would ever return to its former, undrizzled-upon glory.

The delicate, coordinating parasol he'd commissioned as a surprise had obviously been a waste of his blunt—it was bound up tight, *unused*. Everything else dripped and sagged. Her once-new bonnet, her dark blond hair beneath. And the spencer's fur trim? "You have a...dead ferret strangling your neck. What b-brings you here this fine spring...day?"

And damn him for remembering so much about ladies' stylish apparel. Useless information, now that he'd seen his precious Elizabeth matched in a happy union.

All smiles and sunshine despite her disastrous, dripping attire, she swept toward him, pointing that conspicuously dry parasol his direction. "Ridicule all you want. It won't do any good. I'm in a lovely state of mind and have no intention of allowing anything to alter it."

She paused to scratch Cy beneath his chin when he bounded toward her. "And aren't you the most remarkable boy?" Her shining eyes found Daniel's. "Sometimes I forget how good he looks. In my mind, he's still the scrawny bag of bones you described in your letters." Elizabeth had only been in town a short while. Married in the country last fall, she'd spent the time since living on her husband's estate and the majority of time before chained to their father's.

When Cy began snuffing at her hand, Elizabeth laughed and returned her attention to the dog. "I do apologize, Sir Cyclops, but I don't have any treats. Ann's in the kitchen"—she mentioned her lady's maid—"I wager she'll sneak you a dollop of whatever's to be had."

"What he needs. Mmm—" Surprised rather than frustrated when his lips unexpectedly stuck together, Daniel faked a cough into his fist, and then finished, "More food."

Ignoring the scowl in his voice, Elizabeth ushered the dog toward the door and asked one of the hovering footmen to escort Cyclops downstairs.

An identical pair, his footmen were, twins he'd picked up years ago when they were but mere lads engaged in pilfering pockets on the dirty streets of London. One named John, the other James. Only James went by "Buttons", a childhood nickname Daniel knew he'd butcher. B's might not be as bad as D's, but they were close, so he'd renamed the boy "*Swift* John" the day they'd met and to this day called him thus.

While Swift John watched with a knowing grin, Elizabeth whispered something to John before relinquishing the dog into his care. Daniel suspected she went to the trouble because her maid was sweet on John rather than any real desire to see the dog off.

Her matchmaking duties done, she whirled round and came in. "Thank you, Buttons," she said as his remaining footman moved to close the door behind her. Wasting no time, she marched straight to the curtains behind his desk and hauled them open.

The metal rings clacking along the rod sounded like gunfire and Daniel barely masked his wince. But he needn't have bothered. She was busy gathering up the crushed pages and, after seeing the lyrical lines Louise had penned upon them, tossing the whole lot into the rubbish bin.

"What have you been up to? Providing Cyclops new toys

to chase after?" Her tidying efforts complete, she straightened and grinned, her brown gaze fairly shimmering with joy. "Rain or no, it's too glorious a day to shroud yourself up like this."

Coming up beside him, she relinquished the frilly parasol and placed it square on his desk—still spring green, he idly noted, and not the muddy color of Cy's snuff-induced cascade as was the rest of her gown. Next she took off her bonnet, the silk flowers planted among lace and pintucking every bit as wilted and bedraggled as the rest of her. "And I can't believe you'd waste the fuel on a fire, as muggy as it is outside. Don't tell me my big brother is turning into an old maid?"

Granted, along with everyone else he'd been enjoying the unusually mild week, but all that changed with the latest deluge that chilled the air, and his soul. Avoiding the topic—something he excelled at—he plucked at the parasol's dangling fringe, as arid as a desert, and gave her sopping dress a speaking glance. "Useful item."

"Stop that." She slapped his hand away and smoothed the fringe. "It's my very favorite, as you well know. I tucked it under my dress so it wouldn't get wet."

"Ah now." Recalling how he'd just mangled the sound, he took a slow breath before continuing. "Makes...total sense. And the reason for your visit?"

He was curious what would bring her out in such weather. Not that he wasn't pleased to see her. The one member of his immediate family who still drew breath. More than that, the one member who'd never betrayed him—either in fact or by dying too damn soon.

With her customary composure, his sister took possession of the leather chair flanking his desk and evaluated him as one might a captured butterfly. Her brows drew into a frown. "Why is half your face a veritable bevy of purple and green?"

"Half?" He barely refrained from fingering his lip. The

new scab over the old scar had dropped off two days ago. "Ellie, surely you em...bellish."

"Not by much," she muttered. "Covered in whiskers, it still shines through." She rose and approached him. "I fear 'tis becoming unseemly, Daniel, this fascination you have for sporting rainbows." Elizabeth turned his head with gentle fingers to inspect the worst of it. Lips pursed, she released him to rummage in the reticule dangling from her wrist. "When will you realize you no longer need to prove yourself?"

When I stop hiding in here every time it rains.

Hiding in his study, where his mechanical pursuits provided the solace nature denied him. He glanced over at one apparatus in particular and felt a grimace tighten his cheeks. When they worked, that was.

"Silence. I should have known. Your answer to everything unpleasant."

Daniel glanced back at Elizabeth. His bad memories weren't to be laid at her doorstep. Neither was his sour mood. "If I recite p-p-*po*-etry, will you smile?"

That got a laugh from her. "The day you recite poetry is the day I juggle torches standing on my head."

"Unlit ones, I hope." Relieved he could still smile, he suffered through the application of the lotion she'd pulled from her bag. She was always slathering him with some concoction or other "to help with the bruising and aid healing".

He should be grateful, but the stuff put him in mind of an apothecary. Nose wrinkling by the time she finished, Daniel jerked his head back. "What's in there? Smells like a harem."

Elizabeth stumbled in her efforts to screw the lid on. "A harem? My, where your mind veers..." Jar sealed, she slid it across his desk in between stacks of yet-to-be-crumbled-and-discarded pitiful poetry.

"I tried a different blend this time," she admitted without meeting his gaze.

What else had she chopped and crushed and stirred in there? "Ellie?"

"I think it smells rather lovely."

He sniffed again and frowned. There was more to it than that, over and above the smell. "Out with it."

"Oh, very well." A tiny huff and she finally met his gaze. "If you must know, I added a wee bit of honeysuckle. For hope."

"And?" Although, by now, he was almost past caring. His face felt better than it had since the practice round that landed such a fierce chop to his jaw. He was even starting to like the scent—a little light and fluffy for his tastes to be sure, but it did have a spicy undercurrent, a bit of zest.

"Clovesforlove," she said in one breath.

"Huh?"

"Cloves. To attract love."

"Ellie." His sister and her potions. Romantic whimsy, her and her "spells" for happiness—usually his. But she stood there, looking at him so earnestly, so drippingly—and his face felt so damn comfortable—that all he did was tuck the jar into his newly cleared desk drawer. "Thank you."

Her witchy rescue cream accepted, she resumed her seat and fixed him with one of her sunny smiles. "Surely you can cultivate an interest in something *other* than smashing your face into your friends' fists?"

Daniel's eyes again veered toward the orrery collection occupying the bulk of his study. Nothing gave him greater satisfaction than tinkering with the mechanics of the planetarium models he'd collected. But his satisfaction had dimmed considerably since resurrecting and repairing (or attempting to) the pinnacle of all the models he'd amassed: the one originally owned by his grandfather. The one, despite his every effort, he couldn't get to operate properly. Not on his own.

He had an interest other than boxing, dammit—he just didn't know how to pursue it. Not without branding himself a simpleton.

"Daniel," Elizabeth called his attention back to her. "Why can you not find a hobby that doesn't involve being at daggers drawn or going at loggerheads several times a week?"

Feeling instantly defensive, and uncertain why, he sputtered, "I like to bu-bu—" Blast it! He couldn't even get out a simple three letter word: *box*. A fast exhalation and he spit out, "Like sparring."

"You like beating things to a pulp and proving how strong you are."

A pulp? Talk about embellishing!

So he enjoyed a few rounds of pugilistic endeavors every week. Could he help it if he was adept at fighting? If the exhilaration he got from firing off punches and having onlookers cheer him on helped sustain him through the silent—and solitary—hours of his life?

He didn't have to talk in the ring. Wasn't expected to wax eloquent at the boxing academy. Didn't have to jabber over inane comments that in reality meant nothing. All he had to do was strip off his shirt, strap on his gloves—when he and his sparring partners agreed to them—and let his fists talk for him.

It was the one place he could be around his peers without fearing coming across as weak.

"Men!" A decidedly feminine lift of one shoulder accompanied that pronouncement. "Why you cannot all find tamer amusements closer to home that satisfy your manly urges, I'll never comprehend."

What? Had she been reading his mind?

"What's this?" She noticed the advertisement he'd cut out

announcing Mr. Taft's visit to London and presentation on orreries.

Something Daniel had been debating whether or not to attend. "A lecture I'd like t-to hear."

"On what?" She turned the page toward her, then flicked it away with a smile. "Orreries. I should have known. Go. I daresay it'll be a good experience for you." Her gaze drifted across the room. "Have you fixed it yet?"

His scowl answered for him.

"Then go. Learn who else shares your interest. Possibly get Grandfather's machine running again." She gave his face an arch look. "A much better pastime than fighting, if you ask me."

Before he could respond, the bright smile slid from her face. "Daniel. I came because I needed to see how you got on." Her gaze flicked over to the window behind him, then she focused on his face. Her beautiful eyes were somber, sadder than they should be. "I know where your mind tends to dwell on days such as this."

He wondered whether she knew he was expecting her husband. That he had other, even more pressuring, topics on his mind. As always, when in the company of anyone save Cyclops, he carefully considered his words before he spoke. "Meeting someone shortly. 'T-tis what snares my attention."

Well, that and Penry's note.

"Oh, posh." She dismissed his excuse. "No one ever calls this early." Elizabeth rose and gripped his clenched fists. He hadn't realized his fingers were tangled until she applied herself to unknotting them. "When shall you forget all he did?"

He didn't need named, nor the incident in question. They both knew what had transpired that long ago rainy afternoon. Elizabeth had been so young, Daniel marveled that she still remembered.

God knew he'd never forget. After all this time, it wasn't what their sire did that haunted Daniel; it was what he'd said.

'Twas barely a year after his twin brother died; David's sudden absence leaving a gaping hole in young Daniel's life. He'd just seen Robert, his older brother, and their dear mother put in the ground. A child of nine should've been allowed to grieve. But that would have been a luxury in the presence of his austere parent. A parent who had just found Daniel and his sister crying in their mother's abandoned morning room and who quickly made his displeasure known.

Craven bastard. Stop cowering like a whipped cur! It's only a little blood. Father had turned from him then and wiped his riding crop clean while leaving the blood to dry on his only remaining son's face.

"Daniel."

The sound came from far off, far away from the memories gripping him. *Not a day goes by I don't wish you'd expired instead of them. Sodding Fate—took me wife and real sons and left me a useless cripple! The revered Tremayne title, going to a bloody idiot—it makes me sick.*

"B-but, Father," he'd stammered, as he had for years, "you du-du-don't mean—"

Damn imbecile! His sire had rounded on him, crop slashing toward his head for another strike. *You are dead to me, do you hear? Dead to me!* The blows fell swift and accurate, piercing his heart and shredding confidence more than skin, slicing will more than flesh. *Dead! To! Me! Some fiendish plot of Satan may have saddled me with his stuttering spawn, but you will not speak in my home. Ever, ever again!*

Warm fingers plied at his neckcloth, stroked his cheeks. "Daniel. Come back to me, dearest. Daniel!"

The terror receded under the heartfelt pleas of his beloved sister. His arm came round her, and Daniel was startled to find himself standing in the middle of his study with no recollection of having moved there.

"Ah, Ellie, I am... Fine." When she would have gone on smothering him, he pulled her hands down and set her away. "Fine now, thanks to-to-to you."

She gripped his wrist when he tried to escape toward his desk. "What has happened?" Her grasp tightened and she forced him to face her. "What has changed? You've not —not..."

Humiliated, he spun from her hold to finish bitterly, "Not acted the madman?"

"You are not and never were," she cried. "And that wasn't what I meant to say!"

"Acted the-stupid-clunch?" Without thought or intent, the words rushed out, angry bullets peppering the air. "Buffle-headed-chaw-bacon-nnnnnn—" *Noddy!* If his tongue hadn't glued itself to the roof of his mouth, who knew how long he might have gone on spewing self-directed insults? Insults he'd heard time and again from both Robert and his father.

"Not *retreated*." Elizabeth said it as though he'd gone on a mere vacation, a weekend sojourn, when in fact he knew the lapses frightened her. Damned if they didn't frighten him too. Which probably explained, if not excused, his anger. It had been years since he'd lost the present like that, fled inside himself to escape the taunts. "You've not retreated in so very long. Why now? What has happened?"

"I've not been sleeping well," he admitted, startled when the truth slid from his tongue with such ease. "Not sleeping much at all. Not since pa-pa-parting ways with Louise and— D-damn me! I should not have said *that* to you."

Red crept over her sun-tinted features, rendering her as cherry bright as one of the tomatoes she grew with such pride. "Daniel," Elizabeth chided, and he saw how she busied her hands arranging the folds of her dampened skirt in order to avoid his gaze, "lest you forget, I am a married woman now. I daresay you may speak of your...your paramours without any fear of censure from me."

Bemused by her attempt at sophistication, he was nevertheless taken aback when she added, "As to that, if you cannot sleep for the lack, though how one could miss that coarse wretch I cannot fathom, then why not simply find another?"

A single time, well before her own recent marriage, Elizabeth had visited London and stumbled upon him and Louise during one of their rare public outings. A new Egyptian exhibit had opened and apparently both women had fancied seeing a mummified cat. Likely the *only* thing his sister and former mistress shared in common, given how Elizabeth possessed elegance and sweetness and the most tender of hearts, qualities the self-serving, sometimes crude, always lusty Louise could never hope to attain.

"You'd recommend I find another coarse wretch t-to warm my bed?" He didn't try to halt his chuckle at her look of outrage.

"Never that, you wicked fiend!" She swept up her frilly parasol and playfully swatted his shoulder with the side. "You are the best of men and deserve only the best of women. Louise could never be that for you and I'm relieved you finally saw it. I do think it's time you found a wife though. Someone to love—"

"A wife? I think not." He cut her off by snaring the pointy end of her parasol. It might not be one of her hair ribbons he'd filched but it would do. He set off, tugging her round the room as he had when they were younger, swerving between furniture, orreries on display and book-lined walls as he steered her toward the exit. The subject of a wife was not one he chose to contemplate, not today. Especially when he'd yet to respond to Penry's note. "Let me amuse myself with at least one fine mistress 'ere I fall upon the bu-bu-*blade* of the parson's mousetrap."

By design, they'd reached the door of his study. Daniel nudged it open and waved for the remaining footman to summon her maid from the kitchens before he turned back to Elizabeth, who frowned up at him.

"What?" he asked, their laughing trek around the room loosening his tongue. "And why are you shredding me with that affronted look? I cannot indulge in a bit of b-bachelor fare before I am no longer one?"

"'Tis not that. 'Tis—"

"Ah. Tremayne." The masculine voice interrupted whatever she'd planned to say. "Your good man Rumsley told me to come right up and here I find you entertaining my lady wife."

A grin broke free and Daniel released the parasol to take the outstretched hand of his brother-in-law. "Wylde. You made it." An hour overdue. And looking a mite haggard. Odd, that. "Glad to see the latest storm d-d-"—*didn't*, dammit —"failed to carry you off."

"Wylde." Her demeanor subdued, Elizabeth gave her husband a deferential curtsy.

"My lady." Wylde's bow was just as restrained. "I did not expect to find you here."

The formal greeting between the pair wasn't anything unusual. Nor was the flush on her cheeks—Elizabeth pinkened over the slightest provocation. But the sudden anger glinting from her expression? The hard clench of Wylde's jaw when he addressed her? His unpolished appearance, coat buttons askew? Those were definite surprises.

"And I did not realize visiting my brother was disallowed."

Daniel's brows flew skyward at that. It wasn't his place to inquire into the married lives of others but still... "Is all well... between you?"

Elizabeth flashed teeth and eyes at him. Hazel eyes that shimmered with unshed emotion. "Lovely. And now, I'm off. The house does not run itself you know. Oh wait." She cast a cutting look toward her husband. "It does! How juvenile of me to forget."

With an uncharacteristic flounce, she whirled toward the stairs.

"Pardon me," Wylde said swiftly. "I need a word with my wife." He sped across the landing. "Elizabeth!"

Backing into his study, Daniel left the door ajar so he could observe. Trusted friend or not, if Wylde was mistreating Elizabeth, Daniel wouldn't stand for it. But though he witnessed a heated exchange, one that lasted well beyond a "moment", and though he hated the growing look of horror on his sister's face the more Wylde talked—low murmurs indistinguishable at this distance—Daniel couldn't miss the passionate kiss his friend bestowed on her or the powerful way Wylde captured his wife when, at its conclusion, she would've tumbled down the stairs.

Neither could he miss how Wylde ensured she found her balance, then stood stoically with nary a flinch when she steadied herself and delivered a stinging slap to his cheek. One that rang louder than any syllable of their exchange.

Whatever convoluted emotions presently ruled his sister's marriage, the steely look of determination on Wylde's face as he watched his wife calmly descend the stairs, the man's rigid stance only easing once she was safely on level ground, boded well for an eventual reconciliation. Or so Daniel hoped.

What was that all about?

He retreated to his desk, a mahogany monstrosity he rather favored, and assumed The Pose, the one he'd perfected after analyzing how it made his father so intimidating.

What in blazes was going on with his normally refined

friend? The man was always in twig, never such a shabba-roon. Saved from being a dandy by his posture and bearing alone, Wylde spent an inordinate amount of time on his grooming—but not today. Mayhap his valet had quit, belea-guered by the stringent demands of his employer? Daniel's lips quirked at the thought. Wylde had to dress himself and that was why he was late?

An inch or so shorter than Daniel, Wylde nevertheless often appeared taller, being more leanly built. But though the brushed-back dark hair was typically styled to Byronic perfection, today it had the look of stress and sleep.

Wylde returned to the study and shut the door to prying ears. When he turned, Daniel pounced. Arms spread wide, fingertips perched on the surface, upper body inflated and bowed forward, head leading the charge, he roughly inquired, "Wylde? Is there something you want...to...tell me?"

The imprint of fingers flared bright on his friend's surpris-ingly stubbled cheek. "Nay."

Daniel bristled and abandoned the stupid pose to stand. Once the din made by his chair toppling behind him died to an echo, he growled, "T-try again."

A sardonic lift to his lips, Wylde nodded once. "I may not *want* to tell you anything, but I am *willing* to tell you this: I chose Elizabeth for my bride. Despite what she may claim to the contrary, it is not a decision I regret." Wylde brought one hand up to his cheek, the first acknowledgment Daniel had seen of the impetuous slap. "Although, judging by what you just witnessed and I'm still enjoying"—he fingered the reddened skin—"she derides my methods, I assure you I only seek to garner a satisfying and enjoyable union between us."

Which all sounded well and good but told him positively nothing. "That is all you care...to say?"

"It is."

If there was one thing Daniel had taught himself, it was

the art of silence. He employed it now. Occupying himself setting his chair to rights and settling his frame, casually, back into it, he quietly bided his time.

Wylde was here to get something from him—a political issue wasting away in committee he wanted brought to a vote and sought support for, according to the impassioned note he'd sent round yesterday. In fact, he'd requested the ultimate sacrifice: for Daniel to speak—*voluntarily*—in public.

Hell, his prized orrery languished, broken, because he couldn't face a roomful of mechanically minded men discussing their solar system miniatures with relish and great delight, not without revealing himself as a cork-brain the first time he tried to join in, yet Wylde wanted him to make verbose on a topic he could legitimately profess ennui over?

He'd sooner show an asteroid his arse.

Since true friendship was worth personal sacrifice, he'd consider granting the favor. But, gad, the thought of it made his flesh crawl with syllable-spewing maggots.

Before they discussed it further, Daniel expected answers. Ones that explained the strife he'd just witnessed. Perhaps accounted for Wylde's unheard-of appearance.

So he held his peace. Waited.

And without a word, gained what he needed—at least in part—when Wylde, minutes sooner than Daniel had antici- pated, exploded with, "To stop you from breathing fire, because a blind man could see you're about to erupt, I'll share this—where it concerns Elizabeth, I believe she and I both want the same result, to make a go of our marriage. More than a tolerable go if I have my way, but we have decidedly different ideas on how to proceed. Thus far I've tried things her way and I don't need to tell you it hasn't proved success- ful. Now it's my turn." His decisive speech faltered to a musing, "She doesn't like to speak up much, does she? Share what's going on behind those expressive eyes? Like you in that regard but for different reasons, I gather."

Wylde was one of a select few outside his sister who knew of Daniel's ongoing difficulties. "Few" as in two—Penry being the other.

"She wasn't allowed," Daniel conceded. "Not while Father was alive." Not after their mother died. The tyrant who'd created them hadn't wanted to hear a single peep from either of his remaining offspring once the one in his image perished.

"I suspected something of the sort. Tell me—other than dirtying her hands with her prize-winning produce, what might she like? Something she's always wanted to do here in London." Wylde scrubbed one hand down his face and Daniel couldn't miss the lines testifying to sleepless nights. Seemed they had more in common than he'd suspected. "I tell you, I'm at a loss. She's decried attending every ball or soirée almost since we came to town. Afternoon carriage excursions in the park are out because she must be home for callers. Morning rides are met with a sniff because the abandoned patch of garden needs to be readied for planting and heaven forfend she trust one of the servants to do it for her."

"A sniff? That...does not sound like Ellie." Especially considering how much she loved to ride.

"Laugh not over my husbandly peril, for I tell you I've tried everything I can conceive." Wylde took an impatient step forward, made a fist and slammed it into the opposite palm. "We got on well enough in the country, by blazes! It's only since our return to London that she's turned up stiff."

"Theater?"

"She declined that as well." And the exhalation following that admission said more than words that Wylde had neared the end of his tether. "Have you any other ideas? Any at all? I refuse to strip to skin and prance naked through the furrows she's creating but I fear 'tis coming to that."

The fist landed on Daniel's desk this time. "Stop laughing, damn you! My marriage is not a jest."

Nay, but the thought of his fastidious friend frolicking in the dirt—in his altogether—was. "Hold." Daniel raised his hand, asking for time.

After several moments' silent contemplation, he suggested, "The opera."

"She's already refused."

"T-take her anyway."

Once, when they were children and their parents returned from an evening out, not long before their mother and Robert died, Daniel and four-year-old Elizabeth had watched from behind the balustrade on the second landing, their stuffy older brother off on his own. When Mama had waved to them behind Father's back as he loudly proclaimed he'd never again waste his time attending another loathsome performance, the two had stifled giggles. As always, when Father grumped about, Mama attempted to pacify the ogre, her sincere words complimenting the singers and majestic show drifting sweetly up the stairs and causing little Ellie to vow in a whisper, "I declare, the op'ra must be the most splendid thing in the whole world."

"Aye," he'd agreed, "Mama always has loved the op-p-pera."

Then Elizabeth had turned to him and promptly asked what it was.

He laughed at the memory. Upon becoming the marquis two years ago, he'd purchased a box for the very same reason —to honor his mother. And he'd yet to use it, even once. "Take Ellie," he said now, "and use my...box." When Wylde started to protest again, Daniel sliced his arm through the air. "T-trust me. Have you attended together?"

"Nay."

"Then that is the magic you seek. Now come." A deep breath, then, "Tell me of this"—*blasted*—"issue you wish me...to speak for. What and when?" Perhaps he could manage to come down with a bang-up case of severe laryngitis on the day in question?

"Are you quite positive about the opera? Is there not something else——"

"Have you...been?" Damn. He could feel the muscles in his neck and jaw tightening with the effort to talk without faltering. And this was a casual meeting with one of his closest friends.

Aye, but it follows Elizabeth's unexpected visit and wholly unanticipated mention of marriage. It follows Penry's note, your own thoughts of taking a new mistress, two months of sporadic sleep and the worst lapse you've had in years. It also follows almost seeing your sister tumble down the stairs because a sweeping kiss knocked her off balance—or, more likely, her own reaction to said kiss.

Pah! Excuses, one and all.

How was he to get on in public without coming across as a sapskull? How would he get on *tonight*? Gad. Why could he not simply order up a fulsome wench (one whose wattles didn't hear would do nicely) to present herself in his bedchamber? Have her ply sweet words and warm fingers along his lonely shaft?

While that image might have tightened another part of his anatomy, it did relax his neck. Willing his teeth to unclench and his tongue to cooperate, he clarified, "Been together?"

"What? I'm not following you."

No surprise, as he'd bumbled about long enough. Fortunately, unlike those who sometimes tried to finish his sentences for him, Wylde had the wherewithal to wait patiently, regardless of situation or circumstance, and allow Daniel to find his own way, his own words. "The opera. Have you...with Ellie? Ever?"

"If you'll recall, this is our first joint trip to London. I've never really had the opportunity to take her much of anywhere." His face picked up a degree of animation that had been missing since his arrival. "I'd originally planned to shower her with numerous outings. I'd thought to surprise her, But that was before..." Wylde's features froze into a frustrated mask. "Never mind. Just tell me what to do."

"Trust me. Regard-d-*less* of what she claims, she wants to...go." He'd give it a few weeks and see if things turned, if Elizabeth appeared happier and not just resigned with her marriage before demanding more of an explanation. "Now. About this speech you want me to sputter through..."

"You look like a damn Scot." Wylde jumped on the new topic with relish, coming closer to sink into the very chair Elizabeth had occupied a short while ago.

A slice of sunlight beamed past Daniel's shoulder and onto his desk, bright and cheery. The clouds had moved on then, the sky clearing. Might he hope the remainder of his day was to follow? His fingers went to the bristle covering the bruise. "What of it?"

"You'll have to carve that scruff off your face before you speak."

That was the least of his concerns. "And if I...don't acquaint my jaw with the sharp edge of a razor, what then?" *Am I to be exempt from showing myself to be a bumblehead?*

Assuming the whiskers in question would be gone as advised, Wylde took several folded sheets from his pocket and slid them across the desk. "This covers the salient points and history of the matter. It also highlights what I hope you'll vocalize."

"When?"

"The vote is scheduled for next week. Tuesday afternoon, but I'll have to check to confirm the time—"

"I have plans Tuesday next."

Wylde gave a bark of laughter. "We both know you never have plans."

While that was generally the case, Daniel was tempted to shove the advertisement under Wylde's nose. So much for debating the merits of concealing his idiocy versus his desire to hear a man he respected speak on a topic he adored.

Damn. It looked as though Fate had made the decision for him.

Daniel turned to the last page Wylde had supplied and scanned the summary section. It looked like some rot about escalating crime and city patrols.

If he practiced each line a few thousand times, then maybe...

"I've kept them as succinct as I could," Wylde cajoled. "Just take your time, speak deliberately as you always do and I daresay you'll do fine. It'll be over in a trice."

"I still d-d-don't fathom why you or Harrison can't speak for this. Keep me out of it save for the vote." He could promise to show for that, surely. Though he'd inherited his father's seat on the committee along with the title, he'd yet to attend a single meeting. It appeared his cowardice had finally caught up with him.

"Except for your prowess in the ring and your long-standing association with Louise, you're an unknown. If you show up and make a case for this, I'm betting the obstinate pig-heads will listen. Besides, Harry has his hands full with the corn regulations and we both know I have no reputation to speak of."

"I wonder why," Daniel muttered with unmistakable sarcasm. It was no secret that Wylde had left two women standing at the altar. Daniel didn't know the circumstances surrounding the jilts but Ellie did. When Wylde had come sniffing after Elizabeth, once their father was gone and the proper mourning period observed, she'd demanded an explanation before agreeing to his suit. Daniel had left them alone so Wylde could make it.

"Sodding politics!" Wylde exploded. "I only volunteered to serve on this damn committee so I could gain an audience with your father and plead my case for Elizabeth's hand." *That* was news. "The lobprick squashed my hopes in that regard just as he squashed this bill time and again. And now I've come to care—"

"He chaired the commit-t-tee?"

"For years," Wylde grated out.

His father had been *against* this bill? And now Wylde was giving him a chance to *support* it? Knowing that made all the difference in the world.

Daniel waved his arm, indicating the pages Wylde had prepared. "I'll study."

As though Wylde didn't sense Daniel's capitulation, he continued trying to sway him. "I'm set to chime in the moment you've said your piece and a number of others are lined up as well, but we're still in the minority. Too many stubborn, stodgy old codgers hanging on to their old and outdated ways. But we just might be able to turn the tide this time. Every voice will count."

That's what I'm afraid of. Too bad his had betrayed him since birth.

Wylde stood. "Whatever you do, don't be late."

Daniel grimaced. Of course he was going to be late.

He was always late. One of the subtle ways he'd found to avoid people. And especially conversations.

2

TO BE OR NOT TO BE...A FALLEN
WOMAN

❦

"Ah, Mrs. Hurwell, I trust we won't be toppling into any displays today?"

Dorothea Hurwell's companion, who had followed her across the threshold in time to hear the churlish greeting, turned to the clerk manning the bookseller's entrance. "Ah, Mr. Tumson," Sarah cooed back in a sickeningly sweet voice Dorothea knew didn't bode well, "I trust we don't mean to be an obsequious toad? Especially toward someone who indulges in her love of books exclusively at your establishment?"

"Indulges?" The prissy man sniffed, giving Dorothea a nasty smirk as she struggled to close her dripping umbrella—and struggled to resist the urge to gouge the pointy end into the unsuspecting anatomy between his legs. "When she's only indulged in buying *one* book in all the time I've worked here?"

Poised as ever, Sarah efficiently closed her own umbrella without ever taking her eyes off the man. Their unusual color and shape—a stormy grey and uptilted at the outer corners— was rather captivating, and at the moment, the clerk appeared completely snared. "I was speaking of myself, for a slight to anyone I'm with cuts deeper than one aimed at me alone. And we both know I have a predilection toward collecting a positively *obscene* number of books. Now, mind you locate some manners the next time you see us or I'll see to it your subsequent task is locating another position. Are we understood?"

He blanched. "Aye, Ms. Vinehart. My apologies, Mrs. Hurwell." A politely subdued nod to each of them preceded his hasty backward retreat. Right into the downpour.

Dorothea muffled a laugh as he scrambled to circle the customer who'd just wrenched the door open against the flailing winds that had plummeted the temperature in the last hour. "Fitting," she murmured when the rude clerk faltered on the slick cobblestones. "I daresay, that's what he gets wasting time maligning me when he should have been manning the door as assigned."

"You have the right of it," her companion agreed, straightening the fingertips on her gloves. "I vow, if he had any more unwarranted airs, he'd float off like a giant balloon."

"If you'd be so kind as to bottle some of your aplomb, I do believe I'd scrape together the funds to buy it," Dorothea told her sincerely, fisting her chilled fingers in their threadbare gloves around the umbrella handle. "Thank you for coming to my defense."

Having anyone stand up for her, since her dear mother departed decades too early, was such a novelty Dorothea never failed to notice and appreciate.

"Would that it weren't necessary." That she hadn't fallen on such dire times. But alas, every day was a new opportunity

—and one step beyond the smothering silence imposed by her now-deceased spouse. She felt her lips curved in a rueful, embarrassed quirk. "Or that I could defend myself so ably."

"Think nothing of it." Sarah surveyed the ground floor of Hatchards Booksellers. The murky weather had driven a fair number of people indoors, far more than they typically saw this early in the day. "It's too crowded down here. Shall we explore the upper floors?"

Knowing that their presence in the shop was due to its convenience as a meeting place much more than either's desire to select reading material—at least this particular morn—Dorothea gave her umbrella one last shake before placing it in the bucket set aside to collect the abundance of drips. "Of a certainty, let's."

Of medium-to-short height (Dorothea always preferred to put the "medium" first), her feet traipsed up the stairway swifter than her tall friend, as she took two steps to every one of Sarah's.

Unlike most Thursdays when they casually browsed the latest offerings on the street level while speaking in hushed tones on whatever topics struck their fancy, today it wouldn't do to be overheard.

The second they reached the third floor and found a tucked-away corner, Sarah spun in place, an animated expression brightening her countenance. "There now. With prudent people staying out of this dog soup of a storm, our privacy should be assured. So tell me," she ordered, her hushed whisper barely disguising her eagerness, as she grasped Dorothea's wrist to pull her closer, "have you sufficiently considered what I proposed last week?"

At the firm pressure on the recently abused skin, Dorothea's breath hissed outward, but she managed not to betray the discomfort any other way.

"Do you not think it the most viable of solutions?" Sarah

continued, her delight palpable.

Before Dorothea could formulate a reply—she'd pondered little else!—Sarah released her wrist and liberated a napkin from her reticule. "Here, eat this." She pressed a cube of cheese into Dorothea's thinly gloved palm and popped a smaller portion into her own mouth. "Nay. I don't want to hear a single protest. Don't faint as you did last week, and that will be thanks enough."

The additional reminder of that mortifying experience was sufficient inducement, and the crumbling cheese went down as though it were the smoothest of nectars. "You are too thoughtful."

"And you are too young to be fraught with such difficulties. Now tell me—will you take the next step and come tonight?"

Take the next step and admit she couldn't care for herself? Admit she *needed* a man? A rich one, likely a titled one? A difficult task to be sure, when from Dorothea's limited experience, the male persuasion had very little to recommend it.

"Take a lover, you mean? So I can eat? Does it not seem sordid somehow?" Sordid and immoral? But Dorothea knew better than to disclose that secondary concern, given how her friend *lived* the part Dorothea was only contemplating: the part of mistress, of paid companion. Of courtesan... The part of a lover.

Strange to consider, especially for someone who had, as an adult, never felt *loved*.

"Sordid? Not at all," the elegant and older Sarah assured with complete certainty. "And you're not taking a lover for the thrill, though I do hope he'll give you plenty of those, you're taking on a *protector* if you choose to move forward. And that, my dear, is an entirely different proposition."

Grateful for the tall stacks of books waiting to be shelved in the corner they occupied, Dorothea ducked behind a rather impressive one. Reaching for the topmost book, she buried her flaming face in the open pages and allowed her gaze to fix on the lines of poetry. But she saw only a blur. Every speck of her attention was centered on the woman next to her and the illicitly intriguing idea she proposed.

If Dorothea did this, she'd become some man's mistress, possibly by morning. If she didn't, she might as well die because dramatic or not, that was where things were heading. She couldn't go much longer without regular nourishment. Not and have the strength, or will, to fight off her grabby landlord and his unsavory advances.

"I..." Dorothea swallowed the stone that had taken up residence in her throat and quickly turned another page. Still focused on the thin volume shielding her face, she said, "I believe you may have the right of it. Lord knows everything else I've tried has failed to yield results. But how does one not versed in the trade go about finding a suitable protector?" Go about *satisfying* one, she really wanted to ask.

Dorothea had no illusions about her attractions. She had no station, no dowry, no claim to any particular talent—other than a keen interest but unremarkable ability on the pianoforte, an instrument her genteel mother had only just begun teaching her young "Thea" shortly before succumbing to a wasting disease.

How was Dorothea—a woman born of an earnest but impoverished shipping clerk, long since deceased, and wedded to a shopkeeper without any aspirations, more recently deceased—supposed to secure a wealthy patron?

"Mr. Hurwell was the only man I've endured intimate relations with," she admitted in a small voice, rapidly turning pages to fan her heated face, "and our physical relations were..."

Lacking. Disappointing. Sometimes painful.

A cultured female hand eased into view and obliterated

the unrecognizable words shimmering before her eyes. Seconds later, the book slid from her grasp when Sarah determinedly took possession. "Dorothea, child, look at me."

At twenty-six, she was hardly a child, but she did as bade. "You must think me incredibly gauche. I know you only seek to help. Why can I not claim your poise and confidence? The mere thought of attempting to entice a man with this"— Dorothea's empty hands gestured to what she considered a less-than-enticing form—"churns my insides like cream into butter."

Sarah's smile was a balm. "You do have my poise, if you would but believe it. All women have it within themselves to feel confident and beautiful."

Dorothea couldn't help the snorted, "*All* women?" that escaped.

She was plain and skinny and she had no qualms admitting either. Her landlord Grimmett accused her of both and did so with increasing frequency, deriding how she'd likely not find a better offer. Offer? Was that how the weasel described forcing his attentions? And Mr. Hurwell? During the entirety of their eight-year marriage, her husband had naught positive to say on her looks. Or anything else for that matter, insisting the female mind was not adapted to troubling itself with conversation or concerns beyond the home.

Bah! She'd rather not waste thoughts on either of them.

"Aye, all women." Sarah's tone brooked no argument but it was the conviction shining from her gaze that arrested Dorothea's attention. "And that is a gift the right man can grant."

"A gift? How so?"

"A man who values *you*, your words and intellect." Sarah's eyes took on a luminescent glow. "A man who thrives on your passionate nature, why, he can make you feel the most desired and necessary creature on the planet, no matter that you counted three new wretched wrinkles that very morn. And plucked two chin hairs the night before."

Dorothea bit off a laugh. Sarah may have been fourteen years her senior, but wrinkled and blemished she was not. Though a faint line or two was hinted at beneath her eyes, nary a grey hair peeked from the edges of her bonnet, and she had the kindest, most inviting face Dorothea had ever seen. That was one of the things Dorothea had noticed the moment the two struck up their first conversation the previous year, both waiting in line to inquire about the latest Miss Austen book, *Mansfield Park*.

Regretfully, that splendid story was the last time she'd had funds to fritter over something as trivial as reading. But purchased or not, books were usually free to browse, and thank goodness for that, because she continued to cross paths with Sarah.

Mere weeks later, after they'd crossed paths by sheer coincidence an amazing six times, and enjoyed more meaningful conversations with each subsequent meeting, Dorothea had learned of Sarah's profession. Though astonishment threatened to paralyze her lips, curiosity won out and Dorothea, in turn, confided about her own lackluster marriage. A few months later, Mr. Hurwell's fondness for gambling over horse races had made him devastatingly poor—and her a not-quite-devastated widow.

Regardless of what brought Dorothea to this point, the truth was indisputable—Sarah most certainly did *not* look like a woman whose livelihood was dependent upon her ability to seduce men. Warm and friendly, yes. A *coquette*? Not that Dorothea could see.

Could that possibly bode well for her, then? If she were

matched with the right man, would she, perchance, inherently possess the ability to seduce?

"There now," Sarah complimented, "you flush prettily. That is all the gentlemen want—a woman to make blush, and one who will want them back."

"But what if I don't?" The unexpected praise emboldened her. Dorothea stood on her toes to confirm that no one browsed nearby. Their seclusion assured, she voiced one of her fears. "Mr. Hurwell never dwelled overmuch with things in the amorous realm." That was an understatement. "But I sincerely doubt a man who is arranging his pleasures beforehand so they are conveniently available at his whim wants them from a cold stick with no sultry talent or sensuous airs."

"A cold stick?"

Dorothea waved it off as she would a pesky fly. "Oh, bother it. I should not have said that."

"Who *did* say that?" Sarah's tone stated she'd brook no evasion.

Dorothea escaped toward another tower of books.

Books, soothing books, with their familiar-smelling pages, their comforting lines of text. They didn't ridicule or belittle. They didn't snatch dreams away and replace them with soul-stifling monotony. They didn't scare or intimidate. Nay, books, and the words that comprised them, inspired and remained Dorothea's one escape.

"Who?" Sarah persisted.

But not today, it seemed. "Just Grimmett. Something he said yesterday when he came to collect the rent." Grimmett *and* her husband, when he'd been alive.

Sarah moved swifter than a hawk and captured Dorothea's right wrist. "Is that all he managed to collect?" Her fingers whispered across the splash of betraying color on Dorothea's wrist not quite hidden by the ragged lace.

Though she tried, Dorothea couldn't quell the pressure

increasing behind her blinking eyes. "Dorothea. Today is not the first time you've worn bruises where bracelets belong. He's becoming more aggressive, isn't he?"

At that, the first useless tear edged free despite her vain efforts to will it back.

"You *cannot* allow yourself to remain— Oh, dear, and now I've made you cry! Blast me, I did not mean to rouse uncomfortable thoughts. Forgive me." Sarah pulled Dorothea into her arms for a fierce, almost motherly embrace. "I vow, together, we shall make things right."

Dorothea returned the hug while dashing away the remnants of unacceptable tears. Had she not shed enough last night? And over the last two months when her funds depleted to nearly nothing and her efforts at finding employment continued to yield the same?

Sarah eased her hold and Dorothea stepped back. She quickly tugged her sleeve down, muffling a curse when the tattered edge tore. "He is getting rougher, I admit. But I dispatched him soon enough."

"Soon enough to protect your virtue, mayhap, but not the growing fear."

Feeling trapped, Dorothea raised stark eyes to Sarah. "But what if he's harsh or cruel?"

"Grimmett? Hasn't he already been?"

"No, I mean my new protector, assuming one is to be found. What if I fail to please *him* and he punishes me for it, and I've nowhere else to turn because he *owns* me? My home, my attire. Will I be at his mercy? Have I any right to gainsay him?" In truth, this mistress business seemed far more complicated than starving. More frightening on some levels, too. "Or am I being jingle-brained?"

Sarah's laughter brightened their book-warmed corner. "Come now, I talk not of selling your soul to the devil or your body to an ogre. You're still free to say yea or nay, always and with any man." She leaned close and whispered under her breath, "I concede there are vile men walking London and some may very well be in search of a mistress, but not in *my* circle. The people I would introduce you to are known to me, be assured. Please, dither no more. Agree to come to the dinner party tonight and decide for yourself after you meet the man I think could answer all your prayers."

"Oh? You've invited the Almighty?" she somehow managed to jest. "I didn't know He possessed a fondness for turtle soup."

"You wretch!" Sarah chided, but some of the worry shading her gaze fled. "Do come. Penry and I have put our heads together these last weeks and truly think we've found you a perfect match."

"You've discussed me with your... With Lord Penry?" Sarah's longtime protector was married with five daughters, but in the time she and Dorothea had been friends, Sarah had never indicated Dorothea might warrant being a topic between them.

"We have, dearest. From the moment I realized you were in dun territory and all alone, without—"

"I have my mice, don't forget."

Sarah tightened her lips against a smile but continued speaking. "All alone and struggling in your attempts to find a workable solution to your predicament."

Ah, yes. Her predicament—widowed and penniless.

Without tact or fanfare, Dorothea had swiftly learned young women lacking practical experience or applicable references (actually, lacking any references at all) were shown the door of respectable establishments faster than the overhead bell could chime *adieu*.

The meager resources remaining after Mr. Hurwell's inhospitable cousin had claimed the shop—and, by right, her living quarters above—had dwindled to a pittance since her eviction. As the only child of two only children, therefore having no family in London and no other viable choices that she could discern, Dorothea had perfected the art of frugal, solitary living. (She didn't think one-sided discourses conducted with George and Charlotte counted; their whiskers might bob and tails twitch, but as conversationalists, they left much to be desired.)

Yet Sarah spoke of meaningful discussions. How that beckoned to someone who longed for true companionship over and above that of a bursting table. "He talks with you, your Lord Penry? About his day and such? How often does he come round?"

Dorothea knew Sarah's benefactor paid for her lodgings and kept her flush in the pockets, and that Sarah readily traded her body in exchange for the security of her living. But never before had she considered how the two might be *friends*. A mere mistress and a lofty lord. It was an unexpected, exhilarating concept. One that tempted.

"Of a certainty we talk." Surmising Dorothea had warmed to the idea, Sarah's stance relaxed. "We touch upon everything: his day, mine, interesting *on dits*, what event to attend or host next, Prinny's latest foibles, political issues facing—"

"What about Lord Penry's family? His wife?" The words wouldn't be contained. "Do you speak of her? Forgive me if it's impertinent to ask, but I truly desire to know. I mean, what are the boundaries of such a union? How does one avoid crossing them?"

A flash of sadness swept across Sarah's eyes, and then it was gone. "Nay. We do not speak of his wife and only rarely his daughters. But on other topics, I have free rein. As to you and your protector, simply let him set the pace. Like a horse to bridle, you follow his lead. Don't frown at me like that— have you not seen how the men of the ton treat their horseflesh?"

True. So true. Mr. Hurwell had wasted every spare farthing attending—and wagering on—horse races, no matter that the man had never set atop one and professed no eagerness to try.

"But for now," Sarah continued, "when I have a particular someone in mind, you may set *your* mind at ease for he is most certainly a gentleman, one with nary a vile rumor attached to his name."

That brought Dorothea up short. She'd thought Sarah had been jesting earlier when she mentioned selecting someone. "You have?"

"Of a certainty. A marquis, in fact."

A marquis? The mere possibility sent her mind spinning in a disorderly bustle. Yet Dorothea managed to respond, with a lack of sputtering she thought impressive indeed, "Perhaps you aim too high on my behalf?" Thanks to her mother's tutelage, Dorothea knew how to conduct herself and speak with more refinement than many in her class, but she had no right to or expectations of such grandeur. "Would not a second or third son or perhaps a merchant with heavy pockets not be more suited—"

"You measure your worth in drams when you should be thinking in barrels." Sarah sniffed as though Dorothea's concept of a more appropriate protector was preposterous. "Whatever notions you have of unsuitability, discard them henceforth. You exhibit as much grace as any number of other women of my acquaintance and your manner is more pleasing than most. Once you're able to fill your belly regularly, I daresay your countenance will rival that of anyone's. Cease doubting, dear. I would never seek to place you in a situation that would cause you to wish for the gallows."

"I know that, I do. I'm just..." Dorothea's faltering dance toward another stack of books spoke for her. A tiny part of her was fascinated by the very real prospect of enjoying a man's companionship. And if, in turn, he enjoyed her body, then what would be the harm? She groped for something to occupy her hands and reached for the nearest book.

Sarah intercepted her efforts and pressed her palms against Dorothea's restless fingers. "Beset by nerves. 'Tis understandable, so let me tell you more of what to expect so you'll feel as snug as a duck in a ditch."

"Let's hope it's not raining then, for the duck's sake." She squared her shoulders and faced her fate head on. "All right. Tell me the worst of it."

Sarah raised a beautifully arched brow. "Since you put it that way... Tonight's party is at my home. Several of us rotate hosting duties and it is my turn for the chore. There will be approximately a dozen men present and an equal number of women. Women who, by choice or circumstance, are in the business of physically pleasing members of the ton. Several will come with their benefactors; others are looking to make new associations. Others only want to dabble and play for the night. There will..."

Sarah paused as though weighing whether or not Dorothea truly wanted to hear more.

Of course she did! This was a slice of life she'd never anticipated finding herself nudging up against. "What else? Do tell me everything so shock won't send me swooning out the door."

With a comforting pat, Sarah released her hand. "Good girl. I do believe you'll do fine. Since everyone knows tonight is about partnering and pleasuring, either for the evening or beyond, don't expect restraint. While some couples prefer to take themselves off before offing their clothes, others aren't as circumspect."

Dorothea felt her eyes go wide. "I'll be expected to *undress*?" The question squeaked higher than the roof two floors above. "In front of everyone?"

"Most certainly not! But others may and you did say you wanted to know the worst. I'm sure you can ascertain what might come next from any pairs, or groups, who are so inclined."

Groups?! It was a wonder her face hadn't ignited.

In order to speak, Dorothea had to unlock her teeth, which had mashed the insides of her cheeks. "Are you quite certain this is the proper venue for me to meet this man? Would it not be"—*safer for my sanity*—"easier were we to meet elsewhere?" Mayhap at church?

"Ah, would that it were that simple. Lord Tremayne rarely accepts social invitations, especially now that he's seen his younger sister married off. He's not a man given to idle chatter from what I've seen. Prefers meaningful discourse to those of the flittering masses. Penry said we accomplished quite a feat, securing his agreement to attend tonight."

Lord Tremayne. What a strong-sounding name. Dorothea wondered whether his character might be strong as well. In truth, she wondered whether his *body* might be, and her face flamed hotter. "Why did he?"

"To meet you, of course."

"But I... I haven't even agreed to come. And he knows nothing about me."

"Ah, but we knew he was in the market for a new mistress and Penry is one of his oldest friends, so when he mentioned you, Tremayne listened."

"So they're of the same age?" Penry was a year or two older than Sarah; she'd let that tidbit slip one morning when she'd arrived at Hatchards late, hurried and flushed, commenting that the man's stamina wasn't waning with his recent birthday (and appearing rather pleased by the prospect).

"Nay. Tremayne is younger by ten years or so." Sarah gave

a saucy wink. "So he's in his prime too. Very fit. Taller than most, and strong."

"Heavens, Sarah, it sounds as though you're describing a circus bear, not a man."

Her friend's grey eyes sparkled. "I daresay you'll find much to admire about him. As to tonight's gathering, dearest, do keep in mind that meeting him in such a setting ultimately protects you both."

"Protects? From what?" All sorts of dastardly thoughts pelted her.

"You silly pea goose—protects your *pride*. Watch." Sarah slipped two books off a nearby stack and held them up, covers pressed together. "It's a simple matter to engage each other as much or as little as you choose. If either of you aren't interested in pursuing an association, you simply walk away." Holding one in each hand, she whipped the books apart. "It's as uncomplicated as that. Whereas if you were meeting for a *tête-à-tête*, awkwardness might ensue if one of you felt more inclined to proceed than the other." Sarah slapped the two books together as though to indicate the subject was at an end. "So we're agreed? You'll come?"

"Might he have a pianoforte, do you think?"

"A piano?" Sarah blinked owlishly and Dorothea felt foolish for asking. "My dear, a good man will give his mistress expensive baubles as though they were bags of lemon drops. I'm certain he'll provide you a pianoforte if the two of you decide you'll suit."

With every word she uttered, how was it Sarah made becoming a fallen woman sound more uplifting and enticing? And how did one learn the necessary skills to make a satisfactory go of the venture?

"How does a...a..." Dorothea walled off her nerves and shored up her courage. If she couldn't talk about it, she seriously doubted she'd be able to engage in it. "Mistress behave?

In the bedchamber, I mean. And why is it men want a mistress if they already claim a wife?"

After all, she'd been a wife. And from her experience, the occupation had little to recommend it.

"Oh, gracious. Now you're asking questions that go significantly beyond our precious time together. I'm sure there are as many reasons as there are clouds in the sky. An unhappy marriage, an arranged one. A wife who refuses to join her husband in the marriage bed once her duty is done and she's delivered him a son or three. As for those men unmarried, is it not safer—and more expedient—to arrange for a woman you find attractive than risk contracting pox from strumpets on the streets?"

The unsavory aspects of pleasing oneself outside of marriage had not occurred to her. Perhaps because she'd never been much pleased *within* marriage. "You always seem so refreshed. So joyful. As though your time with Lord Penry is not disagreeable. Do you..." Dorothea found her eyes had skittered toward the empty stairwell and she forced herself to meet Sarah's patient expression. "Do you find true enjoyment in the bedchamber?"

Sarah's cheeks pinkened and she looked more like a girl of fourteen than a mistress of forty. "Very much so. It has not always been the case, I confess, with each of my protectors. But I'm very happy with Penry."

And that is when Dorothea made up her mind. Whether this Lord Tremayne indulged in risqué behavior or even told vulgar jokes, whether he changed mistresses as frequently as he did his waistcoats, she'd be a chucklehead not to attempt to find a pleasurable coexistence with such a man. And if not him, then another.

"It will do..." When the words came out hesitant, she cleared her throat and proclaimed with every show of confidence, "I believe I would very much like to find someone as you have. But I admit to fearing I'll not please or satisfy him."

"Lovemaking with someone new is not a race you either win or lose. It's more like...like..." Sarah glanced heavenward, as though casting about for the perfect comparison and hoping an angel would drop it in her mind. She snapped her gloved fingers and looked at Dorothea. "Like crafting the most perfect marzipan. All you need is sugar, almonds and rosewater, but while the basic ingredients might not change from attempt to attempt, the exact amounts and how they're prepared will vary as you tweak and refine your recipe until *voilà*—you land upon perfection, ambrosial bliss upon your tongue. *That's* what perfect lovemaking is all about. The right man knows this and won't expect you to dance on your head the first time you're together. Or even the fiftieth. You'll learn to make your own ambrosia—in your own time." With that unfulfilling explanation ringing in Dorothea's ears, Sarah added, "Have I convinced you? Will you come tonight?"

In the end, the image of dancing on her head while balancing marzipan on her feet was so ludicrous, Sarah's cooking comparison shared so exuberantly, and her own situation so desperate, that Dorothea could do naught but concede. "Aye." Though she might live to regret it, at least she'd live. "I'll be there."

But how? She knew better than to brave walking her neighborhood after dark. Daytime was bad enough.

As though she discerned the reason for the worry on her face, Sarah clasped Dorothea's forearm. "Marvelous. Give me your direction—I'll send a carriage for you at half past six. You'll be the first to arrive and we'll set my abigail to arranging your hair. How does that sound?"

"Thoughtful in the extreme."

"La, 'tis no more than you'd do for me should the situation be reversed. This way, you can be happily ensconced before anyone else makes their bows."

Which meant she had the bulk of the day to press into service her one remaining decent dress. Shore up the seams, make sure above her threadbare gloves the sleeves concealed the bruises without ragged lace falling free, no matter that the dress was hopelessly outdated. "You're too kind. I appreciate all you're doing immensely."

"And I've appreciated your friendship from the moment we met. I only wish I could have done more sooner." With a hand on Dorothea's arm, Sarah steered them toward the stairwell. "You have no idea how relieved I am. I truly think tonight could be the beginning of something wondrous for you. Just like Penry and myself."

Descending the steps next to her friend, Dorothea refused to let the questions beating about her breast take root. Would it be like that for her? Could a cold stick find warmth in the bed of a stranger? And what did it matter that Sarah's "wondrous" man was married—to someone else?

When they reached the ground floor, Sarah indicated the sales counter. "Let me buy you this volume and we'll be off."

"Thank you, but that isn't necessary." Food, she might accept; luxury gifts were another matter entirely.

"Oh, but it is." Sarah brandished the book she'd slid from Dorothea's grasp earlier. "I see you're a great fan of Byron."

Lord Byron, the gadabout poet. One Dorothea didn't like at all. "But I'm not. Wordsworth and Burns, now *them* I enjoy, but Byron is not a particular favorite. There's no need—"

"There's every need." Sarah fanned the book and two loose pages broke free before she stuffed them back inside. "You proceeded to mangle these and several more when I asked about your landlord. So no more protests. I caused your distress, I owe you reparation."

"You most certainly did not cause my distress. Regardless,

Sarah, your friendship repays any debt real or imagined, now and into infinity."

Sarah linked their arms and began making her way toward the clerk. "You're such a dear but I'm still buying you the book. If nothing else, you can use it for kindling."

3

TO CONVERSE OVER DINNER –
OR NOT

———◦○◦———

"Don't be horribly disappointed if the food isn't up to expectations."

Sarah surprised Dorothea with that statement when she returned to Dorothea's side in the main parlor after a brief absence in the kitchens—the second absence she'd made in the short time since the splendid carriage had rolled to a stop allowing Dorothea—with the aid of a servant!—to alight.

A carriage she'd been increasingly grateful for, given how the mild but stormy morning had given way to a chilling afternoon, the kind that heralded a bitterly cold night. How she hoped that wasn't an omen for the evening ahead.

"You're bamboozling me," she said now, unable to fathom such a claim, for any meals or snacks served during her prior visits had always been exquisite.

While she'd been to Sarah's residence a few times during the course of their friendship, it had always been during the day and only when Lord Penry was away from town (hence, no chance of his unexpected arrival). Unlike the lurid den of iniquity Dorothea had half expected a "kept" woman to reside in, relief reigned when she found that Sarah's home mirrored her person: tasteful and composed.

"How I wish that I were. Mrs. Beeson quit to keep house for the butcher and his four sons, and finding her replacement has not proved an easy task."

The plump, gregarious woman had been most welcoming to Dorothea—and the extra fare she always insisted go home with their guest had been delicious indeed. "I'll not complain of any food at this point no matter how ill or illustriously prepared, but what of Mrs. Beeson? She left *your* employ to cook for *five men*? Has she more fleas than sense?"

"He gave her his name. She's to mother his boys."

"Ah, then. Happy for her am I."

"I as well. But not for my table." Her rueful expression made Dorothea laugh. "Off with you now. Here's my girl—" Sarah gestured toward the maid skimming down the stairs.

"Miss Sarah." The bright-eyed, mob-capped redhead curtsied at her mistress and then beamed at Dorothea. "Is this your friend?" Without hesitation the girl, who couldn't have been much over sixteen, plucked at Dorothea's freshly washed hair (a luxury she'd indulged in this afternoon, having hoarded what water she could the past few days; even cold and liable to make her scalp feel like frozen tundra for the two hours it took her hair to fully dry, it had been worth it). "Gah." The girl frowned. "Gettin' this thick mass to take a curl will be a chore, I tell you.

"Don't be sittin' on thorns, none." The girl made shooing motions, urging Dorothea up the stairway. "No time to waste!"

With that, Dorothea was herded into the care of Sarah's capable servant.

Thirty minutes later, declining to don the beautiful dress

the servant tried to coax her into—there was no way Dorothea's bosom would have adequately filled the top nor her shorter legs the skirts—but wearing the stunning evening gloves in kid leather that her friend had left boxed and beribboned, she rejoined Sarah as they waited for the remaining guests to arrive.

"What? Not the dress?" Sarah took up her hands, pulling the leather past Dorothea's elbows and smoothing the fingers in place. "The gloves. At least you accepted those, thank goodness."

"They're lovely." And sumptuous and quite possibly one of the nicest things she'd ever received. "I cannot thank you enough."

"No more purple fingers for you, my dear." And no worries that anyone would see the unsightly bruises, either, Dorothea couldn't help but think with relief. "For these shall keep you warm."

Self-consciously, Dorothea raised one hand to the intricate swept-up coils, in lieu of ringlets, that the servant had miraculously substituted in a trice. "I feel so majestic."

And afraid to move her head lest they topple.

"As you should. Besides, you—" Sarah cocked her head, listening, then smiled and fluffed out her skirts. "If I'm not mistaken, I hear the first carriage now. Chin up, Dorothea dear. The food may not be all that is fine but I can promise the evening will be memorable, and after tonight it is my hope you shall worry no more."

But Dorothea did worry, in her peaceful little shadowed corner, lit only by the candles strategically placed throughout the parlor, as she waited and watched each individual and couple arrive.

Nearly two hours later, though she still claimed the same corner, "peaceful" had been replaced by pandemonium. With every minute that droned by, an increasingly apprehensive weight pressed in on her chest as her thoughts tumbled as freely as did some of the women's inhibitions. And clothing on more than one occasion, as gloves had quickly been stripped, even slippers sailed forth—to her utter astonishment.

Regardless of whatever surprising sights her eyes beheld, the thoughts swirling behind them kept circling back to one unmistakable conclusion: Tonight, if all went according to plan, she would officially join the Fashionably Impure.

It was an unsettling thought. One that had only grown in proportion every moment that she remained alone.

Dorothea surveyed the men congregating about Sarah's parlor, feeling as though her rioting stomach was in danger of expelling what little it held. How she was soon supposed to sit down and act engaging during a five-course supper was beyond her. Nerves held her nearly immobile.

Which of these men would be responsible for her imminent placement into the ranks of London's demireps and courtesans? Would it be a young blood, someone with more pence than sense, who sought to buy favors before his title had to buy a wife? Or perhaps an older, more moderate gentleman, one whose paunch preceded his phiz? Although, really, what did it matter what his face looked like, or his body?

As long as he treated her with a measure of kindness, then she'd be significantly better off. In fact, Dorothea consoled herself, would she not be *raising* her consequence— from starving and practically homeless to protected and well fed? In exchange for simply cultivating a pleasing manner and a satisfactory presence in a man's bed...

She could manage that, surely.

"How are you doing?" Sarah asked in her ear, causing Dorothea to start. She'd lost sight of her friend at some point in the last half hour, hostess duties—and her new cranky cook—demanding much of Sarah's time. "Now that most everyone's descended upon us like a swarm of lusty locusts."

"Rather nervous, I'm afraid," she confessed, wringing her hands in front of her to stop their visible trembling. Why hadn't she thought to bring a fan? (Mayhap because she didn't own one?)

In her element, Sarah looked as composed as ever, her lustrous brown hair done up in loose ringlets about her face and her dress fancier than any Dorothea had ever conceived. In a deep emerald-green fabric that fairly shimmered, the elegant dress barely perched atop Sarah's shoulders, leaving much of her upper chest and all of her arms—above her silk gloves—bare. A profusion of tiny diamonds sparkled about her neck, woven into the most intricate necklace imaginable. A few gems even glistened throughout her curls. With her confident air and bedecked in finery, her warm and kind-faced friend became so amazingly beautiful it almost hurt to look at her.

"Would it be horrid of me to shoo you away?" Dorothea asked, thinking how she definitely needed to invest in a fan. Weren't they useful for hiding behind when one became embarrassed? She glanced down to find that the dull olive fabric covering her chest and arms had taken on the cast of chewed peas in the last few minutes. Ugh! "What was I thinking? Next to your glittering presence, I look a veritable dowd."

The dress she'd thought would serve earlier, especially with its new layer of lace at the cuffs (scavenged from her best petticoat), was easily the oldest, most-out-of-date article of clothing in the room. Even the statuary boasted finer attire—a saucy, beribboned hat perched atop a bust of some bearded Greek fellow, though Dorothea was clueless which one. For the first time in weeks, she thoroughly regretted her decision not to accept when Sarah tried to gift her with a new gown. At the time, it had seemed prudent—walking about her neighborhood in finery was the surest way to invite unsavory notice. Now though...

"Dearest." Sarah placed her hands around Dorothea's and spoke earnestly. "It's not your dress he'll be considering. It's what resides beneath it."

After she laughed, Dorothea growled, "Was that supposed to alleviate my discomfort? If so, I'm afraid you've accomplished the opposite for it's looming ever larger." Her anxious gaze skimmed over the men in the room once more. "Which one is he?"

Was Lord Tremayne the portly gentleman in the opposite corner who puffed on a cigar in the presence of the women— which even Dorothea, with her limited knowledge of tonnish proprieties, knew was beyond the pale? He also, she couldn't help but note, patted the bum of every female who passed within arm's distance, encouraging Dorothea to remain right where she was—bum against the wall.

Or was Lord Tremayne the gentleman with absurdly bushy side whiskers? The one who'd been leering at her since he walked in? Or perhaps the fellow with a deep laugh and a nose so large Dorothea feared he'd poke out her eye were they ever to kiss? Or mayhap the gangly youth who stood, unfathomably, off to the side appearing as ill at ease as she felt?

In truth, none of them appealed.

Nor did the other prattling four, just coming in, talking loudly with the equally vivacious women on their arms. Women who were more colorful than any profusion of rainbows—and just as above Dorothea's own meager station. How could she hold her head up among such lovelies? As to that, how did *they* hold their heads up with such thick layers of cosmetics plastered on their faces? And who was she to be thinking such critical thoughts?

"You neglected to tell me rouged lips and kohl-rimmed

eyes were a prerequisite," Dorothea said softly. "Really, Sarah, given my dated dress and bare face"—*and complete lack of sexual confidence*—"I'm so very out of place."

"I think you worry overmuch. Pay attention because..." Sarah gave her hands a reassuring squeeze, then turned to wave at one of the heavily made-up highfliers. "By the end of dinner that one will be so in her cups she'll find Socrates amusing." Ah, so that was the identity of the bonneted bust. "And Dominique there"—fingers fluttered toward a raven-haired beauty who returned Sarah's greeting with a cool nod —"her accent will start to slip by the third course. Her manners far sooner."

Hearing of their foibles, some of the tightness eased from Dorothea's frame. "But I thought these women were your friends."

Sarah looked right at her, a piercing glance completely void of the artifice she'd just shown the room at large. "You, my dear, *are* my friend. A select few of these women are as well, but most of them are simply competition. That's how they view me and I them."

"Oh." Some of the thawing nerves inside Dorothea froze, thickened. "That's...sad."

"I know it sounds callous, but that's the way of it. Why do you think I delayed hosting for so long, even though it was my turn ages ago? My time with Penry is limited and I guard it jealously. I do not like having to share him."

How Dorothea hoped she might feel the same toward the unknown Lord Tremayne. "Then why must you?"

"Politics. These gatherings give the men opportunity to debate and, if they are successful, sway others to their way of thinking. It's a select few and they're away from the club where others are waiting to pounce in with their own views or agendas. There's a hotly contested vote coming up in Parliament that Penry feels strongly about. As tonight's host, he has more opportunity to guide the conversation in that direction than he might have otherwise."

"Your duty is done," Dorothea told her, "you've adequately convinced me there's more at stake than my ratty dress."

"Then this should comfort you further—despite the breach in etiquette, I've seated you next to me so assistance is only a whisper away if..." A commotion in the hall brought Sarah's head around. "Appears as though Lord Harrison and Anna made it home in time. Wonderful! She's a true friend— I'll introduce you once Harrison takes himself off. They've just returned from Italy. And would you look at that—I declare, her fancy Italian dress looks as though it's from your wardrobe! Her sleeves are long and the cuffs are just brimming with lace!"

Dorothea laughed outright. "Admirable try. Especially as my wardrobe consists of three pegs in the wall."

"Oh look, they brought Susan," Sarah added when a brightly hennaed young woman bounded in after them. "I believe you'll like her as well. There's not an ounce of artifice anywhere and— Fustian! I knew the last few minutes were too calm to last. I see my new cook frantically motioning. Why he abandons the kitchens instead of sending a servant, I know not. I must be off." Sarah kissed her cheek. "Worry not, you'll do fine."

"And Lord Tremayne?" Dorothea squeaked out hurriedly. "Which one is he?"

Sarah acknowledged her cook, indicated she'd be over in a moment, then scanned the crowd.

Dorothea prayed Sarah would point out someone other than the men she'd particularly noticed. There were others, a small, boisterous group of males lingering across the hall in another room, tumblers in hand, but there were as many or more "ladies" in their midst and not a one of the men had cast so much as an inquiring glance her direction. "I thought you said there were only going to be a dozen men here tonight."

Dorothea's count was up to fifteen at least.

"That's what I thought until receiving Penry's note this afternoon. A few others got wind of our gathering and begged invitations." Sarah took Dorothea's arm and casually strolled until she could see into the next room.

Dorothea tried not to be overly critical, tried to remember what awaited her at home: a moldy potato, mice groats—would that her options proliferated as fast as George and Charlotte's "leavings"—and grabby Grimmett. She tried to be grateful, thankful for the opportunity of tonight. But as she evaluated the men present, the ones not melded at the hips to made-up mistresses already, she had to admit not a one of them appealed to her on the physical level she'd secretly yearned for.

"La, that man," Sarah said finally. "I told Tremayne supper was served at nine and not a moment later. And still he runs late."

Upon realizing none of the unpalatable choices before her were the man in question, a surge of relief swept through Dorothea. Mayhap the tardy Lord Tremayne would appeal after all.

Do you recognize the significance of that? a part of her brain seemed to ask.

He's *late*, some imp emphasized.

Late, something her "late" spouse would never, ever have tolerated. Too easily she could recall the disapproving glares should his breakfast, luncheon, dinner—or heaven forfend, afternoon tea—be placed before him even one second beyond the strike of the hour.

My, oh my, Lord Tremayne was tardy. Dorothea smiled, predisposed to like him already.

AT TWELVE MINUTES PAST NINE, Daniel presented his tardy carcass at the home he'd been invited to, doffed his hat, coat, cane and gloves, relinquishing them to the overly officious butler, and prayed he hadn't made a mistake in coming tonight.

At the pointedly assessing look the man gave his jaw—insolent fellow!—Daniel's fingers automatically followed. So he encountered scruff instead of skin. What of it? He'd ordered Crowley, his valet, to trim and refine his whiskers in lieu of shaving them off.

Better to disguise the bruise and scars than to scare her away before ever opening his mouth. *Her* being the woman he suffered through this ordeal to meet.

"My lord, delighted you deigned to join us," the butler said with a haughty air that indicated he took his position very seriously. "Dinner is being held on your account, so if you would..."

The man set off at a marching pace before the first syllable of Daniel's "Lead on," made it past his lips.

No out-of-the-way narrow nook for Penry's lovely light-skirt, Daniel saw, the home he was escorted through being as genteel and grand as anything one would expect to find in Mayfair. Only they weren't in Mayfair, the upper echelon of abodes, but a neighborhood or three away.

"Here we are, my lord."

Nodding his thanks to the impertinent fellow, Daniel paused before entering the formal dining room, keeping out of sight of most its occupants. Though the space was absurdly large, a slightly low ceiling coupled with the crowd inhabiting it gave the room an intimate, almost cozy air. Elaborate candelabra spaced evenly over the table's surface ensured adequate light—a sort of subdued, shadowed light that invited one to lean their head toward their closest companion for a romantic *tête-à-tête*.

He cast his gaze back the way they'd just come and unease threatened to crawl through him. Penry certainly hadn't spared any expense outfitting his mistress, had he?

Daniel hadn't yet seen the lodgings he'd secured for his potential paramour, wanting a fresh start in fresh surroundings with a—hopefully—fresh woman. He'd had his man of affairs take care of it and hadn't bothered to inspect the townhouse himself. Hadn't his man assured him it was just the thing?

The nip of unease promised to metamorphize into an onslaught, fixing him—and his neck muscles in place.

'Tis nothing, he assured himself. Only a willing wren of a widow in need of protection and your pipe in need of her attention. Three fortifying breaths later, he braved crossing the threshold.

Excellent.

Everyone was seated. Just as he'd hoped. Less chance of getting tangled in the trap of idle chatter before supper if people were hungrily anticipating it.

Silently acknowledging the greetings he received from the group at large, Daniel smiled and nodded at several acquaintances as he made his way around the giant oval table to this evening's hostess to make his apologies. He wouldn't put it past Penry to have purchased the huge slab for the occasion —and for the occasion of plowing into his mistress on top of it after everyone went home.

Penry sometimes talked a little too freely about his lusty interludes with the serene brunette. Ready for his own lusty interlude, Daniel scanned the women present, more than a little curious as to the identity of the well-hyped Widow Hurwell.

Penry had teased him with enough hints of subtle beauty

and true refinement to pique his interest. But it was hearing of her strained circumstances that had ultimately tipped the scales and caused his carriage wheels to roll this way tonight. No money meant no options, and Daniel was desperate enough in his own right to take advantage of her situation, desperate enough to at least put himself forward. If she was truly as cultured and untarnished as he'd been led to believe, some lucky man would snatch her up and it might as well be him.

"Forgive me," he said to Penry's Sarah, coming up to her and proffering a slight bow, knowing he owed her his sincere apologies for his tardiness but unable to stop himself from avidly inspecting the woman by her side. She was the only female he didn't recognize and the only person who looked more than a little out of place, discounting the pup at the far end who gazed with his mouth agape toward the arched doorway Daniel had just entered through.

In the muted candlelight, she shone like an undiscovered jewel, her wealth of dark hair piled and looped on the back of her head in a manner quite at odds with the simplicity of her dress. But he cared not to analyze her attire for the faint stirring in his loins boded well indeed.

Faint? Putting to rest any concerns he had about not being attracted to her, at the thought of bedding the lovely widow, his body stirred more than a dead man's falling down a ravine —which is what Daniel started to think he'd been for staying with Louise for so long. Dead to any finer sense.

Determinedly, he fixed his gaze on the frowning Sarah. He started to carefully explain his fabricated, rehearsed excuse for being late. His mouth not yet open, already the tension climbed up his neck and squeezed inward—

Not now! he wanted to rail.

But Penry's woman unknowingly saved him.

"Do sit down, Lord Tremayne. I'm grateful you decided to

finally grace us with your presence," she told him archly, gesturing to the lone empty seat at the table which, not coincidentally, was next to the woman he had hopes of claiming. "But I've held back supper long enough. Hopkins," she called out to a servant hovering at the ready, "tell Cook the first course may be brought in. *Finally*."

"Yes, madam."

A FRISSON of awareness swelled through Dorothea the moment the latecomer came into view. When Sarah called him Tremayne, the subtle tingling became more of a lightning spike.

Of what, Dorothea couldn't say. The gruff-looking man didn't appeal exactly, but he most definitely *attracted*—both her attention and greetings from many of the men present.

"Glad to see that munsons muffler didn't lay you out for long."

Munsons muffler?

"Nay. Not our man—way to work it till the ringer!"

"Jolly good show, Tremayne."

What? Did he perform in some venue? What an odd occupation for a peer. But apparently, instead of diminishing his standing, it only served to enhance it.

Yet...as he surveyed the room and his gaze alit upon her, she didn't think Lord Tremayne needed any more enhancement when a surge of—

What exactly? Interest? Appreciation? Speculation? A surge of *something* foreign to her experience came into his eyes, something hot and banked glittering from the depths of deep amber. Being the recipient of such focused potency drove some part of her to contemplate jumping from her seat to proclaim she was ready to retire with him straightaway.

The other part of her, the heretofore sensible part that

seemed to be undergoing a most peculiar change—into sultry?—commanded her lips to curve into a welcoming smile, her melting body to stay put and her eyes to narrow (she feared losing them if they opened any wider) as he made his way to the available chair next to hers and she undeniably drank him in.

He was a big man, powerfully built yet somehow tamed by the trappings he wore—a rich brown tailcoat over a waist-coat in a muted burgundy stripe, with tan buckskins below. A cream-colored cravat, meticulously tied, and rebelliously straight hair. Rebellious, because all the rage was tousled curls for men and sausage ringlets for the ladies, as she'd been informed when Sarah's abigail had tended to hers.

She liked the silky-looking, thick strands adorning Lord Tremayne's well-shaped head (Mr. Hurwell's had been rather narrow; his head, that was. His hair, somewhat lank.). She liked Lord Tremayne's confident air and strong-looking body too.

She especially liked the way he smelled, now that he was close enough to inhale, clean and spicy, with just a hint of the outdoors.

What she couldn't yet claim to like was his beard. And how he appeared intimidating beneath the bristle, all hard, flexing jaw and tendon-filled neck—she'd glimpsed a couple inches below his chin and above the cravat when he cocked his head in a peculiar stretch just before taking possession of his chair.

And until she had reason to like *him*, rather than land herself further into the suds, Dorothea knew she'd bide her time. Wait and discern what manner of man he truly was before agreeing to proceed with a liaison between them.

But oh, how she liked the flood of warmth that beset her every limb when he joined her beneath the table, his long, powerful body coming within inches of hers as he brought his chair forward...how she admired his forearm encased in expensive superfine she'd never thought to view up close— much less consider touching, as he reached for his wine...

TAKING advantage of the slight commotion when several servants began tromping in carrying silver-domed trays, Daniel dodged further introductions by settling himself next to the woman he suspected he was here to meet.

And to bed.

Briefly her eyes flicked to his and a ghost of a smile touched her lips before it faded like a breeze. But the damage was done—one covert, up-close, lash-shrouded glance and all he could do was gape and goggle.

Soft tendrils of her luxuriant midnight hair framed a heart-shaped face. The flickering candlelight caused shadows to dance over her slightly angular nose and jaw. She was a mite thin for his tastes, but any hint of hardness in her features was belied by the bow-shaped mouth that commanded his attention.

So easily he imagined those plump lips against his, parted and welcoming, where he would sample the passion he hoped was packaged inside this delightful exterior. He'd like to see her dark hair rid of its pins, his fingers tangled against her scalp as he guided her lips lower...

A hot spike of lust wound through him and Daniel smiled.

Rescuing Sarah's little widow would prove no hardship. Indeed, could the timing have been any more fortuitous? At long last, his long lance would undoubtedly sleep snug and satisfied, and, finally, he'd *sleep*. Snugged against the lithe body he suspected resided beneath the atrocious dress.

Closer now, he couldn't help but notice its shortcomings. Her olive gown had obviously seen better days. A thin fichu was tucked into the low, squared-off bosom, concealing her attributes completely. After the overtly stimulating attire Louise typically wore, the widow's outfit was almost puritan in its severity. Puritan yet provocative...encouraging visions of divesting her of the drab layers and uncovering what lay beneath.

Giving his body a moment to relax, he turned to his meal. A task which proved surprisingly difficult when, moments later, he was fully aware of her slight wrist grappling with the overdone mutton on her plate. His was already neatly severed. So with nothing more than a lift of one brow and an inquiring *Hmmm?* that had her pausing in her efforts, he deftly switched their plates, quickly sliced her serving and had them swapped back before anyone took notice.

A well-timed bite between his choppers ensured all he had to do was nod after her quiet but appreciative thanks and he was off—inspecting her again (for it was a significantly more enjoyable endeavor than chewing overcooked mutton).

A servant came between them bearing gravied asparagus. A particular and unwelcome scent—one he'd suffered enough of thanks to his prior inamorata—wafted strongly from the dish, and Daniel declined.

The man turned to the widow and offered to ladle some on her plate. Daniel watched her nose wrinkle.

"No, thank you," she said quietly. "I'm not fond of onions."

Better and better.

As his eyes skated over her features in profile, another rush of warmth filled his loins. No haggard-looking widow, this, as he'd half feared based on Penry's continued attempts to gauge his interest in Sarah's friend the last week or so. No, this woman looked more like an innocent maiden than a well-used widow.

And just think—if he could deal adequately with the

onion-loving Louise for several years, how long might his interest in this divine little morsel last?

"Meezes Hurt-weel, I zee you are new to de trade?" The jewels about her neck as counterfeit as her accent, one of the single females addressed the woman at his side with a bite to her voice. Jealous cat.

"Trade?" his dinner partner queried. "Whatever do you mean?" Thrilled at having her identity confirmed, he was a bit stymied when his widow sounded suitably vague. Was she dense—or only pretending?

"Zee trade of selling *your* wares." With an unmistakable emphasis on "your".

"*My* wares?" Mrs. Hurwell managed to sound both startled and impressed. "You've heard of my work, then? Why, Sarah..." His widow pointed her empty fork at their hostess in a teasing gesture. Daniel wasn't sure anyone but him caught the slight wavering in her arm before she retracted it. "You didn't tell me you'd shared about my mercantilian efforts."

Amazingly, she made it sound like *rep*tilian. And now instead of a phony-French doxy questioning his mistress-to-be, all Daniel saw across the table was a blowsy viper in fake rubies.

He set his fork down and leaned back in his chair, ready to be amused.

Sarah, he thought, masked her surprise plausibly well. Reaching for her wineglass, she took a delayed sip. Stalling? For herself or the friend she sought to shield? Returning the glass to the table, she met and held every gaze intent on the byplay. "Aye. But I could not resist. Forgive me. I know your wares are exclusive to Mr.—" A quick gloved hand made its way to Sarah's lips, as did a soft blush to her face. "Pardon me. His is a *very* select shop and promised anonymity to my dear friend if she would but consent to sell her work exclusively through him. I can offer no less." Sarah placed one finger to her lips and appraised the group at large. "May I have your assurance of secrecy?"

Several heads bobbed and the woman next to him choked off a snicker.

When she was again composed, and keeping her voice low, the widow leaned forward and addressed the rapt crowd. "I do thank everyone most sincerely. Now let us talk of topics we've not sworn to secrecy. Dominique," she spoke directly to the vixen in forged finery, "do tell us of what ever book you now enjoy. I so love literary recommendations from new acquaintances."

"I do not read." Dominique bristled, looking as though she had no clue how the topic had escaped her grasp and segued back to *her*. (Daniel wasn't sure he knew either but it had been great fun witnessing the little charade—for he had no doubt one had just been enacted.) "Not your English drivel."

"Don't read at all, I vow," his companion-soon-to-be-mistress whispered beneath her breath. Then brightly, to the table at large, "Of course you don't," and before Dominique could take umbrage—for no one seemed inclined to come to *her* defense, he noted—Mrs. Hurwell turned the focus yet again. "What of you, Sarah? Have you finished either of those two volumes you purchased at Hatchards last week?"

"Yes—what did you buy?" Harrison's beauty vaulted in with sincere interest. "I just completed Byron's *The Corsair* and found it easier to put down than his other works."

"Oh, did you?" Sarah said with a sly look at the woman seated between them. "Mrs. Hurwell practically fawns over Lord Byron. I could hardly *rip* the pages from her grasp the last time she beheld them."

"Perhaps so," his widow demurred, "but once they'd served their purpose I relinquished them easily enough..."

And so it went. Most of the table's occupants engaging in light, meaningless banter with the lovely Mrs. Hurwell chiming in as appropriate.

Daniel found himself more than pleased.

She answered promptly and with an undercurrent of wit not everyone circling the table seemed privy to. Her responses, while intelligent and entertaining—to him at least —were concise, he noted with no little degree of appreciation. Neither did she instigate conversation but only responded when posed a direct query.

Exquisite. Could he have asked for better?

LORD TREMAYNE'S admiring analysis and pleasure over Dorothea's lack of verbosity would have most certainly been mitigated had he but known how she battled the inner longing to turn to him and inquire fifty and one assorted things: Was he always this quiet? Did he truly like the glazed shoe leather on his plate? (He must, he'd downed it with nary a blink.) Which poets did he find particularly fascinating? And what in heaven's name was a munsons muffler?

The servants brought out another course, this one glazed duck—she thought. It was a bit difficult to tell as the poor bird was so raw it was practically still swimming. Foregoing the foul fowl altogether, Dorothea picked nimbly through the macaroni noodles—they seemed safe enough, if a trifle undercooked—and allowed herself to admit what she *really* wanted to ask: Why had Lord Tremayne neglected to shave his chin whiskers?

Was he growing out his beard or did he not care enough about meeting her to bother? And did he always smell so nice? (A curious combination of cloves and honeysuckle that made her want to forego the filling noodles and lick him instead. Shameful, she knew, but the urge was undeniable.)

What did he do with his days? Did he want *her* for his mistress? Had he any inkling yet, one way or the other? How often might he visit? *Was he married?*

Heavens to Hertfordshire, but just thinking of everything she wanted to ask him was enough to keep her mute. Well, her chaotic thoughts *and* Sarah's counsel: *Take your cue from him.*

So this was a man who wanted quiet? She shoved aside the pang of disappointment at not finding a boon companion in her first foray into the demimonde.

Then she fortified her resolve because *quiet* she could do; wedded to Mr. Hurwell, she'd lived in it long enough.

HOW SOON COULD THEY LEAVE? Blazing ballocks, but he'd guillotine Penry if he'd arranged some drawn-out shadow play as he'd done the last time Daniel consented to attend one of these asinine public affairs. That one had been years ago at Sarah's standard-strumpet townhouse, before his friend had invested more than common sense recommended in his high flyer's accommodations and purchased her this near mansion. Louise had been enamored with the salacious shadow play and once they'd returned to her lodgings, had wanted him to perform a strip behind a sheet, backlit by the fire, for her amusement (he'd sooner swim the Thames —*bound* in a sheet).

He cringed at the memory. Thank God she'd found another protector, some American captain more flush in his pockets than his crown office had swept her off to his ship. She'd sent round a perfumed note before they'd sailed to make sure Daniel knew she wasn't pining for him. He grunted. Not hardly. Who would pine for that bird-witted bird of paradise—when Paradise of another kind waited in the chair beside him?

A good night's sleep after a good round of frisking! He'd sing if he could, bellow out his delight—

What? Yammer out the tune of your faults?

By damn, he'd nearly forgotten.

A stunned, strangled groan worked its way free of his throat.

When she looked at him directly, the very source of his amazed consternation, a puzzled expression on her face, Daniel realized he'd gone practically the entire meal without uttering a word.

Gad, he was an arse.

4

BIRD-WITTED AS A CUCKOO OR LUCKY AS A LARK?

A voice so thrilling ne'er was heard
In spring-time from the Cuckoo-bird...

William Wordsworth, "The Solitary Reaper"

————————⊷∘⊶————————

IN THE DIMMEST part of the large drawing room, Dorothea pressed her back into the wall so hard she heard it snap (her back that is, not the wall).

Escaping to make use of the necessary directly after the sliced fruit course had seemed a good idea a quarter hour ago; rejoining the ribald social scene seemed anything but. Because once her eyes adjusted to the reduced lighting, over half the candles being extinguished, she beheld the most startling sight on a settee not ten feet away.

So much for the men savoring after-dinner port and the women idle gossip. Dorothea gulped and tried to merge her spine into the wall. Mayhap she could close her eyes and pretend to vanish—

"*He* really laps *her* like *he* means it, don't 'e?" a spirited voice asked in a conspiratorial whisper.

Startled to realize her secluded spot had been discovered, Dorothea nevertheless smiled when she realized who'd joined her. She'd met Susan before dinner and if the young woman's pronunciation wasn't consistent, her friendliness and sincerity of manner were.

Glad for the company, Dorothea promptly answered the H-heavy high flyer. "That he does."

Goodness, but she sounded woefully out of breath. Not taking her eyes from the couple both she and her companion spoke of, Dorothea filled her lungs and tried again. "I say, do all er, um..." How did one properly describe that which was so improper? Blazes! She could practically hear the saliva-induced suction from here! "Ah...do all titled gentlemen nurse themselves with such vigor upon the bosom of their paramours?"

"Wot?" The young woman's attempt at elocution slipped yet again. "Oh, you mean are they all so game when they suck on diddeys?"

"Um-mm..." When he switched his attention to the neglected nipple on the other side, she saw it was the gentleman with the large laugh and even larger nose.

Dorothea averted her eyes from the scandalous sight. But as though the unfamiliar tingling in her newly awakened breasts controlled her vision more than her sense of modesty did, her head immediately swung back. "I don't know that I've ever seen"—*or considered, and certainly haven't experienced*—"how such an activity might be done for so long and with such painstaking effort and zeal," she whispered to her companion. "He's very thorough, isn't he?"

Susan sighed hard enough to ruffle several of the gentleman's protruding nose hairs.

While Dorothea swallowed both laughter and dismay, her new friend answered with more than a hint of wistfulness. "Aye, Donny's—oops, I mean Lord Donaldson." Susan leaned close to confide, "'E told me to only call *him* that when we were naked. Well, *he's* one of the best I ever *had*. That man likes nipples more than a dry scone craves bacon-grease gravy, an 'e can kiss on 'em for a long while before *he* goes diving lower."

Another sigh made her fond recollections clear, though Dorothea wasn't quite clear on what "diving lower" meant.

She had an inkling, an incredible, too-shocking-to-be-accurate inkling but decided 'twas best to stay mum. No need to shock Susan with her ignorance—or herself with the improbable, impossible truth if *lower* did not mean one's umbilicus.

"'E don't like just bein' with the same woman over an' over, so 'e never keeps a mistress but 'e'll pay you well fer a night or two—and damn me if I ain't goin' and fer-*forgetting* my proper speech with you, Mrs. H. You're not as *hoity-toity* as some of them others."

Flattered, if surprised, Dorothea said, "Thank you. I'm the last one to put on airs. I'm rather new at the trade myself."

"I figured that out when Dominasty went after you at dinner. She's a real bitch, that one is."

Dorothea barely managed to stifle her gasp at the vulgar word she'd never heard another female utter—discourses on breeding dogs notwithstanding. Certainly, no one had ever said it knowingly in her presence before.

"She's a miserable rip to anyone she sees as a threat," Susan continued. "Don't pay her no, I mean, *any* mind. Crikey, but these things won't quit droopin'!" Susan bent over and hauled up her skirt, revealing an indecent amount of thigh—thanks to the drooping stocking.

Dorothea politely averted her eyes. Only to encounter several other indecent sights.

About the *only* decent thing remaining was the cluster of men congregating near the hallway and spilling into the opposite room. The more plentiful wall sconces that direction lit them clearly. Lord Tremayne was among their number and these gentlemen, unlike the others closer to her, remained vertical and clothed.

Sarah waved and caught Dorothea's attention. A quick lift of her brows inquired how Dorothea got on, a slight tilt of her head asked whether she needed immediate rescuing.

Feeling infinitely more at ease now that she and Susan were engaged (and she no longer held up the wall alone), also curious what else the young woman might impart about "Donny" or diddeys or any other formerly forbidden topic, Dorothea smiled encouragingly. *I'm all right*, she hoped her expression conveyed. *Betwattled to the gills but still breathing. Hostess away...*

After an understanding nod, Sarah headed toward the nearest servant to confer over something, leaving Dorothea where she was—which was swallowing her surprise over Susan's continued actions (really, she balked at a raised skirt, given what else currently went on?). "Those are the most lovely stockings," Dorothea told her honestly. "I don't believe I've ever seen that shade of lavender before."

Certainly not on stockings. Dorothea's feet fairly lit up at the prospect—would lavender stockings feel any different than ordinary ones? Hers, all two and a half remaining pair, were dingy beige—years ago, they'd started out white—and sporting more than a snag or two, she was shamed to admit.

Task finished, Susan straightened and fluffed her skirts. "Aren't they the most rum color? Lord Denten got them for me when—"

At a shout, Susan glanced up, then her eyes fairly

sparkled. "I 'ate to run off but looks like Cecilia's found us two gents fer the night." She squeezed Dorothea's elbow. "Now stop wringin' your hands and no one'll know how bedeviled by the jitters you are."

"Be well and thank you." Dorothea's parting words were lost when Susan's friend tromped over and grabbed her arm to drag her toward the waiting men.

Alone. Again.

Well now. That had been a refreshing exchange.

But Dorothea was still of two minds: Was she excited about the imminent physical prospects facing her later tonight or dreading them? Did she want this evening to be over swiftly and the die cast, her fate sealed, or did she want the minutes to eclipse slowly, giving her time to make the right decision?

Were the growing tingles in her abdomen anticipation over what might come? Or was her stomach simply seizing in a cramp because she'd not consumed enough food today? Or perhaps because it protested its recent and disastrous dinner?

Bah. Watching women abandon all sense of decorum because they enjoyed—nay, *encouraged*—the roving touch of a man was proving enlightening. Even thrilling, if she were honest.

Dorothea wanted to be scandalized by their behavior— she *should* be scandalized. But a heretofore unrecognized part of her found the couples' actions arousing. She was enticed to stare, even as part of her was compelled to turn away. The conflicting urges confused her almost as much as the man she'd come to meet.

Her eyes sought out his form again, though in truth, she'd been acutely aware of him all night.

Wretched man! Lord Tremayne hadn't attempted to converse with her during dinner, not once! Neither before nor after he'd so thoughtfully, so unexpectedly, sliced through all her misconceptions about peers when he'd adroitly severed the tough mutton for her. But still—not a word!

Did that mean he wasn't interested?

She sincerely hoped not. For if she were to indulge in sexual congress with another man—if some nipple-licking lord was going to place his hands and lips on her—then she desperately hoped *he* would be the one. Unlike her late husband, who had, all things considered, been rather nondescript, Lord Tremayne commanded attention without effort. The very air about him seethed with a dangerous excitement that made her feel both on edge and eager for another tantalizing taste.

"Well? Will he do?" Handing her a goblet of ratafia, Sarah came up and asked the question in a quiet but urgent voice, looking at Lord Tremayne who stood slightly apart from the crowd surrounding Lord Penry.

Grateful for something to strangle with her wayward hands, Dorothea took the glass by the stem and downed half the contents before coming up for air. "Sarah, why ever did you not introduce us? I believe without that formality, Lord Tremayne did not feel at liberty to address me directly."

"Oh, please say he didn't harp on that!" Sarah laughed without malice and her gaze found Dorothea's. "I deliberately left that to him so as not to embarrass you. Until you and he come to an official arrangement, I doubted you wanted it announced to the world at large that we'd intentionally matched you. I believe he's acquainted, at least by sight, with most everyone else, so I thought that the best way to proceed."

"Of course. Thank you, then, for your consideration." Dorothea couldn't stop her eyes from seeking him out.

At the sight of his tall, broad form, at contemplating

pressing hers along it once they were alone, a strange mew of longing filled her.

Quite the opposite of what she experienced when Big Nose gained an armful as Dominique landed on his lap—and his hand promptly disappeared under her skirts. (So much for ardent bosom worship; now he seemed intent on, indeed, diving *lower*, in every sense of the term.)

"What do they discuss so animatedly?" she asked Sarah when one of the other men rounded on Lord Penry and gesticulated as she imagined might a newly headless chicken.

"The recent riots," Sarah answered gravely. "They've caused much contention to erupt in Parliament, as members debate the corn regulations. Penry and a handful of others have brought petitions, signatures numbering in the tens of thousands, and have spoken against the Corn Bill as it stands, but their protests have gone mostly unheard. As public unrest has grown to such a violent state, he's rallying support, hoping to prevail."

Dorothea had heard mention of the riots that swept through the city days ago. Angry mobs protesting in the most violent way, attacking the homes of specific peers and members of both Houses. Hearing of the tumult the morning following was a far cry from watching those directly involved discuss the issue with such heat.

The House of Lords. The House of Commons. The king— or in the current clime, his rascally son. Powerful men whose decisions shaped, for good or ill, their country. Never before had Dorothea reason to consider what all went on, how a single conversation at a small dinner party might change the course of history. It brought home how far her station was from those present tonight.

A clock seller, a watchmaker. That's who she'd been wedded to. Someone who lived by the ticking turn of the big hand and demanded she do the same: up at five dings, breakfast at six dongs, open the store at eight chimes (or, when she wasn't swift enough to misalign something after he repaired it, annoying cuckoos), and so on...until bed twelve hours later when again those horrendous cuckoo birds sang (for by now, Mr. Hurwell would've fixed them). Only to do the cycle all over again the following day. To the *minute*. For in Mr. Hurwell's eyes, untimeliness was akin to thievery, murder, and idle chatter.

The only time things ever varied was when a nearby horse race was to be had, and Mr. Hurwell abandoned his me*tick-tick-tick*ulous dignity for the thrill of equestrian gambling.

She'd made the mistake, once, of teasing him about it—his fascination with clocks and all things that dinged, donged or gonged—early in their marriage. A simple comment which led to a setting down of monumental proportions and the severe admonishment that "Levity has no place in the life of a hard-working Englishman. Or his wife's." Bah.

She'd soon come to adore the races he closed the shop to attend, for those were the only days Dorothea enjoyed any freedom, didn't have to plan her every action according to her husband's methodical, ding-dong dictates.

Come to think on it, she hadn't seen Lord Tremayne consult his timepiece even once tonight. *And* he'd been sufficiently unmindful to arrive late. How wonderful was that?

But she was beginning to wonder if he'd ever deign to glance at her again.

Wretched, intriguing, wonderfully tardy man!

"They'll be a while, I'd wager," Sarah said. "Though I daresay Anna is bursting at the seams to visit." Sarah gestured toward the pretty blonde of middle years occupying one of the chairs farthest from the men. "She's increasing," Sarah explained sotto voce with a smile as they made their way toward her. "Or she'd be in the thick of the debate."

Dorothea didn't know what stunned her more—that a woman might dare argue politics with not just a man (which was shocking enough) but an entire group of them *or* that her pregnancy seemed a joyous thing. Wouldn't that mean an end to her protected situation?

With a light touch to Sarah's arm, Dorothea halted their progress. "Her benefactor—Lord Harrison. He isn't angered by her condition?"

"On the contrary. They're both delighted. She lost an unborn babe last year, and I gather Harry's ensuring she takes every chance to rest this time around. Now don't look so worried... This is a joyous thing—for them. For *yourself*, simply practice what I told you each time you have relations with Tremayne and your chances of conceiving will be drastically reduced."

They'd be *completely* reduced unless he approached her.

A circulating waiter came by for their empty glasses and after placing hers and the one she had to pry from Dorothea's fingers on the tray, Sarah started forward again. "They were *trying*, dearest. Both of them want this child."

A second later she was being entertained by the *enceinte* woman.

The next few minutes flew by in a startling blur of whispers and laughs, which did much to calm the quadrille-dancing butterflies fluttering about Dorothea's middle. Anna was a joy, as pleasant and welcoming as Sarah if more critical toward those she had no tolerance for.

Hearing her blast the absent Louise as a bubbleheaded ninny who deserved the coarse American she'd sailed off with, thereby informing Dorothea the woman most recently in Lord Tremayne's bed wasn't someone she need fear crossing paths with, greatly eased her chest. Laughing so hard when Anna launched into a diatribe about Italian accommodations only made it hurt anew but in a wonderful way.

Finally the men's talks wound down, due in part she was sure, to the enticement of several bored strumpets who took to climbing all over a few of the stragglers. Lord Harrison soon drifted over to steal his woman away after thanking his hostess.

"Hold tight to this one," Sarah told Anna after Lord Harrison effusively complimented dinner. "The devilish twinkle in his eyes tells you when he's spouting clankers. But he's so very sincere about it, I cannot help but approve."

Once they were gone and several other couples (*and* a couple of trios) followed—and once Sarah excused herself to ask Big Nose and Dominique to hie themselves off before soiling her settee—Sarah and Dorothea stood near where she'd begun the evening—the darkened corner, surveying Lord Tremayne and Lord Penry. Though the other men had drifted away, the gangly youth had joined them at some point. They were the only three still in earnest conversation.

"He's rather a magnificent specimen, is he not?" Sarah was staring straight at Lord Tremayne, leaving Dorothea in no doubt of whom she spoke. "And the way he fills out his inexpressibles..." Sarah made a sound of appreciation. "Impressive, to say the least."

Dorothea floundered. She wasn't used to discussing men or their attributes in detail.

Her murmur was noncommittal; her blush was not.

Sarah laughed quietly. "Don't mind me. Penry keeps me more than satisfied, financially and physically. I wouldn't be human, though, if I hadn't given a thought to being with Tremayne. Men like that don't seek to feather their love nest every day, which is why I've championed for the two of you to meet. Tragically, it so often seems the attractive ones are either insanely boring or horribly depraved."

"Depraved? You mean wicked? Lord Tremayne?"

Now why did that thought not have *her* hieing off? Mayhap, after years of restrained living, she craved a little wickedness—along with lateness—in her life.

"Certainly not. At least, not that I'm aware of. Tremayne keeps to himself more than most, but I've always found him sincere. A bit rough around the edges at times but charming nevertheless. Penry speaks highly of him. And the entire time I've been with Penry, Tremayne has only had the one mistress. Does that not bode well for your extended future?"

Rather than contemplate the future, Dorothea voiced her present concern. "I'm not sure he's interested in me. He hasn't said much." That was an understatement.

"Oh, posh. Have you not noticed the way he's devoured you with his gaze on multiple occasions?"

She hadn't. With a slight shake of her head, Dorothea commented, "He is very handsome in a ruggedly appealing way." Another understatement—and when had she begun to think of him thus? A powerfully built hulk of a man who towered over her by nearly a foot and had thick, coffee-colored hair—and whiskers—along with a propensity for sparse conversation...

How could she find that attractive? But then her nostrils flared and her mouth watered at the memory of his divine scent as though her other senses overrode that of sight. Aye. She found him easy on the eye, *if* easily intimidating.

But initial impressions were often erroneous. After all, hadn't she found Mr. Hurwell pleasant and agreeable during their first few meetings? Enough, certainly, to countenance a marriage to the man when her father pushed to secure her future.

Perhaps time with Lord Tremayne might soften his harsh edges (and ultimately find a razor blade scraping those whiskers to perdition).

Was she as bird-witted as her former husband's stupid cuckoo clocks? For beginning to yearn for a man she knew nothing about? Or could Sarah's earlier claim possibly be correct—was she fortunate enough to have found the answer to her unspoken prayers?

"Can you do this, do you think? Be intimate with him?" Sarah asked intently. "It's not too late to call a halt, but I truly believe he's a gentleman in every sense. He isn't addicted to drink nor to gambling. Doesn't overindulge at the table and isn't a pinch farthing when it comes to the ready—he kept Louise dressed in style and she always had pin money to fritter." Sarah gave an indulgent snort. "From what I can tell, his worst vice is his propensity toward tardiness, a minor inconvenience at best."

Now that she'd seen him, been intrigued by his manner and enticed by his scent, something akin to panic squeezed her chest at the thought of *not* going through with her intended plans for the evening.

"Aye! I want to go home with him tonight." Good heavens. She sounded overly excited about the prospect. This was supposed to be something she *had* to do, not something she *wanted* to do. Dorothea tempered her tone. "Well, if I absolutely *must* have a protector, then I believe Lord Tremayne will do."

Quite nicely.

"If you're sure?"

Why was Sarah expressing doubts now? It had been her idea to begin with! Dorothea might have been brought up to never remotely consider such an arrangement, but she also knew hunger. The newly added lace at her cuffs reminded her she also knew fear.

After finally meeting a titled gentleman in want of a mistress, one who took pains to considerately make mincemeat of her mutton, was she sure? She was positive that being with him far surpassed any other alternatives open to her at present.

"I am," Dorothea said with an emphatic nod, guilty excitement tingling in her belly. "But does he not need to approach me?" And before the clock struck midnight? She'd been acutely aware of the eleven resonant bells a while ago, chiming out her doom if he didn't get on with it.

"Fie! More often than not, men must be shown what they need. Are you game?"

Before Dorothea could nod her assent, Sarah grabbed her hand and was resolutely tugging her in the direction of the three men.

A short while earlier...

"WHO's THE RUNT?" Daniel nodded toward the lanky kid grinning at him from a distance. It was a touch eerie—the cub didn't appear to be gawking at anyone else.

Now that Penry had spoken his piece and Harry echoed the points with convincing—and enviable—ease, and between them they'd managed to sway at least three of the others to give their cause due consideration, it was past time to secure his little widow.

But something about the way the kid had been staring at him all evening set off alarm bells. Like the ticking of an overloud clock one couldn't ignore, Daniel had the feeling an explosion was about to detonate.

A feeling he shrugged off—why borrow trouble that didn't exist?

"That's Everson's youngest." Penry waved the cub over. "He's a huge admirer but you need—"

"Admirer of what? Loose women?"

"Tell me I didn't just hear that." Penry shot him a dark look. "You're under duress else I wouldn't let that slide without a slap."

A slap? As in challenge him to a duel? Over a jest? A quip barely slighting the man's mistress? When had Penry become so protective? And what was he nattering on about now?

"...to meet you." Penry spoke so low, Daniel saw his lips move more than heard him. "Fair warning, though, he—" Penry broke off when the boy raced the last few steps and reached them in a blink. "Tremayne, this eager fellow here is Thomas Everson, Jim's youngest. But he prefers to go by Tom," Penry said with the ease of long acquaintance.

With not more than a score of years under his belt—if that—the young buck stood taller than either of them, six-four or better, and his lack of muscle made him appear as long and thready as a weed. He had a shock of red hair and the type of fair skin that blushed abominably. Young Tom also had a smile wider than Penry's slab of a dining table.

"Tom, as you already know, this here is Daniel Holbrook, the Marquis of Tremayne."

Daniel gave a slight bow to acknowledge the introduction. Very slight—he wasn't used to looking up to anyone. Not since reaching his majority and the height of six-three, not since escaping the estate and his brute of a father.

Tom didn't look anything like *his* sire. Everson was a stout, beefy fellow well into his fifties. Without a daughter to his name, he was known more for his brood of nine sons than his talent in the ring, but Daniel had always found him a jovial, good-natured companion when they sparred. One who'd bluster on about anything with a smile on his face—even when Daniel's fist had just connected with it.

Everson was often accompanied by a son or two, but Daniel didn't remember ever seeing this one. Tom beamed at him and thrust his hand out in a casual show of greeting not found among mere acquaintances, never found from a pup to a peer.

Startled by the gesture as much as surprised to find himself grinning back, Daniel clasped Tom's outstretched hand. But holding on to the smile almost killed him when the boy started to speak.

"Muh-muh-muh-mmmmu-mmmmmm-ister Hollllllllll-brook, ssssssssir," Tom forced out Daniel's seldom-heard surname while holding his gaze, the boy's own expression as guileless as could be.

Kaboom! The bomb went off. Pieces of shrapnel, of syllables, exploding around him.

"*Ahmpa.*" The nonsense syllable blasted through the debris. "Mmmmmeannnnn Lllllllord-lord T-t-t-t-t-tr-trey-*mayne!*"

Was this a joke? A cruel jest? Penry getting in a dig after that thoughtless loose-woman crack? But no, Tom continued his laborious speech—and his clutching of Daniel's hand—with both enthusiasm and unbridled excitement.

"I've ad-mmmmred you *ahmp* sin-sin-since that-that-that-that match in Do-Dover."

And Penry, when Daniel shot a panicked glance his direction, only looked apologetic. His expression screamed a guilty *I tried to tell you.*

Realizing there was no help from that quarter, Daniel felt his head fight against him, his neck muscles objecting when he forced them back, returning his gaze to the boy's. Who was still smiling, still exuberantly massacring everything he uttered. Still gripping Daniel's hand.

"Fffffellled Thomp-*ah*-son fas-fas-faster than lightning, you did." A garbled breath, a few unintelligible sounds, then, "'Twas a beaut, my lord, a beaut of-fa-fa a fight, it was. Made me pa-pa-pa-*roud* to see it-t-t-t!"

Daniel was exhausted. Simply listening, without cringing,

required so much strength. He didn't know how much longer he could hold himself together. Every muscle screamed in protest, bunched tight from his ankles to his armpits.

But the kid wasn't finished—with his speech or with pumping Daniel's arm. "Yessirreee, ever since that-that-that-jab-you-you-lan-lan-landed in the fourth round, I've been affffffff-ter Papapapa to 'duce me..."

Tom went on, haltingly at times, furiously fast at others but always exuberantly, putting to shame the agony Daniel experienced each time he even thought to open his mouth.

He endured more accolades than he deserved, more praise than he warranted, but through the remainder of the painful recitation, the inarticulate articulations, he never tried to retrieve his hand and he never—not once—allowed his gaze to falter from the young man's.

It was excruciating.

As though he watched a mirror image of himself—though one nearly half his age who truly had things worse off than he did. A reflection that hurt, not so much because looking at it made him uncomfortable—which admittedly, it did—but because seeing *this* side of it, seeing how *his* image could have been projected into the world had he possessed a father like Everson, someone encouraging instead of cutting, someone constructive instead of destructive, made Daniel long for what he'd never had. Never *have*.

A different father and older brother. A different childhood. Acceptance, tolerance, lack of self-consciousness.

It made him long for a different life. A past not punctured with doubt and shame. A future not burdened with the expectation of failure.

It made him long to be anywhere but here.

Tom's speech was riddled and rutted with so many stops, starts and stumbles, it was a wonder he still stood. Still garbled out admiration that only scraped Daniel raw.

Finally, after his jaw had already started cramping in sympathy, the boy wound down. And just then noticed he still maintained possession of Daniel's hand.

"Oh-oh-oh-suh-suh-suh-*suhrry*, so sorry!" Tom's grip had tightened during his monologue and Daniel suspected it had been totally involuntary. Holding on to a lifeline so he didn't drown. One he now dropped like a hot coal. "Geh-geh-geh-geh-*get*-t-t-t 'cited and for-g-g-get-t-t."

And still the kid was smiling.

Deuced amazing.

Damned impressive.

How was he still going? Daniel couldn't fathom it. Tom had to be exhausted, the lack of air caused from all the muscles in his mouth and larynx seizing up on him, freezing out his breath, starving his body...

But dammit, he kept charging forward.

"Seen you at other b-b-b-b-bouts-bouts, I have-have-have*eh*. Never miss one if-if-if-fff-I-can-help-help-help-*ah*-it but that one's mmmmmmmmmy-my-my fav'rite!" He glanced at Daniel's hand and his cheeks flushed crimson. "Ap-p-ologize, I do! *Ackpm*. For-got-got-got myself."

Giving his mangled fingers a ginger stretch, Daniel raised his beleaguered hand to the boy's shoulder when Tom paused for a breath.

He gave a gentle squeeze. *Forgiven. Nothing to forgive, in fact,* he wanted to say. But he couldn't. Not after witnessing—after *living*—Tom's butchered speech.

So he nodded. And thought fast. But talked slow. "Hon-ored." Daniel brought his hand back to his side and felt strangely bereft. "High...praise you..."

Deliver? Bestow? Dammit! What else? *Think, man, think. Don't start mumbling like an idiot!*

5

PAST VS PRESENT VS PASSION

"Father, father, where are you going?
O do not walk so fast!
Speak, father, speak to your little boy,
Or else I shall be lost."

The night was dark, no father was there,
The child was wet with dew;
The mire was deep, and the child did weep,
And away the vapour flew.

William Blake, "The Little Boy Lost"

————————————◆◆————————————

DON'T BE AN IDIOT!

Oh, God. Memories swamped him, made his ears ring.
Strangled his tongue.

How many times had he heard that in his youth?

Don't mutter like a dolt! Stop yammering like a fool! Only idiots can't speak their mind. Guess that makes you an idiot, then, don't it? Get out of here, idiot-boy, can't stand the sight of you!

It hit him like a lightning bolt. One that flashed fierce and hard, sizzled through his veins as though his blood had caught fire. Not once had he thought of young Everson as an idiot. As something to belittle. Not once!

But himself? At the mere possibility of tripping over a letter or two, Daniel started thinking like his father. Condemning and cruel.

Nausea roiled through his gut as the force of his memories outweighed the knot of dinner by a stone.

And Tom Everson was still waiting. Penry still watching his every move like a mother hen protecting chicks from a fox.

"High p-praise— *Arghem.*" He cleared his throat to mask the fumble. As though he swallowed metal spikes with every sound, it felt scratched raw. "You shower on me," he somehow managed to say without mangling. Without running for the carriage as though Death chomped at his heels. "High... praise...in...deed."

When would he ever be rid of the old man's legacy? When, goddammit?

Peripherally he caught sight of Sarah and Mrs. Hurwell, heads together in conversation, eyes darting his direction. By damn! He'd forgotten all about her. His new mistress.

If he hadn't blundered that beyond salvaging. Ignore her during dinner. Neglect her afterward. Go home empty-handed and mistressless. Listless. Lonely.

Again.

But he couldn't abandon the boy, not even if it meant missing out on the pretty widow. Not after the courage the kid had just displayed. Was still showing, in fact.

"Wellllll deserved, mmmmy-my-my lord, well de-

deserved! Muh-muh-muh-*ight* you work with me, Lllllllllord Tremayne? In-in-in-the-the-ring?"

Only a heartless bastard would turn the boy down. Would be so cruel.

"Will-will-will you t-t-t-t-*teach* me?"

"Absolutely not."

And don't look at me like that. I can't be around you and be reminded.

Of what I never had.

That I'm turning into him.

Devil take me! I'm turning into him—the man I loathe most in all the world. I'm sitting like him, thinking like him, acting *like him.*

Fire burned along his lip, the old scar reminding him he'd never be free.

But he had to say something else. Couldn't leave it at that. Couldn't bear the dimming of the eager features, hated seeing the excitement falter into embarrassment, the hero-worship turning to hurt.

'Tis nothing to do with you, Daniel wanted to shout at Tom. But in truth it had everything to do with him.

Daniel couldn't be around Tom Everson and not constantly remember, not forever compare. He couldn't interact with the boy without seeing the life he *could've* had, had his father not been such a loathsome monster.

Daniel fought the constriction in his throat to force out, "Not just you...boy. I...don't...train." Mayhap not, but he did sound like a hard arse. "New fighters. Only spar with ...those ex...p'renced." He'd left off a syllable or two but couldn't bring himself to care. He only wanted to escape.

By damn, his insides had been dipped in burning coals, his whole body overly warm in places, searing hot in others. His neck burned, blistered by the fear. He had to get away before the rest of him turned to ash.

A light, joyful laugh drew his reluctant gaze across the room. Mrs. Hurwell, flushed from wine and he knew not what else, looked more fetching than ever. She caught his glance and gave him an encouraging, if timid, smile.

His fiery gut clenched with the renewed thrum of desire. Oblivion—for a few moments at least. That's what time with her body promised.

But he couldn't stomach *talking* to her for God's sake, not now. Not for the amount of time required to do the pretty before he plunged inside her to pound away his past.

Damn. He balled his sore hand at his side, contemplating: the woman or his sanity?

Who needed a new mistress? His bruised fingers should be sufficient for the task. If he yanked his pipe long enough, maybe he could jerk the growing pain right out the tip along with his spunk.

"Tremayne." At the unmistakable warning from Penry, Daniel wrenched his gaze back to Tom.

The kid was blinking fast, trying to hide the hurt. He didn't quite succeed. The smile he flashed was as wide as ever, but it didn't come close to reaching his eyes. "I-I-I-I-I unnnnnnnnn-der-der-sta-sta-sta-stand," he spoke softer and without any inflection. "Should've known beh-beh-beh-ter-ter-ter. *Mmmmmmmnnnnnnn. Ap. Ap. Mmmmnnnn.*"

Daniel missed the eagerness that'd characterized Tom's earlier efforts. But God help him, he couldn't miss how Tom's elocution had faltered, grown worse, less comprehensible. Leading him to believe the boy now shuffling back and forth on his feet had practiced the lines beforehand, rehearsed what he'd come to say.

But never thought to rehearse a rejection.

"Un-un-understandstandstand, I d-d-d-do. Papa told me not-not to pester you-you-yyyyyyyyyou. Should havvvvvvvvvv-*eh-eh* listennnnnned. *Mmmmmm...*"

When the word refused to come despite several seconds' effort, when his lips persisted in staying glued together despite his obvious efforts to pry them apart, Tom jerked his head to the side and reached up to slap his face, a hard *thwack* Daniel felt slam across *his* mouth. The slash of a cane instead of a palm. He bit the inside of his cheek to keep from crying out.

Tom looked back at Daniel, unshed tears welling in his eyes. The sight punched him in the stomach harder than any blow he'd ever received. "F-fa-fault. Meh-meh-meh-*mine*."

Daniel wanted to take the rejection back. Wanted to offer to meet the brave young man next week. To teach him everything he could.

He wanted to offer to be his friend.

But he did none of those things. Throat tight, neck aching with the strain, teeth and tongue trembling, he fisted his throbbing fingers tighter and inclined his head in a curt show of acknowledgment or dismissal—he knew not which, and he wasn't about to linger long enough to figure it out.

Before he could stop himself, Daniel pushed past Penry and stepped around Tom.

"Tremayne!" Penry called him back. But he kept moving forward, blindly racing for a way out.

You'll burn in hell, Satan spawn, his sire had screamed at him once (more than once if he were honest). He very well might burn, Daniel knew. But it wouldn't be for the sins his father falsely attributed to him. It would be for running away and crushing a young man's spirit. For sacrificing another man's dreams to preserve his own delusions of manhood.

In seconds, he reached the main door and waited impatiently while the grim-faced butler retrieved his coat and other paraphernalia. The moment it was within reach, Daniel coiled his fingers tight around the shaft of his fancy walking stick, as though only it could keep him from drowning in the quicksand the night had become. His elaborate walking stick —a useless item, but Elizabeth had given it to him years ago, claiming she'd blessed it with all manner of herbs and enchantments, and he'd brought it tonight for luck.

For luck. What a laugh.

He transferred the cane so he could shrug into his coat, his damn hand missing the armhole on the first two attempts, no matter that the butler held it out for him.

"Lord Tremayne!" The feminine voice bit through the haze of guilt prodding his frantic actions. "Are you off so soon? And...and *alone*?"

Wrenching the coat from the butler, he shoved it over his arm and gripped the walking stick. Smoothing his hand over the cool ivory ball at the top, seeking a measure of composure anywhere he might find it, he turned to face the obstacle. For now, all he wanted was *gone*. Gone from this place. Gone from his damnable memories.

Sarah and Mrs. Hurwell.

It took a second to register that it was the widow who'd called out to him, who gazed at him inquiringly, no doubt seeking understanding.

Daniel opened his mouth to send her on her way, to say he'd changed his mind. But with one good look at her, he snapped it shut.

Because instead of accusing condemnation, as her friend's expression held, the widow's countenance reflected a remnant of the wounded look he'd just caused on Tom Everson's face. Instead of angry, she looked baffled, disconcerted by his inexplicable retreat.

Hell. He was disconcerted by the whole damn evening.

Being this close to her again only brought home how much. He was attracted to her, of that there was no doubt. He wanted to know—nay, *feel*—what she could do with her mouth. So easily could he imagine how heavenly it would be to banish the hell brimming in his mind by hammering into her soft and welcoming body. "Ah, the lovely Mrs. Hurwell..."

Well, that came out flawlessly. Maybe *she*, rather than his ivory-handled walking stick, would prove to be his good-luck charm. "I am d-delighted...to mmake your acquain...tance."

And maybe she wasn't.

Blast it! The scene with the cub had definitely addled his mouth.

Fortunately, some sauced fancy piece—half her bosom modestly covered, the other half bouncing with abandon— chose that moment to run by, an indiscreet lordling hot on her heels. Her squeals and his shouts camouflaged Daniel's massacred greeting. Any other time the vulgar display might have made him frown; tonight he was hard pressed not to blow the trollop a kiss.

He turned back to the widow. As though the bawdy exhibit of bare breast had never been flaunted, she stared at him with calm, pale eyes the color of the underside of a velvet leaf. Beautiful eyes, oddly haunting, threatening to drown him in curiosity and uncertainty.

If any decency resided in him at all, he'd pay her for the month and give her to Tom Everson. Salvage his pride with the gesture.

But he was too damn selfish.

Mrs. Hurwell had come here for him. Dammit, she was meant to be *his*.

He knew he'd disappointed her, taking off the way he had. Yet still she gazed at him with something akin to hope. The wary stance she employed, the perceptible, if squashed, optimism—as though poised to run herself but reluctant to do so —put him in mind of Cyclops when he'd rescued the dog. She might put on a brave front, but he couldn't shake the notion she was quaking inside.

It only endeared her to him.

Though Sarah hovered right behind her, a fierce frown pinching their hostess's forehead, it was the widow who commanded his attention. She had a way about her that drew him mightily. A pliableness to her features, a soft hesitancy to her eyes as she stood there after chasing him down as he tried to escape his past...

By damn, he might not be as brave as Tom Everson, but he was man enough to speak up for what he wanted—which was her in his bed. Posthaste.

"Shall we depart?" The smooth delivery put him on his guard; he didn't trust his mouth to be so cooperative again.

Damn, his neck ached abominably. He just wanted to prig her and go to sleep. In her arms if she'd let him.

Hoping to alleviate the growing tension climbing up his jaw, he stretched his neck under the guise of transferring his walking stick to his opposite hand. He proffered her his free arm, the one unburdened by his haphazardly folded coat. "I"—*desire you fiendishly*—"wish to be off and would prefer we...go...to...gether."

When she hesitated, her gaze darting between him and her friend, Daniel intentionally relaxed his jaw, softened his posture. If he was scowling at her as he feared, she'd be a noddy to go anywhere with him.

As casually as he could manage, he lowered his arm. "'Tis your choice of course...but I would...be honored should you..." *Decide?* Nay! He quickly cast about and finished in a rush, "Choose-accompany-me."

Giving her a moment, trying not to berate his brain for panicking, he ordered his heart rate to slow. Deliberately, with every appearance of one with idle time on their hands, he strolled past her and approached Sarah to make his bow.

"Mm..." *Miss? Mrs.?* Blazing ballocks, he had no clue what her last name was, *Penry's woman* being how he typically thought of her—*if* he thought of her at all.

Wholly aware of the woman staring at his backside, the woman likely debating whether she wanted to see it bedside, he took a desperate breath and prayed his mouth wouldn't seize up. He started anew. "Sarah. Thank you for including me...tonight. Most gracious of..." Hell, he was growing hoarse. A hoard of frogs having jumped in his mouth along with his foot. "Of you."

He heard the widow shift in place and angled his head, silently watched the byplay between the women. Sarah's brows rose inquiringly and Mrs. Hurwell gave a slight nod, then stepped forth, ready to accompany him.

But then Penry's woman stood on tiptoes, pressing on his shoulder until he tilted his head, whereupon she whispered something to him that had *his* brows shooting skyward.

And the scowl returning full force to his face.

―――――――⊷◦⊷―――――――

LIKE A CANDLE THROWN on a frozen lake, Lord Tremayne waxed hot and cold.

When he swung back to face her, his frown once again in place, Dorothea feared this time the downward tilt was etched in stone.

What had Sarah just said to cause its return?

She faltered as she reached him, her already shaky confidence wavering at the unholy glower he leveled her way. Fierce, then fiercer still, yet she couldn't bring herself to walk away. Or to truly want to.

Because in the brighter entryway, the bruises hiding beneath his whiskers were unmistakable. And despite the hint of a scar on his lip, despite his formidable presence and fearsome grimace, she instantly felt an accord with him.

Had she not sewn lace on her cuffs for the very same

reason? To mask unsightly bruises—though she doubted *his* were from a grubby, grabby landlord.

Suspecting the reason for his facial scruff lessened her dislike of it.

On the surface, she worried whether Sarah had landed her with a ruffian, a man inclined to shows of temper. But deeper, almost instinctually, her mind contradicted that assumption: Would a ruffian slice her serving? Would a royster have so many of his peers jockeying to greet him upon his arrival? Or monopolizing his attention after dinner?

Admittedly, Lord Tremayne possessed a most distinguished countenance, when one troubled themselves to look beneath the angry façade. The side whiskers in front of his ears and angling toward his jaw were shaped most adroitly, tempting her fingers to smooth along their contours, to seek out that tiny indentation bisecting both lips on a slant.

His posture was exquisite, the breadth of his chest impressive. His deep, somewhat gravelly voice, when he chose to bestow it, reverberated through her in the most invigorating way. And really, given the placid years that stretched behind her, was she not due some invigoration?

Dorothea shifted in place, considering.

If she wasn't meant to be with him, would she still feel so inexplicably jealous upon seeing where his gaze had landed mere seconds ago—on the voluptuously exposed breast of the circling cuckoo in their midst?

Regardless! Dorothea chose not to evaluate how her own less-than-charming charms compared in the size-and-bounce arena.

She'd counter his every frown with a smile as long as his actions didn't pose a threat. But lay one finger on her in anger and she'd take a boot to his crown office, then one to Sarah's posterior for placing her in jeopardy.

That image fortifying her, Dorothea smiled past her

nerves and allowed her reckless enthusiasm to show. "Lord Tremayne, I would very much like to accompany you, if that is still your wish."

His expression inscrutable, he grasped her gloved hand and pulled her forward as he bent to place a kiss just above the bend of her wrist.

"Mistress Hurwell?" his deep voice intoned as he looked past the length of her arm and sought her gaze. "My wishes have not changed."

This close to him again, with his big, strong hand holding gently to her fingers, the warmth from his breath reaching through the leather, her arm practically melted. "Call me Dorothea, please."

His grimace tightened perceptibly.

What? Had she crossed some line? Her fingers flexed within his.

He immediately unclenched his jaw and swallowed. Giving his head an abrupt shake, he stroked his thumb over her trembling fingers. "Thea, I think. It suits you...better."

Who was she to argue? At the heated look in his amber eyes, she feared she would've agreed if he'd suggested her new name be "Turtle".

Sarah stood a short distance away, foot tapping on the floor, arms crossed, eyebrow raised, waiting for more—from both of them, Dorothea sensed.

She looked back at Lord Tremayne (looked *up*, more precisely, given how he'd straightened). Her smile came naturally this time. "Thea. Would be lovely to hear it again," she told him. "'Tis what my mum called me when I was a girl."

"Are you agreeable?" Lord Tremayne cleared his throat and his gaze drifted to where he maintained possession of her hand. "Ah...to our union?"

Her palms were sweating in her gloves. She longed to rip them off and touch—

Places she likely shouldn't.

Was she agreeable? Goodness, he'd already seduced her entire arm; she was eager for him to seduce the rest of her.

"Aye." Her head jerked in a nod. "Quite."

As *Thea* (how appropriate—a new name to go with her new life) closed the distance between them, Sarah gave her a relieved nod and glided away. Now it was just her and her new protector—and the hovering butler, his eyes painstakingly averted, her reticule dangling off one finger.

Lord Tremayne saw it as well and released her.

While he put on his greatcoat, Thea reached for the small purse. "Thank you, Simms."

Free of the feminine burden, Simms nodded toward a footman who opened the large door. A blast of icy spray swirled inside, nipping her feet with the threat of frost. Dorothea stamped them in place. "I am ready, my lord."

"Your cloak?" Lord Tremayne sounded incredulous at the lack.

Her "cloak"—the coat of Mr. Hurwell's she'd taken to wearing after his demise, being both warm and worn, thereby easily overlooked in the stews.

Rather than admit she'd chosen not to wear the tattered rag—one sleeve ripped completely off thanks to the most recent tussle with Grimmett—she pretended she hadn't heard his question. Winding the strings of her reticule through the fingers he'd so recently caressed, she queried, "I'm to accompany you home, then?"

"I've arranged for your lodgings." He stilled the nervous gesture by placing her arm on his. Her eyes swept from the sight of the new cream-colored gloves—thank you, Sarah!—atop his muscular forearm covered in dark wool, up to his face.

"We could retire there now?" His lips quirked in what she suspected was meant to be a reassuring smile.

Reassuring to a tart in truth, perhaps.

Thea swallowed her apprehension. "I would like nothing better, my lord," she said rather convincingly, she hoped. "Lead on."

Which he did, the large man with the intimidating scruff and inviting scent escorting her out of the safety of Sarah's home and into the dark, damp unknown.

With nary another word.

IN MOMENTS they were ensconced in his magnificent carriage, a grand conveyance far surpassing any other coach or hack she'd ever climbed into. The night air was thick from the day's rains, the cobblestones slick, but as the horses pranced forward and the well-oiled wheels turned smoothly, Thea couldn't help but marvel how she was—wonder of wonders —snug and safe.

If at sixes and sevens over how to go on from here. Lord Tremayne remained stubbornly mute and she claimed not the courage nor the fortitude to break the silence.

In such close confines, his alluring scent was stronger. Or perhaps she still reacted to the lung-expanding whiff she'd stolen when he handed her up and had seen her comfortably seated on the plush bench before settling his large frame into the one across from her.

Four feet, mayhap five. 'Twas all that separated their upper bodies. But it seemed a mile.

A single lamp lit the interior. Lit one side of his harsh face and the ivory knob of the walking stick his leather-encased thumb methodically stroked.

Lit her lap where she twined and tangled her fingers as she battled two horribly opposed notions: her gloves or the door?

Her gloves, she was sorely tempted to rip off so she might

touch his whiskers, could learn whether they were prickly as she suspected, or possibly, absurdly, soft to the touch. A most contrary yearning, given how she also contemplated opening the coach door and hurling herself into the night, fleeing the intensity of his presence...

Wholly aware of his speculative gaze evaluating her person, Thea was riddled with self-doubt now that they were alone. It was nearly time to lie in the bed she'd recklessly made.

The bed he'd bought, as surely as he'd bought her favors.

Uncertainty besieged her. She lifted back the curtain and focused on what she knew lay beyond the security of his richly appointed carriage: Grimmett, hunger...and unsavory mounds of mice doodles.

IN THE MEAGER light afforded by the dwindling lantern, Daniel studied the subdued Widow Hurwell. *Thea.*

Seemingly immune to the frigid air, she sat with her back straight against the squabs. Both feet, encased in scuffed leather slippers, were placed firmly on the floor and her hands were knotted in her lap.

If he didn't know better, he'd think she was on her way to her execution, not her new home.

Did she seek to avoid him? Or was she simply interested in their destination? With rapt fascination, she gazed out toward the darkened streets, tilting her head to survey both where they headed and where they'd been.

The action exposed the pale skin of her cheek and throat.

A throat sans woolen scarf. A body—now trembling—attired in anything but a fashionable state.

"Your...belongings?" he asked. Other than the small reticule hanging from her wrist, she didn't have any personal effects. *No cloak?* No cape, nor pelisse? *Nothing?* He was still baffling over that discovery.

A slight movement of her head indicated she heard his question although it was a moment before she answered. "I'll retrieve my things tomorrow."

He thought to offer assistance, but she continued before he could phrase the words. "There isn't much, really. Only a few articles of clothing." She glanced at him and added, "Nothing I'd miss if everything vanished during the interim." A shy smile, then she returned to contemplating the view beyond the carriage. And he returned to contemplating her skin.

Delicate, smooth, inviting... Inviting his touch, his lips?

Sarah's parting words rose up to haunt him. *Mind you moderate your passions with her, Tremayne. Don't rush your fences and let your ardor overwhelm her.*

What the devil had Penry's woman meant by that caution? The one she'd whispered frantically in his ear just before they'd left.

Moderate his passions? Talk about interfering with his plans for the night.

He shifted in his seat and Thea jumped.

She turned from the window, letting the curtain fall back, and fixed her gaze on him. Her large, surprisingly pale eyes met his in the feeble lantern glow—the fuel needed refilling. But he was glad for it. Some of the starch seemed to go out of her spine the more the flame flickered.

He was acutely aware how his arousal increased as her steady regard lengthened.

Those eyes of hers did things to him. A soft jade green, her gaze held his without wavering. He'd only seen that exact shade once before, during a trip to the coast when he was a boy and his family still intact.

He and David had loved splashing in the ocean, watching the waves break upon the mossy, rock-crested shore.

She blinked, her expression unchanging, and Daniel shook himself.

Gad. He hadn't thought of that time in years. Robert had been off at school. He and David barely seven and, as always, inseparable; Ellie but a babe trailing after them. It was so clear he could taste the salt coming off the ocean, feel the chill of the water, the roughness of the rocks as he and his twin competed in a crab-catching contest, Mama laughing at their antics while Father indulgently looked on. That was before their sire had become such a beast.

The memory threatened to turn him maudlin and Daniel blamed her—Thea, with the moss-colored eyes. The refined features. The full lips.

Blasted ballocks—temper his passions? When all he wanted was to banish that lace fichu out the window and plunder her mouth with his while he plunged his hand down her dress to plunder the rest of her?

So he could fondle a handful of pointy-tipped breast and stop thinking of mossy banks, ocean discoveries and *moderating* his bloody passions.

His well-sprung carriage gave an uncharacteristic lurch as his driver hollered at another.

Instinctively Daniel's arm shot out to steady Thea but 'twas unnecessary. She'd done no more than bobble in place, as though staring at him silently, unnervingly, somehow gave her inner strength.

Disconcerting, it was. Desirable too. Deuce—

Another sharp swerve cut off the thought.

"Sorry, milord!" Roskins called out. "All's right now, it is!"

To acknowledge the apology, Daniel tapped the head of his walking stick on the roof twice, then replaced it beside him, all without ever taking his eyes from hers.

And still she watched him watching her.

The constant *clippety-clop* of the horses filled the gently swaying carriage. That and the sound of his and Thea's breathing. Gad, she was quiet. Louise would have blathered on enough to wear out his wattles.

He reached up to rub one, just to make sure his hearing was still intact.

How many times had he been grateful there was no void for him to fill? Conversely, how many times had he wished for a latch upon the hinges of her jaw so he could stop the incessant chatter?

He'd tolerated the tavern-grade soliloquies on bonnets and baubles and butterflies, pleased naught was required of him in response. Yet he'd yearned for silence on occasion, to be blessed with a modicum of restful, peace-filled companionship.

Did he not have his wish now? Silence.

Peaceful, horrible, grating silence.

One that threatened to allow the guilt from earlier to swell and—

No. None of that now. He wouldn't think of Tom Everson or how he'd treated the boy. Wouldn't remember the crestfallen look on his face or feel bloody responsible. Not tonight.

Daniel cast about for salvation and found it seated across from him.

What did Thea like?

Byron, he recalled from dinner, with an automatic twist of his lips. Poetry. Something he'd learned early and well to detest. Especially from poets whose names began with "B".

Byron...*Blake*. For those, he held a particular abhorrence.

William Blake, the word-wielding rascal, had gifted Daniel's father with a rare volume of his works. A volume his sire revered but that he and his twin thought better suited to post chamber-pot wiping than recreational reading.

Sadly though, young boys had little say in their education especially when their elders held a particular engraver-turned-poet in high esteem. As a consequence, their childhood tutor forced him and David to study and recite the lines *ad nauseam*. To this day, Daniel regretted how he could not block them from his memory.

He was *not* a "Little Boy Lost", by damn! Neither was he a man who needed to moderate his bloody passions!

But damn his infernal curiosity, he did want to know more about his new mistress.

Did she have a bonnet collection numbering upwards of thirty-seven? Did she waste considerable time cataloging baubles enough to fill fourteen jewelry cases? (Nay, for she wore not a single one upon her plainly dressed person.) What of butterflies? Was she, perhaps, enamored of their wing colors?

Enamored to a sufficient degree to spike a pin through their hearts and tack them in a padded box? To retrieve and carry with her a broken, iridescent wing and tell the milliner *that*, precisely, was to be the exact shade of the ribbons on her next bonnet?

All atrocities his former, fancifully dressed fancy piece had indulged in.

Daniel couldn't see it, none of it. Not from Thea, the composed, if absurdly, *annoyingly* quiet woman across from him. But by God, he wanted to *hear* it from her lips.

So he pried his open. "Tell me of yourself."

She jumped as though a cannon blasted from his mouth.

"What would you know?" she said after recovering her composure. "You have but to ask and I am pleased to share, though I fear you will find me an uninspiring topic."

She was wrong, so very wrong.

Daniel thought a moment, determining the best way to inquire without revealing his weakness. No longer could he expect rescue from a top-jiggling trollop. "How long ago were you widowed?"

Now that was brilliant. First question he poses is about the other man most recently in her life? Hell, he might as well have asked her if her husband was a good lover.

He bit his tongue to still the plethora of other thoughts yearning to break free. *Had* her spouse been a good lover? Was there anything she particularly enjoyed in the bedchamber? Anything she wished to avoid? Would she, perchance, be amenable to amorous convincing, should the need arise? (His need had arisen, achingly so, now that she was close and they were alone.)

"Just over a year, my lord."

A year what? His mind blanked, too busy conjuring thoughts of her splayed across his big bed.

Daniel ground his teeth and cast about for another query, minus any troublesome letters.

"We were married nearly eight," she saved his tooth enamel by offering. "I knew Mr. Hurwell most of my life. He and my father were friends."

Which told him much. He and her *father* were friends. Not her.

As though she'd shared more than she meant to, Thea's eyes sought the closed curtain. Her hands fidgeted—a flurry of movement that wound his gut tighter than the strings of her reticule.

Hurwell. Hurwell. *Mr. Hurwell.* Why did that name sound familiar? Why did his mouth burst out with, "So it-it wasn't a love match?"

She mashed those lovely lips together before freeing them to say, "Nay. 'Twas a match of convenience. *Their* convenience. My father and Mr. Hurwell's, that is. When Papa fell ill, he urged me to accept the proposal, which had been repeated more than once. I finally did so, to give him some reassurance at the end."

She was talking now, which was all very well and good but not at all what he wanted to hear.

The gulf between them threatened to widen, from a carriage to a chasm. "It won't do."

His deep, gravelly murmur surprised them both. She gasped at his intensity; he smiled because it came forth without hesitation.

"What won't, my lord?"

"This...ah..." Regardless of the convenience of making her his convenient (which made him no better than her deceased husband, he realized on a groan), he was curious about Thea, about her past, her dreams. About her missing coat. *About what lay beneath the drab olive gown.* It won't do. Nay, not at all! "This..." Divide? Distance? "*Space* between us. Won't...suffice."

The exposed skin of her neck beckoned once more. Would it be as cold as the air between them or, if Ellie's bewitching cream had truly blessed him, hot like passion?

The seats creaked as he rose and transferred to the one she occupied. Her startled glance flittered away. He wasted no time stripping off his gloves. With one hand, he covered the tangled fingers in her lap. With the other, he cupped her cheek and turned her to face him.

Warm. Even in the cold night air, her skin was heated, giving him his answer. *Passion.* No frigid miss could have skin this warm.

He bent his head to press his lips to hers and the fingers beneath his tightened further.

Giving in to his body's urging, he opened his mouth and slid his tongue over her lips.

She jerked back with a gasp, staring at him with overly bright eyes. A sharp trembling besieged her limbs.

His heart sank.

If she scared this easily at his touch, how was he supposed to bed her?

He wasn't in the habit of supplying lodgings for just any female off the street. Neither could he imagine taking his pleasure with someone who shrank from his touch.

Sliding his hand from her face, the other from her lap, he leaned back against the seat and expelled a breath. Then another. He turned his head, eyes seeking hers, expecting condemnation. Instead, finding only her outline, the interior lantern having burnt down to fumes.

He unclenched his jaw to inquire, as silkily as he could manage—no need to scare her further— "Problem?"

She'd raised a hand to her mouth. He saw a hint of her fine, pale glove when she lowered it to her throat. "What-what do you mean?"

"Is there a...prob...blem?" He waited a moment. When she didn't respond, he clarified, "With my t-t—" *Deep breath, Daniel,* he remembered his grandfather saying, *the words will come when they're ready.* Well dammit, he needed them ready now. "You have issues with my...touch?"

"Nay!" she said emphatically, convincingly. "Not at all. I, um...ah..." The hand at her neck took to fanning her face, tiny, panicky puffs of air he felt a foot away. "I'm not used to kisses such as yours."

Gad. Even his kisses were wrong. Too passionate? he wondered and then discounted the insane notion. He'd barely touched her.

Despite his attraction, he was becoming concerned. If she couldn't stomach his kisses, how would she tolerate his cock? "What t-t-type of kisses are you used to?"

"Are you laughing at me?" She sounded stiff, hurt by the thought.

"Laughing? At you? *Never.*" When she remained defensively quiet, he ordered, "Thea. Answer me."

How else would he know how to please her?

"None at all. I'm not used to any manner of kiss." The words were a shameful whisper, one that lashed at his conscience for demanding she admit it. But he couldn't regret the urge when she tore off one glove and gripped his hand, halting his retreat back across the squabs. "Pray, do not fault me for the lack," she implored into the shadows between them. "I've not had ample opportunity to receive nor bestow such affection."

Ample opportunity? "Oh?"

"*Your* kiss—'twas not unpleasant, only unexpected. I...."

When the lantern flame flickered and faltered, fizzled to nothing, she clutched him harder—the hand that hadn't suffered a mangling previously—and Daniel sensed she was winding up to confess all under the cover of darkness. "Earlier tonight, I watched Lord Big No—*ahem*, Lord Donaldson —lick...ah, *intimate* parts of his partner, but I failed to consider your tongue questing upon my mouth. Silly of me, I know." Her laugh was self-mocking. "It was my omission. I do apologize."

Her fingers pulled at his, but he was too startled by the halting revelations to do more than enjoy the way she plucked at the naked skin of his palm while she haltingly said, "Please be assured, and I mean this most sincerely, Lord Tremayne, you may feel at liberty to place it there again."

It? His tongue? She invited him to place it upon her mouth?

Though beyond tempted, he had to clarify, "What 'intimate p-parts' exactly?"

"You knave!" A muffled giggle escaped as she tossed his hand from her. "Now I know I hear laughter in your voice."

She heard laughter when he felt lunacy? That would do. Would do famously. "Nay, 'tis curiosity."

"'Tis most ungentlemanly of you," she accused with breathless abandon, "to mock my ignorance thus."

'Twas most ungentlemanly of him to delight in her admitted ignorance but he did, oh how he did. So he told her. "You de-delight me."

"I delight your funny bone, you mean."

It was true.

He found, the more they bantered in the blackness, that he *was* suppressing laughter. What a freeing experience. "T-tell me"—he fisted the recently abandoned fingers to keep from groping her in the dark—"if not your m-m-mouth, where d-did you consider my...tongue upon your person?"

The perplexing widow (Was she one *in truth*—in the fleshly sense? Had her horse's arse of a husband truly *never* kissed her?) refused to answer what Daniel most avidly wanted to hear. Although what she did next was infinitely better: she blindly raised her ungloved hand to his cheek, skimming it up his chest to map the way. He swallowed thickly when her fingers glided up his neck and again when they settled upon him.

She feathered her thumb across his lips and he felt the imprint of each individual finger cupping his jaw as she guided his head down while lifting hers.

Their lips touched a second later.

This time he kept his tongue to himself, wanting to see how *she* might kiss, given ample opportunity (which he had every intention of supplying her, every chance he could). In fact, he was more than willing to let her experiment on him, as much as she wanted, as long as he could entice her.

"Whoa. Whoa now!" Roskins brought the horses to a decisive stop. Their bodies lurched in tandem with the carriage. "We're here, milord."

Damn.

Did their mouths cling, reluctant to part, or was that mere folly on his part? A breath later, her lips were gone. The hand on his jaw flexed, then fled.

Thea edged away with a tiny whimper.

Of what? Frustration—that they weren't continuing? Fear —of him? Of what awaited her in the townhouse he'd procured?

What *did* she feel at the too-brief kiss? Irritation it hadn't deepened or relief at the interruption?

Daniel knew what he felt—twenty stone of pure lust. Another forty of regret—that he hadn't claimed her lips sooner, as in the second they'd entered the carriage.

When he moved to open the door, Thea stayed his arm. All humor had fled from her when she spoke. "Please. Do not hold my lack of experience in mistressing arts against me." *Mistressing arts?* "I remain very aware of the honor you do me, granting me the chance to please you. And once we arrive inside"—her voice cracked, giving lie to her words—"I'm ready for you to take me, my lord."

6

TAWDRY OR TITILLATING? 'TIS A MATTER OF OPINION...

———— ❦ ————

UNCERTAIN AS TO the protocol for one in her position, Thea stood just inside the door of her new home. Upon first glimpse, she could tell it was grander than any place she'd lived.

Grander and golder and, well, *gaudier*. And she absolutely loved it.

The lower walls were painted a rich scarlet; above the wainscoting, they glimmered bronze in the flickering wall sconces. Flush against one wall and flanked by two ornate chairs, a rectangular table was draped with a red and bronze, fringe-trimmed brocade. Several ceramic figurines cavorted on one side of the table (carnally, if she wasn't mistaken) and a gleaming oval tray occupied the other, its polished surface conspicuously empty. Awaiting her correspondence?

How very indulgent!

The unexpected décor lent an opulent feel to the very air. Inhaling the lavish scents of decadence and relief—had she ever been privy to such a sumptuous, *safe* home?—Thea paused at the table to remove her remaining glove, placing the pair near the glittering tray.

Above the table, an arched mirror reflected her pale face and drab dress, along with two coordinating paintings on the opposite wall—her escort had stalled in front of one—each showing a voluptuous, artfully nude female in a very suggestive pose. Thea found it easier to focus on those wicked images rather than her own plain one.

The resplendent, if debauched, excess—from the obscene figures to the stark naked models adorning her new walls—were the exact opposite of the pallid squalor she'd been reduced to the last few months. Naughty or not, Thea knew a home this splendid surely boasted more than moldy potatoes in the larder.

And that made it very fine indeed.

After shedding his coat and slinging it over the arm of one chair, Lord Tremayne came up behind her and caught her gaze in the mirror. He placed his warm hand low across her back and cleared his throat. "Not what I—"

He choked off what sounded like a curse and his fingers flexed just above her hip. The added pressure incited a tremor that quaked through her legs and down to her toes. Thea's feet stretched in the cold slippers as heat blossomed.

"I like it," she said before he could deride her new abode, turning against his large form to look up and capture his gaze directly. "I like it exceedingly. It's more beautiful than I imagined." And to think—she'd only seen the entryway!

He grunted—and slid his hand a bit lower.

Her breath caught in her throat but then a strident bird cry arrested her attention and his hand fell away when he stepped back.

Cuckoo—cuckoo—cuckoo...

Through twelve interminable seconds, they both stood

transfixed. Because instead of a sweet (or annoying) chirping bird extending out and bobbing sprightly, their eyes were greeted with two figures, one unmistakably male, the other female. Female *and* on her knees, mouth open and bobbing over his...er...um...

"Gracious me," Thea said when she could garner a breath. "That's...that's..."

"Filthy."

His ragged growl drew her gaze away from the clock. Was that embarrassment flushing the tips of his ears?

Thea's eyes darted over the portraits, the figurines, the cuckoo clock, and finally settled on the man in front of her.

"I was thinking funny," she said lightly. "Wretchedly funny."

The dark scowl faded to be replaced by a slow and knowing grin. "Funny? Aye, Thea, we'll...d-do—" He broke off on a slight cough, muffled quickly by his fist. "Shall we?"

Extending his arm, he indicated the prominent staircase that stood off to the right. If this townhouse was arranged as most, the split stairway led down to the kitchen and up to the bedchambers.

Thea nodded and he gestured for her to precede him, placing one hand on her waist as their feet followed the ascending path of the crimson runner. Though acutely aware of the gentle pressure of his fingers curved near her hip, Thea had to bite back a laugh.

If a scant hour in his company had taught her that mayhap she didn't hate *every* cuckoo clock, what other surprising revelations might her new association bring?

AT THE TOP LANDING, only one door stood ajar. Lord Tremayne steered her toward it.

"My, how lovely and-and—" She gasped, stumbling to a

stop just over the threshold, barely muting her *monstrously huge*. Without doubt, this chamber alone had to be the size of the entire living quarters above the clock shop.

With none of the ostentation found below, the elegant cream-and-pink room possessed beautifully carved furniture. Painted roses trailing on vines decorated each piece of the matching set: armoire, a dresser along one wall, and a pair of chairs at a circular table occupying a corner.

There were few adornments beyond the furniture itself, simply the large bed, a vase of real roses atop the armoire— how extravagant—and lit candles sprinkled liberally throughout—how doubly extravagant.

As he hovered closer, Lord Tremayne's heat scorched along her back. Under his direction, Thea stepped farther into her new room.

"May I have a moment of privacy?" she asked, surreptitiously looking for the chamber pot.

He indicated a shadowed door across the expanse. "I... believe what you seek is through there."

"I'll hurry," she promised, edging toward what she realized was an adjacent dressing room. "Just please, ah...give me a moment—"

"Thea." He held up one hand and gestured between them and then to the bed, his gaze never leaving hers. "This is...not a race."

"Then I won't hurry," she assured him. At his raised eyebrow, she blurted, "But neither will I dally."

Her cheeks heated at the amused look he gave her and Thea rushed to the promised respite, swiftly shutting the door behind her.

Only to find the windowless room completely dark.

Completely, as in pitch-black.

She blinked and waited—to no avail. She wouldn't have known if a herd of mice were juggling grapes at her feet.

Thea eased the door open. Lord Tremayne hadn't moved. "A candle—" She pointed as she sped toward the closest one. "I'm afraid I need it."

"B-by all means." The wretch was laughing at her again, but she couldn't seem to mind, not when his eyes twinkled too. He clasped his hands behind his back, and when she raced past him again, candle in hand, he winked.

Face flaming, body thrumming, Thea escaped to the sanctuary of the dressing room where she found not only the chamber pot but also a basin of water and more personal necessities than she knew what to do with. And, unmistakably, what she was expected to don for the night—a long, ivory gown hanging next to the washstand.

Knowing she mustn't tarry, she quickly disrobed and took care of her ablutions. Rather than linger over the task, one made especially pleasant by the warmed water and soft towel, Thea made do with as expeditious a cleaning as she could muster, ever aware of the strapping six foot plus of utter masculinity waiting only a few paces away.

Once her skin fairly sizzled from the brisk scrubbing, she reached for the voluminous night rail. "Heavens, there's enough fabric here to sail the Royal Navy."

Shouldn't official Mistress Apparel be more...scant?

Thea laughed at herself. What had she expected? To be attired as the buxom beauties in the paintings downstairs—in absolutely nothing at all?

"You noddy! Be grateful for the long sleeves that'll hide the bruises!"

That fortified her and she pulled the gown over her head, inhaling in surprise when the filmy fabric caressed her bare skin. Practically choking when she realized the wealth of froth was in direct opposition to what it concealed—or didn't conceal.

Every shadow and cleft of her body was more than apparent. But before she had time to wither in mortification, Thea saw how the waves of diaphanous fabric hinted at curves and a womanly softness she knew had long deserted her limbs thanks to the meager rations she'd come to subsist on.

The capacious gown had obviously been sewn for a woman much taller than she. The neckline rode low on her shoulders, the sleeves hung inches past her fingertips, the hem pooled on the floor, but the nearly transparent mistresswear only enticed Thea to stand tall. (It was either that or bemoan her lack of needle and thread, and she'd never been one for moaning over what couldn't be changed.)

It was past time to begin "earning" the right to her new accommodations and the lovely nightclothes. If she spent any more time *thinking* about what she'd be doing in the next few minutes—with a man she'd only just met—she'd likely barricade the door and that wouldn't do, not at all.

Done with dithering, she leaned over to blow out the candle. As the smoke wafted by her in the dark, Thea decided she must learn to conduct herself as someone used to such lavish surroundings.

That thought fortifying her courage, Thea bunched the lacy cuffs in her fists, held the overlong gown off the floor so she wouldn't trip, took a deep breath for courage and barreled through the door. "I'm ready, my lord."

THANK GOD. The avocado abomination she called a dress had been abandoned in favor of an alluring night rail.

She'd left her hair pinned in place, but the provocative confection she emerged in more than made up for it, a confection he'd happily appreciate—off her—at a later date.

At the moment, damn his infernal luck, he had a bravely trembling mistress-to-be to soothe.

For despite what she claimed, he knew better. She wasn't ready. Nowhere close.

She might not be a stranger to sex, but she was definitely a stranger to kissing. And to sex *with him*, and he'd be damned if he'd "rush his fences" and ruin a potentially grand thing.

Striving for control he was far from feeling, Daniel allowed his attention to drift over her shoulder to the door she'd burst from. He'd hoped the time alone might work a miracle, that her inhibitions, along with her ratty dress, might be cast onto the coals upon her return. But judging by the quickness of her breaths, the shaking of her person, that was too much to wish for, at least for tonight.

While she'd been gone, he'd taken a moment to appreciate the scrupulously clean environment. The furnishings below stairs—and in the master chamber down the hall, he'd noted when he'd escaped to find his own chamber pot—were tawdry beyond belief.

But the couple his man of affairs had hired to staff the place promised to make up for the prior occupant's lack of taste. They knew their duties: the chamber was cozy from the banked fire, the bed was turned down (in here, not the master's rooms he noticed; seemed he wasn't the only one who found the garish vulgarity off-putting, given how *this* was the room they'd readied). The perfect number of candles were lit—enough to see by but not so many the intimacy was shattered.

Add to that, they knew how to disappear—he knew they resided in the servants' quarters on the lowest floor, but he hadn't heard a peep.

Thea's "I'm ready," shook him from his stupor.

What was he to do with her? Or with the need filling his loins?

THEA SKIDDED to a halt at the sight of Lord Tremayne standing patiently near the bed.

He was fully clothed save for his tailcoat, which he'd draped over the dainty bench at the foot of the massive bed.

At her appearance, pleasure flared in his eyes but the look was squelched so quickly she wondered if she mistook his approval.

Would he stay the night? Sleep here after her mistress duties were done? She'd lain in the same bed nightly with Mr. Hurwell and it had been a singularly...uneventful experience. Unless actually copulating, her late husband had taken pains to remain on his side—and instructed her to do the same (the one time she'd drifted near, Mr. Hurwell had taken exception to her "cold extremities" upon his person).

Lord Tremayne didn't seem a man to be put off by frigid feet. Though, Thea reflected, curling her toes into the thick rug, they didn't feel the least bit cold now.

What to do? What to do?

Her fingers clenched the delicate fabric and she made a conscious effort to relax. Tossing her head as though she did this sort of thing every night, she repeated, "I am ready, my lord."

Ready for what, she wasn't quite sure.

Him to kiss her again, certainly.

"On the...bed." Lord Tremayne spoke the command quietly.

Having him tell her what to do was a relief. Thinking mayhap he'd kiss her there, she crossed the room under his watchful gaze.

The bed itself was fit for royalty, standing far above the floral rug and supporting a sumptuous mattress. Thea marveled at her new circumstance as she perched warily upon the edge and ran her fingertips over the crisp sheets. Amazing, from sleeping on rags piled on the floor to this?

Pristine and unwrinkled, the linens bespoke of purity. A whimsical notion, yet not sufficient to detour her thoughts from the direction they'd gone all evening...

What kind of lover would Lord Tremayne be? Slow and tender as she'd dreamed of as a girl, spinning fantasies about her future husband? Or abruptly efficient as Mr. Hurwell had been? Or possibly masterful and commanding as she longed for several years into her lackluster marriage?

Anything other than the tepid, perfunctory matings she'd known would suffice. It seemed Mr. Hurwell had thought it his duty to have congress with her monthly, whether he wished it or not. More than once, he'd even fallen asleep in the middle of the act—was it any wonder she'd questioned her ability to seduce and satisfy?

Thea sensed Lord Tremayne evaluating her and left off admiring the sheets to gaze up at the man she was here to please. Was he? Pleased at the sight of her? At the notion of bedding her?

Brooding silence aside, she hadn't a clue.

He stood near the foot of the bed, his formidable shoulders slightly hunched, fists clenched, staring at her and not looking very much like a man pleased.

But also definitely *not* on the verge of sleep. Quite the opposite, in fact. He studied her with an intensity she might find alarming from anyone else. But there was no mistaking how her body responded to him, growing restless in the strangest places... "Lord Tremayne? My wish..."

She couldn't hold his gaze a moment more, so she looked down and was reminded how prominently the sheer gown displayed the summits of her breasts, the shadowed triangle between her thighs.

Shocking—how this much loose fabric managed to reveal. Shocking, that the sight of her nearly nude body didn't send her scurrying for cover but instead gave her a measure of confidence she'd lacked moments before.

She risked another glance at him. Surely, even in the dim candlelight, he could see her beaded nipples through the thin fabric. See how she didn't shrink from him. See how she was agreeable to pressing forward. Then why did he not move toward her? Take what he'd bought, what she freely offered?

Was he waiting for her to lie back amid the fluffy bedcovers? Waiting for her to crawl beneath them? Or, mayhap, the opposite?

Think like a mistress. "I wish to please you. Shall I"—*gulp*—"remove my gown?"

"NAY. LEAVE IT."

For if she didn't, Daniel feared he'd pounce on her and banish to the rubbish bin his good and wholesome intentions of giving her time. In truth, he was of two minds—take her anyway, despite Sarah's counsel, or depart Temptation's presence. Return home and palm his staff as he'd been doing nightly, only this time, to the vision of Thea.

What circumstances brought her to this place? Because it assuredly wasn't an honest desire to barter her body, not the way she trembled more than a leaf in a storm.

He half-wished he hadn't snapped when Penry dangled the bait. Thea was a young, fresh-faced guppy swimming in shark-infested waters, not at all the experienced, older widow he'd been led to believe.

He ought to cut his line and throw her back.

Daniel's tongue pressed against the roof of his mouth as their too-brief kiss flashed through his mind. He wanted to taste her again—everywhere. *Everywhere.*

If he tossed her overboard, someone else would catch her up.

The thought of anyone else swimming in her waters—
"God-d-d-*dammit!*"

Thea jumped a foot and Daniel realized he'd cursed out
loud. His infernal mouth!

"My lord?" Her face was flushed and her body quaked as
though the bed balanced on a high wire. But her eyes, those
soft, mossy eyes met his valiantly, as if she didn't abhor the
thought of him taking her. As if she was amenable to it,
mayhap even anticipated it with something other than dread,
but she wasn't *comfortable* with the idea.

Not with him. Not yet.

And when she gave a solemn blink and a hint of hurt
entered those pretty eyes, as though she sensed his hesitation
and had concluded he found her lacking (patently preposterous!), it all caught up with him: the whole entire aggravating
day...

Wylde's asinine request, Ellie's tears, the damn orrery he
couldn't get working. Add in the weeks of sexual frustration,
his own agonizing over Sarah's "party" and meeting a potential mistress...

Tom Everson.

And there it was. The one thing troubling him more than
anything else—save for Thea's trembling—how effectively
he'd crushed the young man's spirit.

Bloody hell.

Bloody, bloody hell! Where was the ease a man's mistress
promised? The refuge from life's travails? The night of *sleep*?

By God, he'd paid for the right to use her body and use it
he would!

And it had nothing to do with that wounded look in her
eyes. *Nothing.*

"T-turn over." Even a paltry two-word request was beyond
him? Double dammit!

"Pardon?" He could tell he'd startled her.

Too damn bad. "Over," he ordered harshly, gesturing with his arm, sick of dithering. "On your stomach."

Confusion wrinkling her brow, she complied, bringing her legs to the mattress and then rolling to face the bed. He took advantage of the moment to prowl the edges of the room and extinguish every candle save the one burning closest to her bed.

Mayhap the shadows would help alleviate her nerves.

They sure as hell didn't mitigate his desire, not when he returned to her side and found her resting on bent elbows, upper body propped over a pillow.

She didn't look at him, didn't ask what he had planned, just resolutely waited.

Waited for him to join her, to take her.

Well, take her he would—*his* way. The lewd way he'd begun envisaging after his former mistress dragged him to one of those wretched shadow plays which illustrated the arousing act in all its unnatural glory. The bawdy way the same former mistress had permitted a time or two—just enough to whet Daniel's appetite for more.

Thump. His left boot hit the floor.

Snarl and *thump*, he wrenched the right one off as well. Then he tore through the buttons on his trousers and pushed them and his drawers down, kicked them off.

He was stiff as a pike, his poker ready to *poke* but damn him if he'd settle for *resolute*. No, by God, when he finally took his *new* mistress, really took her as a man did a woman, it'd be because Thea *wanted* him to. Needed him to release the torrent of desire he'd build into a writhing ache...

But not tonight. Tonight was for him. To ease *his* relentless desire

The mattress dipped when he placed one knee near her hip. And because he couldn't wait any longer, Daniel smoothed the night rail over the small of her back and the flare of her hip. Savoring how the material felt sliding over her warm skin, he lowered his open palm to the swell of her backside, settling it firmly atop the cheek closest to him. She made a faint sound in her throat, not a whimper, not a protest (he didn't think), perhaps something between the two.

He wanted to ask her. Wanted to haul her upright, take her hand in his and *talk*. Ask her if she feared him (and assure her she needn't), ask why Sarah had issued that blasted caution, why circumstances had dictated a change in her fortune (because that...that...that maggoty dress had no business covering the form of such a well-mannered young woman).

He wanted to ask her whether he could stay the night— and where the blazes was her cloak.

But Daniel knew better than he did his own name if he opened his mouth and started the imbecilic spewing before he ever had a chance to give her a different impression first, all would be lost.

Just as he was lost—lost to reason and any finer sense when he watched his fingers travel downward over her legs until they gripped the hem of the frothy night rail and, by a will stronger than his own, whipped it up her body until the fabric ballooned at her waist. So his eyes could drink her in.

The gentle flare of womanly thighs, the anxiously flexing toes and muscles of her calves, the sweetest little *derrière*— clenched so tight he couldn't mistake how appalled she must be, knowing he looked his fill.

Relax, he murmured in his mind, shifting the rest of his weight onto the bed and straddling her thighs as both his hands stroked the halves of her arse.

His heart gave an unfamiliar lurch when she let him, her ragged breaths the only sign of her distress. That dark seam between his fingers beckoned, especially now that she'd unclenched, and Daniel edged his thumbs inward, beyond pleased when her hips tilted as though inviting him to explore further...to delve into deeper, damper territory.

But his own territory had grown damp—the small circular spot darkening the tail of his shirt where it drifted past the tip of his rod glaring the evidence. His cock was past ready to spend.

Without giving himself time to debate further, Daniel firmed his grip on her cheeks and slid the opposing sides of her bum apart, groaning at the musky, dark pink flesh the action exposed.

WHAT WAS he *doing* back there?

"Ah..." Thea gulped down the apprehension threatening to close off her air. She was a grown woman. She'd had amorous congress before, she consoled her growing nerves.

But not like this!

Never like this!

She trusted him, Thea reminded herself. Trusted the understanding man in the carriage who had kissed her so tenderly.

But still! "Lord Tremayne?"

With his broad hands holding her posterior in a most objectionable way, his heavy and hot lower half hovering over hers, Thea's insides were a pure muddle.

Outrage, uncertainty, perhaps a bit of passion in the mix, it all boiled together, churning her stomach in a most disturbing manner. She strove to look over her shoulder. "What, ah, are you—"

"Hush," he growled, lowering himself on top of her. At the first feel of his erect male length against the sensitive cheeks of her bottom (*between* them actually!), Thea felt her hips flinch away, then press up to meet him. Her mind might be screaming protests, but it seemed her traitorous low country had other thoughts.

Without further ado, his long legs blanketed hers and his upper body settled over her back. He arranged his arms around hers, bracing the bulk of his weight on his elbows, and cradled her fisted hands within his large palms. Large, strong hands she couldn't help but stare at, their heat seeping through her skin and igniting an unfamiliar sizzle in her belly.

Hands, thank heavens, that were no longer groping her posterior.

Though why that reality gave her a pang of disappointment instead of relief, Thea couldn't have said, not now, not when so many new sensations were bombarding her nerve endings.

Her breath—what she could catch of it—came in tiny pants.

When he nuzzled his cheek next to hers, she caught the subtle aroma of the wine he'd consumed with dinner. That and, now that he surrounded her, the elusive, sweetly spicy scent, the one so uniquely his. And an understated reminder of the outdoors, pine or juniper perhaps. Again she thought of the aborted kisses they'd exchanged in the carriage.

Kiss me again.

But she couldn't ask, not when he'd just told her to hush.

As though he couldn't be bothered to remove it, he still wore his shirt. Her eyes fixed on the cream-colored linen blending with the gossamer sleeves of her gown as he relaxed his weight against her and started to move, that part of him rubbing so insidiously, so illicitly between the crease made by the lobes of her bottom.

The deliberate motions of him burrowing along the crevice pressed her deeper into the bed. Rather than give in to maidenly hysteria (her first inclination, which was definitely not appropriate Mistress Behavior), Thea concentrated on the masculine hands bracketing hers, the knuckles raised and rough-looking, and tried not to think about how gently those hands had just caressed her in such a personal place. Tried not to think about the foreign texture of his groin snugged flush against her posterior.

Devil take her to Devonshire, it proved impossible.

How could one *not* think about something so intolerably titillating, so very wickedly stimulating? Especially when a curious tingling began in her abdomen, one she'd felt a time or two but never quite this strongly.

She wanted to roll over, to curve her legs around his and hug him to her. To experience his bare chest pressed against hers, to feel the full weight of him as she looked into his stormy, amber eyes. Despite her misgivings, Thea positively had to express that desire. "Lord Tremayne, I—"

"Shhhht!" It was a grunt this time but he softened it by kissing behind her ear. A lingering kiss that moved leisurely down her neck and stopped when confronted by the lacy edge of the night rail.

He reached between them to pull the neckline lower. The delicate lace resisted and several threads snapped.

"D-damn me," he muttered between kisses. "Buy you another." And then his lips plastered themselves to the groove between her neck and shoulder and he kissed her with more feeling. Her head dropped to rest on his bent arm as she surrendered her inhibitions to the divine assault of his mouth.

His legs slid between hers, forcing them to part. The action widened her thighs and slanted her intimately into the mattress. His thrusting motions continued, prompting Thea to squeeze the halves of her bottom together. For if she didn't, he might slip and accidentally enter her—*there*.

The fast motion of his pelvis rocking into her became

hard to follow. Confused beyond reckoning, Thea simply held on, enduring the irregular position, enjoying his kisses, wondering...

Didn't he want to be *inside* her? To put his long stalk in her delicate flower? Mr. Hurwell had used those words once, early in their marriage. She'd not paid them much mind then.

But now, she sensed her flower pearling with dew, preparing to bloom. If only Lord Tremayne would—

He gripped her hands tighter as his breathing became erratic. His weight bore down and her hips began to rotate on their own, to move against the mattress, angling so that the bed provided friction to her center, even as her traitorous backside pressed up into Lord Tremayne's groin. Giving herself up to the moment, Thea rode the waves of his undulating body, consciously relaxing in order to move in tandem with him.

"Thea." Another grunt, the whisper of her name, but one that touched her. She might be perplexed by his unexpected actions, but she felt unaccountably cherished by the way he said it.

He stopped kissing her shoulder and exhaled harshly near her ear. A drop of sweat rolled off his face and landed on the bed sheet. Again he rasped, "Thea."

His side whiskers rubbed against her temple, abrading her skin, when he said it.

The force of his movements increased. His hips jerked hard into her several times before stilling. And Thea knew the warmth of his seed upon her back.

Other than a slight twitch of his spent erection, all was frozen: time, her pounding heart, even the restless yearning centered in her woman's flesh.

He shifted against her and his long exhalation stirred the loosened hair near her ear.

Would he tell her to face him? To roll beneath him? Would he now thrust into her rose? End the persisting ache in her abdomen?

Anticipation wound through her.

Abruptly, he released her fingers, pushing up on his arms and away from her. He eased off her bottom. The air hit her newly exposed skin and caused chills to erupt along her spine. The sticky wetness remained on her back.

"Lie still," he commanded, climbing from the bed.

Thea had to stifle a giggle. What did he think she might do? Offer to rush downstairs and bring him a brandy? Jump up and dance a quadrille?

As soon as it formed, she longed to share the jest with him. But the wall of silence he'd erected stayed her tongue. Wondering what would come next, she held her breath as he stepped into the dressing room.

While she awaited his return, she repeatedly smoothed the sheet beneath her fingers, searching out the spot where his drop of perspiration had landed. The simple motion calmed her, though the wetness remained elusive.

Seconds later, Lord Tremayne approached the side of the bed. He ran a cloth over her lower back and bum, even swiping once between her cheeks!

Now would he come back and join her? Finish the act?

Aye, for she heard him removing his shirt. A sigh of relief, of nervous excitement escaped as Thea languidly rolled to her side—only to find him pulling his shirt not *off* but his trousers *on*.

"Lord Tremayne?" Thea hurriedly lowered the night rail and spun to her back. She hugged a pillow to her torso, vexed to see his attention focused on his garments—and not his mistress. Why, now that he'd finished their erotic exchange, he wouldn't even look at her! Was too enamored with wrestling his tailcoat after snatching it from the bench.

"My lord? You're leav*ing*?" Her voice squeaked at the last, making her sound needy indeed.

Definitely not the impression she intended to give her new benefactor. "Of course, you must leave." She attempted a credible, casual laugh (and feared she failed miserably). "You have a home to return to, after all."

A home he likely shared with a *wife*.

Thea nearly choked on that unpalatable thought. Why had she not thought to ask Sarah? After all, Lord Penry was married. Chances were Lord Tremayne was too.

Emotions too plentiful to name, too punishing to endure threatened her outward calm but Thea resolutely shrugged them off. *Dwell on him, you ninny, and your new safe existence.* "Thank you again for providing me such beautiful accommodations and—and—"

Why did her throat thicken and the words come swiftly, as though trying to outrun tears? Why were the carnal urges storming her insides stronger than ever before? She barely knew the man, knew even less *about* him. She only knew that she wanted to again feel his body upon hers, this time without the barrier of their clothing. To explore his broad chest, feel his skin, slick with sweat, against—

Thea sat up and clutched the pillow tighter. She'd put on a confident air or her name wasn't Dorothea Jane Hurwell, the dashed Best Mistress of 1815!

DANIEL KNEW HIS DUTY.

Send the woman a bauble first thing tomorrow. A sparkly trinket delivered straight from the jeweler's with his name attached to the box.

That's what men did for their mistresses—the requisite token of appreciation; something tangible, something expensive that paved the way for the next encounter.

Next encounter? Hell, he wasn't satisfied from *this* encounter. Not even close.

He might have melted across her back, gained some measure of release, but it wasn't the one he wanted—to mount her Venus mound and ride them both to heaven—nor the one he promised himself he'd take—

Damn his cowardly hide! He hadn't been able to do it— breach that virgin territory of hers. Not and maintain his honor. *Coitus per anum* might be well and good for a man's raunchy mistress, but Thea didn't act like one and he'd be damned if her first introduction to sex with him was an act of sodomy guaranteed to drown any tender feelings she might ever harbor for him before they had a chance to float to the surface.

Though he wanted to doff his vestments rather than don them and hunker down in that pretty, feminine bed, he didn't trust himself to exercise restraint if he stayed the night through.

Ignoring the inner promptings to linger, Daniel snagged his tailcoat from the bench and shoved his arm into it just like he shoved away his yearning—ruthlessly.

He might know his duty but the vague notions that brimmed in him now confused the hell out of him. Duty mixed with not-quite-filled desires and an odd eagerness to please. To convince Thea she'd made the right choice, choosing him as her protector.

Mayhap he'd compose a note, a sincere and personal "thank you" to accompany the trinket.

Pen her a missive? The asinine thought had his arm missing the second sleeve twice.

What was he thinking? He was a grown man with physical urges, not a damn suitor for her hand!

Never before had he thought to send a gift because he *wanted* to. He hadn't even left her bedchamber—and yet he was already acting like a lovesick swain, anticipating his return...

Pining for more time with her. A time when he might tup her properly.

A time when he might hold her, sleep with her in his arms... A time when he might stay the night.

He thought to kiss her, to stroke the fallen hair from her flushed face and tell her with the touch of his lips how much he *wanted* to stay. But he knew his own limits as well as his duty.

So, without sparing her another glance, he picked up his boots and crossed to the door. Hand on the knob, he stared at the dark wood in front of him. "Thea." Just the act of saying her name soothed the rasp plaguing his neck. "May I visit you again?"

"Certainly, my lord. You are welcome here anytime."

She answered too swiftly for him to mistake her reply. *Of course* she could do naught but agree. After all, it was his money buying the house. Buying *her*.

The tenor of their association gave her no other choice. His fingers tightened on the brass knob.

This wasn't how he wanted it! Not between them.

Risking a glance, he angled to catch her gaze. She looked so damn inviting, hair mussed, plump lips curved in a tremulous smile—one that didn't quite make it to her eyes and therefore kept his hand in place, strangling the knob, so he wouldn't lunge for her. That and the reddened patch the torn neckline revealed—where his damn whiskers had abraded her soft, soft skin. "Thea."

It was a sigh. An apology, a question. All he couldn't say.

One she answered simply with, "I will never turn away your company."

But would she welcome it?

When she offered, "In truth, I will eagerly await your next

visit," words she needn't have uttered, his pride was soothed and he decided she just might.

Mayhap his earlier actions hadn't botched things beyond repair. "Very well."

He wanted to tell her how much she pleased him. How he'd enjoyed laughing with her in the carriage, holding her within the cage of his arms so very briefly. How he looked forward to more time with her alluring backside, more time with *her*.

But of course he could attempt none of those things, not with *his* damn mouth.

After a final, abrupt nod, he wrenched the door open and escaped.

NOW THAT SHE WAS ALONE, the finality of the latch clicking into place sounded disproportionately loud.

Thea was positive he'd wanted to say more before he plowed through the doorway. Twice, he'd opened his mouth but both times slammed it shut.

Had she displeased him? Nay, because he'd expressed his desire to return.

Releasing her worries on a sigh as she sank deep into the sumptuous mattress, Thea heard him pause outside the bedchamber to pull on his boots. A moment later, he pounded down the stairs.

So this was it? Her first night as a fallen woman. Curious how she felt so very *elevated*, then. So very—

He raised his voice, calling out. Thea cocked her head and heard the low rumble of conversation before Lord Tremayne exited the townhouse.

Afterward, someone shut the door and locked it—from inside.

Which could only mean that, in addition to securing the

house, he'd also procured a servant? *For her?* Though in her youth she'd experienced such, since her marriage, Thea had learned to depend solely on herself, money for servants something Mr. Hurwell decried as an unnecessary luxury.

But now it seemed she had someone else to depend on. Goodness, that would take some getting used to. Time enough to greet them when she wasn't so befuzzled.

Perplexity over Lord Tremayne's disquieting behavior and excitement over her new lodgings battled in her breast.

Breasts that felt heavy and acutely sensitive.

She slid her fingers over their tips, still tight and hard. Though she'd never touched herself outside of bathing before, Thea couldn't stop her growing curiosity. Given the added knowledge she had thanks to Sarah, the added awareness thanks to Lord—

What *was* his given name? "Lord Tremayne" seemed so inappropriately formal now.

Now that he'd awakened new urges.

Thea allowed one hand to wind down her stomach. When it reached the juncture of her legs, she pressed inward. Even through the gown, undeniable moisture greeted her fingertips. That and the insistent longing gripping her loins told her she'd *wanted* the sex act tonight.

It was more than she could have hoped for.

Tomorrow. How she hoped Lord Tremayne visited her tomorrow, for she ached to be with him again. To laugh with him again. To have him, not just on top of her, but *inside* her.

Of their own accord, her fingers delved farther into her cleft. Never before had she felt so saturated. Thea scrambled to raise the gown out of the way. When she did, the warm slickness covered her fingers as her inner muscles pulled them deep. With the palm of her hand, she rubbed against her core, flinching from the pressure.

Determined not to recoil, to brave the new sensations as

she knew a Proper Mistress (what a combination!) ought, she moved her hand, pushing her fingers higher, and rocked her pelvis against her palm. Instead of bringing relief, the motions only heightened the ache.

Uncertain what to do next, feeling so tightly wound she wanted to burst, Thea eventually slowed the motions, then pulled her fingers free. She wiped them clean with the washcloth he'd left by the bed. Considerate man. She wished the bounder hadn't left.

At some point, she slept.

But only after counting the two hundred and forty-seven rose petals painted on the armoire (the remaining candle burned out before she could finish). And only after reaching the surprising realization that in addition to her body craving Lord Tremayne's return, her mind craved his company as well.

Though she was his, technically bought and paid for, when he looked at her, he didn't make her feel cheap or tawdry. Unlike the insulting glare of her former landlord, her new protector's gaze didn't brand her as his possession. Instead, being with him made her feel like a person. And a desirable one at that.

Gracious. She'd only just met the man and already felt indebted to him, thankful he'd given her something she hadn't even realized was missing these last difficult months—her dignity.

II

LUSTY LETTERS

A note...speaking peace and tenderness in every line.

— JANE AUSTEN, *NORTHANGER ABBEY*

7

WHEREUPON THINGS PROGRESS NICELY – AND NAUGHTILY

Get posts and letters, and make friends with speed.

William Shakespeare, *King Henry IV*

THE FIRST ATTEMPT (the strip of paper it was on cut away, now balled up and swept to the floor):

Mrs. Hurwell–

What a horrid beginning. Did he *want* to instill more distance between them?

Second attempt:

Thea,

Please accept my most humble thanks——

"Humble thanks?" *What am I? Her deuced hat maker?*

Fourth attempt (currently being batted about by Cyclops, along with the other three):

Thea,

I count the hours until next we meet—

"Ballocks!" He wasn't ready to pen poetical-sounding odes to her either.

"Woof!" Cyclops agreed as yet another piece of crumpled paper was relegated to the empty grate.

Seventh (and final) attempt:

Thea,

Thank you for an enjoyable evening. I recalled someone mentioning you have a particular fondness for Byron. In all honesty, I cannot tolerate poetry (his or any others') so please accept this volume with my sincere wish that it brings you pleasure.

Until tonight, Tremayne

———————⸭———————

THEA LIFTED her gaze from the missive to the servant who'd delivered it. Along with the note and a book of poems, he'd also handed her a bow-adorned box.

The spry young man had introduced himself as, "Buttons, miss, since I was caught eatin' one, with loads of others found missing. My papa told me once that our ma despaired but I don't remember, on account of being jus' months old at the time."

"What is etiquette in this regard?" she asked, smiling at the informative Buttons and gesturing toward the gifts and letter she now held. Thea hoped he knew—for she surely didn't. "Is Lord Tremayne expecting a reply?"

Not quite twenty, the youth was broad as a barn and twice as sturdy. His blunt-featured face was turned charming by the decisive cowlick that flipped up a good portion of his sandy-brown hair on the left side of his forehead. He'd told her, when he swiped the offending cowlick for the third time, that he had a twin, one whose hair misbehaved on the opposite side. "Expectin'? A reply?" He pondered a moment. "That I cannot say certain-like, but I do be thinkin' he might be hopin' fer one."

"Oh?"

"Aye." The young man dressed in formal livery stepped forward from his perch on the small landing just outside her townhouse. He tilted his head toward her ear, as though about to impart a confidence he didn't want her hovering new butler to overhear. "I was told to take my time in returnin'."

Assuming the ornate desk in the sumptuous drawing room was as well supplied as the rest of the residence, Thea was confident her eager fingers would have no trouble locating paper and ink. "Would you mind waiting in the kitchen while I compose one?"

She'd met the married couple hired to serve as caretakers and knew Mrs. Samuels was downstairs baking this very moment.

With a glance at Mr. Samuels, who had summoned Thea to the door once informed Lord Tremayne had requested his servant place the missive directly into her keeping, the spiffy footman stepped back a pace and diffidently crossed his arms behind his back, giving her a casual shake of his head. "I'll jus' wait here, ma'am. Take what time you need."

"Outside?" When intermittent rains thundered down for the second day in a row, making the uncovered porch damp and dreary? "Poppycock!"

A quick look at Mr. Samuels—and the nod he gave her—confirmed Thea's intuition, and she tugged the visiting servant over the threshold by one sleeve and pointed. "The kitchen is tucked at the back of that hallway, down the single flight of stairs. Mind you ask Mrs. Samuels to let you sample her lemon tarts."

When the young man smiled wider than the Thames, Thea suspected he had a fondness for baked goods. Either that or he'd caught sight of the painted nudes.

His next words illustrated how very wrong she was. "I'm right glad he found you, miss."

He being Lord Tremayne?

Well, of course. Who else could the footman mean? But to be told so directly—that a servant was glad his master had "found" *her*?

It was...unexpected, unusual.

It was flattering to the point that flutters abounded in her belly as Thea situated herself at the angled writing desk. She used the familiar task of readying the quill as she contemplated just what to say.

How did one answer the first note from their new protector? (Dare she hope it was the first of several?)

More importantly, how did she respond to the man who'd spent his seed on her back in the most intimate of acts but who hadn't spoken more than a paragraph to her all evening? And a paltry paragraph at that.

"Just reply to him as he addresses you," the words were

out before she'd thought them through, echoing a semblance of Sarah's previous advice. "Same tone, same length."

Aye, that should suffice.

THIRTY MINUTES LATER, a significant portion of which she'd wasted staring at the blank sheet, Thea had finally managed to fill it in, not quite to capacity but close. She wafted the page through the air, encouraging the ink to dry.

Lord Tremayne,

I delight in finding common ground, for despite public opinion to the contrary, I do not find much to appreciate in Byron. Based on the works I've read, he's overly dramatic for my tastes. Robert Burns, now, I adore and admit to a frisson (a small one, I assure you) of dismay at learning you hold no particular fondness for poetry. None at all? Are you quite certain? (I must clarify, you see, as it is something I find nearly incomprehensible.)

As to the volume you sent, I will treasure it always (are not gifts meant to be treasured?) though I will admit I am already in possession of this particular volume—and through no purchase of my own. I come to think mayhap Hatchards put it on sale?

Please, I beseech you, read the next few lines with your mind unfettered by past opinions:

> *Wee, sleekit, cow'rin, tim'rous beastie,*
> *O, what a panic's in thy breastie!*
> *Thou need na start awa sae hasty,*
> *Wi' bickering brattle!*
> *I wad be laith to rin an' chase thee,*
> *Wi' murd'ring pattle!*

Do these lines not speak to you? Are you not curious to know more? To learn the fate of this dear, wee beastie?

What of the incomparable Mr. William Shakespeare? Do you find anything in his work recommends itself to you? Oh, dear. I believe this must be a magical quill I employ for it has quite run away with my tongue. Do forgive me. (But here, I must interject: this new home I find myself situated in feels magical indeed. It is lovely. More serene than anywhere I've lived before. I do thank you, most sincerely. And will endeavor to please you in exchange.)

I anticipate tonight with a smile.

~~Dor~~ *Thea*

"Same tone, same *length*?" Bah. Brevity had never been one of her particular talents.

Frowning at herself, Thea folded the paper and sealed it with wax and the generic stamp she'd found in the desk. "You'd better hope that during the reading of it he doesn't nod off."

———————◦∞◦———————

DANIEL LAUGHED AND LAUGHED AGAIN.

The demure little chit had taken him to task! That would teach him to deride all poetry in one unwarranted swoop.

And serene? She found that garish abode *serene*?

Another chuckle escaped.

He checked his pocket watch. It was scarce after 2:00 p.m. Hours yet until dark. Hours yet until he could feast his starved eyes on her again and see whether she was truly as lovely as he recalled.

"Rum fogged, I am," he muttered, reaching for another sheet.

Ah. I see now.

Like a pokered-up prig of a tutor, you've decided I shall admire poetic lines or else? Is that it?

As to the verses you so, ah, eloquently shared, might I put forth a request for future examples to be in <u>English</u>? My beastie-gibberish has fair run amok, you see. And the longer I attempt to decipher what causes your wee beastie's breastie to panic, I fear my own crown office has been split asunder by a "murd'ring pattle" (what, pray, is a pattle, murdering or otherwise?).

No doubt, now you'll be regretting the bargain we've made, your fair, <u>fine</u> breastie in a bickering brattle (though what the deuce that is, I haven't a clue) over your benefactor's lack of appreciation for lyrical, metrical prose. What can I do to redeem myself in your eyes?

Aha! Inspiration strikes...

He jumped up to scrounge his library. After a thorough search, he retrieved several leather-bound volumes from one of the topmost shelves. Volumes that sent dust motes dancing in the air when he dared blow on them. Volumes that protested when he opened the aged spines for the first time since inheriting the London house along with the title but that practically sang to him when he started reading...and searching...

Mayhap I should illustrate <u>my</u> tastes in poetic literature? If nothing else to set your concern to rest.

To borrow a bit from the glorious Bard himself...

> *HAMLET: Lady, shall I lie in your lap?*
>
> *OPHELIA: No, my lord.*
>
> *HAMLET: I mean, my head upon your lap?*
>
> *OPHELIA: Ay, my lord.*
>
> *HAMLET: Do you think I meant country matters?*
>
> *OPHELIA: I think nothing, my lord.*
>
> *HAMLET: That's a fair thought to lie between maids' legs.*
>
> *OPHELIA: What is, my lord?*
>
> *HAMLET: Nothing.*
>
> *OPHELIA: You are merry, my lord.*

Me? A merry lord? I confess it's not something I've ever thought of myself—until just this moment. Perhaps it is your poetical prompting that makes it so.

Ergo, as I inappropriately must point out (or could it be considered <u>appropriate</u>*, given the intimacies inherent in our liaison?), where it concerns country matters pertaining to the beautiful female of my recent acquaintance, I find much to admire in Shakespeare. As I find much to admire in her (You, should you be at all unclear).*

Pity the verses I tend to admire are not of the socially acceptable variety. Therefore I shall endeavor to find something more proper:

Shall I compare thee to a summer's day?
Thou art more lovely and more temperate...

"Shall I compare thee to a summer's day?" Oh, how could you try
to bamboozle me with that one?

I doubt anyone with half a modicum of any brain matter at all
would be unable to pull that out of their hat. But you do earn
points for entertainment (if not for effort). And I must commend
your penmanship as well. It's bold and sprawling (much like I
surmise your shoulders and chest would appear sans shirt if I were
given to considering such a thing).

"Dorothea Jane, should you be so vulgar? Hinting that
you want to see his chest..."
Hinting? You came right out and wrote it!
"And blast me to Bedfordshire and back if I'm not about
to leave it!" With a hearty (and unfamiliar) feeling of
burgeoning confidence, she continued...
After all, he'd started it.

And though I should be shamed to admit it to anyone save you, I
find your inappropriate, illicit Shakespeare much to my liking. The
thought of your head upon my lap sounds lovely indeed. Have you
a picnic in mind? Gazing overhead at the clouds as they skitter
past?

Or perhaps you have something more earthy in mind?

I—

Thea's quill leapt from the page as though blasted backward from the mouth of a musket. "Nay, I cannot write that."

She couldn't. Shouldn't. It was wicked. Wanton beyond measure. But oh, how the naughty thought tempted...

Follow his lead.

Thea reasoned, given the sage advice Sarah had imparted, she could really do no less. After all, if she couldn't be boldly flirty with him in person, then why not indulge the urge now, when he'd been the one to include the erotic wordplay?

Determinedly, Thea re-inked the tip and continued.

I confess, upon first reading, my eyes skimmed your letter so quickly they fairly skipped over part of Hamlet and Ophelia's exchange. Imagine my astonishment when I thought I read of your head lying between my legs. (Forgive me! I most ardently intended to write his head, his—Hamlet's—between a maiden's le— Oh, bother it!)

Face flaming, Thea lifted the quill and watched her shaking hand hover above the page.

She should cross it out. The entire last paragraph. It was completely beyond the pale.

Nay. She should trim the page and start anew.

She looked at the thick stack of fresh paper, then back at the sheet before her, only half filled in.

Starting anew would be very wasteful. And had Thea not learned economies, in every aspect of her life, the past few months?

Tell yourself the truth, girl. It wasn't thrift that had her continuing on the same page. It was the tingling awareness Lord Tremayne's presence had brought to her body last night. The awareness that had only grown in hours since he'd left...

You see in me a pokered-up prig of a tutor? My lord, how you wound me with such a comparison. Could you not think of me more along the lines of a spruced-up sprite of a governess? Or a buttoned-up— (Fiddletwig! I must cry off here. I cannot think of any suitable, single-syllable B-word that might meld with "barmaid" which is where I was going—though please do not stop to inquire why. Assuming you've remained awake through the reading thus far.)

Madness. Sheer madness. It's this magical quill, I assure you.

So have you decided Mr. Shakespeare might, after all, suit your stringent literary tastes? How wonderful I am sure. (And I vow that's not a single speck of sarcasm you perceive. Not a single, solitary one. All right, perhaps a half.)

Shall I share a few lines of my own with you? Ones composed during my childhood? Or might you think less of me when you see how very, ahem, <u>less</u> is my talent?

I will refrain from troubling you with them unless you ask.

Thea (who vows she hasn't smiled, or written, this much in an age)

———————◦○◦———————

THEA WAITED and waited (and waited) for his response, growing ever more appalled by her actions. With every second that passed without a pithy, entertaining reply, she worried she may have overstepped not only the bounds of propriety but the boundaries of mistress as well.

So it was with complete and utter dismay, and an impressive (and instantaneous) elevation of spirits, that she received not one but *two* notes in response.

Both delivered at the exact same moment.

And both *by* the very man she'd been afeared of offending.

DANIEL WAS GREETED at the door by Samuels, a strapping man of early-senior years possessed of a barely perceptible limp and few hairs atop his balding pate. He'd met the couple briefly upon his leave last night. Recognizing how they'd roused themselves from sleep upon his departure, Daniel had simply thanked them for having the room prepared on such short notice and bid them good night. Now that it wasn't after one in the morning, the latest servant in his employ seemed inclined for a more effusive greeting.

"Come in, my lord, come in," Samuels encouraged without preamble, opening the door wide. "Horrible rains we've been having today, just horrible." It had been raining? He hadn't noticed. "Glad to see it didn't tamper with your plans tonight."

Before Daniel could acknowledge the man—or the weather—Samuels was circling to help remove his greatcoat, talking all the while. "Molly and I have been looking forward to your visit. You'll join Miss Thea for supper this eve?" Samuels came around and reached for gloves and walking stick. With a slight rub of his thumb over the ivory knob, Daniel released it, delighted to find the man so given to jabbering. "Lovely woman, Miss Thea. Hope you don't mind the informality, but she asked us to call her such."

Daniel nodded to indicate his approval. Patting the outside of his pocket, reassuring himself the two folded squares were neatly tucked inside, he inquired, "Where is she?"

He was promptly ushered toward the drawing room. "In here, my lord, in here. Miss Thea?" Samuels called upon reaching the doorway. "Lord Tremayne here to see you." With a polite nod at both, he said, "Refreshments can be served any time you wish. Ring if you have need of us, otherwise we'll be below. Enjoy your evening."

Then the butler was gone, acting as though he didn't know the sole purpose of Daniel's visit was convenient fornication.

The moment she saw him, Thea scrambled from the small writing desk located across the room. Twin spots of fresh color stained her cheeks but he was comforted to see that her smile came naturally and the trembling that had been so very apparent last night was absent.

"My lord." She gave him a deep curtsy, then spoiled the effect by rushing toward him with every appearance of eagerness. Eagerness she checked just three steps away, as though unsure of her reception.

Thinking how easily her inherent splendor overwhelmed the ratty state of her dress—he really needed to buy her a new wardrobe—Daniel covered the distance in one long stride and took hold of her hand. "Thea." He lifted her arm and bowed low before her, straightening and tugging her closer. He'd rehearsed in the carriage so the words came—almost—easily. "Would ask how you spent your day but think I know."

He couldn't help the grin nor the glance toward her writing desk.

Her feet shuffled in place. He still maintained possession of her hand and she looked at where they were joined instead of his eyes. "Sleeping in, I confess. Then making the acquaintances of the wonderful Mr. and Mrs. Samuels. Exploring my new home." All of that came out in a rush. Only afterward did she meet his gaze, and her breath wafted out on a sigh. "After that I enjoyed the most unexpected afternoon."

Her fingers fidgeted in his and he reluctantly released them, reaching behind his back to clasp his palms together—

it was either that or thread his hands through the luxuriant spill of dark hair that was piled up again, but not nearly as intricately as the night before. "Oh?"

"Reading." Her eyes flashed at him. Wondering if he would take up the bawdy banter in person?

With every appearance of boredom, Daniel spun on his foot and walked sedately toward a garish red settee, frowning at the velvet upholstery—at the entire room—once he realized how very vulgar it was, echoing the gold and crimson tones, and the illicit décor, from the entryway.

Upon reaching the settee he planned to banish as soon as he ordered her new furnishings, he sank into a corner, crossed one ankle over the opposite knee, and very casually commented, "Reading? How...droll."

She snickered and he knew she saw right through his act. "Not today. Today I had the most thumping time turning page after page. However"—she started heading toward him, slowly—"just when I was reaching the exceptionally good parts, I'm saddened to say, they disappeared."

"Vanished?" He made a sound of dismay. And decided it was time to share the contents of his pocket. Before he made a cake of himself by talking too much.

"Completely! How shall I ever know *how* the story unfolds if—if—" She stumbled to a halt, both in words and in walking, when he held out the folded squares. "For me?"

Deuced amazing. One would have thought he'd given her diamonds instead of mere dispatches.

"For you," he concurred, making sure she saw what he'd written on the outside of each before relinquishing them into her control.

THEA LOOKED AT THE NOTES, one marked *For Now*; the other labeled *For Tomorrow*.

Two more letters to cherish! How could she be so fortunate?

Not attempting to disguise the smile lifting her cheeks, she tucked the one designated for tomorrow in the pocket of her dress and unfolded the other. Standing just shy of the settee where Lord Tremayne sprawled, she began to read, not realizing until she was partway through the first paragraph, that she was doing so out loud.

"*Dear Thea, It occurs to me I was remiss. Unaccountably callous, in fact, and for that I beg your pardon.*

"*Last eve you so kindly saw to my needs while I—*" Here she paused to glance at him over the sheet. Looking solemn but unembarrassed, his gaze unwavering on her face, he nodded for her to continue. She did, unable to help the lowering of her voice as though they shared a secret. "*While I selfishly ignored your own.*"

Her own needs? The page shook—following the tremor of her arm—and Thea resolutely stiffened her betraying limb and her resolve. Her resolve *not* to give in to any missish vapors. Of a certainty she did have needs! How wonderful of this man to recognize that. To *acknowledge* them. Something her late husband had never, never been considerate enough to do.

Granted, she'd not thought to contemplate her needs so soon, given how she wasn't yet attired to receive Lord Tremayne in the boudoir. But she had reveled in the first sit-down bath with hot water she'd been treated to in ages, thanks to the efficient and indulging Mrs. Samuels. The sweet woman had even washed and pressed her dress. Though really—to greet him wearing the same ugly dress? It was not what Thea had planned. But she was clean, her hair simply but neatly arranged, and Lord Tremayne had looked as pleased as she'd felt when Samuels had shown him in.

Taking solace in that, she firmed her voice and read on,

again admiring his fine penmanship (which was easier than fully processing what she was saying). "*May I rectify that now perhaps? I need to, you see, for I did not mean to present myself as such a selfish lover. It was most insensitive of me, to begin our new association that way, and I would like to presume upon you to give me this chance to show myself in a better light.*"

Thea was intrigued. Just what was he planning? Eager now to find out, her voice hurried along as she no longer attempted to read with any great skill. "*While I have a prior engagement this evening and regret I cannot stay long, I don't doubt we have ample time for me to illustrate the merits of my apology in the way—*"

Though there was still a sentence or two remaining, Thea lowered the page. After the titillating exchange they'd carried on this afternoon through Buttons, she'd reached a level of comfort with their relationship that perhaps she shouldn't have. She'd assumed he'd stay for several hours, if not the entire night.

How foolish. Just because she'd remained at home all day, rather than trek to her horrid room across town to retrieve her meager belongings (something she'd put off a fortnight if she could), she had to remember Lord Tremayne was a peer. A man with responsibilities and associations far removed from her narrow place in his life.

Take heart, he's here now. "I'm disappointed to hear you cannot remain but I hope your social activities tonight prove enjoyable. It was very kind of you to stop by given your commitments else—"

"Kind?" he laughed. "Nothing of the sort." A look of mischief entered his eyes. And his posture wasn't quite so sanguine. "Read on or I might lack sufficient...time."

She muttered through the last line until she found her place. "*Illustrate...merits...of my apology in the way of <u>your</u> interpretation of Hamlet and his maiden—*"

The page fluttered from her fingers. "Lord Tremayne!" That was all she said. All she could say, for he surged to his feet and caught the note before it hit the floor.

Holding her gaze, he refolded it, precisely creasing the corners before slipping it into her pocket along with the other. Then he promptly took up her hand, placed it in his, and led her out of the room and directly up the stairs—after no more than a single wink.

HE KNEW he'd shocked her speechless. Good.

Five hours of swapping stimulating raillery had him stiff and ready and craving the taste of her. Had him stopping by now, *before* his dinner engagement, instead of after, when he'd be too tempted to stay the night—and be selfish all over again.

He'd gotten off to a rotten start last eve, Daniel knew. But he thought their exchanges today had more than made up for it. Beyond his wildest dreams, in fact—her replies had him smiling and laughing and watching out the window for his footman's arrival like a callow youth in the throes of his first passion.

Daniel thought Thea might be beginning to *like* him and damned if he'd do anything to interfere. So if last night was for him, then tonight was for *her*.

Tomorrow night could be for them both.

They reached the landing and he turned toward her bedchamber.

"Nay," she gasped, digging in her feet and pointing down the hall. At his raised eyebrow, she released her bit-upon lips and said in a breathless voice, "The master chamber. I— You — There's a *mirror!*" she finished on a hushed squeak.

A mirror? Grasping her meaning immediately, her hand still tucked snuggly within his, he marched down the corridor until coming to the room he'd briefly glimpsed in shadow the night before. The candles were already lit, several of them, and the bed was turned down.

He released her near the giant canopied bed and leaned in to look up. Sure enough, a large mirror hung overhead, securely fixed beneath the canopy. Five by six feet if it was an inch, and Daniel's body responded as any red-blooded male's should. "D-d-damn."

She'd come up behind him and placed one hand on his shoulder. But her exclamation of "'Tis something, isn't it?" had gotten severed by his curse.

She jerked back in surprise and met his gaze when he straightened. "You don't like it," she said flatly. "You hate it. Forgive me. My room is fine. Let's—"

He gripped her around the waist when she would have fled. Pulled her spine flush against his chest and leaned down to whisper in her ear. "Love it, I...do." He fancied a tremor racked her frame from the breathy caress of his words. Or perhaps it was caused by his hand, the one not across her middle and edging toward her breast, which couldn't help but mold to the firm flesh of her right buttock and thigh. "I'm upset...at not having...time to make long and loud and lusty use of it...tonight."

At his explanation, his kneading fingers, she melted into him. "Tomorrow night, then?" she asked on a lilt, one that had him cursing again—this time his sister and Wylde for tonight's dinner invitation issued last week. Given the strained relations he'd witnessed yesterday—God, had it been just yesterday?—there was no way he could avoid going this evening.

Nothing that would keep him from returning tomorrow.

In answer, he kissed that delicately sweet spot where her neck met her shoulder, ready to swear anew at the high, unyielding neckline of the deuced dress. "Wardrobe," he murmured as his fingers started crawling over and lifting the dense fabric of her skirt higher and higher. "Need to b-banish yours to the grate."

"Aye, likely I do." It was a heartfelt sigh and he was thrilled when his erection rubbed firmly against her back and she did no more than lean in closer to him. "But—but I haven't changed yet into—"

She went rigid. A second later she spun to face him and put her arms in between them as if to ward him off. "Wait! The night rail you sent this morning—I forgot to thank you in all the fun of our earlier exchanges. I wanted to put it on— wear it for you—"

"No time." Gad, if he saw her in that scrap of nothing, he'd never get out of here.

GLOSSING over her forgetfulness as though it mattered naught, Lord Tremayne curved his hands around her waist and boldly tossed her straight on the bed. A coil of naughty desire wound through Thea.

It intensified when he climbed up after her.

She scurried backward until the pillows against the ornate headboard prevented further retreat. Instinct—and modesty—had her clutching her dress near her hips, had her protesting. "You cannot mean to—"

"I can." He pressed inexorably forward, advancing until he grabbed her ankles and spread her feet so he could settle his bulk between her splayed legs. Her skirts rode up as he did so, obscenely so.

Feeling vulnerable, Thea told herself she should protest more stringently, claim she wasn't ready for such perverted intimacies, not without at least *some* preliminaries. She should cry out that she truly did not want this—his powerful torso forcing her legs wide.

But all of that would have been a lie. For she'd already admitted, when she shamelessly wrote those illicit lines this afternoon, that she *did* want this, was vastly curious about the sensations his mouth on her might bring forth. She wanted to experience the scrape of his whiskers in a place that had never known the light of day—much less the lust of a candlelit bedchamber.

So Thea did the only thing she reasonably could—she looked upward.

And what a sight she beheld.

His cigar-brown tailcoat, fitted to perfection across the broad expanse of his shoulders and practically glued to the slope of his tapered back; buff breeches molding to strong thighs... His elegantly attired masculine form—so very dignified for an evening out—so indecently centered between her stocking-covered legs.

Legs that quivered beneath the upward stroke of his hands. "Can and will," he said in a low rumble that sent a fine tremor through her. "For *you.*"

"But I don't—" Thea broke off, seeing her white-knuckled grip on her skirts slacken. Seeing her knees bend, her thighs stretch to welcome his proximity even more. Seeing him pause, tilt his head toward hers.

"Thea?"

She refused to lower her gaze, transfixed by their reflection. Too busy watching his fingers, strong and powerful, slide higher until they gripped the skin of her thighs above the aged stockings. Feeling his hands tighten, then tighten again, until she was persuaded to lower her gaze from the mirror and meet his.

This strong, handsome protector (aye, *handsome*, for the short beard troubled her not a whit tonight) whose penmanship and the personality it portrayed snared her interest when they were apart, but not nearly as much as his presence captivated her completely. Enticed her mind until she thought of naught but pleasing him. Pleasing herself.

Soulful brown eyes narrowed even as he climbed his fingers upward, honing in on that unexplored territory. A quick, fumbled, under-the-covers mating from Mr. Hurwell, with him in his nightshirt and her in her gown, compared naught to *this*.

"You," Lord Tremayne said deliberately, his face looming closer as he closed the gap between his fingers, intensifying the depth of carnal awareness between them, "...don't...?"

Thea's lashes slammed down. Her traitorous, treacherous hands abandoned their hold on her skirts and instead curved over his shoulders, latched on to the solid muscles there. But that wasn't enough to stop their restless wandering and soon they were plucking at his immaculate neckcloth. Tendrils of arousal weaved through her, growing tighter every silent second.

"I don't..." *Want this.*

Liar! You know *you want this. Precisely this. After what you saw at Sarah's party, what the verses made you think of today— after what* you wrote *to him! You want* exactly *this.*

Aye, but I didn't expect it tonight!

One of his large hands left its intimate mooring high upon her thigh and Thea whimpered at the loss. Only to feel those same fingers edging past the opening in her drawers.

Her eyes flew open.

He was still staring at her face. "You say..." One fingertip brushed lightly down her cleft, barely making contact, fluttering through the tight curls and making her feel the caress deep inside. "Say 'no', and I shall stop." Then it brushed upward.

Thea's pelvis tilted forward a fraction, determined to receive the caress again.

When his head flinched, she saw her fingernails had

embedded themselves in the skin above the starched silk neckcloth. She relaxed her hands and brushed back a thick lock of coffee-colored hair that had made its way across his cheek.

"Nay, I cannot say 'no'." At his supreme smile, she confessed, "'Tis all so very new to me though."

He slid another finger inside the slit and whispered them both down one side of her sex.

"I know." His breath brushed over her abdomen as his other hand released her thigh to part the placket shielding her, exposing her completely. Thea gulped as he hitched his entire body closer.

But her legs had no such reservations, widening to make room. As though compelled, she returned her gaze above, to the sight of her stark face, eyes luminous and larger than she'd ever seen them, and his broad-shouldered body, his head only inches from where she craved his touch so very much...

"Let me?" The warmth of his words stroked her damp flesh and Thea jerked a clumsy nod.

THANK THE SAINTS. He couldn't have waited another second. Not with her clean, musky scent luring him onward.

Daniel couldn't believe he was here—with her—on a bed and keeping his clothes resolutely *on*. The linen cuffs of his shirt extended from the tight sleeve of his evening coat, emphasizing how absurd it was—his rough, callus-worn fingers upon her satiny skin. Or mayhap, instead of absurd, he meant *arousing*.

Had he ever arrived at the abode of his mistress with the intent to keep his cock tucked away while dancing attendance on *her* body?

With his thumb, he stroked the smooth, white skin of her

upper thigh, nearly choking on his desire when she whimpered and a fresh wash of dew coated the fingertips grazing her furrow. As though determined to thwart him, her thin drawers kept her mound hidden. But the sex-swollen folds were readily apparent, moist and silky and so, so inviting...

He pressed one finger deeper and was rewarded when her nails gouged his neck again.

Her musk grew stronger, his fingers damper, and he slanted his hips until his erection pressed firmly into the mattress, wishing it was her velvet recesses he stroked with his cock.

Alas, his tongue would get the pleasure tonight.

He withdrew his fingers and spread the placket open. Just before he made contact with the honeyed folds he'd revealed, a stirring raised the fine hairs on his nape. Daniel glanced up, only to find her gaze focused not on him—as he'd suspected—and not *closed*—as he'd expected—but instead, her wide-eyed attention was riveted to the canopy overhead. Directly where the giant mirror was secured.

So his new mistress liked to watch?

That knowledge sent flares of desire spiraling through him. Her plain stockings were already in shambles, her drawers freshly washed but old and thin. He planned to buy her new ones anyway. So, without a speck of remorse, he let his primal side have its way.

"Here..." he breathed, leaning back to grip both sides of the slit in either hand. "Shall I..." *Improve the view?*

Rrrrriiiiiip! It was nothing to tear the fragile seam. Nothing to push her dress high toward her waist, nothing to lift one of her thighs over his shoulder and angle his body so she could truly see the show.

But, oh gad, oh God, was it something to hear her shriek turn to a moan when he lunged forward and plastered his lips to her wet heat.

Was it something to finally taste his new lover's flesh, the salty essence of her ardor.

Like a demon possessed, his tongue sought out her flavor, working up one side of her passion-soaked labia and down the other. Availing itself of every drop of silky want she exuded.

Blazing ballocks (his were, of a certainty), she *wanted* him tonight. Wanted what he could give her—his body thrusting into her, creating its place in hers. Wasn't beset tonight by nerves that inhibited her innate response.

Nay, oh nay. She was passion personified, pure responsive female in his arms tonight. And after nothing more than the transfer of a few titillating letters?

He should take pen in hand more often.

Her slippered foot rubbed frantically over his back. Her hands swept over his head, through his hair. Her hips rocked, matching the avid sweep of his tongue as he licked his way to the top of her sultry sex where he delved deeper until locating the tiny pearl secreted within.

While circling the hard nub with the tip of his tongue, Daniel parted her downy folds with several fingers. He discovered her wet and ready, ravenous even—if the encouraging little gasps she made were anything to go by as his mouth silently spoke for him, in all the ways he usually couldn't.

The faster his tongue lashed, the more she tried to clamp her legs together, to escape backward. But his unrelenting hold prevented retreat, kept her in place for his dining pleasure. By God, his mouth might betray him at every turn but not tonight—not in this. When it came to sampling her body, enticing her cream to flow thick and hot, for once, his lips and tongue were in command.

And demanding surrender had never tasted so sweet.

Keeping a firm grip on her thighs, he coaxed the pearl out and placed his lips firmly around the responsive bundle.

"Oh, Lord—" The words were a delightful little whimper, soft and full of air.

He slid two fingers into her damp passage, reveling in how the warm walls drew him in, the muscles of her channel clasping hungrily at him.

"Oh, Lord—" Louder this time.

Daniel started to massage her from the inside, nearly smiling at how she was calling on divine deliverance.

But as he sucked hard on the tiny knot and swiveled his fingers against their own sweet heaven, it was as though his shaft and not his hand plunged through her depths. Amazingly, his primed pipe felt every squeeze and contraction his fingers and lips experienced. Felt her reactions intensify just before she rewarded him by exploding on a scream.

A scream of, "Tremayne!" and he realized she'd been calling on him, praying to him for release. Every sexual atom of his being—the nonsexual ones too—seized in a pleasure so intense, so unexpected, damned if his hips didn't flail, his body bucking against the restrictive garments as he rode the damn mattress until he screamed and creamed too.

Right in his bloody breeches!

Deuced amazing.

But it was her shout of satisfaction that roared through him more than his own release—embarrassingly satisfying as it'd been—because she was still clutching at him, his head, his shoulders—his back with her leg. Her sex still convulsing around his fingers, vibrating against his tongue.

Her mouth murmuring shakily, "L-Lord Tre... Lord... Tremayne. Come...higher. Please."

With one last, lingering kiss to the pink and pouty valley —a kiss of promise to return soon—he answered the frenzied motions of her hands, the sultry plea in her words, and crawled up over her chest, pressing her deep into the pillows.

"Aye?" His own syllable was tellingly breathless. "You rang, milady?"

Her bright eyes found his and she circled her arms around his neck, pulling him down. "Oh, thank you! Thank you," she exclaimed into his ear. "I didn't know—hadn't ever—oh!"

Lower, her abdomen lurched toward his body and she gasped and trembled yet again. Hugged him tighter, with both arms and legs, as her pelvis ground solidly into his groin. "I-I didn't know."

He'd suspected as much but having it confirmed made him hurt—for her.

Daniel tugged one of her strangling arms away from his neck and rose on to his elbow. With his free hand, he smoothed the fallen hair from her sweat-dampened face, ran his thumb over her plump lower lip. Which wasn't so plump, after all, upon such close inspection.

In actuality, her top lip, though alluringly curved, could be described as thin. It was the difference between the two that captivated him, the gentle and unexpected swell of the bottom lip that made him hungry to touch, lick and taste. To explore, plunder and plunge within.

Gad, how he wanted to dive inside her mouth, kiss her with everything he had—his tongue, his heart, most of all his cock.

Hearing her admission touched him deeper than any release—pending or otherwise—and he knew tonight was not the time. "Your husband was a..." *Bastard! A doltish grout-noll.* Not to cherish and charm such a pleasing, passionate creature. Words he would have loved to utter. But he settled for, "A chub."

She gave a tiny shake of her head but didn't try to subdue

the blossoming smile. "Nay, he was decent enough. Just uninspired in the bedroom." Her lashes veiled her eyes when she added, "In everything, truth be told."

"A clump," he told her with conviction. Then he dropped his forehead to rest on hers. "Thea." Daniel licked his lips, tasted her all over again. His softening erection surged against her honeyed center, so moist and receptive—thanks to his efforts and her wondrous response. Had a man ever been blessed with such an exquisite mistress?

He forced his hips back and she instinctively followed, wringing a deep groan from his throat, one that originated in the vicinity of his blazing ballocks. "Thea! I must go. I..." *Don't want to.*

Damn, how he didn't want to. But it was for the best—if he stayed, they'd talk more. Either now or later, and he could only hide his defect for so long.

With Louise, it had been easy. She prittled and prattled on about anything and everything, not really caring, and certainly not curious what his views were—on anything—or how he spent his time. With Thea, soft, sexually un-awakened Thea—though he'd certainly awakened her tonight, he couldn't help but acknowledge with a surge of pure male pride that had his cock stiffening within its sticky confines—with her, he had an urge to *discuss*. To ask for details on how she occupied her day. To seek her advice on matters troubling him.

To beg her to massage his shoulders and neck—much as she was doing now—but with his shirt and coat *off*, with him not feeling the pressure of the upcoming evening in the company of two people he cared about and had *thought* happily settled.

"Gad, how I d-d—" *Don't want to leave.* He masked the slip by kissing her nose, then by whispering his new favorite word. "Thea."

Had he ever loved forming syllables as much?

She leaned forward and pressed her lips to his jaw. "'Tis all right. I know you have commitments outside of our...um...ah..."

"Friendship?" he hazarded, rewarded immeasurably when she nodded beneath him, when she stroked his shoulder down to his biceps as though she wanted more than anything else for him to linger all through the night.

"Aye, friendship," she confirmed without a hint of hesitation. "*Passionate* friendship."

He laughed and kissed her cheek, then hauled off her. As it was, he'd need to return home for new breeches before venturing out again, and if he didn't leave Thea's presence now—all tempting and warm and flushed from release—he'd surely miss dinner at Ellie's...and that wouldn't do.

He already had enough guilt heaped upon him by his wretched conscience, based on how things had gone with Tom Everson the previous night, to invite more regret.

Marshaling his strength, Daniel gained his feet and turned to her. She'd flung her dress down to hide the treat he'd just dined on and her color was as high as ever. But she held his gaze. "Thank you, my lord, for a most, um...erotically enjoyable evening."

"'Twas my...pleasure." He gave her his most formal bow, even clicking his heels together to the accompaniment of her chuckle. Straightening, he vowed, "Until...tomorrow."

"You'll be back tomorrow?" Every blasted minute he had to endure in his release-ruined drawers was erased right then by the solace of her sweet smile. "Wonderful."

"In...deed. I shall count the hours."

"As will I."

8

EXPECTATIONS MOUNT, ONLY TO BE
DEALT A CRUSHING BLOW

——— ⋈ ———

7:21 a.m.
Though the looming clouds promised another drizzly, grey day, Thea awoke feeling as though rays of sunshine frolicked across her bed, as though a flock of songbirds chorused within her breast.

7:37 a.m.
"Has there ever been a lovelier morning?" she greeted Mrs. Samuels as she descended the stairs.

"The follies of youth must be upon ye, to welcome such a morn with open arms."

Undeterred, she patted the pocket that held the two folded notes Lord Tremayne had given her the night before. "Folly or a blind eye," Thea excused, pausing when she reached the bottom of the staircase and noticed the laden tray the woman held. "I confess, my attention 'tis on a letter I must compose. My, you've been busy, to cook so much this early."

Her new housekeeper's smile contained a wealth of understanding. "I hoped the scents of a hearty meal might lure you awake. And *must* compose?" The woman chuckled. "Like as not you cannot wait to begin. Aye, I know to whom you're writing with such haste. Think ye I missed that rascally Buttons sitting in my kitchen twice over yesterday? Here now, I was bringing up your breakfast—"

"For *me*?" Why, there were no less than five full plates: fried ham, shirred eggs, tarts (strawberry this time, judging by the heavenly scent), kippers, high stacks of bread and more. "I thought all that was for Mr. Samuels and yourself."

"Ye'll please both me and my Sam by making a noble attempt to clear each and every plate." While Thea sputtered, the housekeeper surveyed her with grandmotherly affection. "Child, a brisk wind would keel you over. Breakfast first and then I'll see you settled at your desk with a pot of hot tea."

"You're too kind." When Mrs. Samuels would have headed toward the formal dining room, Thea stopped her. "Nay. I'd prefer to eat in the kitchen. With you both."

"Kind?" Mrs. Samuels clucked, spinning around and heading back down the stairs. "You're easy to care for, I daresay. Our last mistress, God rest her rotten soul, was a crotchety crone. Always ready to harp a complaint but nary anything else. You're twice the woman she was even if she did have the title 'Lady' before her name."

8:24 a.m.

The hearty breakfast consumed (between the three of them once Thea persuaded the couple to join her), Thea slipped into place at her writing desk and readied her quill, letting the anticipation mount. She couldn't wait to read the remaining missive from Lord Tremayne.

She opened the *For Tomorrow* page and, after smoothing the creases with a palm that tingled as it came into such close proximity to his words, began to read.

Thea—

Never fear that <u>anything</u> you care to impart would be unwelcome. As to poetry by your own hand? I am agog with impatience to read what shall no doubt be a sublime and impressive effort. Write on, fair one...

Pertaining to the barmaid comparison you so indelicately suggested —put those pesky one-syllable B's to bed (or perhaps let me escort you there instead?) for you're much too refined to ever be considered thus.

I pray you have fond memories of last evening.

I await with breath bated (and mouth longingly recalling your taste—I hope) for your entertaining reply.

He'd signed it "T", casually, as though they truly were friends.

It was but a moment before Thea's quill was soaring across a fresh page.

For shame! Talk of escorting me to bed, tut-tut. (Though I must be shameful as well for I think of the same—with a frequency I might find alarming had you not mentioned it first.) For double shame: mentioning—and <u>before</u> it even occurred—what your mouth did last night, where it ventured.

Really, Lord Tremayne!

With naught but a parenthetical aside, you whisk me upstairs and beneath the mirror, my limbs quivering so that one would think I am cold. Alas, no. You heat my insides to sweltering with the bold strokes of your pen (and your tongue) but I shall endeavor to cool myself off.

Quickly now.

There. I've raised the window so the invigorating breeze can blow hither and thither my overheated yearnings. Yearnings that only deepen as memories (yes, I confess to many where last evening is concerned) besiege my brain, rendering me—

"Aaaaa-chooo!" As the wind turned frigid, the unexpected sneeze caught her off guard.

Ack! Rain droplets pelt the sill and now the floor and—

8:41 a.m.

When a second sneeze followed the first, she hurriedly closed the window, coming back to her chair and seeing with dismay three ink blotches caused by renegade rain, as well as how much of the page she'd taken up—with lurid flirting!

What would her mother say?

She'd be pleased pink you've found someone to be yourself with and you know it.

"But such a naughty self?" Thea whispered, blotting the worst of the mess from the page. "Who knew?"

There now. I've ceased allowing the rain into the room and onto the page, and now I must cease my chatter. Else how will I ever complete this missive during daylight hours?

You state without equivocation (I feel compelled to remind you)
that you would like to be privy to my early compositionary efforts.
Please bear in mind, they came to the fore shortly after I celebrated
my ninth birthday.

And so, my lord, due solely to your encouragement, I shall mitigate
my pending embarrassment and share my poetical talents,
minimal though they are:

> *Drip. Drip. Drip it goes.*
> *All day long, it grows...*
> *The pile, the dripping,*
> *Gluey, sticky pile...from his nose.*

A sonnet (or is it an ode?) dedicated to Mr. Freshley of the Dripping
Nose.

Thea (who will hurriedly blow hers and hope she's not given you a
dislike for her magical quill—or her taste in literature)

8:53 a.m.
　　She sat.

8:56 a.m.
　　And sat some more.

9:02 a.m.
　　Prowled across the room. Looked out into the empty hallway, scowled at the stairs leading down to the footmanless

kitchen. Scowled again toward the closed front door. She returned to her drawing room and sat down again.

9:04 a.m.

She waited. Contemplated. Huffed a hearty sigh. Drank a delicious cup of the rapidly cooling tea.

9:11 a.m.

She stood and crossed the room again (twelve times to be precise). Then her posterior greeted the chair once more where she cogitated further on exactly *what* to do with her reply.

For once, there was no one waiting in the wings to deliver it. No exuberant, button-eating youth ready to speed it to its recipient. No stern-faced, kind-hearted man reaching out to receive it in person.

Nay, there was simply one lone (and swiftly growing frustrated) "virgin" mistress wondering what the deuce she should do.

9:18 a.m.

Her foot tapped a jittery tattoo upon the rug. Her fingers drummed upon the sealed note—and with sufficient agitation to rattle the desktop. Her breath heaved forth like an angry horse blowing steam.

9:41 a.m.

"Hummmmmmmmmmmmm."

Drat. Only thirteen seconds.

. . .

9:42 a.m.

Deep breath. "Hummmmmmmmmmmmmm."

Better. Seventeen this time.

9:43 a.m.

Here we go. "Hummmmmmmmmmmmmmmmmmm-egck! Eeegkk!!"

Knock. "Why, Miss Thea, you're turning blue! Here now, borrow one of my shawls. And I'll warm ye some more tea."

9:50 a.m.

9:51 a.m.

Did she smell peaches?

9:52 a.m.

9:53 a.m.

9:54 a.m.

Had she ever checked a clock as frequently?

9:55 a.m.

Hated contraptions.

9:56 a.m.

She should have dismantled this one an hour ago.

9:57 a.m.
Well now.
Just what the devil should she do with her note?

9:58 a.m.
Ball it up and have a snack with her tea?

By 10:07 a.m. Thea had swallowed her nerves and snatched up her letter and marched down to the kitchen to inquire whether Mr. Samuels had Lord Tremayne's direction.

"I have an inklin' of his neighborhood but not an exact address," he'd told her. "Before movin' in, we dealt with the agency and his man of affairs, Miss Thea, not his lordship directly. I could inquire, run round to the agency and—"

"Nay. That isn't necessary," she responded, reached for a peach scone hot from the oven, and furtively crept back to her writing desk (perhaps there were unspotted raindrops she could scrub from the rug or the wall).

By 10:26 a.m. Thea had also declined Mr. Samuels' offer of inquiring via his lordship's man of affairs. She'd paced the room another twelve times (times twenty), and watched the clock tick with wretched slowness.

She'd also declined another pot of tea, another scone, and feeling sorry for herself.

Self-pity would never do!

Of course Lord Tremayne would send Buttons by soon. Last eve, he'd seemed as eager as she for their lighthearted correspondence to carry on. She was just being an impatient ninny.

By 10:52 a.m. she was plucking at her dress. Though Mrs. Samuels had laundered it (and even mended the lace Thea had so expeditiously sewn on two days ago), she'd still rather be wearing something else when Lord Tremayne came to call.

He'd surprised her last evening, arriving before she changed into the beautiful night rail he'd sent. What if—

Pure excitement raced through her veins. What if he meant to retrieve her reply personally? What if he were simply waiting until a socially acceptable time to call?

Was she truly expected to wait the entire day before "posting" her note?

Horrors!

AT 11:06 a.m. she jumped up, thinking to dash to her rented room in the unsavory part of London to gather what few personal items she retained. Everything of value had long since been sold, and though a single one of Lord Tremayne's leather gloves (if not a *single* finger on a single glove) was surely worth more than the sum total of all she possessed, the thought of greeting him in something other than her old olive dress drove her onward.

But the reluctance to return there made her pause...

The thought of visiting the dingy room threatened to suck dry all the joy she'd felt today. Yet there was one item she'd grieve were it to disappear, which was more than likely to happen the longer she left the space abandoned: her hairbrush, a gift from her mother when Thea was but twelve and right before her doting parent succumbed to a swift illness. The handle was fancy, the boar bristles soothing.

That was surely worth retrieving.

But what if, during her trek across town, she missed his arrival?

At 11:08 a.m., conflicted, she dropped back down.

11:16 a.m.

"No, thank you, I still have this last cup."

11:17 a.m.

"I'm glad my color is better, and aye, the shawl is quite warm. I appreciate the loan of it." *And aye, I've learned my lesson about timed humming.*

12:24 p.m.

"Thank you. Lunch would be lovely."

"I saw yer eyes spark at those scones. Making a peach cobbler now, I am. 'Tis my duty to fatten ye up."

12:47 p.m.

"Please don't think it's your bountiful offering; I'm simply not hungry. Such a large breakfast, you know."

Such worry-induced indigestion, you know.

1:03 p.m.

If that clock doesn't start ticking with more alacrity, I'll wring its scrawny neck...

1:20 P.M. (and fourteen s-l-o-w ticks of the second hand)

Oh, doom me to Devonshire! I'm turning into Mr. Hurwell!

That unpalatable thought ringing in her mind, Thea returned the shawl (she didn't want the damp weather messing with the fine yarn) and asked Mrs. Samuels if she could spare a hunk of cheese (which the woman did, her perplexity only growing when Thea explained it was for George and Charlotte).

Moments later, she set off, refusing Mr. Samuels' offer of escort, insisting her errand would best be conducted alone. In truth, she would have been comforted by the company, the thought of confronting Grimy Grimmett nearly enough to make her embrace Clock Watching as a full-time occupation, but she was made of sterner stuff than that.

Asides, knowing—and with a great degree of certainty— that she had Lord Tremayne's arrival to look forward to upon her return only hastened her feet once she left her new residence.

Hastened her down one damp street and then another.

Hastened her a bit faster when the tiny drizzle turned to a full-out downpour...

Until Thea realized, more than a little taken aback, that she was totally and completely lost. Lost and without the fare to pay a hack—had she any notion of her new address. Which she didn't.

Middlesex could've been Mercury for all she recognized through her dripping lashes.

Surely she wasted half the afternoon searching for a familiar landmark, but she might as well have taken the slow coach to Scotland for all the good her wandering did.

EARLY THAT MORNING, Daniel received a letter—just not the one he was anticipating.

Dan—

Jackson's — 10 a.m.

P

And people thought *he* was abrupt?

The summons wasn't entirely unexpected. But the timing was. Disappointing, if not downright disheartening.

So instead of whiling the morning away, fiddling with that pesky gear, the one that hung up every time he tried to get Uranus orbiting properly, while awaiting Thea's next missive, he packed up his pugilistic paraphernalia and hied off to #9 Bond Street. Ready to get his face boxed, if not his ears.

———————————⬦———————————

IT WAS NEARING NOON and Penry had yet to put in an appearance. Or grace Daniel with the ragging he knew was coming.

Slam! Daniel got in a solid jab, then danced back on his toes to the cheers of several men who'd gathered to watch when his latest opponent had issued the challenge over twenty minutes ago. Hell, it was the third person he'd sparred with today and he'd hardly even broken a sweat.

Certainly didn't know the name of the prig he currently shared the ring with, some young blood back in town after his Grand Tour. A cocky upstart who'd insisted they fight gloveless, and without wrapped hands, so Daniel would "feel the wrath of my every knuckle plowing into your flesh, old man."

Old man? Who did this coxcomb think he was dealing with? Methuselah?

Daniel owed it to every male with less than three and a half decades in his cup to take the blustery fribble down a notch. And he'd been doing it in style.

Child's play, really.

Ducking, spinning, landing a nice one-two on the chap's not-so-cocky-anymore chin, slowly but surely wiping that smug expression off his face.

Giving his mind way too much time to ponder his friend's unexpected absence.

Was Penry trying to serve some sort of mangled justice by not showing on time? Doubtless, given his cryptic note, he had an earful to deliver concerning the Everson boy. And even though Daniel was no longer a grateful lad of eight, he respected the man enough to listen to any advice he cared to impart.

After all, hadn't it been Penry, back then known to a young Daniel simply as Will, his older brother's best friend, who was the one person at home—outside of Ellie and their mother—to come to Daniel's defense once David was gone?

"Lookit what we have here," Robert had drawled one afternoon shortly after David's death, sliding from his heaving horse and approaching Daniel, who might've sniffed a time or two but was tearless. "A little c-c-c-c-*cry* b-b-b-b-ba-baby!"

"Stop that, Rob," Will had ordered, jumping to the ground and following a bit slower, leading his horse who wasn't breathing nearly as hard. "Quit mocking him. You know he can't help it."

They'd come upon Daniel while riding over the extensive Tremayne estate, lands that, to a playful boy, had once meant fun and freedom but that now provided only silence and solace. Silence from his father's accusations; solace in the form of memories.

Daniel, still grieving the loss of his best friend and twin, had returned to the scene. Only this time, instead of climbing the tree and laughingly daring David to follow, he'd hunkered down at the base and tried not to cry. Tried with such agonizing effort, he'd bitten his lips so hard, two teeth pierced skin.

"M-m-m-m-mmmm*ocking* him!" Robert had chortled, waving a thin stick in Daniel's face, perilously close to his lips. The very branch he'd been using to whip his horse into a lather moments before. "Stupid t-t-t-toad. I still cannot believe I'm saddled with the imbecile for a spare."

Robert used the branch to slap Daniel on the head, prompting the little boy to scramble to his feet. But he held his ground, proud. Not a single tear had fallen. Not before and not now. Turning to his friend, Robert continued, both his attack and his hateful tirade. "Papa's livid *he* wasn't the one to fall—"

"Rob, I said to stop!" Will snatched the weapon and snapped it in half.

By now, the stick had landed twice more on Daniel's cheeks, leaving twin red welts. "Hate you!"

"Very good," Robert said snidely, bowing as though he were at court. "You managed that without stammering like a fool. Care to try again? B-b-b-b-bet you can't do it t-t-t-twice!"

"Come on." Will gave Robert a friendly shove toward their grazing horses. "Quit being such a bastard. We don't want to miss—"

"Leave off. He doesn't mind, hardly even notices. Too stupid to care." Robert whipped around and snaked back to Daniel. Where he kicked one tiny ankle, causing his younger brother to stumble to his knees. "D-d-d-d-don't stay out t-t-t-t-too late. You might get l-l-l-l-lost."

"Good God, you're an evil one sometimes, Rob."

Daniel couldn't miss the look of sympathy Will shot his way before he convinced Robert if they didn't leave now, they'd miss the big race.

Evidently seeing whether Lord Woltren's new phaeton

could stay upright on a particularly sharp curve surpassed the enticement of plaguing a younger brother.

Will mounted his horse—and after one last, lingering and compassionate glance at Daniel—turned toward Robert. "You arse—there are days I detest your mean streak."

Robert just laughed and whipped his horse with the reins.

Seconds later, the older boys rode off.

Leaving Daniel no longer feeling like crying. Just angry.

Angry that David had died while Robert lived.

Mean, snide Robert who made fun of Ellie too. Because she dared to be a *girl*, one who'd started sucking her thumb again after the burial just days ago.

Already back on his feet after facing Robert's taunts, only somewhat mollified by the continued influence Will Penry had on his rotten brother, Daniel turned back to the tree.

This time, though, he didn't climb it. Didn't sink down beside it to mourn.

No, this time he *attacked* it. Slapping and pummeling the bark until the skin on his knuckles and palms scraped off and drops of blood flew along with every flush hit. Scratching with his nails at the living embodiment of the one thing he could blame who couldn't take him to task. Who couldn't talk back—or mock him if he was dumb enough to say a single, stupid word.

And then he was crying. Crying so hard he couldn't breathe, could only pound at the tree while sobbing out his sorrow.

Thunk! The side of his right fist slammed into the bark. *I hate my dumb mouth.*

Thawk! He hit again, just as hard. *So I just won't use it.*

Whack! Bam! The left fist followed suit, pain radiating up his arm when it greeted the tree. *Who needs to talk?*

Pow! Despite the broken finger, both hands clawed and

fought the offending monster where once two boys had laughed and played. *Pow-pow!*

Oh God. David's gone.

I miss him so much!

Stinging from the punishing blows, his arms slowly gave out. It took everything in him to raise the right one again and land it against the strong tree. *Bam!*

How I miss him.

BAM!

Daniel feinted left when he should've gone right and leaned directly into the oncoming fist.

"Ompfff!" Everson clouted him harder than expected. And he *had* been expecting it, purposefully angling into the hit.

It was only what he deserved. A thorough beating for his sorry-arse actions toward the man's son a couple days ago.

Unknowingly or not, with Penry's continued absence, Everson had stepped in to fill the void.

It was nearing 2 p.m. At least by now, he knew what had happened to his missing friend: rumor was Penry's second eldest had received three offers this week—two this very morning. For a man with multiple daughters, this was accounted a very good thing.

No wonder he hadn't put in an appearance even though Daniel had lingered beyond the appointed time, sparring with several others before inviting Everson to join him, only slightly reluctant when Everson had suggested they wrap their hands.

Laughingly, the man had claimed he didn't want Tremayne to be at a disadvantage, sparring with so many today. He had no inkling how lucky he was about to feel, by stepping into the ring with the guilt-ridden lout who'd disrespected and disillusioned his youngest son.

Smack! He twisted to the side, just in time for that one to glance—heavily—off his ribs.

Daniel had been more than a little surprised Everson treated him with the same respect and friendliness as always. So young Tom had kept his mouth shut, hadn't shared what a bastard Daniel had been. Likewise, Penry hadn't said anything to Everson either. Which meant it was up to Daniel to make amends.

Which he'd do, as soon as he could trust his conscience had suffered sufficiently, by way of his body.

Thunk!

"Ay!" exclaimed Everson, shaking out his gloved fist. "Sorry, Tre...mayne." The man was out of breath. Also likely knocked askew by how many he was landing. No matter what side of the fist one was on, a sharp punch was jarring.

Just thinking about Thea kissing things better almost made it worthwhile.

Thea.

His smile bloomed even as Everson landed an unexpected punch solidly on his cheek.

"Eh, now..." Daniel shook his head, rolled his shoulders. Sweat flew from both. "B-been practicing?"

Everson grinned. "That I have."

Good man. *Let him get in a powerful one.* Daniel knew he deserved it.

So he suffered another. Then another.

Then finally started weaving and ducking, fighting back, if only to a point.

Responding automatically now, his body doing what he'd trained it to for more years than he could count, his thoughts flitted back to dinner last night, to Elizabeth's startling observation during the second course...

"So tell me, brother dear, what's put that smile on your face?"

Wylde cleared his throat. "I'm wondering *who* put the gouges in his neck."

Rather than sputter or blush prettily, as she would have in the past, his sister gave him a frank look, one of curious appraisal. "I believe Wylde has the right of it." Though he still sensed a definite air of reserve about her, she left off frowning at his neck and glanced at her husband as though seeking his advice. All evening, Daniel had sensed a new awareness between them. "What think you? Could it be the same person who did both?"

Wylde grinned like a court jester. "Aye. Most definitely. Tremayne—care to enlighten us as to her identity?"

"I would not." And though it galled him to be the source of amusement for anyone, he could withstand the discomfort given how his predicament seemed to bridge a bond—however tenuous—between Ellie and her husband.

"It matters not who she is," Elizabeth said warmly. "If she makes you this content, I like her already."

Content? Was that the strange emotion besieging him since yesterday? Contentment? Nay, for it didn't come close to conveying the hunger he felt to be in Thea's company again—and he'd just left her—"their"—mirrored bed an hour ago!

"Daniel," Elizabeth's enthusiasm arrested his attention, "shall I apply myself to conjuring you a happy ending with this mystery woman?"

Wylde gestured with his fork and his voice held a bit of a bite. "Before you go spreading herbs and blessings to all and sundry, best conjure up one for yourself, wouldn't you think?"

"Wylde!" A sharp tide of crimson swept up Ellie's neck.

He stared at them both. Wylde appeared indolent, relaxed yet alert, his concentration fixed solely on his wife. Elizabeth was ill at ease. Not mad exactly but definitely irritated about something.

Daniel unglued his back teeth. (Easier to snarl that way.) "*What* the d-d-deuce is"—*going*—"on?"

"What's wrong with us?" Ellie interpreted incorrectly. But the gist was the same.

"Eh." A single-syllable grunt that didn't come close to expressing his worry and concern.

Ellie waved her napkin (probably hoping to cool her face off). "Nothing a little time won't cure, dear brother."

He didn't believe that for a moment.

Wylde put in wryly, "Nothing a few good tuppings won't fix."

Now *that*, Daniel believed.

But the way Ellie was strangling on her last breath told Daniel he'd best lighten the mood. So he twisted his lips into a semblance of a smile. "Pr-pr-pr—" Deep breath, think it out. Quickly now. *Problem?* Nay, already tripped over that one. *Trouble? Difficulty?* Nay. Nay. *Bad time?* Nay times infinity! Shit.

So he barked, "*Things* not flowing 'tween the sheets, that it?"

"Daniel!" Elizabeth shot a panicked glance behind him.

He looked over his shoulder and saw the footman, eyes deliberately averted.

Damn. "My ap-p-ologies."

As though it didn't matter whether everyone was privy to the situation between him and his wife, Wylde lounged back in his chair. He took up his wineglass, letting it sway from a loose hold, giving the appearance of a man without a care in the world. "If you must know, old chap, the problem isn't what happens *between* the sheets, it's *getting* her there: between them."

With a cry, Ellie jumped to her feet, outrage and embarrassment mingled in her expression before she fled, leaving

Wylde to plead his passion for all things political, the servants to clear the table around them (neither gentleman being inclined to move, the wine within easy reach and relocating elsewhere an unnecessary effort).

Leaving Daniel to worry over the affairs of men and women—did the course *ever* run smooth? But mostly leaving him to nod and pretend to be listening to Wylde's natterings while instead, he was thinking of Thea. Imagining the following day when they'd again carry on their budding flirtation, thanks to her bewitched quill and his bemused footman...

Boom! Ker-thump!

Pain exploded behind his cheekbone.

Everson put out a hand to steady him.

Daniel blinked. Damn. That'd been the hardest one yet—what he got for woolgathering.

"I'm think...ing," Everson panted, "that's...enough for... one day."

Daniel slung an arm around the other man's solid shoulders. The gesture was one of friendship; in truth, he was still seeing stars and didn't want to land on his face this close to exiting the ring.

The men made their way to a corner and toweled off. Still standing, Daniel addressed his companion, who'd sunk wearily onto a bench. "Everson?"

Everson looked up from where he unwound the wrapping on his left hand, fingers flexing with each freeing revolution. "Aye?"

Daniel opened his mouth to apologize. To confess how rudely he'd treated—

But no. Wasn't that the coward's way out?

It was the man's son he owed an apology to. "Would like...

to call. Is t-t—" He scrubbed the damp towel over his throbbing face to muffle the words. "'Omorrow a'reeable?"

"Call? At my *home*, my lord?" He'd obviously flustered Everson. They'd known each other for years and had never once socialized outside of Jackson's or during a rare sit-down over brandy at their club.

Daniel quit hiding his mouth and tossed the towel to an empty spot on the bench. He nodded once. Tried not to look intimidating. Wasn't sure whether either of them could accomplish that feat—they both sported the beginnings of bruises—and where Everson had landed that last hit, Daniel felt the skin below his right eye pulling tight as it swelled; the rest of him felt like he'd been dragged over rocks.

Despite his surprise, Everson grinned. "Certainly you can, Lord Tremayne. The household comes alive early, so anytime after nine?"

As always, Daniel felt the stiff formality that surrounded him. He wanted to ask the man to dispense with his title, to call him by his first name. Or skip the honorary and use "Tremayne". But habit kept him silent. His name was the absolute worst. Couldn't pronounce it once without mangling the bloody hell out of it. So he settled for, "Eleven?"

"Fine. Fine." Everson shrugged into his shirt, only wincing once before emerging from the neckline. "You're, ah, not planning on having another go at me for that last punisher?"

That brought a smile. "Hardly."

Unwilling to linger now that he'd accomplished the first step of the objective that had been weighing on him, Daniel quickly drew on his street clothes and pulled on his boots. Before parting ways with Everson, he glanced across the bench. Waiting until the man glanced up, he said deliberately, "Have your...boy...Tom there."

"Thomas?" Everson reared back as though struck, his eyebrows soaring. "I didn't know you'd met my youngest…"

But by now, Everson was talking to air.

———◦◦◦———

It was sheer luck that brought Thea into safety and the comfort of Sarah's carriage. Well, luck and Thea's lack of a cloak.

"I still cannot believe I saw you!" Sarah exclaimed, using her warming blanket to blot water from Thea's head.

Moments earlier (as Sarah explained the second she hauled Thea inside), she'd spotted a woman who had taken refuge from the rain, hunched and shivering in the doorway of a closed haberdashery. Recognizing her friend, she'd screeched at her driver to halt and had the carriage door open before the wheels stopped turning. "For once you can thank that dress of yours. Even wet that atrocious color is unmistakable."

"Unmistakably ugly?" The words came out near frozen, but inside, the chill of fear that had gripped Thea the last two hours was rapidly giving way to peace. *It would be all right now.* "Th-thank heavens for friends who love to shop!"

Sarah tried to frown but it came out upside down. "How you can jest when your hands feel like blocks of ice, I'll never know." Sarah transferred her attention to chafing Thea's palms. "Gloves, child! How you could go off without those too is beyond me!"

She hadn't. Thea had (stupidly, she realized after the fact) traded them to a street urchin who swore she knew the way to Hatchards, only to lead Thea a merry chase down several streets—ones without a bookstore in sight—before disappearing.

Thea opened her mouth to apologize, for she truly

regretted the loss of the beautiful gloves her friend had given her, but snapped it shut when Sarah started up again.

"Why you won't take the cloak and dresses I've offered..." Now that Thea's fingers were flushed a nice tomato color—and stinging like the devil—Sarah took to bundling her in another blanket. "Offered time and again!"

A few months into their friendship, Sarah had positively insisted Thea take a couple of her dresses once she'd realized how sparse Thea's wardrobe. Thea promptly insisted Sarah take them back. When one eked out an existence in the dingy slums of London, one did *not* arrive home wearing fine quality silk and fur. Not and live to wear the wares.

"'Tis of no matter. Truly, I'm fine. Thanks to your timely rescue," she said and her teeth hardly clattered at all. "Just so relieved to see you."

"You can thank a carriage mishap two streets over. I was heading home but we had to detour through here—what ever are you doing?"

Thea had emerged from the blanket and pushed open a window to view the soggy sight of decent homes rolling by. Shielding the stray but determined raindrops with one arm, she kept her gaze on the houses while explaining, "Looking for my home. Have you any notion where I live—the town-house I mean? The one Lord Tremayne secured?"

When no answer was forthcoming, she glanced back at Sarah.

For a moment, her friend gaped like a caught carp. "You mean you don't?"

Wet hair streamed in front of her left eye. Thea blinked and hooked the soggy strands behind her ear. "Not the address, precisely. I've been there since the night of your party. I just left today for the first time but failed to note the street and number. Reckless of me, I know..."

Laughter at her own folly, and because she couldn't help

but smile as she recounted the last two days, Thea shared much about her time since leaving with Lord Tremayne (but certainly not everything; some intimate memories—and mirrored reflections—were best kept to oneself).

She also shared the last few bites of George and Charlotte's cheese.

"I cannot believe you meant to waste this quality Stilton on two rodents," Sarah said, a true grin on her features. "Especially after how hard you worked to rid yourself of them."

"Not *them*, specifically, just their offspring and aunts and uncles—"

"Enough!" Sarah held out a hand, choking a bit as the last laugh—and piece of cheese—went down the wrong pipe. "Shall I be practical? It seems as though one of us must and due to your mouse mania, the task turns to me. I could bring you home with me, see you dry and warm in a trice, but based on how you've practically fallen through the window twice—"

"I have not!"

"Searching for a landmark, I think I'd serve you best by helping you find your street. Come, tell me what you remember. When you left the party, which way did you travel?"

And so, after ferreting out a few facts and knowing Lord Tremayne wasn't one to scrimp, Sarah proclaimed, "If I'm not mistaken, that townhouse with the overdone Grecian garden you described belongs to Dunlavy's mistress. It was in Belgrave Square. I'll have Peter drive around that way and you can tell me if anything strikes a chord."

The clouds had parted, letting in a few, nearly horizontal weak shafts of sunlight and Thea eagerly agreed.

"But I warn you," Sarah cautioned, "it'll be full dark in less than an hour."

Ever pragmatic, she acknowledged the time. "I know full

well the futility of keeping you and your coachman out much longer. If we have to, you could write to Lord Penry and he could fetch Lord Tremayne—"

Sarah was laughing again. "Penry fetch Tremayne? Which means you have not his address either?"

"Guilty." A flood of heat washed over Thea. "There's more to this mistress business than I bargained for, I admit. I—"

"Tell me of that," Sarah interrupted with an air of urgency. "You spoke of Buttons and the Samuels and delicious meals, but what of Tremayne? Was he gentle with you? Patient?"

"More than necessary, in truth. Why?" Every moisture-laden particle of air settled heavily on her lungs. At once, the confines of the carriage combined with the sudden suspicion and her soggy self had Thea suffocating under her uncomfortable garments. "Did you have anything to do with that?"

"Me? Perish the thought. Now tell me how he's been treating you. Are the two of you getting on?"

Just like that, as though her fairy godmother had waved a wand, the air shimmered and sparkled with all the excitement Thea couldn't contain. "Positively lovely! Oh, Sarah, he's everything I could have hoped for. Considerate and kind—and how he makes me laugh. He possesses a wicked sense of humor."

"Tremayne?" Sarah sounded intrigued. "I know he can bite off a pithy remark on occasion, but I've never thought of him as a mirthful man."

"With me he is. I believe I make him laugh as well; we're well matched in that regard." She thought of their ribald Shakespearian exchange the day before and didn't attempt to subdue her own smile. "And the home he procured for me? It's the grandest place I've ever lived. All gold brocade and crimson velvet and giant—"

Mirrors. Which Thea swallowed at the last second. "To be sure, I find Lord Tremayne thoughtful and generous and his inexpressibles you mentioned—" She heard herself prattling on but couldn't seem to stop, not even when venturing toward such an inappropriate subject. "Well, I needn't expound upon how happy he makes me in that regard."

Granted, she'd yet to actually experience the full measure of his "inexpressible", but she had no doubt when the time came (which she assumed would be soon—tonight?) that the particular encounter and resulting sensations would rival what he blessed her with the night before.

Instead of being delighted at Thea's good fortune, Sarah only eyed her critically. A look of censure—or was it resignation?—found its way to her friend's expression. "It's only been, what? Two nights? And you're waxing on as if you've fallen— Nay. I won't tread that path. But, Dorothea, mind, don't lose your heart to him."

She waved the concern away. "Of course not! We've only just met."

But was he married? She opened her mouth to ask but Sarah cut her off. "Heed me well, dear. Take joy in your new circumstance and pleasure in his company, but don't mistake your interactions for anything more than what they are: he's *paying* for your services. It's naught but a business transaction, though I admit, a singularly intimate one." Avoiding Thea's gaze, Sarah spread out one gloved hand and began straightening the soft leather where it stretched over every fingertip. "We can delude ourselves and paint it up pretty as a tulip but it doesn't change the facts—women who are paid for sex are, at heart, nothing more than whor—"

"Don't say it! Really, Sarah," Thea remonstrated, more than a little astonished at hearing her friend speak thusly. "*At heart*, I was a woman in need and his money has provided for those needs. 'Tis all."

"Well, make sure you don't lose yours."

"Of course not," she said again, turning once more to gaze out the window. "I know better."

Oh, but hearts to Hertfordshire, she was playing herself for a fool if she truly believed that.

YET AGAIN LORD Tremayne came to her rescue. For not five minutes, and at least fifty unspoken self-recriminations later, she spotted not her new townhouse exactly, but the man who'd leased it for her.

"There he is!" she said urgently, so relieved every concern about her heart took wing. "Walking up to the porch— Lord Tremayne!"

While Thea gestured wildly as though she could halt the horses herself, Sarah knocked on the roof, alerting her driver, and leaned forward so she could see. "'Tis him all right. His silhouette is rather splendid."

They neared and Thea's shouts captured his attention. Though the evening light was hazy, and his face shadowed by his tall-crowned hat, when he swung round, she could easily make out the grimace distorting his features. "Oh, dear."

"What is it?"

"He looks angry."

"I'm sure that's simply worry over where you got off to," Sarah consoled, already relaxed back into her seat. "Oh, I've been meaning to tell you, I'm journeying to Bucklesham to visit my sister. She just sent word her baby came early and—"

As they rolled closer, Thea saw that worry was the least of it. "Egad! It looks like someone took a mallet to his face!"

"What?!" Sarah flew forward and jerked the curtain aside. "Dammit, Penry!" she swore, startling Thea's head back around. "He *promised* he'd exercise restraint."

"Did Lord Penry do this?" Thea was aghast. She'd never

before heard her friend curse and couldn't fathom Sarah knowing about— Actually *condoning*...

But what did it mean? "What reason would Lord Penry have to attack his friend? To hurt him so?"

Explanations could wait for later! The second the carriage rolled to a stop, Thea was fighting to get the door open. "Lord Tremayne!"

9

ODE TO MACHINES

Happy the Man, who in his Pocket keeps,
Whether with green or scarlet Ribband bound,
A well made Cundum.

Generally attributed to John Wilmot, the Earl of Rochester; from *A Panegyric Upon Cundum*, circa 1720s, a pamphlet extolling the virtues of condoms.

———————◦◦———————

IT ONLY HURT when he breathed.

So the unexpected gasp his lungs expelled when Daniel caught sight of Thea flinging herself from the carriage and racing toward him cut like a sword slicing across his ribs.

She looked like sunshine, even when the spontaneous smile on her face transformed into a flat line, even when she came close enough he could see that the depths of her mossy eyes were drowning in worry—over him. But neither her fading smile nor the growing alarm dimmed how she lit up his entire day. Amazing really, considering her bedraggled state.

Sludge. Her ugly dress, now soaked and muddy—and torn near the hem, he couldn't help but note, when a fair amount of ruined stocking showed—put him in mind of sludge. Sewer bracken.

Yet Thea outshone it still.

"My lord!" she exclaimed, reaching him with breathless abandon. She immediately lifted one ungloved hand to feather fingertips over his cheekbone. "Whatever happened to you?"

Granted, his eye was halfway swelled shut, but nothing was broken—not even cracked, or so Crowley had assured him when Daniel washed up and suffered the man's thorough inspection before departing his bachelor residence to make the jaunt to Thea's. His tiger had already taken his carriage round back.

Daniel had considered sending his regrets and staying home tonight—not dismaying her with his freshly beat-upon visage—but it seemed his mouth had other plans, ordering his team and driver made ready before he was even dry from his bath.

But Thea—

Dear, battle-worn Thea...

Daniel pulled her fingers from his eye and ran his opposite hand down the back of her head. Straggly strands of saturated hair fell over her shoulder, left an increasingly damp spot over one breast. A breast with one very beaded nipple. "And you?" he intoned, trying—and failing—to keep the concern from his voice. "You look a fright."

"Me?" She blushed, turned to wave Sarah on and just as swiftly took his hand in hers, opened the door and hauled him inside. "Never mind me, my lord. Your face. What—"

"Oh, Miss Thea." At the sound of them entering, Mrs.

Samuels came bustling. "Land sakes, child, we thought to have ye back hours ago. About ready to call out the Royal Navy, we were— Oh." Catching sight of Daniel, the woman skidded to a halt. "Lord Tremayne? We weren't expecting ye so early." Her gaze swung to Thea and she forgot all about him. "Look at ye, child! All—"

"I am fine, truly. Would you send up some warm wash water? Start the fire in my room if it hasn't been already?"

The housekeeper hurried off to do her mistress's bidding and Daniel, silently bemused at seeing this calm, capable side of Thea, waited to learn what she might do next. He was stunned when, rather than direct him to wait in the parlor while she changed, she swirled back to him and cautiously touched the cut beneath his eye. "How you must be hurting. Come with me. I'll see that you're taken care of."

He didn't tell her his face was so numb he couldn't feel a thing. Didn't tell her Ellie's witchy cream had taken away the worst of the sting and blessed him with more relief than he deserved.

Didn't tell her that having her fuss over him nearly made the pain in his ribs and the guilt weighing his heart all worth it.

Nay, for once, Daniel *gladly* kept his mouth shut. Was at peace to meekly follow Thea's guidance, thanks to her hand wrapped gingerly around one set of swollen knuckles, and let her lead him up the stairs.

FINDING LORD TREMAYNE bruised and battered upon her doorstep had chilled Thea more than her icy dress. When they reached her bedchamber and she saw that though the makings of a fire were in place, the hearth was cold, she drew him straight into the windowless dressing room, which tended to be warmer especially when outside temperatures threatened the windowpanes.

Releasing him, she busied herself lighting candles and then turned to shut the door behind them to preserve what heat remained.

"Well now." She swung back, gazed up. And the look in his unswollen eye—the sight of him, so big and so close—elevated her temperature ten degrees. "Well."

He leaned back against one wall, arms crossed negligently in front of his chest. His neckcloth was as carelessly tied as she'd ever seen it, as though tonight he couldn't be bothered with the intricacies of doing it up proper.

Although "proper" was hardly an applicable term when one considered the rest of him: his face had suffered the repeated application of someone's fist, that was for certain, and he'd used her preoccupation with the candles to dispense with other formalities—removing his greatcoat, tailcoat, and waistcoat. The lack left him looking indolent as he lounged against the wall, more compelling in his shirtsleeves than any man had a right to be.

Thea knew she should be wary of him, feeling guarded and distant. Especially given his ravaged state and Sarah's recent warnings of love and whores (nasty business, that; Thea decided to put it promptly from her mind).

How could she be expected to erect walls between them when his very presence made her both secure and aware all at once? Secure of herself and aware of him. When he made her feel more feminine than she ever had, made her want to be closer to him? Had her, in fact, marching forward and pulling one of his hands free to inspect the damage done to his knuckles.

Before she could *tsk* more than twice, he curved his broad hand around hers and tugged, inviting her to meet his gaze.

What she could see of it, the flesh surrounding the one eye so puffy a good portion of it was obliterated.

"There is so much gentle strength in you," she said quietly, feeling the power in the blunt-tipped fingers that held hers. "I don't know *how* I know it, but I know I'm safe, even though your demeanor is so fierce and fearsome."

He tried to smile, but with the swelling pulling his skin it looked more like a sneer. "Would never hurt you."

"I know that, silly man. You chopped my mutton."

"Eh?"

"The night we met, you chopped— Oh, never mind it. Will you tell me how *you* got hurt?"

She waited but he said nothing.

Her hand grew hot within his hold; her entire arm simmering as he feathered gentle caresses over her skin, parts south flaring to life at the heated look he gave her. But he'd yet to explain. "My lord?"

"Mmm?"

"Did Lord Penry do this? Attack you? Pound your face?"

He shook his head once.

"Are you going to tell me what happened?"

He thought a moment. "I walked into a d-d— *Ow!*" He hissed when she squeezed his fingers at the lie. He finished wanly, "A...door?"

So he didn't intend to tell her? All right, neither did she relish confessing how her blunder-headed afternoon had gone. "A door? One with a nasty streak it appears."

"And you?" he inquired silkily, taking up her other hand and spreading both her arms wide so he could survey her from fallen hair to mud-splattered hem. "Where— What of your...day? Stroll into the ocean? Embrace a shark or...two?"

"Oh, that..." She whirled from his loose hold, too embarrassed to confess her folly while standing beneath his inspection.

"Aye, that." Lord Tremayne came up behind her, halting her retreat by pulling her spine flush against his chest.

"My lord. Stop. I'm drenched." But she couldn't stop herself from sinking against his strong, stalwart body and her protest was halfhearted at best. "I'll ruin your clothes—"

"Hang my clothes," he said hotly, his breath tickling her ear. He pulled her tight to him with one arm snug across her middle. "Thea—were you set upon by footpads?"

"Nay," she rushed to assure him. "Nothing so dire."

"Attacked by angry geese?"

That had her laughing and hugging his arm. "If you must know, you wretched man, I became lost. Lost in the rain the first time I ventured out and it was—it was—" She swallowed the growing lump of fear, determined not to give in to unrealized *what-ifs.* "'Twas..."

So very frightening. Wandering the streets for what amounted to hours, wondering if I'd ever find my way back. Back home, back to your arms—

"Alas!" She shoved his comforting touch away and broke free, scrubbing at her eyes. "'Twas no fun at all. I detest feeling so very helpless and alone." Hearing what she'd divulged, Thea rushed to cover the admission. Edging farther away, she shrugged. "Though I hadn't realized it, I must have wickedly awful compass sense and—and—"

The heavy gait of his steps shadowing her gave but a second's warning before he spun her to him again, this time chest to chest.

He flinched and his breath hissed out. But he only held her more securely as his fingers went to the buttons at her nape. "So you d-*did* have a fright."

He swore, but his fingers remained gentle. She stared at the column of his throat, again catching that elusive scent of his and drawing it deep into her lungs. A faint memory teased—

Once several buttons were undone, he curved his hand around the base of her neck. "You're freezing." It was a growl. "Where's that water—"

As though summoned, Mrs. Samuels knocked and forged inside at his brisk "Enter."

She started to step back but he kept her in his embrace.

Both Mrs. and Mr. Samuels came into the small room, carrying steaming pots, which they placed on the washstand. "We'll be but a moment and I'll have refreshments brought to your chamber as well," she told them, kindly keeping her eyes averted. "Sam already has the fire going and the room is warming nicely. Will there be anything else, Miss Thea? Lord Tremayne?"

She let him answer in the negative as her mind was working feverishly, thanks to the spicy scent of cloves and something else, something faint but sweet, taking her back to when she'd first seen him—when he'd arrived late to Sarah's and had drawn such a chorus of greetings just before sitting next to her.

"Wait." Recklessly, her mind on two different paths at once, Thea called to Mrs. Samuels. The woman popped her head back in and Thea said, "The master chamber down the hall. Please heat it as well."

"Certainly, miss."

Once they were alone, Lord Tremayne went right back to undoing her buttons and she returned to resolving what kept niggling her brain. Astonishingly, the experience of being undressed by him paled as she pieced a large part of the Tremayne puzzle together.

"There now. Lean..." He coaxed her away and started tugging the sodden, tight-fitting sleeves of her dress down her arms. "Forgive me."

His words arrested her from the fact that the bodice of her dress had just drooped forward, leaving her upper half covered by only a damp chemise. That and long, stubborn sleeves, adhering like glue to her elbows. "Forgive you? What ever do you mean?"

"I've..." Though it appeared all his energies were focused on peeling down her left sleeve, Thea had the sense he didn't see his efforts at all, that his attention was aimed inward. "Remiss. Horri...bly so. Not to have stationed a footman here or...assigned you a coachman or—"

"Stop." She was practically giddy. He felt guilty over not giving her *more* servants? "Remiss? When you've blessed me with so very much? 'Tis I who needs to learn directions. You fight for sport, do you not?"

"There." The left sleeve finally free, he pierced her with his one good—and one swollen-narrowed—eye. "What?"

"You. The bruises." She was so relieved to have figured it out. "Like cockfighting—you fight for sport."

She'd heard of men who wagered on roosters or dogs trained to fight to the death. Knew how popular boxing had become, men actually enjoying hitting each other. She'd just never seen anyone who'd done it, timepieces and Mr. Hurwell's droning diatribes about equestrian races being the extent of her "social" interaction the last few years. "Pugilism," she said with satisfaction. "I'm correct, am I not?"

A slow, crooked grin spread across his mouth as he nodded. "Aye. Like cockfighting," he confirmed, "only with fists."

"As opposed to your cocks?"

Thea couldn't believe she'd said that.

She knew the word, of course. Living in the slums had enlivened her vocabulary if not her life, but she'd never before uttered it.

Lord Tremayne didn't seem able to believe it either.

He stared at her a moment, eyebrows raised, breath held.

Then they both laughed. He winced, then laughed again. Thea howled so hard her stomach hurt.

How grand her life had become since meeting him.

———◦∞◦———

IN THE BEDCHAMBER, Mr. and Mrs. Samuels shared a surprised look.

She silently deposited the tray with wine, fruit and cheese and several wedges of roast beef upon the dainty circular table while he—not so silently—set down the bucket of coal beside the hearth and beefed up the flames.

Together they turned and exited the room, securing the door behind them.

It wasn't until they were approaching the bottom of the second set of stairs that Mrs. Samuels spoke. "Didn't his man of affairs lead you to believe that Lord Tremayne was rather a somber fellow?"

"That he did."

"He doesn't sound somber to me."

"Someone needs to teach that boy how to duck."

———◦∞◦———

FUNNY HOW BREATHING without her hurt but laughing *with* her only tickled his ribs. She'd surprised him, this mistress of his.

Had from almost the moment they met.

But something surprised him more when he freed her right arm—and was confronted with the bruises lining her wrist.

For a split second, Daniel thought he'd been too rough on her that first night. But then sanity prevailed. Lord knew he'd seen enough bruises in his life to know these weren't fresh.

Had to be several days old. There were individual finger marks as well as some deeper yellowing, indicating it hadn't been the first time someone had used force on her.

Rage stormed his gut; he hated seeing anyone abused by bullies. He'd lived with it enough as a child, seen how cowed Ellie had been around their father, experienced his own fortitude and will draining away too many times to count to stomach it happening again—to anyone he cared about.

The overpowering need to protect Thea flooded through him.

Her eyes were still sparkling with their shared laughter while he had to exercise every bit of restraint he could summon. Keeping his grip on her loose, he raised her arm between them. "Who...did...this?"

She looked completely startled for an instant, then her eyes flicked to the discoloration before jumping back to his. The laughter withered and she pressed her lips into a tight line.

"Thea?" His thumb smoothed over the old injury, his gaze pinning hers, demanding answers.

He watched her gather determination around her like a cloak. "Nothing you need concern yourself with."

He refused to let her get away with that. Unintentionally, his hold constricted until the subtle start she couldn't hide reminded him to temper his anger at her unknown assailant. "I *am* concerned."

"Just my troublesome old landlord." She tossed her head as though to prove how unaffected she was. The gesture was ruined by a long hank of damp hair slinging onto her shoulder, bringing to mind the day she'd had. "He won't bother me further."

Daniel purposefully gentled his grip, giving no indication how ferociously he wanted to throttle the absent man. "You're sure?"

"Positive."

Despite her tone, he could see the thought of the bastard flustered and frightened her. Daniel would make damn certain no one would ever put that look in her eye again. He'd send Swift John to her first thing tomorrow, tell the boy to stay. From now on, if she needed him, he'd know in a hurry.

Before he could reiterate she was to use the servant as her own, Thea leaned down to step from the sludgy dress. Then she stood, not quite shivering, in her chemise. Instead of meeting his gaze, she addressed a point some three inches above his shoulder. "If you'll wait in the bedchamber, my lord, I'll wash and be out to join you directly."

So that's how she intended to play this? He glimpses a teeny bit of honest fear and she pokers up stiff and pushes him away?

Not hardly. Blocking the door with his body, Daniel jerked at his neckcloth, wincing when his knuckles protested the stubborn knot. Working it loose, he leaned to the side and snared her gaze. "We'll wash together."

He watched comprehension sink in as he dispensed with the neckcloth and undid his shirt cuffs, the mild protest of his ribs worth it when he ripped the shirt overhead and tossed it behind her. Worth it because the prim, detached look dropped from her face and she exclaimed over the fresh mottling on his side.

He'd never thanked a flush hit more.

Stripped to the waist, he reached for her chemise—ready to bare the rest of her—but she hauled out of reach. "Wait. Do you care to tell me *why* Sarah thought Lord Penry did this to you?"

So he is out to smack some sense into me?

Daniel smiled grimly and sidestepped her question. "Never saw him."

"My lord..." There was a threat in her tone, as though she

chastised a sword-wielding grasshopper bent on terrorizing her begonias.

The image had him laughing again. "'T-tis true. Crossed paths not at all with him—"

"Nor with a door, I'd imagine."

He had the grace to look ashamed. Why hadn't he just *told* her he sparred?

Because Elizabeth always made it out to be so much more? *Father beat it into you until you came to believe it—you think you deserve being punished because you lived while David died.*

That wasn't true. Not anymore.

However, an uncomfortable piece of honesty made him recall how he *had* thought he deserved a pummeling today for his treatment of Tom.

The sudden burst of clarity was startling.

But it paled when she stepped forward and touched an old scar on his shoulder. "There now. I shall badger you no more. Only tell me what—or who—caused this..."

It was a ragged, several-inch line that Louise had never once noticed or remarked on. Not in all their years together.

"Trouble with a tree branch." When Thea rose up on her toes to rain kisses over the puckered and drawn skin, the rest escaped without forethought. "The day my brother died."

How easily the confession slipped out—physically and emotionally. Part of Daniel wanted to question why it was that touching Thea seemed to loosen his mouth, to make the words come easier. The rest of him simply marveled at the flash of compassion in her expression when she leaned back to stare into his eyes.

"Climbing," he explained. "We were eight."

"Both of you?" She grasped the significance immediately. "He was your twin? Oh, Lord Tremayne..."

The soft sympathy was nearly his undoing.

Daniel, dammit! He wanted her to use his name.

But then her gaze and the light graze of her fingers moved to his lips.

"What about this? How did you scar your mouth?"

Instead of tightening as they always did when he thought of that day, Daniel found his lips opening, confiding, "My father."

"He did this? On purpose?"

He jerked a hard nod and his hands flexed on her waist. How long had he been holding her?

Rather than drop to her feet or back away, she came closer, blessing him with her tranquil presence. Like a man addicted to drink, he craved more.

"I can tell the memory pains you." Her voice became a whisper. "Shall I kiss it away?"

Too stunned to speak, he nodded.

This beautiful, bedraggled woman then began searching out every mark and blemish his exposed body possessed, kissing each, murmuring words of comfort and solace... incredibly, not shying away from his "fierce and fearsome" self.

He was tempted to tell her the truth. All of it. His dreadful difficulties with speech. His—

Don't be stupid! You've known her less than a week.

But still, he was tempted...

Do you want her to think you a fool before you've had time to convince her otherwise?

And still her kisses and caresses continued, up his chest, across his shoulders, down his arms...

It felt as though she were courting him. Courting his mind as she wove a spell over his body. Her unabashed acceptance made him want to give her something in return. He wanted to buy her jewelry and furs, maybe a dainty horse and—

His mind backtracked. Jewelry and furs. "A coat," he interrupted her journey over his raw knuckles to ask. "Have you one?"

"Nay. And my gloves slipped away today I'm afraid."

"Slipped away?"

"On the heels—or should I say fingers?—of an unhelpful beggar..." Once again, she tried to laugh off her troubling excursion.

They hadn't known each other long, but Daniel didn't think Thea was a female given to vapors. She'd obviously had a trying day, and after what she'd just done for him, replaced past hurts with present approval, putting aside his selfish wants was the least he could do.

His entire body tingling from her exploration, he grasped both her hands and brought her fingertips to his mouth. It was his turn to cherish her.

He'd help her bathe. Then he'd take his leave. Let her sleep.

She deserved no less.

"Let me wash your hair." He led her to the basin where the no-longer-steamy (but suitably warm, a quick dip of his finger told him) water waited. There was an empty pail for rinsing as well.

Thinking through his words, he guided her to kneel. "You've had a harrowing...day. I shall..." *Tuck you in bed and bid you* adieu *with a kiss. Dream of you all night long.* "Finish here and leave you...to rest."

Giving in to the pressure of his hands, she ducked her head over the basin so he could dampen the mass.

"By all accounts"—the words were muffled by her position—"I should be exhausted but I'm not." When the warm water streamed over her scalp, she made a low murmur that had his body tightening. "Likely it'll all catch up with me tomorrow. For now I'm quite awake."

THEA BARELY HID HER ASTONISHMENT. He was washing her hair!

A man, a *marquis*, was patiently working soap over her scalp and rinsing the suds away. He was brushing through tangled strands with his strong fingers and massaging her head long after the water ran clear.

Who knew one's scalp was so susceptible to stimulation? Brushing her own hair was a calming experience; having her mother brush it when she was a child, a very pleasurable one. But this?

This was beyond fantastical.

With every touch, shards of lightning struck from the tips of his fingers and blazed a path straight to her stomach, and lower.

From the moment she'd seen him standing on her doorstep, she'd felt invigorated. Now she just felt aroused.

Thea yearned to swing her head back as he blotted the length with a towel, yearned to grasp his muscled arms, pull his chest to hers and assuage the heavy ache in her breasts. The ache his thorough hair washing had created.

And he planned to *leave her to rest*?

Not when the soothing stroke of his hands had energized and enlivened every particle of her body. Not when she wanted him to kiss her and not stop.

Not when she wanted *him*.

"There now," he said as though the task was finished, giving one last squeeze to her hair. And giving her the sense he was about to make good on his promise and depart.

Removing the towel from his grip, she faced him squarely.

After inspecting his body earlier, trying to look dispassionately at each of the imperfections carved into his skin and instead only seeing the man beneath the hurts, she hardly registered the swollen eye or bruised side anymore. What she saw before her was a spectacular specimen of masculinity.

What she wanted was every square inch pressed against her.

Seeing his look of steely determination tempered with a frown of self-denial recalled to mind Sarah's curious words in the carriage. All Thea could think was how he'd not yet truly bedded her. Not completely.

And he was set to deny them both? *Again?* Not if she had anything to say about it.

She'd had enough of being quiet. Enough of not stating her wishes, of blending into the background, first with her husband and then without him. Enough of not being clear about what *she* wanted.

Time to change that, starting now. "Just so we have clarity between us, Lord Tremayne, I am quite willing—more than willing actually—to have you...have you..."

Why was she dithering? *Just say it, Dorothea Jane.* "I would prefer you stay. Would like for us to come together fully." He looked a bit nonplussed. While her fingers strangled the damp towel, she forged ahead. "To be perfectly blunt, I don't want you to leave—and leave me aching again. And after being confronted with your magnificent chest, I'd like to see the rest of you naked, to feel you pressed ag-*ahummm*—"

Without having to finish her pathetic recital, he *knew*. Knew and took command.

His arm went around her back and molded her to him. His mouth sang a symphony of lust against hers.

This kiss was nothing like the exploring ones in the carriage, nothing at all like the sensual one he gave her after bringing her to orgasm last night.

Nay, this kiss was hard and hot, urgent, and just a touch shy of savage.

This kiss boiled her blood and dampened her loins faster than she could think *he has on too many clothes*. As he plundered her mouth with primal intent, her nails scored over the fabric covering his posterior.

With a smothered chuckle at her eagerness, he gave her lips one last bit of intense suction before releasing them. "Shall I?"

While she struggled to comprehend (and kept clawing at his frustrating pantaloons), he dragged his hands past her bottom to grip the hem of her chemise and hauled it over her head.

"Ah, Thea." He gasped at the sight of her, one unsteady hand going to the ribs discernible beneath her slight breasts. "You're so thin. So dangerously thin..."

She didn't take offense, didn't panic that he found her lack of womanly flesh distasteful. How could she? When the look in his eyes said the concern was *for* her.

He swiftly used the washcloth to cleanse every inch of skin with the remaining water, and then he scooped her up, carrying her through her feminine bedroom and into the hallway where he unerringly made his way to the master chamber.

She spared scarcely a second to wonder at his murmured, "Like Cyclops...just in t-time..." because upon reaching the trysting room, he placed her on her feet and kissed her again passionately. From her lips, to her shoulder, working his way down until his tingle-giving mouth reached her wrist and then to the tips of her fingers. After sucking not one but two into his mouth and rousing an even deeper hunger, he released her, straightening and raking his gaze over her naked form.

She trembled from the heat in his eyes. Trembled more when he bent to bestow a tender kiss on the bruises above her wrist. "So lovely."

A blush threatened but there was no time for modesty. "You still have on too many clothes."

She reached for him but he reached her first, fusing their lips as he used his grasp on her waist to place her square across the mattress. Thea stretched her arms to receive him but he was already skimming his lips down her body as he unfastened his pantaloons, then wrestled with his boots.

His lips stayed busy on the skin of her stomach, tongue circling her navel. She heard the sweet thump of one boot hit the floor. "Hurry," she ordered, that achy sensation growing between her legs. "Just shove them off and—"

He licked lower and her hips lifted off the bed, her nails scoring the counterpane at her hips, wishing they were sinking into his skin.

And then it *was* his skin when he finally shed the rest of his clothes and came down over her, the smooth, smooth skin of his shoulders greeting her fingertips.

She welcomed the weight of his body pushing her into the bed, welcomed the reverent slide of his hand up her stomach until he was moving his fingers over the sensitive peak of one tightly bunched nipple.

"My charms are rather...minimal at the moment." Why did she go and mention that? Even when eating regularly, her "charms" weren't much above *minimal*—but did she have to draw his attention to the lack?

Embarrassed, avoiding what she might see in his gaze, Thea flicked hers overhead. Then promptly forgot to worry about her bosom deficit. Because she was staring at the shadowed reflection of his naked buttocks!

So very pale, so very muscular. So *very* sinful of her, to be salivating over the salacious sight.

Heavens to Hampshire, thank the blazes for the glowing hearth and what it revealed. Her first look at a nude man most definitely did not disappoint. In truth, the titillating sight tripled her ardor in an instant.

Lord Tremayne drew her focus from the mirror when he climbed up her body, wicking his tongue along the path of his fingers until he licked up one barely mounded slope, sending all manner of delight from his tongue to the far reaches of her body. He applied his tongue to the puckered areola and murmured, "Not the size that matters..."

Looking pointedly from her breast to her eyes, he curved his mouth in a slow grin. "It's the cherry on t-top."

Holding her gaze, he closed his lips around one aching nipple and delivered sufficient suction to have her back arching off the bed, her hips toward his, and her neck up so she could watch. Where she blinked in surprise, seeing the length of her body bracketed by his.

Miraculously, she looked every bit as voluptuous and alluring as her paired portraits downstairs, only instead of burled wood, she was framed by Lord Tremayne's hands and body.

For once, *she* was a naughty nude, and how it made her smile. Made her eager for more, impatient for the length of his erection now pressing into her thigh.

Breathless whispers of encouragement escaped when his lips sucked fiercely on her breast and his tongue flailed over the tip, the flat of one palm coming up to massage the other. "Aye, like that."

Whimpering at how easily his attentions fired her blood, she grazed her hands over his shoulders, coasted them over the powerful muscles and passion-warmed skin, craving him closer...ever closer.

He transferred his mouth to her other breast while his splayed palm glided down her stomach and below her waist. She tilted toward him and was rewarded with the first probe of his fingers.

"Mmm." She dug her nails into his back and crawled them lower as though she could bring him higher, entice his shaft to slide inside.

But wait—

As he stroked over her labia, her thighs widening in welcome, her fingertips encountered more than one straight ridge low across his back. Despite the growing pressure, the languid urgency building in her abdomen, she deliberately traced along one wicked line until encountering a host more, numerous thin welts parading across his flank the farther she slid her palms.

Understanding made her gasp.

Noticing where her hands had frozen, he grew rigid.

"Your father?" she whispered.

A full three seconds later he nodded against her breast.

"That insensitive bastard." Curving her fingers over the scarred flesh, Thea swore aloud for the first time in her life. "How could he—"

Lord Tremayne lunged upward and silenced her with his lips, with the raggedly voiced, "You wonderful woman."

You goddamn wonderful woman!

The taste of Thea, the feel of her slick passion coating his fingers, her untutored body's response—and her reaction to the old scars—practically stealing his wits, Daniel recalled himself without a moment to spare.

"Stay." The order was instinctive. Rude even, as one hand drifted over her trembling thighs when he reluctantly slid from the bed to retrieve one of the machines purchased the day of Sarah's party.

Another second and he would have forgotten to armor himself.

Startling because after years of regular and consistent use, he never forgot. Never.

He'd started donning the machinery years ago after it made the rounds when Lord Tims' trusted mistress gave him not only an hour's pleasure but a screaming case of clap (after dallying with a visiting French count, or so the story went).

Not one to risk his ballocks for a quick tup, especially after hearing about the pain and blisters, it had been a worthwhile sacrifice to avail himself of the plentiful preventatives. More than that, it became easy to justify their usage when long-time Louise started hinting at something more permanent between them, offering to bear his heir. Egad. The lunatic ideas she had espoused made it easy to suffer a bit of sensation loss for the sake of his sanity.

So it was with no little astonishment Daniel found himself nearly forgetting a habit so well ingrained. Habit or no, his blighted hands fairly shook at the task, his need for her so great.

At his continued absence, she sat up with a whimper, not understanding his departure. Until seeing what he was about, pulling the device over his cock and tying it firmly at the base.

"Oooo—is that a preventative?" She leaned forward as though to inspect the contraption covering his shaft. "I've heard them hawked in the streets but not seen one up—"

With a growl, he shoved her back and grasped her ankles, one in each hand. "Later."

He tried to apologize and explain a world of information in those two syllables. *Later*, she could inspect the armor if she was of a mind. *Later*, he'd make it up to her for being abrupt. *Later—later—later*, maybe his patience would return.

For now, a savage beast controlled him. A sexual beast she'd roused. One that needed appeased.

"Later," he said it again, softer this time, but it didn't seem to matter. She wasn't pouting—prettily or otherwise.

Nay, she was writhing on the bed, her hands stroking up his arms, nails scraping over his skin, legs tensing within his restraining hold, as he slid his grip along her calves, unable to miss her feminine folds weeping, begging for satisfaction. His recently neglected body was past ready to please her.

Yet he knew if she laid a hand on him again, if she dared caressed his ridged buttocks once more with her delicate touch, it would be over before it began. So he braced his legs wider on the floor and readjusted his hold until he could pull her forward. Positioning her groin right where he wanted it—and his arse out of reach.

Instead of fighting him as he thought she might, Thea only stretched back upon the mattress and urged him on. "Aye, please."

One of her hands fluttered above her stomach. A second later those very fingers came down to knead her breast. Her other hand flew to her mons, then jerked backward two inches, anchoring itself just above her downy curls.

"T-touch yourself for me." He was shaking, his entire body vibrating as she did as bade, her eyelids at half-mast as her fingers edged past the dampened midnight thatch and disappeared into the honeyed well between her legs.

"Ohhhh," she breathed, sounding excited and pleased and more than a little surprised. "I'm *ready* for you."

Meaning she hadn't been with her husband? Or had never been given leave to touch herself to know?

Either thought had pride—and fury—storming through him. That such a responsive, passionate woman would go unappreciated...

"Thea." The cry turned ragged when he saw her fingers emerge from her depths, slick and glistening, only to disappear back inside.

Timing his advance with the steady pace she set, he released one leg to grasp his cock and run the tip over her cleft. For once he hated the cover shielding him from feeling all sensation. So he nudged his thumb forward, let her heat and viscous fluid coat his skin, and imagined that those silky juices of hers flowed over all of him.

Gripping his staff just below the crown, he pressed forward, stroking between her spread labia.

"Yes, please." If one discounted the breathy way she said it, she sounded so very polite and proper, he almost laughed.

But when the leg he wasn't holding curved behind his thighs to bring him intimately closer, deeper—

Thoughts scattered.

Overridden by the sight of her hands delving between her thighs, stroking up his shaft, coaxing him to enter. Eclipsed by the urgency her touch conveyed.

Her lilting cries gave him the strength to advance slowly and then she was killing him, the walls of her sheath opening with such exquisite reluctance as he forged deep, then deeper still, her passage closing in around him and clasping so tight, damned if he didn't spend before ever lodging the full way inside. Before ever pumping out a single stroke.

Damned if skill and experience didn't flee as his cock tunneled inside her rippling sheath with a series of short, clumsy paroxysms that left him gasping for breath—and his balance.

The orgasm tore through him unlike any other.

Tensing his ballocks and his neck as Thea's bawdy bits tightened like a vise, squeezing his cock, his heart, and every other part a man *thought* were his.

Leaving Daniel gasping and shaking—and wanting to tup her all over again.

10

OH, TO BE AN ASS

And will as tenderly be led by the nose
As asses are.

William Shakespeare, *Othello*

———————◆———————

"Oh my," she said when Daniel eased, regretfully, reluctantly, out of the snug haven of her body in stunned, stupefied silence. "Is that all?"

How could he have blasted off so precipitously?

Daniel looked at his recalcitrant cock. Still stiff. Still erect though totally spent. Still primed for more though unmistakable proof of its unruly tendencies filled the reservoir.

Damn me.

Not since first partaking of the sins of the flesh had he stayed so achingly solid after such a powerful ejaculation.

Damn me, he thought again, unsure how to react. The muscles of his legs quivered until he locked them in place.

Ground his heels to the floor. He'd be damned in truth before he lost his footing, fainted to the floor like a fribble.

"All right then." At his lack of response (he was still staring at his flabbergasting phallus—until her disappointed sigh pulled his head up), Thea hugged a pillow to her breasts. She was visibly shaking—and not at all satisfied he knew. Thanks to his impudent penis.

"Well," she said with false brightness, "that was, um...intense."

Intense? *That* was how she described their first time together? Not exceptional or pleasing or exceptionally pleasing or—

He must've scowled.

For she immediately added, "*Memorably* intense. Which is a good thing, I vow." Her gaze drifted to his chest and a hint of color flooded her cheeks. "Wonderfully intense, to be perfectly clear. Much, much better than uninspired or uninteresting or...lethargic."

Lethargic? That lummox she'd been married to, no doubt. The man obviously didn't know how to appreciate a woman, even had she been glued to his prick.

Anything but lethargic herself, while holding tight to the pillow with one arm, Thea scrambled for the sheet with the other, giving every indication of jumping from the bed and retreating to her personal chamber.

Time to make something clear.

"Thea?" His voice was gravel but it had the desired effect. Her motions halted. She sank back onto the mattress, still choking that pillow.

She blinked up at him. "Aye?"

"Think you we're finished for the night?"

"We're not?" A hint of confusion came into her eyes before she caught on and a quick smile curved her lips. "We're not. Oh, good."

Aye. He intended for it to be *very* good.

As though she read his thoughts, her mossy gaze fairly sparkled. She released her hold on the pillow. Angling her elbows behind her, she propped herself up and asked brightly, "May I inquire what's next?"

Chuckling over her undisguised relief, he tore off the soiled machine and retrieved another. No time to wash the blasted device now. Not when his lady lust lay waiting.

What was next? she asked. Let him number the things...

FASCINATED BY THE INTIMATE SIGHT, Thea watched Lord Tremayne exchange the used preventative for another. It looked innocuous enough, simply a thin, flesh-colored membrane topped with trailing ribbons. What she knew of the popular machines was garnered from the street hawkers who extolled their various virtues. ("Won't chafe ye partner nor make ye pecker burn!" or "Jumbo superfines, right 'ere, milords! Best armor yer coinage can buy!" and "The finest machinery in London! Double scraped and rinsed thrice! Sold by the fives.") But hearing about them paled upon seeing one up close.

Seeing Lord Tremayne's personal parts up close.

Seeing him cloak his erect shaft with the device, and so soon after she'd touched the sides of it, after having it in her —if for so short a time—brought all the passion and pressure and persistent ache plaguing her loins storming to the surface.

He muttered something like, "Damn me...not supposed to lose my mettle like that," while wrestling with the scarlet ribbon weaved around the opening. His self-directed flagellation made her smile, but she was too enraptured watching the sway of his ballocks, the crisp hair of his groin, the thick erection he handled with such ease, to respond.

Shoving the pillow to the side, she scooted around to recline on the bed properly, with her head near the head-board, where she waited for him to join her.

The room was warm and her body on fire, so she was surprised to see gooseflesh pimpling her skin. Perhaps that was simply a result of lying full-out on a bed—naked as a loon—waiting for her lover to join her and feeling no shame at all. (Well, such a small amount of shame that it was practically nil.) What a marvelous concept.

Finished with his task, the ribbon tied in a surprisingly adept bow, he approached the side of the bed where she waited. Instead of joining her, he stood surveying her, one fisted hand on his hip, the other cupped around his generous, aroused anatomy.

"Thea." Actually, he stood *grinning* down at her. Incongruous, given the swelling surrounding his right eye, the deepening bruises on his ribs.

Her heart gave a flutter at the look of mischief his misshapen smile somehow expressed, one side pulled up slightly thanks to the stretched skin of his cheek.

"Aye?" She shifted atop the coverlet. Had she done it wrong? Did he want her back at the edge of the mattress so he could keep standing?

Drat everything to Dartmoor. How she wanted to feel his weight on her again, to touch the silky covering of hair adorning his chest.

His chest. If one discounted the discoloration, his torso was a work of art.

Merciful God in heaven. How blessed she felt, for never in her imaginings had she known such an amazing sight could exist: her benefactor, strong and manly; at once both powerful and yet protective. Saliva began to accumulate in her mouth the longer he stood there, and she wanted nothing more than to run her hands over his impressive physique.

The sight of him waiting calmly next to the bed—ready to be intimate with *her*—sparked sensations in her breasts, belly and loins as all three places tingled and yearned for his touch.

But that was all he did—waited.

So she *had* mucked things up?

"My apologies." She pushed to sitting and swung her feet toward the floor. Unfulfilled urges made her a tad cranky else she never would have huffed, "Would you have said something, I wouldn't have changed positions—"

Cutting off her efforts, he swept her into his arms and lay down—with her solidly against him. With his body *beneath* hers. "You're p-perfect."

His words were muffled as he flipped her over and arranged her directly atop his limbs—face up. Shocking notion, that.

Bombarded with stimulation from all sides, it was all she could do not to swoon. His strong, muscular frame supported her posterior, the backs of her thighs, her spine and shoulders—her suddenly flexing and twitchy bum.

But her sensitized bottom wasn't where her attention stayed, not when she looked up. Where before her eyes, in the giant mirror's reflection, she saw herself—*stark naked* —for the first time.

Thea started to sweat.

Ladies, even gently bred females without an official "Lady" preceding their name, were taught never to look at themselves unclad. One learned early and well that *skin* was akin to *sin*.

One might bathe, might change clothing two or three times a day, might do all manner of intimate or necessary tasks to their person, and all without *ever* forgoing modesty. Only loose and fast women reveled in lewdness, in the lush sight of exposed limbs and blatantly revealed areas in between.

"Oh my." She had just made a staggering, and somehow satisfying discovery—fast and loose must also equate with fun and lusty because gazing at herself in all her slender splendor brought only positive feelings to the fore.

A sound of supreme something—excitement or pleasure, maybe—came from his throat when Lord Tremayne slid both his hands up her ribs to the under swell of her breasts. A similar sound came from hers when he dragged first one thumb and then the other over each nipple.

As though the desire battering her insides were happening to a stranger—the one in the mirror, perhaps—she saw her legs shift restlessly, felt the answering nudge of his erection.

Peering over her shoulder, he caught her reflected gaze overhead.

"Thea." It was sighed, giving her but a moment's warning before he extended one muscled forearm down her stomach to settle his hand just over her abdomen, fingers spread wide at the border where pale skin met dark curls.

Could one expire from desire? The sight of his hand, deliberately paused in such a place, was so forbidden, so arousing.

"Shall I—" She swallowed hard, her hips rocking ever so slightly, answering the thrilling call of his trespassing fingertips. "Turn around?"

How she wanted to.

Wanted to bury her lips against his neck, hide from the brazen female staring down at her, the pointy-tipped breasts being massaged and plumped by one strong, brown-fingered hand, the feminine length of leg pressed securely to hair-dusted thigh muscles.

Who was the lush wanton staring back at her? That

woman in the mirror—she was a stranger. One Thea wanted to know better. And after only days in his company...

The man at her back made her feel things, see things, differently than ever before. His broad hand kneaded her left breast, then he widened his fingers, placing his thumb on one nipple while stretching his pinky over to the other. He pressed down, just enough to make her gasp.

"Please." It was a plea this time. "Let me face you."

His hot breath brushing a "Nay" across her ear was all the answer he gave. Well, that and his other hand moving lower, fingertips probing, parting—

"Bless me to Middlesex." Her eyelids squeezed shut; she didn't need to see, only to feel. The drift of one lone fingertip delving, venturing deeper, finding and then gathering moisture... The deliberate glide of that same finger, back up and over...over...around...

"*That's* where your tongue—last night—" She garbled to a stop when her pelvis jerked away from the soft invasion. Then jerked right back for more.

"It is." His tone was as tantalizing as his touch.

"Feels, um..." Her abdomen convulsed. "Ah—"

"Intense?" She swore he almost laughed and couldn't help but peek, that naughty, indulgent mirror drawing her gaze like a patch of sunlight did a lazing cat, staring at the place where her thighs spread wide, thanks to her feet propped on either side of his powerful legs. Focusing on where his fingertip circled and petted and coaxed...

Her internal muscles wanted him to return. She wanted his body surrounding hers, her loins surrounding him, needed him plunging inside again where she could feel him deeper than she had anyone before.

She tried to roll over and tell him, but he stopped her with one arm across her waist.

He kissed her shoulder until she relaxed, sank back on

him. "Hmm-mmm," he complimented wordlessly and kept trailing his mouth toward her neck, unhurried, sensual applications of his lips that beckoned her to leave everything up to him.

True relaxation was impossible. Given how his fingers continued their advance and retreat over that part of her that grew at turns tighter and acutely sensitive blossoming into something soft and receptive. Over and over he rubbed and stroked her to whimpering abandon, inciting the exquisite, unbearable pressure to build, always halting or changing the tenor of his strokes before she jumped from that dashed cliff her body sensed loomed closer and higher.

"Tremayne," she cried at last, frustrated, eager, so wrung out from walking the tightrope his fingers pulled and swung at will that her mind finally gave up. And she gave in to begging. "Lord Tremayne, *please*. What—"

Only then did he loosen his hold on her waist, halt the torture between her legs.

"Why did you sto— *Ah!*"

Before she knew what he was about, he curved both hands under her arms and hefted her higher.

The new position angled her head awkwardly toward the mattress, and it was too much effort to raise it. Too easy to concentrate on sensations instead of sight. On his arm sliding between their bodies, fumbling for a second, then firming as he positioned his erection at her entrance.

"Like *this*?" At the first nudge of his penis, her confusion cleared and she grasped the previously foreign concept. Still... "It's possible? From this direction?"

But already, her feet were moving over the mattress to give her more control, her abdomen pressing down, pushing her lady bits against the crown of his hard flesh. Her hips twisting and tilting to accommodate the silky glide of his staff pushing into her, wedging itself more securely inside.

"Oh...my." The sensations he wrought within her majestic. Unreal.

It was being split apart and made whole all at once. It was terrible, aching pain and incredible, awesome pleasure.

It was rainbows bursting across her closed eyelids and storm clouds gathering strength.

It was so good and so different and— "Wicked or not, I want to see."

When she tried to raise her head, her neck protested. Then his hand was there, his palm cradling her nape, his fingers supporting her skull. It was the sight of their heads, close together, both staring above, at each other...

It was his other hand reaching past her stomach, fingers splaying around his thrusting shaft, the heel of his palm digging into her, finding *that spot* and riding it...

Her pelvis vibrating beneath his touch, her feminine muscles clamped on for the ride of their life...

And it was her body balancing between restraint and release, hovering between power and weakness...

Her mouth forming a breathy string of high-pitched sounds, encouraged by his deep-throated murmurs...

And finally, shockingly, it was her loins winding into a coil of painful passion, so strong that when the crest finally came, it burst on a wave of wet release, a visible shower of—of—of, she didn't know what, but one that had his fingers flying swiftly over her intimate flesh, had him groaning approval and praise with barely discernible words, the only thing she had the presence of mind to comprehend, the husked, "You're a d-delight," which was more than enough.

She gasped, strove for breath.

Sweating. Crying. Heaving as air and delight coalesced and bathed her insides as surely as her body had bathed his fingers.

His renewed thrusting and swirling touch made it clear

that the rush of dampness she'd found so startling—and embarrassing, by the only part of her that wasn't reveling in the glory he'd brought her to—was something *he* certainly reveled in.

Just when she thought it was over, that she was descending into the replete and utter bliss he'd first taught her last night, that mayhap she could catch her breath, it began again—right beneath his dancing fingertips...

An urge.

A need that was more. Fierce. Nearly unbearable. "I cannot—"

"Aye." He used the hand supporting her head to bring her face to his. "You can."

His lips ravaged hers, his mouth taking possession in a manner more demanding than anything that had come before.

WHAT A TREASURE!

Daniel couldn't believe the unrestrained passion in the slight package writhing over him.

She wasn't experienced enough to hide her responses; wasn't jaded enough to fake them. No mistaking that sweet, sweet flood of her climax, proof their bodies spoke the same language.

Knowing beyond a doubt he could give her this—carnal pleasure, a true appreciation of herself as a vibrant, sexual being—was one of the greatest gifts Daniel had ever received.

Giving to his precious Thea made it clear how he'd reduced sex to habit, done it by rote for too long, going through the motions without any feeling at all. For he'd never been more pleased by pleasing a lover more.

Never been more thrilled than when she splintered in his arms—under his command, around his cock.

And now—the taste of her honeyed mouth? The reciprocal surge of her tongue stroking his?

Her response lent steel to his shaft, fluidity to his strumming fingers...

Her Venus mound bloomed again.

She was close. He knew it. And she was scared. Shaking again.

Pushing his tongue from her and whimpering, "I can't. Not—"

Her body thought otherwise. He wasn't even moving his hand now. Wasn't pumping his cock into her. Nay, despite her initial hesitation, Thea's inborn instincts had taken over.

Now she was rocking into him, swiveling her hips frantically, her tiny fists clenched, nails dug into his wrists, keeping his fingers firmly on her.

Her primal keen blessed his ears as her responsive flesh engorged, jerked, and dampened his fingers yet again as her sheath rippled along his shaft.

Only then did he release his control and surrender to his own climax, his essence jetting out in time with her inner constrictions, her near-shouted pants of, "Intense. Aye. *Intense.*"

Scant minutes later, just when he'd thought she'd drifted off, Daniel occupying himself with the simple act of holding her, she surprised him by rolling to her side and fixing her gaze on his. "You've rendered me speechless. 'Intense' is all I can offer."

His smile told her it was enough.

"Who's Cyclops?"

The unexpected question confounded the truth right out of his mouth. "My dog."

"Your dog?" She digested that for a moment. One elegant eyebrow arched in a show of pique, but her voice was only curious when she asked, "And I remind you of him?"

"What?"

"You said earlier I was just like Cyclops."

"Oh." Blast it. Had he? He loved the ugly, dribble-drizzling mongrel but wasn't sure sharing that would get him out of the doghouse or not. Hard to shrug lying down, but he made the attempt. "Rescued him. That's all."

"Hmmm." The eyebrow lowered, the lush lower lip pouted out, and Daniel was afraid he was about to be severely taken to task.

"I never knew," she began, suddenly shy, "there could be such tangible evidence of passion. Both before...and at the culmination."

He'd heard tell of it but doubted. Until now. Until her glorious release. Praying he didn't butcher it, Daniel said, "You were, *are*...beau...tiful."

That shy smile blossomed wide and she snuggled against him once more. For about thirty seconds. Then she popped up to one elbow. "Did you know—Mrs. Samuels made peach cobbler earlier."

So he was forgiven for comparing her to his dog?

"*Peach. Cobbler.*" Thea repeated as though the very concept was akin to flying to the moon. Perhaps, to her, it was. After all, fresh fruit was a rarity for most. "I didn't smell it on the tray she brought. Dare we race to the kitchen? Winner claims the biggest piece?"

Race a mistress to the kitchen?

After the most *intense* sexual experience of his life?

Daniel considered the time. He considered all he had to do the next day. He considered his empty bed at home. "By all means."

———◉———

THEA WOKE ALONE.

Warm and snug beneath the thick coverlet in her rose-adorned room, her face and the one arm that extended beyond chilled from the morning air. Sufficient light streamed from behind the curtains, telling her morning was well underway.

Regrettably, she had no recollection of Lord Tremayne's departure. She did, however, possess the sated, sore and sublime sensations of a well-loved woman.

Even better (or possibly not *better*; how could *anything* be better than how her body felt at this precise moment?), she had the memory of sharing peach cobbler in the deserted and dark kitchen, of feeding each other, of his mock complaint over *where* was her reply to his last missive?

"For I long t-to read *your* p-poetry." He'd laughed when she stuffed the last of her cinnamon-spiced bite in his mouth, giving him no time to swallow before she was kissing him, and he her. Wiping crumbs off his lips as he swept her into his arms and carried her up to her room, to her bed, where he lay down and pulled her against him, cuddling her close until Thea drifted off...

Only to wake this morning with a smile on her face. One that faltered when she sat up to be confronted yet again with her dress, laid out over one of the chairs in the corner. Dear Mrs. Samuels—the woman was a marvel. She must've snatched it from the dressing room floor and cleaned it during the night because the hem was clear of mud, the skirt freshly pressed. If wearing the same thing again didn't thrill Thea to the core, then the clean underthings stretched out beside it certainly did.

She pushed back the covers and braved the cool air, feet hitting the floor and stretching against the rug, reluctant to cross cold wood over to—

"What's this?" Stacked boxes on the circular table obliterated any reluctance and she fairly bounced across the room, where she paused. Savored. *Gifts*.

Drawing out the anticipation, she inspected the boon. There were four in all, ranging from one that nearly covered the entire table, to three smaller ones atop. Simple boxes, devoid of any wrapping save soft green bows tied around each.

Heart hammering, she watched as her arm reached out to caress one satin bow. The delicate fabric yielded beneath her touch. Her stomach dipped. Had she ever been this happy? Felt this secure?

For a certainty, not since her mother was alive.

Unsure where to start, she chose the second-largest box, and in moments stared, to the accompaniment of her astonished gasp, at a pair of quality half-boots. Made of dark leather and lacing up the front, they were the most fashionable boots she'd seen since childhood. New stockings were rolled and tucked inside. As though seeing another perform the actions, her chilled feet were tucked inside the stockings and then the boots in a flash, toes turning toasty.

Moving the box aside, she heard something clank. "More?" She riffled through the paper. "Oh, Tremayne..."

Shock nearly held her immobile as she spied the metal and wood pattens he'd thought to include, ready to be attached to the bottoms of her new boots any time rain made sludge out of the roads.

Blinking back amazement, she numbly opened the largest box which yielded a lined cloak. A stunning, hooded garment *with a matching pelisse*. Fairies to Flintshire, she must be in a magical land herself, for surely she would sprout wings and fly. As she tugged on first the pelisse and then the cloak, she doubted her feet would ever return to earth.

The sleeves were only slightly too long, she realized, as

she sat there cozily wrapped, staring down at her booted toes, all manner of delight and disbelief coiling through her.

Not to be forgotten, the smallest two boxes seemed to dance on the table, drawing her gaze.

"What else could he have sent?" Saving the smallest for last, she retrieved the remaining box. "He's already done so much."

Reverent fingers slowly untied the bow and lifted the lid. "Gloves!"

Thrusting her hands inside, she closed her eyes. The supple leather and fur lining stole her breath as surely as her protector had stolen her wits. *Dorothea, he's surely secured you now, bought and paid for.*

Trouble was, she didn't seem to mind. Not any longer.

After basking a few seconds more in her newly reduced and wondrous "lowered" status (ironic, as she'd never felt her spirits soar higher), she roused herself to open her eyes and her remaining gift.

Which contained an unmarked jar.

What commanded the largest smile yet, as she sat at her table bundled to the gills in her new winter finery, and lifted out the jar, was the folded square of paper that resided beneath. Setting it aside, still folded, she unscrewed the lid and a familiar, spicy-sweet scent greeted her.

Lord Tremayne's fragrance? She sniffed again. Nay, the crisp outdoors was missing, but it still smelled like him. Why send her—

"Read the note, you ninny."

Dearest Thea,

I trust you'll find these items useful, especially the lotion. Put it on your wrist and arm and I can promise the bruises will fade in no time. As to the other items, if anything does not fit or is not to your liking—

"Not to my liking? Has he windmills in his upper garret?" She wiggled one hand free of the fur-lined gloves to stroke bare fingers over the soft leather of the cloak. "Indeed, I like very much."

Pulling off the second glove as though it was the most precious of Meissen porcelains, she pulled up one long arm of the pelisse and rubbed the cream on one wrist. Whether the bruises disappeared or not, knowing she smelled vaguely like him made her old injuries vanish into the ether.

She inhaled, the scent of him in her lungs taking her back to taking him in her body, when he—

"Thea," she said tartly, "stop thinking of last night. Read on, missy."

Oh, but 'twas difficult when every shift of her legs brought to mind new sensations from last night. Grinning like a goofy goat, she slid her fingers back into the gloves and picked up his note.

...not to your liking, I trust you'll let me know so I can provide something you prefer.

Now, woman, make haste—if you're reading this, then Swift John is waiting for my promised reply.

I do believe there's the matter of a poem you're supposed to share?

Tremayne

PS. I found much pleasure in our evening together. Thank you.

In only as much time as it took to remove the gloves,

ready the quill, and add a postscript (or two) to the letter she'd composed yesterday morning, she sent Buttons on his way. But only after asking for clarification first:

"Swift John?" she queried the footman. "I thought your name was Buttons."

"It's actually James, ma'am. But my brother and me—we're twins, you recall? *He's* John."

"Which explains naught. How do you then come by Swift John?" And why did Lord Tremayne not simply call him James or Buttons?

The servant gave her an unrepentant grin. "On account of when we tried to snaffle his lordship's pocket watch, I'm the one who ran the fastest. My brother, John? Now he got hisself caught."

"You attempted to steal from Lord Tremayne?"

Buttons rocked back on his heels and gave every appearance of one who loved divulging this particular tale. "We did indeed. Only he wasn't his lordship back then. Nine, we were, and not particularly adept at the trade but hungry after havin' just lost our folks to the fever."

"Oh, James..." Just imagining two boys, so young, alone and grieving—

"Don't go worrying on about us, Miss H. His lordship's a real square cove. We couldn't have picked a better pigeon to try an' pluck—though we were the ones caught. After chasin' down my brother, Lord Tremayne stood in the street holding tight to John till he finally caught sight of me. Told us we could keep stealing and like as stretch for our efforts, or we could come with him and do honest work for food and pay without ever having to worry about a noose around our necks." His chest puffed out. "An' I've been *Swift* John to him ever since."

DANIEL SMILED and read again beneath the raindrop-smeared ink...

> Drip. Drip. Drip it goes.
> All day long, it grows...
> The pile, the dripping,
> Gluey, sticky pile...from his nose.

A sonnet (or is it an ode?) dedicated to Mr. Freshley of the Dripping Nose.

Thea (who will hurriedly blow hers and hope she's not given you a dislike for her magical quill—or her taste in literature)

P.S. The cloak, pelisse, gloves and boots are <u>lovely</u>. And though the sleeves are a fraction long (which I only confess because you'll see this for yourself since I plan to wear my new garments henceforth when I leave the house), I vow your gifts are <u>perfect</u>.

Perfect! Though you are dreadfully spoiling me, I fear, I quite refuse to give them up. Thank you a thousand times over.

P.S. Again. Bruise Fading Cream? What a concept for a pugilist. Are you secretly an apothecary? Or have one in your employ? I adore how it smells on you and will gratefully slather it on my arms. Thank you, kind sir!

P.S. III. I cannot express enough my appreciation to you for sending Buttons to join our household. Though I feel horribly overindulged, I will cherish his presence nevertheless (and perhaps request he give me directional lessons with all due speed).

P.S. IV. I too found great pleasure in our coming together last night. (My face is about to flame at how I'm putting this to paper, but may I reiterate, <u>Great</u> Pleasure?)

———◦———

...I'd much rather slather it on for you...

...I said you were too refined to be considered any sort of tavern wench? Another error in judgment it appears. Thank you for pointing it out, as I am one who can appreciate the fine, enthusiastic qualities a tavern wench (or in point of fact, my lovely mistress) might show when we're together and the bawdy sense of humor she might exhibit, and share, when we're apart.

As to your ode-worthy companion, I do hope you provided the remarkable, rememberable Mr. Freshley with a handkerchief?

———◦———

Alas, no. The grizzled Mr. Freshley would have scratched me ere I tried. He was the neighbor's cat, you see. I wanted to be friends, but he had differing definitions of friendship. (If I approached without a fish head or bird in hand, he wanted nothing to do with me.) 'Twas a true pity. Would you care to know what I penned to commemorate my first scratch?

———◦———

I shall be turning blue from lack of air until you share.

(Remarkable coincidence, that; it rhymed without effort—and 'tis obvious, eh?)

Once again, after sending Swift John off with his response, Daniel returned his attention to the areas Wylde wanted him to cover at the committee meeting. He'd put this off for days and could no longer justify avoiding it.

Trying to keep an open mind, because if his throat tensed along with his thoughts, he'd never get the words out, he applied himself to succinctly rewriting each salient point and then practicing the words ad nauseam—both in his head and out loud—until he deemed himself ready to move on to the next one.

With every phrase he committed to memory—phrases absent of pesky letters and sounds—he tried not to think of the other meeting he'd miss, the one he'd longingly thought to arrive right as it began and remain near the door, if only to catch a smattering of the brilliance that was Mr. Taft.

Mr. H. B. Taft, a gentleman Daniel had yearned to hear speak for years who was making a single London appearance. 'Twas no hope for it now; both events were scheduled for the same afternoon.

Disappointed anew, a heartfelt sigh shuddered from his lungs. He reminded himself of the good he was doing for his friend, if not for London.

Hell, poor Wylde had to have been desperate to ask *Daniel* to help him out; any words out of his mouth were bound to be a cheap bargain. But by God, he'd give the man his pennyworth.

For upon taking the time to really study what all Wylde had prepared, Daniel had experienced a major change of heart. Once he realized the earnest passion in the arguments presented, and recalled the primary reason why his friend cared so much, Daniel was determined to do his best.

After all, if any man had cause to see an organized police roaming the London metropolis, it was surely Wylde.

———◦◦◦———

My dear Lord Tremayne, you may not be so quick to condemn
your own literary attempts once you read more of mine.

> *Mr. Freshley, pussy so fine*
> *Why on my arm must you dine?*
> *With teeth marks and hisses and scratches galore*
> *I must stop trying to befriend you. No, no, nevermore!*

Before you ask, I regret to admit we never made nice. He was a
rotten mouser; I think I became better at it than he. I always
suspected the (is it too indelicate of me to say "snot"? I fear it might
be; please forgive me for asking) phlegm drip-drip-dripping from
his nose might be the culprit. How can any feline be expected to
sniff out prey if they're always sniffing snot? (Well, knock me over
with a black cauldron, this pen does have its own way at times.)

I've only just recently forgiven Mr. Freshley for snacking on me
when I was delivering fish heads. The skin he took from my arm
was not given willingly, I assure you.

———◦◦◦———

AFTER EXTENDING the latest message from his master, Buttons
blotted the sweat from his temple with a weary-looking handkerchief. He didn't fare much better.

"You're flushed." Guilt crawled up Thea's throat. "We've
been selfish, sending you hither and yon with scarce a
moment to rest. Forgive—"

"Ma'am, if I may?" Buttons interrupted, stuffing the handkerchief deep in a pocket.

"Certainly."

"'Tis no hardship, I promise you. Me an' John—the other

servants too—why, we haven't seen his lordship this animated in years. Even ate luncheon at his desk and I know he's beyond eager for your next one." Buttons pointed to the note she held. "I'll go down an' see what Mrs. S has cooked up this afternoon and grab me a quencher while you pen him back, eh? Be ready to run back to his lordship's in a trice."

The enthusiastic, sweating footman was off, racing down the stairs, leaving Thea to marvel at the fortune Fate had dropped in her lap and excited to read the latest missive Buttons had dropped in her hand.

Trust me, something as simple as a four-letter word, be it <u>snot</u> or any number of others, will not offend. In fact, I count myself honored that you feel at sufficient ease to talk thus with me. May it always be so.

Although once the question was posed, my mind would not rest until I'd applied it sufficiently, ascertaining what other possibilities you might have considered: snuffles, sniffles, sniveling...hmm, are you familiar with Captain Grose's Dictionary of The Vulgar Tongue? I proudly own a useless copy and took the time to peruse its pages. Tell me what you make of this:

> *TO SNIVEL. To cry, to throw the snot or snivel about. Sniveling; crying. A sniveling fellow; one that whines or complains.*

> *TO SNOACH. To speak through the nose, to snuffle.*

I trust you could come up with a rhyme or two that would work companionably with snoach. (Does anyone ever—in actuality— use that word?) Although since first reading about your dear Mr. Freshley, I do have it in my head that he's a snivler (aye, I just coined that one myself). Do you not agree? "To throw the snot or snivel about"—does that not describe your fiendish feline foe?

Now tell me more about your mousing talents. On that, I am aghast with curiosity.

━━━━◆◆◆━━━━

EARLY THAT AFTERNOON, her written reply arrived. Only instead of regaling him with the most welcome and anticipated jovial rehash of her mouse-catching escapades, it contained one simple paragraph.

A simple paragraph with a relatively simple suggestion.

One that struck the fear of God into his heart.

Snoach! How could I have gotten on so admirably with such a lack in my vocabulary? You are quite right. Mr. Freshley was definitely a snoaching snivler! How could I not have seen that on my own? Perhaps, when next we meet, we should apply ourselves to joint compositionary efforts?

Pen some lyrical odes together?

What the devil?

Together?

His eyeballs burned as the syllables threatened to detonate in his brain, explode in his misbegotten mouth.

Oh Gad.

What was he doing? Thinking? *Saying?*

Idling his day away—flirting? And with *words*?

Now his new mistress wanted to write poetry—together? In *person*?

As though a serpent had just sunk fangs in his arse,

Daniel bounded from the chair. The back smashed into the window behind him, shattering glass.

His canine's howl of surprise couldn't drown out the incriminating crash.

But the whining dog scampering toward the door and the singing shards decorating his floor were nothing compared to the black blanket of dread that swooped over him. Enshrouded him. Pressed him down, back into the righted chair, hands between his knees, head bowed.

Pray God, what have I done?

Forged a friendship on a lie? Wiled away hours, if not days pretending an interest in something that could never be. Damn him! Damn his mind for veering on to this blasted path. Damn his heart for jumping in head over heels. But most of all, damn his goddamn mouth!

SOME TWO HOURS LATER, after the glass had been cleared and the vacant window area boarded over, Daniel realized he was *still* staring into space, conjuring visions of Thea occupying his ornate bed upstairs, her hair splayed over his pillow, her body sprawled over *his*. By damn, he wanted to howl like Cyclops.

He was *not* some naïve Othello to be led around by *his* nose. Or by his frigger, by God.

What was he thinking? Imagining her occupying the London home he inhabited, the bed that had just paraded through his brain box, sporting images both lurid and lusty? In the very chamber where his revered grandfather had once slept, in the home he'd inherited from the venerable old man he'd not only wished was his father but the man who had taught him more about *being* a man than any other. About goodness and kindness. Sacrifice, even.

Distracted, feeling guilty because he *wasn't* feeling guilty at the idea of parading his paid paramour through these honored halls—and straight into that bedchamber—Daniel balled up the page that tormented him so and tossed it toward Cyclops, straight into the languorously extended paw that clamped over the missive.

"Woof!"

Instead of smiling at the dog's tail-thumping antics over "catching" such a treat—and with so little effort expended—Daniel found himself hard-pressed not to race his carriage to Thea's, toss her inside and return with her—upstairs. To his bed.

To make his vision a reality.

And that wouldn't do.

Wouldn't do at all.

No SMALL AMOUNT of time later, a time during which he hadn't moved, not physically from his position, nor mentally from his fanciful musings, there came a knock upon his study door. A knock significantly subdued to indicate it didn't herald another letter from his mistress.

After rousing himself to retrieve the latest note—the one still languishing beneath Cy's paw—Daniel bade his servant to enter and quickly resumed his seat, smoothing out the page bearing the delicate penmanship and equally destructive suggestion. Joint compositionary efforts? Bah. He'd rather be roasted alive.

"This was just delivered, milord." Far different from when his brother bounded in bearing Thea's banter, John sedately placed a wax-sealed note upon the corner of his desk. "Buttons was curious about a reply? He swung back around just to check. I told him I'd bring it when—"

Daniel shook his head.

"I'll tell him nothin' yet." With an ill-disguised frown, the servant backed out.

Why did that look of disappointment make Daniel feel all manner of regret? What of it if his footman had lost the eager mien of a courting compatriot? Was disappointed his master was no longer flirting with a mistress?

"Goddamn waste of t-time," Daniel muttered with conviction as he reached for the just-delivered note, determined to convince himself.

"Woof!"

"So you want me to open it? T-to see who—" Upon noticing the formal presentation, the fancy wax-seal on thicker paper than he and Thea had been using, something tugged at the back of his mind. He broke the seal and looked straight at the bottom, identifying the sender. Dread reached down from his throat to seize his innards in a clawed grip.

Lord Tremayne—I trust you are well and not under the weather after yesterday's bout. I only write at the prompting of my son who insists *something dreadful must have befallen you (ah, the anxieties of youth).*

I myself claim the only thing that has befallen either of us is my memory. I must've mistook our appointment time. According to my wife, 'twould not be the first lapse.

Regardless, I remain at your convenience and heartily hope all is well.

Everson (& Thomas, who persists in looking over my shoulder)

Gads. How could he have forgotten? He never forgot appointments. Never. He didn't make enough to clutter his schedule, ergo, the ones he committed to he cared about keeping.

Ballocks! *His* should be seized in a clawed grip and twisted.

But what to do about Thea?

"D-dammit." One problem at a time.

All the self-castigation in the world couldn't make his pen fly fast enough.

Everson—

My sincerest apologies. Something unexpected occupied my morning and put me off my plans for the day. I do apologize, to both you and to Tom, for my unpardonable rudeness.

If you'll indulge me once more, I will be at your residence tomorrow morn at eleven. Nothing will keep me this time save your preference for another... You have only to specify.

Sincerely, Tremayne

Forty minutes later, still feeling like a horrid heel whose ballocks were in need of a good stomping, Daniel received Everson's reply acknowledging their newly set appointment.

"There. 'Tis settled till the morrow. Now to you, my d-dear."

So Thea wanted to compose poetry? Suitable punishment, that, after his deplorable disregard for his day's schedule.

Lesson learned—*Don't forsake your commitments because you're in rapture over your new mistress. In alt over pen-and-ink frivolity.*

Blazes. He felt like a total clodpate.

Definitely time to tone down, institute some distance

between him and his new inamorata. Why, with the last one, what's-her-name, he routinely got by seeing her once a week, sometimes less. With Thea, the thought of skipping *one day* without her company spiked a shaft of angst straight through him.

And that wouldn't do at all either.

So turning his nose up at their earlier literary whimsy and completely ignoring her suggestion—the absolute *last* thing he needed to do was whimwham with her over words—he wrote...

Thea—

I regret I cannot meet with you this eve; a prior commitment calls to me. However, I should like to make it up to you tomorrow afternoon or evening. Where may I escort you? Anywhere in London. Consider the city and its environs at your disposal. Where would you like to go? What would you like to do?

There. That should prove suitably penitent (for lying about having something else to do tonight) as he was, in essence, giving her free rein. Pray God, whatever she chose was not his undoing.

I hope you enjoy yourself this evening, that your commitment is a pleasant one.

Pertaining to the morrow, I thank you for the generous offer but I am quite content to entertain you here. Mrs. Samuels is a fabulous cook; would you care to join me for dinner? What time may I look for you?

———————————◦◦————————————

WHEN SHE'D no doubt want to "compose lines" together, whether he arrived before dinner or after. The woman already tied his brain in knots, no need to hand her his tongue on a platter.

Especially where there was nothing to distract them save each other. An outing would provide a buffer. When he brought her home and they were alone, *that* would be the time to rush his fences and rush her up to bed.

Pen in hand, doubts hovering, he wrote:

Nay. I insist. It's beyond selfish of me to keep you stashed away.

Selfish, mayhap but smart.

Come now. Name your pleasure... A drive in Hyde Park? Perhaps a picnic?

Hell. With either, he'd be expected to chat. To converse. To reveal himself as a word-stumbling, bumbling idiot and that wouldn't do. Not with her. Never with her.

Gripping the pen tighter, he attempted to recover.

~~*A drive in Hyde Park? Perhaps a picnic?*~~ *Strike that. I hear thunder rumbling near—*

He didn't.

so the ground will likely be too wet for an agreeable outing.

If it wasn't, he'd spit from here to Sussex to ensure that it was.

Damn. Where could he take her? An outing where *she'd*

have a chance to sparkle and shine and he could blend in and be unnoticeably mute? Where she could visit with someone other than his stammering self? Somewhere he could keep his bone box shut and just watch? Allow her presence to soothe his soul without vocalizing his inadequacies. Where he could simply sit and enjoy the enchanted bounty that was Thea?

Needing ideas better than his own, he rang for John and instructed him to bring up the latest round of invitations. Everyone knew the "reclusive and barbarian Lord Tremayne" wouldn't attend, but his title ensured the blasted things kept pouring in.

When nothing remotely palatable presented itself—a ball was out of the question, even one where a man's mistress might attend; he'd plant a facer on any bounder blighted enough to ask Thea to stand up with him—Daniel requested the morning papers he'd discarded earlier. There had to be *something*.

Ten minutes later, he'd settled on the theater.

A nice, relatively safe option. The performance would entertain so he didn't have to. It'd be the carriage ride there and back and any intervals during. Did the theater even have rest intervals? He didn't remember. Wasn't sure he'd ever gone. But what did it matter?

Thea would love it and when they arrived back at her townhouse, he'd love her.

A bang-up solution all around. And if she started nattering about poetry in the carriage, he'd just kiss her quiet.

Daniel congratulated himself on his perfect plan.

He finished composing his missive and sent it off, feeling light in his chest. And heavy in his groin.

So it was with utter dismay that, shortly thereafter, he read her most unexpected response.

———————◦◦◦———————

Nay. I do apologize for having to insist upon this, my lord, but I will not, I cannot attend the theater with you (no matter how much I might wish to).

———————◦◦◦———————

Do you?

———————◦◦◦———————

Do I what, my lord?

———————◦◦◦———————

"Oh, for God's sake." This conducting a love affair through letters had blossomed from asinine into absurd.

L-l-l-love? *Love* affair?

Forget his tongue, his head tripped over the thought.

Choosing to shoo away the unpalatable concept by stuffing it deep, deep into a dark corner of his soul where time would surely snuff it out so it never warranted further contemplation, Daniel gripped the pen hard enough to strangle. He had to, in order to still the sudden trembling in his fingers.

Printed so heavily the nib poked through the page in two places, he wrote:

Do you wish to attend the theater with me tomorrow night?

If "Aye", then why will you not agree? If "Nay"—

"If 'Nay', then I've half a mind to lock you into your b-bedchamber—and lock myself in there with you. Pun-punish us both."

If "Nay", then, for the love of God Almighty, woman, what would you like? What can I do for you?

And if, upon ordering John to deliver yet another missive, as daylight eased into dusk and limped straight into dark, Daniel salvaged his conscience by pressing an extra coin or two into his footman's palm, well then, he could be forgiven.

John or Swift John? Hell, he'd seen them both so many times today, he was no longer certain who stayed at his residence and who resided at Thea's.

"Owe you new shoes," he muttered as the man grabbed the folded letter with a grin so wide, Daniel exerted real effort to avoid wiping it clear off his servant's face—with his fist.

At least one of them was finding his new situation amusing.

THEA'S REPLY, when it came later that night, staggered him.

What can you do for me, you ask, astonishing me to the point my eyebrows ascend to my hairline?

Lest you forget, you spectacular man, you have already given me the world: A safe home, one that I'm not constantly defending against mice nor men. Plentiful food and wondrous hands to prepare it, so that my empty stomach no longer wakes me during the night.

You have given me so very much that I hesitate to trouble you for anything further.

Yet, you have requested so little from me in return. So now that you have posed the question, I feel compelled to answer from the heart, with the same earnestness with which it was asked.

I would like to spend more time with you. For our time together to flow as my magic pen does across the pages you've seen fit to so generously provide.

I would like for the hesitance that often characterizes our in-person interactions to ease and the inviting, invigorating tone of our written correspondence to take its place. You make me laugh so easily, in person and on the page, yet I find, reluctantly I admit, that I do not know you at all.

How do you spend your days (other than getting beamed on the nose and clobbered on the ribs, if you will forgive my impertinence)?

What matters concern you? Matters of state, matters of your own holdings and responsibilities? Matters of family? I would listen to it all, if you would but share.

What things do you like? Rainy days by the fireside or walking in the sunshine? After-dinner port or evening brandy? Strolling in the countryside or shopping in the busy streets? Arm-scratching, nose-dribbling cats or rescuing playful, barking dogs?

Have you any personal interests? Any favorite pastimes or nonsensical enjoyments?

What do you dream of? (Whether you wish your nosy mistress would squelch her inquisitive nature and leave off pelting you or your life dreams...I wish to know them all.)

~~I wish to know whether you're married, possibly have children~~

That last, she'd crossed through so much that he had a devil of a time making it out.

In all honesty, I wish to know so many things about you, but I quite wonder whether you've continued to read this far.

Aye, I would <u>very much</u> treasure attending the theater with you (most anyplace, in fact).

But I simply cannot, my lord.

And please do not laugh at my reasoning. I don't claim to know how things are conducted in the upper reaches of society, but I assure you, I exaggerate not my situation. The bald truth is...

The reason why I cannot accompany you is...frankly...

Well, to be perfectly blunt, I haven't a thing to wear.

11

SQUINTING QUINT'S QUALITY QUIZZING GLASS

Squinting Quint's quality quizzing glass is queerish fine;
before he got it on Quarter Day,
the quaint, quaking man had been in quite a quandary
when queried to dance the quadrille!

Thomas Edward Everson, *Lyrical Lines for Education, Elocution and Entertainment*, circa 1820s

———◦———

THE NEXT MORNING, Thea nimbly ran her fingers over the keys of the pianoforte they'd found stashed away, along with a host of older, unused furnishings, in another bedroom upstairs. Mr. Samuels and Buttons had liberated the shrouded piece and shuffled things around so Thea and Mrs. Samuels could give the old instrument a thorough cleaning.

Those efforts had defined Thea's day after she'd sent off the final, unanswered note to Lord Tremayne. Now, though, even the reality of the pianoforte failed to make her smile.

The sounds it made when she picked up speed weren't quite enough to make her cringe—but they were close.

The sun sliced in through the open window, promising a warmer—and drier—day than the preceding few. It was still early enough she wasn't yet worrying over what Lord Tremayne's response might be to her last missive, nor was she agonizing over why she hadn't she heard from him yet (not overly much, anyway). But it was late enough she was definitely wishing she'd added one more request to her brazen list of what all she wanted.

If she was going to pelt him with a plethora of requests, she might as well include everything.

A piano tuner. By Jove, she'd neglected to ask for a piano tuner.

She played a little harder, a little faster. A lot louder. And then she did cringe—*how could she?*

A new mistress didn't rail at and complain to her protector, not when things were going rather swimmingly, and not if she sought to retain her intimate position in his life. Which she did, oh, how she most definitely did.

The discordant notes that followed echoed her uncertain mood.

"Miss Thea!" Buttons burst through the open doorway. "Down...stairs..."

He was out of breath, both hands dangling at his sides, neither extending a folded square in her direction.

So, no note, then.

Disappointed, apprehension growing at her no doubt offputting forwardness, she tried to whip beautiful music out of the stubborn old pianoforte. (All she whipped were both their eardrums.)

Her fingers never breaking stride, she asked, "What is it? Something certainly has you in a dither."

"You're needed downstairs," he repeated in a more normal

voice and she glanced up in time to see a secretive smile flash across his lips before he wiped it clear. "You have guests."

Her fingers fell from the keys. "Guests? Plural?"

"Aye."

"Who?" She reached the doorway but hung back, leery of venturing out into the unknown. What kind of guests visited the abode of a mistress—other than its master, who arrived most definitely *not* in the plural?

"Come and see." Buttons' posture urged her to hurry. "You won't be sorry."

Taking the trusted servant at his word, she sped down the hallway and flew down the stairs, only to come up short at the sight of Mrs. Samuels beaming at her.

"Get yourself settled and I'll bring them in." The woman stood in the entryway, all but blocking the closed front door. She pointed toward the morning room near the back of the residence. That particular room was airy and inviting, decorated in simplicity and pastels. (Not at all like the sumptuous squares of decadent debauchery of the entry and master bedchamber.) "Go on with ye now, can't keep them waiting."

Them? "Who?" Thea tried again.

But the bustling housekeeper had already slipped outside through the narrowest crack in the door. Thea heard her telling someone it would be but a moment.

"Ah, miss?"

Not yet to the morning room, Thea halted when Buttons spoke. "Aye?"

"You'll want to read this first." Winking, he tucked a familiar-looking square into her hand. "I'm goin' back out to help Samuels get the mare settled."

"The mare?" Thea's fingers trembled on the unopened note.

"Callisto, ma'am."

Callisto? What manner of lord named a mare after one of Jupiter's moons?

"His lordship sent her an' a small carriage 'round too."

A mare. And a carriage? When she'd half expected her *congé?*

Bemused, she quickly claimed a seat and unfolded the page, trying to give the appearance of a lady of leisure—one accustomed to receiving surprise guests—while inside, her heart set up a distinctly unsettled rhythm.

Forgive me, Dear Thea. I've been negligent, inexcusably so, forgetting to tell you that you have accounts arranged in your name at a number of establishments, that you are free to spend, within generous reason, to your heart's content, outfitting yourself and your home.

For today, I beg of you, my proud girl, work with Madame Véronique. She'll see you grandly clothed and I shall see you this evening. Be ready at 6 p.m.

Daniel

Daniel. His given name was Daniel.

And he hadn't taken offense at her requests. Hadn't taken her to task for the audacious listing of them. Had, in fact, responded with even more consideration, more generosity. He'd sent her a horse and carriage, and, more amazingly than an unexpected invitation to dine with their rotund Regent, signed it with his given name!

Thea had no time to savor the realization, not when "Madame Véronique Rousseau, exquisite dressmaker to London's elite" immediately presented upon her doorway.

A tall, handsome woman with mounds and mounds of brightly hennaed hair, Madame V, as she said "Meezes

Hurwell" could call her, spoke with an unmistakable French accent. Unmistakably fake, Thea suspected, but the words were delivered with such arrogance, she doubted very few ever quibbled with anything the haughty "French" woman might want.

With entourage in tow, comprised of three assistants carrying boxes piled high, she swept inside as though she were a tornado that made no allowance for anything in its path. And tornado was a perfect comparison, for within a matter of seconds, Thea found herself surrounded by a profusion of books, patterns, bolts of colorful fabric and swatches of even more, lace, trims, edgings, ribbons, hats... the previously sedate morning room becoming a storm of productivity.

And that was only the first trip!

After the second round of all three bringing in yet more boxes, aided this time by Buttons whose arms were piled high as well, Thea's startled gaze flitted from girl to girl as they pulled forth dresses in various stages of completion, each more beautiful than the one before. Once the final box was emptied and the last dress swished softly into place atop the settee, Madame Véronique clapped her hands imperiously. "Come now, girlz. Yvette, clear zee floor. Josette, find a stool or crate for Meezes Hurwell to climb upon. Suzette, ready yourself to take zee notes." A snap. "My measuring tape!"

Trying not to laugh at the false accent or phony names proved surprisingly easy once the first dress was held up to Thea's form and she was shoved in front of the mirror Mrs. Samuels brought in. (Hard to giggle when one is gasping.)

Time passed in a haze, fittings and pinnings interspersed with various pronouncements from Madame V...

"Zix p.m.? He expectz zee miracle!"

"Suzette, for the last stinking time, leave off making cow eyes at that footman!" (In her exasperation, as this was the third such warning, Madame V's accent took a tumble.)

"Tsk, tsk, Meezes Hurwell, you are a stick, a twig! Theez will never hang right! You are a weed, a—"

By now, Thea had heard enough mutterings and criticisms about her shortage of natural padding to vex even the most patient of saints. She might be down to only chemisette (a peach-colored silk, it should be noted) and bare feet, but in recent days, she'd finally learned to stand on them—and stand up for herself. "Madame V, I appreciate all the work you're doing on my behalf, but where my figure—or lack of one—is concerned stop comparing me to spindly vegetation! I vow, pretty dresses and unmentionables aside, if you don't harness your nettling opinions forthwith, I'll eject you all."

After that, the fittings continued much more silently, and if Suzette caught Thea's eye and gave a nod of approval that caused Thea to blush, then it was all for the better. Blonde and buxom and so very English, Thea thought she might've stepped right off a dairy farm in a neighboring shire; there was *no* conceivable way that girl came from across the Channel. And if she had a fondness for Buttons? Well then, Thea liked her already.

"Six p.m.? Never!" The accent had been long discarded. "I'll never have it ready. 'Fit for a princess' he orders..." Madame V complained from her kneeling position near Thea's feet.

"Lord Tremayne?" Arms straight out, Thea had been

forced away from the mirror and off the stool as the hem was checked and rechecked.

"Lower them. Aye, Tremayne." As though coming to a decision, Madame V left off fiddling with the hem and stood. "Yvette, ball up some cotton. I need to fill in the bodice."

Madame might have abandoned the accent but Thea wasn't ready to falsify her bosom. "I'm not sure—"

"I am." The woman was adamant. "If I had designed this for you from the beginning, 'twould not be necessary, but alas, he orders you clothed like a queen *for tonight* and I am left with altering what already exists. I positively cannot have one of *my* creations fitting so ill. You're not a scrawny scarecrow without a *hint* of curve"—at least she'd unbent that much in her assessment of Thea's form—"and it would do no credit to my reputation to have your dress hanging on you as though you were."

"Mum always said that all a girl needed was to pop out a babe or two and her bosom would plump out right nicely," Suzette said helpfully.

Madame tugged the neckline forward and Thea frowned at how much it gaped.

"I shall make a temporary fix," the dressmaker announced. "The padding, it will be removable, hmmm?"

She shoved the small, rounded wad of cotton Yvette handed her behind one side of the bodice and smoothed the fabric over it, then leaned back to evaluate. Stepping in front of the mirror, Thea had to admit the addition did help the dress flow across her figure better.

Behind her, Yvette confirmed the theory. "She's right, Sally Ann is. My sister done got poisoned by the groom's seed and she's grown two inches in the bosom already!"

"Poisoned?" Thea whispered, glancing toward Suzette. Madame had dropped to her knees again and was humming over the hem, a nice, calm tune that told Thea she much approved.

"'E got her with child," Suzette explained, "with no plans to claim her or the baby."

Not to be left out, Josette poked her head between them. "Well, my mum told me that after you suckle your first babe, the pair of 'em will be drooping an' saggin' down so far on your chest, you'll wish—"

"Josette! Zee lips—zey are to be shut!" Madame V was back, the relaxed interlude over. "Hush zee mouth or I shall pin it shut with zee hammer!"

"A pin? Don't you mean *nail* it shut?" Suzette asked, and Thea laughed, earning a glare from the dressmaker and another round of grumpy fittings when the perfectionistic seamstress decided to start over by modifying an altogether different dress.

"IF YOU WANT this finished for tonight," Madame V gritted out some time later, "you best leave off talking and twitching!" She grumbled a curse, then seemed to realize this wasn't the best way to address a new customer. Stretching her lips into a semblance of a smile one might expect to find on a beached barracuda, she added, "Zee rest will be ready for zee fittings three days hence. I will ezpect you at zee shop during regular hours."

"At your shop?"

"*Wee*, Meezes Hurwell. Henceforth, you'll come to my place of business, in Leicester Square, for zee remainder. For even zee indomitable Lord Tremayne, I refuse to close shop for another full day. Further business will be conducted there, and that is *final!*"

"Yes, ma'am. Aye, aye."

"One could wish your arse had as much cheek as your

mouth," Madame muttered beneath her breath, her head bent over a delicate seam she was taking apart.

Thea caught Suzette's gaze and the two shared another smile.

"One could," Thea said clearly, barely suppressing a laugh at the audible *rrrriiiippppp* that followed.

"DOES HE DO THIS A LOT—ORDER fittings?" Thea asked, the next time Lord Tremayne's name was mentioned, this time by one of the girls, who was complimenting his manly physique (to the titters of the other two, and the narrowed gaze of Madame). It had been in response to Thea's curiosity over the vast array they'd brought, which she was informed he'd had a hand in. "Make selections and choose fabrics and patterns?"

It seemed an odd occupation for the man she was coming to know.

"For his sister, he did," Madame answered distractedly, pinning in the sides so the dress didn't *hang like zee sack*. "Before she was married."

Before she was married.

Which still didn't tell Thea if *he* was...

———⟡———

"ONLY MOMENTS AGO, my son confessed his folly," Everson said without preamble when Daniel was shown to the book-lined study where both men waited.

After nodding at the butler who pulled the door shut after Daniel entered, Everson, he continued. "In his overzealous-ness, I regret Thomas badgered you unpardonably. Please be assured, Lord Tremayne, it will not happen again."

Everson's proclamation totally threw Daniel's carefully rehearsed opener out the window.

Twice he opened his mouth; twice he closed it. A heavy silence filled the air as they waited for him to respond. Tom snuck covert glances toward Daniel, his expression alternating between guilt and ill-concealed adoration. Everson looked at him steadily, confident that his son wasn't about to be raked over the coals any more than he'd apparently seen to.

The stalwart support in this family continued to astonish him.

Leaning his walking stick against the back of a heavy chair, Daniel caught each man's gaze with his own. "Aye. Well." He stalled, thinking swiftly. "I owe...both you fine gentlemen a sincere ap-p—" Dammit! "'Ology," he finished, trying not to curse aloud at the blunder.

All blasted morning he'd debated on how to proceed. Debated on whether to confess *his* badgered B's, destructive D's, and all-around abhorrence of public conversation. Well, ever since he'd dispatched John with the proper purse of coins and folded notes to ensure Ellie's most favored dressmaker's presence at Thea's.

Did he now accept Everson's apology and bow out? Escape home with none the wiser? Even though he was the one in the wrong (arriving a day late, being unpardonably rude)? Or did he go against everything instilled in him since earliest childhood and—

Tom made the decision for him. "L-l-l-lllord Tremayne, Fa-Father is rrrrrrrrright-t-t-t, he is. I knew better than-than-than to ac-c-c-c-cost you but I-I—"

All it took to halt the eager and contrite youth was a wave of Daniel's hand.

When Tom fell silent, Everson nodded to his son. "That will be all, Thomas. You may—"

"No. P-please," Daniel said, determined to face his unmasking like the man he strived to be and not as the coward his father had made him. "Stay, Tom, please. I have words for you b-b-both."

He could see Everson's eyes narrowing, as though he suspected foul play was afoot, about to be brought down around his cherished son. Oh, to be that loved and protected!

The muscles in his neck clamped into a block. His next two attempts at speech were garbled beyond recognition. Damn.

Damn-damn! He would *not* let his body betray him again. Not now. Too much was at stake.

He might only face two men and not the several that loomed, but *these* were men whose opinions mattered. Whose respect he wanted to deserve. Needed to earn.

Those noddies in Wylde's committee? That was duty.

This? *This* was honor.

Daniel picked up the walking stick, determined for once to be "charmed" by his sister's incantated concoctions and, despite the fiery siege laying claim to his throat, he forged onward.

"Nay. Please—" Daniel tried to speak swiftly, to explain before he was tossed out on his ear. And for all that, taking longer than ever. "'T-tis not a trick or jest I pl-*play*."

He turned to Tom, his face as unguarded as he could make it. "You, T-Tom Everson, are the b-bravest man I have ever met. I regret I could not t-t-tell you the other night bu-but..."

Unable to face either of them the more he stumbled about, he clutched his walking stick and spoke to the ivory knob hidden beneath his fingers. "I was t-t-*taught* to hide it, t-t-to not speak—have the b-beatings to show for it." He smiled grimly and risked an upward look at Everson, only to find comprehension and compassion coming from that quarter.

Though he spoke to Tom, his next words were for the

father. "I p-p-pray, should I ever b-b-b-be blessed with children, I can be as good a father as your own."

Making sure the youth knew he meant it, Daniel said what had been milling about his garret for days. "And, T-Tom, if you still have an interest in p-pounding me to a pulp in the ring, would b-b-be honored to work with you. But your father isn't—" *A bad hand*, he was about to say, but was overshadowed by Tom's response.

"Wwwww-*would* I!" The exuberant young man started to rush forward but checked himself. "Cap-cap-capital! And I pr-prom-prom-ise, no one will-will-will hear from me." He indicated Daniel's head, then his own mouth. "'Tis your-your bus-in-in-ess."

"Nor I." Everson weighed in, coming forward to cover Daniel's hand, causing him to realize the strength of his hold was about to shatter the ivory. "And you have no idea how relieved I am, in some selfish ways, you understand." The man patted his hand once, then released him. "I always suspected you never liked me, just tolerated boxing with the big lout who never could learn any better."

"Never that," Daniel vowed, finding his hand gripped in a strong, comforting shake, almost as though Everson hugged his entire body with that simple touch of curved fingers and palm to palm. At least now he knew where Tom had learned that!

A nod of understanding and accord passed between the two men and their hands separated.

"Now," Everson began, after taking a deep, relaxing breath, one it seemed Daniel's lungs automatically echoed, "Thomas told me *what* he asked of you and that it had been done in a social setting. But he failed to tell me exactly *where* you two met—"

"'Twas-'twas at L-L-Lord P-P—"

"Hold up, Thomas." Everson cast a fond glance at his son,

then caught Daniel's gaze. His lips curved in a gentle smile that spoke volumes. "Let's all sit, shall we? I think this may take a while."

Daniel laughed. He actually laughed.

And so the story came out between the two of them, haltingly slow, furiously fast, in bits, starts, stops and stammers, but it came out. Gratifyingly, for once in his life, without a speck of aggravation.

It was simply a conversation that took a rather long time (a *really* long time), and that was just the way of it.

A pleasance he hadn't anticipated buffeted the day's exchange, the ease he experienced conversing with these two fine gentlemen nothing short of remarkable.

Positively remarkable.

At some point, after first taking refreshments and then lunch with them, talk naturally turned to Thomas and Daniel's difficulty. "I had a cousin who stammered as a boy," Everson explained. "He eventually grew out of it, but a physician his parents consulted made several recommendations..."

As Daniel idly listened, he couldn't help recall how the only physician he was ever paraded in front of wanted to slice out his tongue, sever off the nerves in his lips. Father had supported the notion and an all-out brawl ensued when one very determined ten-year-old made his escape. The sour taste that tarnished his saliva was too easily evoked and he swallowed hard. Bad memories best forgotten.

He renewed his interest in what Everson was saying. "... favorite suggestion was that he practice reciting word puzzles and poetry—"

The word *poetry* set off an unwanted visceral reaction. But instead of casting up his accounts and heading for the coast, Daniel made himself calmly inquire, "Word...puzzles. What are they?"

Everson nodded to Tom who quickly—and surprisingly—rattled off, with only a hitch or two:

Naked naughty Nancy natters on like a ninnyhammer
while knitting napkins for the nob's nozzle.

There once was a man, not a priest,
who fancied for himself a fancy piece.
So he counted his coins
through his stiffening loins
till he could buy himself into her crease.

While Daniel chuckled, Everson frowned. "Thomas, what have I told you about the bawdy ones?"

Thomas assumed a glum expression. "Nnnn-not while-while Mum is home." Turning to Daniel, he brightened. "But-but they're grand fu-fu-funnn."

"Helpful, too," Everson put in. "We don't know if it's the cadence or song quality, but with practice, he's able to spew these out like a geyser. They've really helped with his regular speech too."

Helped his speech? Daniel couldn't fathom it, the poor lad. Evidently his expression gave him away.

Everson laughed so hard he choked. "Truly, my lord. You should have heard him before."

Nodding enthusiastically, Tom added, "But these are mmmmmy favorites, the p-peh-personal kind. Roses are red. / My name is Thomas. / Follow my lead, / I'll be your compass. And one mmmy brother wrrrrote: Roses are red. / My name-na-name is Sir Henry. / There's no time to waste. / To the privy I make haste." He finished on a grin. "Now-now you try."

As though housed in a glacier, Daniel's mind froze. But Tom looked at him so expectantly, he pried his lips open, determined to give it a go. Only what came out was a disgruntled, "Don't like p-poetry."

Everson smiled, that indulgent, fatherly smile Daniel hadn't received in years, not since his beloved grandfather passed on. "Here now." He scooted his chair toward his desk and pulled a sheet and the ink toward him. "I'll jot down a few of the others and you can practice at home, hmmm?"

"Much obliged."

While Everson wrote and Daniel tried not to be embarrassed by his lack of participation, Tom entertained them with several more surprisingly competent recitations.

Buxom Betsy bouncily brings brimming buckets of butter
to bossy, balding Bob in the big, bug-filled basement.

Roses are red,
The birds they do chirp,
the worms, they do squirm.
But they don't eat the dirt.

"They do, really, but-but couldn't get it to-to-to rhyme."

Daniel smiled encouragingly and Tom finished off with two more.

Roses are red.
Words can be fun.
No matter what people may think.
I am not dumb.

Touched, because Daniel had no doubt Tom's father had written that one for him at a very young age, he was hard-pressed to maintain his smile. That was, until Tom's rendition of:

Jane Jubilee jubilantly jiggles with joy when Jack Johnson,
a jug-bitten jackanape, jumps over with jacks. Just jolly!

"Bravo." Daniel applauded.

"It may be jolly, son," Everson said, still writing, "but you're going to wear out his lordship's wattles."

"'Tis fine. And call me D-Daniel, both of you." Another deep, pray-I-don't-muck-this-up breath and he exhaled. Resting his arm along the back of the couch, attempting to appear completely casual, he announced, "All right. I'll give it a whirl. *Ahem-hem.*" How long could he stall? His neck already felt rawer than squealing bacon. "Roses are red. / My name is T-Tr-*Tremayne.* / Think we've all lost our marbles. / *But* at least we're not lame."

"Good!" Tom practically cheered. "Do-do anotherrr."

"Here you go." Everson passed him the sheet. "Try the top one."

He read over the lines to himself: Dashing Delbert, with pockets so deep, diddles his days away, while pretty Patty ponders by the pond, pitching puny pennies to dog-paddling puppies.

Gads. I'll destroy it.

He didn't realize he'd said it out loud until Tom said, "You're among fr-fr-friends, mmmy lord. 'Tis part-part of the fff-ffun!"

Everson gave him a reassuring pat on the shoulder. "Take your time, Daniel. There's no censure here."

12

COUNTERFEIT CHARMS CHARM THE TRUTH

For they breathe truth that breathe their words in pain.

William Shakespeare, *King Richard II*

─────────◦──────────

"*EXQUISITE.*"

The rasped compliment raised the fine hairs at Thea's nape. Lord Tremayne's voice was deeper tonight, more rugged—if that were possible.

She hadn't needed the words to know he was well pleased with her appearance. The sudden gleam in his eyes as he surveyed her when she came down the stairs told her clearly enough.

She was too aware of the late hour—significantly past six —and too aware of her changed appearance to meet his gaze for long and hers veered away to focus on the rail where she placed her gloved hand to steady herself as she descended. Watching her satin-covered fingers slide down the mahogany banister was much easier than contemplating the forceful presence below.

A quick, lash-veiled peek told her he looked remarkably handsome, if somewhat different. She couldn't quite identify why, but it must be his clothes. She'd never seen him attired so impeccably, in formal evening dress, everything ink black save for the snowy cravat and white silk stockings beneath his knee breeches. Even his waistcoat was black beneath the snug-fitting tailcoat. Her heart gave a distinct lurch when she glimpsed the strong thighs—and impressive parts between— shown to exquisite perfection by the absurdly tailored breeches (if there was an extra wrinkle of fabric to allow for movement, she couldn't discern it).

A few steps from the bottom, a self-conscious hand went to the back of her hair where "Suzette," upon asking Madame if she could remain (under the guise of reboxing everything they'd brought), had offered to weave in a feather or two.

"It's all the crack," she'd told Thea, unearthing two iridescent feathers that shone with the same inner fire her dress did. The dress Madame had finally settled on, a rich, shimmering sea-blue confection unlike anything Thea had ever seen, much less worn.

It was also, to her dismay, the one with the falsified bosom.

No drawers either! Just beautiful silk stockings tied at her thighs. "Drawers will ruin the glide," Madame V had imperiously informed her.

Thea felt so very debauched, and he hadn't even touched her yet. Oh, but she was primed for it. For their entire night together, for how it would end. With them in her bed, skin on skin, hot, slick, sweating—

She gasped as her left foot slipped on the step.

Lord Tremayne jumped forward but she waved him

back as she regained her footing, determined to make it to the bottom unscathed. "Silly me. Best I watch where I'm going."

Buttons and Mrs. Samuels had hovered about all evening, laughing with Sally Ann (who'd professed to preferring her real name over the fancy "Frenchy" one) while Thea quietly endured their attentions. They were all excited about her first night out with "his lordship", and though she portrayed the epitome of ladylike composure, inside she was a fluttery, flustered wreck.

The look he gave her when she reached the landing didn't help. Trembling, she allowed Lord Tremayne to tug her in front of the mirror.

Where had the servants gone? Just as his hands settled heavily on her shoulders, a startled glance told her they'd disappeared into the woodwork.

Leaving two of them very much alone. And she was *very* aware of his tall and powerful presence brushing up against her as he snared her gaze in the mirror.

At the picture of her low—dreadfully low—neckline, Thea struggled to smile. Had she ever before exposed so much skin? (Discounting their mirrored encounters upstairs, that was.) The padded corset plumped up the swells of her breasts to the point they were actually visible. It was a miracle. And oh, mercy to Mercury, there was a hint, just a hint mind, of shadow between them.

What dismayed her most was how her *nipples* (she thought the word on a whisper) nearly promised to peep over the edge of the deeply rounded bodice if she so much as sneezed.

She noticed her reflected image quivering and resolutely locked her knees. Over her shoulder, Lord Tremayne captured her gaze. Above those piercing eyes of his, thick, coffee-colored hair was brushed back with careless abandon, tempting her fingers to muss it further. "You look extraordinarily handsome tonight, my lord."

He gave an abrupt nod. The hard line of his jaw firmed. "You...are a jewel."

The swelling had gone down, both eyes were blinkable, but the bruising looked bad, deep purpling surrounding one eye and part of his cheek.

"What of that cream, my lord? The one that fades bruises?" She tsked. "It doesn't seem to be working."

"Almost out," he told her with a forced smile.

His face must be paining him, poor man. Why he seemed so strained.

"Then I'll just run up and grab what you gave—"

Tightening his grip on her shoulders, he pointed to the cuckoo clock beside the mirror. "Later."

Which she surmised meant they really needed to be on their way. "Very well."

She watched the motion of his Adam's apple bob once after he nodded grimly, the flexing of his tight jaw, the strong column of his throat—

"You—you!" Thea spun in place, her fingertips going to his chin. That's what was different about him. Not his attire at all. Not just the reduced swelling, but his face. "You shaved!" she accused, too surprised to temper her tone.

A muscle jumped in his cheek. He inclined his head.

Her eyes skimmed every feature as her fingertips echoed the same path, rubbing over the squared and stiff jaw, the discernible cheekbones, the strong jut of his chin. In truth, she was met with a countenance she could study for hours.

Every speck of skin his thoughtful action revealed lured her touch to linger. That is, until he frowned. "Thought you'd..."

Be pleased sounded in her head, conveyed by his eyes.

She wound one arm around his neck and pulled him

down. Rising to her toes, she placed a deliberate kiss on the newly smooth skin. "I do like," she told him, leaning back and lowering her arm while keeping her gaze focused on his, "very much. Excessively much. It's just..." She darted a quick glance behind her and to the side, making sure the woodwork hadn't sprouted servants' ears.

When she remained silent, one of his dark brows lifted.

She spoke to his right earlobe. Good thing too, because she whispered so softly the confession was barely audible. "Just that I was never overly fond of men's beards until yours. I, ah, enjoyed the feel of it, *you*, ah...betweenmylegstheothernight."

His hearty laugh rewarded her courage. Taking her hand in his, he bowed over it. "It will grow."

And there he went, laughing at her again, *with* her now that she was laughing too. Gracious, but she'd become audacious since meeting him!

"La, sir," she said in her best "lady" voice, wishing she had a fan to playfully *thwack* on his arm, "how you love to mock me."

His expression was suitably stern when she garnered the courage to face him again. He straightened and Mr. Samuels magically appeared to open the door. Lord Tremayne took up his walking stick in one hand and extended his opposite arm to Thea as she retrieved her reticule. Nodding at the butler, he escorted her to the waiting carriage.

WHAT WAS WRONG?

The carriage ride, contrary to everything Thea expected, was fraught. Lord Tremayne hardly spoke. He barely nodded when she profusely thanked him for the lovely dress she now wore and the new wardrobe on order. Scarcely smiled when she shared about George and Charlotte, her efforts at first eradicating and then befriending the friendly rodents.

Only just acknowledged her laughing mention of poetry and how much fun she'd had bantering with him over noses and cranky cats. In fact, each topic seemed to pain him more than the one before until she was left confused and clueless, her fingers plucking at the reticule strings as she cast about for more to say, distraught that he might be tiring of her so soon.

But nay, he didn't seem disinterested, merely distracted, painfully so.

Once they left her neighborhood, the horses moved so slowly she thought they might be rolling backward. The seven—yes, seven—additional attempts at conversation she made were met with near grunts or hardly any response at all.

Night shrouded their meager progress, but the carriage's interior, unlike their last ride together, was well lit.

She knew he was pleased with her appearance. (He couldn't seem to take his eyes off her sham of a plumped-up bosom, which only made the scant pressure of the cotton feel like a ton, weighing on her conscience.) She knew he wanted to continue on because when she'd suggested they return home and stay in, some time after the silent ride commenced, he barked a nay.

The carriage rocked in place as one of the horses snorted. A huge sigh heaved from her lungs. She tried to look away, to focus anywhere except his newly revealed countenance but couldn't.

How could she ever have thought him unhandsome?

As THOUGH AN OUT-OF-CONTROL bonfire threatened utter destruction, Daniel sensed all his efforts, all the relaxed time they'd spent together going up in smoke.

What a blighted evening!

At the townhouse, it had been all he could do to eke out his understated appreciation of Thea's glorious appearance.

His neck and jaw, throat and tongue, hell even his teeth and tonsils, were all weary to the point of exhaustion. He never should have done so much talking at Everson's. Not when he had plans this evening with Thea. But the afternoon had been so easy, once he'd moved past his initial reluctance, so...fun, dammit. Aye, *fun*.

Laughing over brandy and port, playing with words and letters, testing—and massacring—some of Tom's many tongue teasers. Once, when a maid brought in jelly-filled scones, all three of them had stuffed their mouths to over-flowing and tried to sing Tom's Q list. *Squinting Quint's quality quizzing glass...*

Crumbs had spewed, coughs ensued, and the whole effort proved hilarious. He didn't know when he'd ever had such a rum time with someone he'd, for all intents and purposes, just met. He'd been himself, his habitual hesitance all but vanishing the longer he stayed in their presence.

Though he'd hurt at the time, he'd thought it a puny price to pay. Figured all would be fine in a trice.

Hardly!

For once he'd said his goodbyes, after making a boxing date with Everson and a lesson date with Tom, once he was alone and heading back home, it hit him: a pervasive tight-ness that seized his voice box and every muscle between his neck and his nose. Near excruciating pain that punished him —by gads, *him*—for talking too damn much. Talking!

Daniel assured himself a couple hours of rest would turn things around, soften the soreness and soothe the sting. Which was why he'd gladly agreed when Madame Véronique sent Swift John round with the message there was no plausible way Thea would be ready at six.

Seven, eight, midnight, Daniel didn't care, was happy to wait.

Maybe one of the remedies Tom had shared would help. He sent down to the kitchens for some precious ice, rubbed it all over his neck until he went numb. But when his flesh thawed, he was as sore as ever.

One remedy? Why not try them *all*?

So he sipped boiled water with honey, ate a lemon, lay on his bed and hung his head off the edge. Flipped over and let it hang from the other direction. Tried napping, gargling, and more stretching (who knew a man's tongue could extend so far?). And still, with each swallow, at the merest inclination of speech, agony screeched through his muscles.

Rest, we need to rest! they railed at him, embedding sabers and swords from the inside out, jagged blades that cut through tissue and bone until he stilled the urge, released and relaxed the fatigued muscles, silenced the desire to speak.

And sat mute, once again, like an idiotic imbecile.

Thea was aware of the change in him. Acutely aware, and she was baffled by it. He could feel her discomfort in every worn-out particle of his being. Twice he'd touched her in the carriage, once on her hands, once on her knee. Both times, she flashed him a grateful smile, as though saying, *It's all right.*

But it wasn't.

He couldn't lose her before they'd barely begun. And that dress! It bedamned and bedazzled. Befuddled his senses like—

"Season's in full swing, milord," the voice of his driver proclaimed at full volume. "Can't light a fart in this crush!"

"Roskins!" Daniel scraped out and banged on the roof as

the woman beside him choked on a laugh. At least he hoped it was mirth and not disgust. Did the man forget 'twas not Louise he squired about?

As though he'd leaned close and lowered his voice, a muffled, "Beggin' your pardon, milord! Milord's lady friend, I meant no disrespect."

"None taken," Thea hollered back to his driver, "I assure you." Her lilting voice reassured *him*. Then stole his wits when she continued, "Had I a lucifer and the bodily urge, I might try it myself!"

Both men chuckled. And the carriage lurched ahead yet again.

Silence descended.

Weighed heavily.

Threatened to drown him.

Had air always been this thick? Or was his throat truly that swollen?

Long minutes later, when the horses had done nothing but inch forward a foot, Roskins yelled that there was no hope for it. He eased from the crush and took a sharp turn, coming to a complete stop (which was rather hard to discern, given how little they'd progressed). The man jumped down and opened the door, asking to confer with Lord Tremayne who gratefully stepped out at the unusual request.

Jointly, they moved toward the horses, out of earshot of the door, where Roskins continued. "The roads are clogged tighter than Prinny's privy, milord." He nodded toward his elevated seat. "Don't see it getting none better, either. Here's wot I'm thinking..." The man went on to offer several suggestions: take a longer route around, choose a different destination, try again another night.

Daniel latched on to the second option. "Anywhere," he told his trusted driver, waving his arm and encompassing the whole of London. "Any p-p-pu-b-blic—"

He tripped over the words so bad he was surprised his tongue didn't flap out and flay them both. But Roskins had been with him a long time, knew how to interpret. "Another playhouse, milord, instead of the one we was aiming for? Will that do the trick?"

A nod and they each returned to their previous seats, Daniel only partially jealous of his driver's freedom up top, and alone.

How could he regret even one moment spent in her presence?

Easily, when he worried every one might be the last...

"Orreries!" exploded from his mouth as Roskins took off, the sudden forward motion jarring the occupants—and likewise his jaw. "Like orreries," he said more sedately in belated response to Thea's last note.

He wasn't yet ready to talk about family. (What would he do? Tell her his sister fancied herself a witch?) Neither was he comfortable with the notion of declaring what he dreamed about. (Did he even dream? Other than a good night's sleep and a fetching, accommodating mistress to help bring it about, Daniel didn't think he'd dreamed of much in years.) But he *could* tell her of his interests (if he could talk, that was).

Though the planetary models he'd loved since childhood had been popular for decades, they were definitely playtime fodder for the privileged class. Not something those untitled were often familiar with. Rather than assume she knew what he meant, he'd better explain. "They're pl-pl—" He licked his lips, tried again. "Pl-pl—"

Goddammit! The multiple, massacred efforts met his ears and he cringed. Even now, years later, there were times he had to remind himself a sharp birching wasn't on the other side of a hashed-up word.

Why in blazes had he decided to start answering her litany of questions *now*? When they were stuck in such a confined space? Where all he was left with was dreaded, deathly silence? Or...or he could kiss her senseless, toss her silky skirt over her head and plunder her pu—"'Lanetary miniatures!"

"Orreries," Thea responded in a delighted tone as though he hadn't just been flailing about in a stupid stew of his own making. "You have an interest in them? I'm familiar with them too, especially the inner workings."

Especially the inner workings?

She couldn't have stunned him more if she'd been a bolt of lightning. "Y' are?"

"Fancy trappings powered by clock mechanisms. That's the part I know about—the turning mechanism. I've seen a number of the smaller ones operating above clocks and a tabletop model or two"—she sounded wistful—"but I've never seen the larger, floor models."

"How?" It didn't seem to bother her—that he'd been reduced to monosyllables.

"My husba—" But she did seem to think better of that beginning because she immediately started over. "Mr. Hurwell operated a clock and watch service, you see."

Recognition snapped. *The Time Piece.*

That's why her name had sounded vaguely familiar when they'd been introduced. She'd been married to *that*? An older, slightly effeminate man who was bland nearly to the point of offense.

Daniel had stopped by the establishment twice, once to ask advice (which was given only grudgingly, even after the proffered coin was swiftly snatched away) and a second time to inquire whether the man would come to Daniel's residence and look at the broken arm on Uranus. *I don't make house calls*, he'd been dourly informed. *I'm a watchmaker, Lord Tremayne, not a physician.*

Damn. To think he'd been so close to her and had never

known what a treasure the disagreeable Hurwell had stashed upstairs.

"My bosom!" Thea suddenly said, startling him away from the shadowy, crowded, ticking emporium he remembered and back to their brightly lit and now swiftly rolling carriage. "It's not, not this, well..." Her hands waved the air in front of her chest, fingers fluttering incriminatingly toward the creamy expanse of skin above the neckline. Skin he'd admired from the moment he'd seen her. The graceful neck, the beautiful, beckoning area below—luscious skin he should have thought to adorn with a jewel.

Damn him again, why could he not seem to remember the most basic rules around her? Of course he owed her a bauble (after forgetting to outfit the woman, he likely owed her an entire jewelry store), but more than that, he wanted to see a stone he'd picked out, one that shone brilliantly and was cut to perfection, decorating the exquisite creature at his side.

In fact, he'd love to see her wearing jewels he'd ordered made up and nothing else.

But lack of a gemstone-encrusted necklace didn't appear to be the root of her dismay.

Thea stared at him, guilt in her eyes, a frown on her lips. "It's a complete deception. These..." She looked straight down and scowled at the gentle swells hinted at by the fitted dress. Then she looked back at him. "They're fake. Cotton. *Padded!*"

Mashing her lips together, she ruthlessly clasped her hands and stared off to the side. "Forgive me. I told Madame V 'twas not honest, to counterfeit my charms, but she wouldn't heed my opinions. Not on this. But there. I've told you now." She shot him a fast glance. "So why do I still feel as though we've tricked you? Lied about my form?"

I've seen your form, he wanted to tell her. *Have you heard a single complaint cross my lips?*

Other than her thinness, which was lessening by the day it seemed, he had no objection to anything about her. And yet, she was so obviously worried he might take offense. At something he had no doubt half the women who would be present tonight did as a matter of course.

It was charmingly sweet, Thea's earnestness. When had anyone so cared about warranting his good opinion?

He gave her a smile meant to reassure.

She still looked unconvinced.

"Thea." He had to waste time giving thought to his words. Preparing not to wince at the pain. "Know of men, re... spected ones, who enhance their own ana...tomy with filling."

For a moment he thought he'd have to try again. Then, simultaneously, her gaze dropped to his crotch and her cheeks flamed scarlet.

"You don't mean—" Lifting her lashes to face him, her blush deepened. "Oh, heavens to hades, you *do* mean. But you..."

Her arm stretched out between them as though she intended to test whether he did or didn't. Daniel would have let her. Would've been happy to have her hands on his body, but she snatched her arm back on a groan.

"I mean, you don't. *I know you don't.* Not that I would have any complaint if you did, you see, because I have tonight— have padded my bosom as I've just admitted. But I know you don't. Of course *you* don't. I've seen you up close, remember?"

By the last, her voice squeaked so high, it was a wonder the glass around the lantern didn't shatter.

Daniel couldn't help it.

He shoved across the carriage to sit next to her. Taking one gloved hand in his, he promptly placed it atop his non-enhanced masculine attributes.

"No...filling," he told her, gently curving her fingers around his hardening flesh. "Just you."

"Me?" The query was a soft sigh.

"Want of you enhances me," he eked out, hearing the harsh edge in his tone. "'T-tis all I need."

At the slip, he wanted to curse his blasted mouth. But she obliterated the urge the second she raised her head and meshed their lips.

He felt her smile against his mouth, couldn't help smiling in return.

He released his loose hold on the back of her hand—she caressed him now without any encouragement—and brought his fingers up to her shoulder, her neck, tilting her head as they jointly deepened the kiss, lips opening, tongues touching.

Like a spectacular display of pyrotechnics, desire exploded through him—

"Here we be, milord!" Roskins called out as the carriage bobbed to a halt. "The King's Theatre."

King's Theatre. The Royal Opera House. Where he had a private box, Daniel thought with supreme satisfaction. Where they could continue the kiss and, if they were both feeling bold, even deepen the intimacy...

"We don't have to stay," Thea breathed against his chin as they reluctantly broke apart. "Take me home and—"

"Nay. Show you off. Your new..." Dress. Gown. Attire. Gads, every word had an abhorred letter.

Easier to let it hang, especially when Roskins climbed down and opened the door. Especially when Thea playfully grumped, "If you insist," then jumped to the ground as though she were seven and a candy store awaited.

Aye. She deserved a fanciful night in her fancy new dress.

And Daniel? Well, he'd just count the minutes until it was time to take the blasted new dress *off* her.

III

DARING DECLARATIONS

Then pray speak aloud. It is of all subjects my delight.

— JANE AUSTEN, *PRIDE AND PREJUDICE*

13

BOTH PLEASURE AND SUFFERING

Voi, che sapete che cosa è amor,
Donne, vedete, s'io l'ho nel cor.
Sento un affetto pien di desir,
Ch'ora è diletto, ch'ora e martir.

You who know what love is,
Ladies, see if I have it in my heart.
I have a feeling full of desire,
That now, is both pleasure and suffering...

Le Nozze di Figaro (The Marriage of Figaro), a popular opera
first performed in 1786

————⟡————

THEA WAS AFRAID TO BLINK. *What if she missed something?*
Bypassing the ticket booth, Lord Tremayne conferred
briefly with an employee before guiding her straight through
the foyer and up one of several sweeping staircases.

Muted music indicated the performance was well underway.

Mayhap arriving late was to their benefit? (No one to see her gawking like a chicken.) Of a certainty, the large rounded lobby they came out at on the second level was only sparsely populated.

Lord Tremayne paused before entering either of the two opposing corridors that she assumed led to the private boxes, some costing in excess of two thousand pounds per season she'd heard. That was a vast sum more than most people earned in years, abundantly more than she'd ever come across—and she was *here*, as his guest. An occurrence he still seemed less-than-thrilled about.

"You have a box?" She hazarded conversation once again.

Stone-faced, he nodded, then gestured toward refreshments available for a coin.

"Thank you, but no," she told him, far too uncomfortably aware to eat or drink anything. She patted her hair, afraid the feathers might incinerate if his glare became any fiercer. For a man who insisted he *wanted* to be out with her, he seemed remarkably disgruntled. "I'm not thirsty, but if you—"

He grunted and took off toward the right, her light hold on his forearm whisking her down the passageway as effectively as if he'd picked her up and tossed her ahead. Practically skipping to keep up with him, she prayed the figure-filling padding would stay put. The last thing she needed was to leave a trail of dropped cotton marking her every step.

Narrow doors flanked the corridor, spaced every few feet. They passed a dozen or more before he slowed to find the one he sought. Like most, it was closed. He turned the handle and stepped back, gesturing for her to precede him.

After the well-lit hallway, it took her eyes a few seconds to adjust to the darkened interior. In that short time, she was showered with a wealth of impressions.

Smaller than she'd expected, the box itself was a cozy space, extending only a few paces in either direction. From about waist high, it opened out in the front, overlooking not only the massive stage currently occupied by twirling ballerinas—what an unexpected boon!—but the opening also allowed a glimpse into the noisy gallery below and beyond that—

Thea gasped at the magnitude of it all. Why, there had to be five levels of private boxes, all filled with an assortment of gaily dressed people. Branches of candles extended out every few boxes, illuminating some areas better than others, but everywhere her flitting glance landed, a new and dazzling sight met her eyes.

The spinning, jumping ballerinas cavorting across the stage; a full orchestra playing in front; and behind the musicians, the writhing pit of masculine voices and shapes, only half of whose attention was focused on the performers, the others—like Thea—craned their heads to inspect the individuals lining the boxes on either side.

Some of the occupants stood near the openings, gazing raptly at the stage, others conversed, paying no heed to the spectacle they'd come to see, and others...well, more than one box had the curtain pulled for complete privacy and if she wasn't mistaken—it was difficult to be certain, given the distance and amount of smoke the many candles gave off— but across the expanse, in one of the highest boxes, she *thought* she glimpsed a pair of exposed breasts just before they were covered by two broad palms and both bodies disappeared into the shadowed recess—

Thea swallowed hard and quickly returned her attention to the private box *she* was privileged enough to enjoy tonight.

Chairs. There were several. She blinked as they came into focus.

Oh Lord, levitate me right to Lincolnshire! Lord Tremayne

had barged into the wrong box—for two of the chairs were occupied.

The impressions of grandeur still brimming in her mind, one thought screamed above the others: *Escape!*

She reversed direction but he'd come up behind her, his hard body preventing retreat. His breath caught audibly as he took notice of their company.

Then everyone spoke at once.

"Tremayne?"

"Daniel?"

"Ellie!" burst from the man behind her, the immovable force who curved one hand around the side of her waist with a tense grip that should have hurt—but oddly didn't. "Wylde. What..."

The other man gained his feet, giving the impression of pure, lean elegance. He was immaculately turned out, not a strand of dark blond hair askew. But his lips? Those were definitely off-kilter as he shot her a contemplative look. A single look that conveyed various emotions: curiosity, speculation, censure perhaps? (And she'd thought Lord Tremayne had an intense manner?) Stepping toward them, he said, "Appears we both chose the same night."

When the woman stood and came to his side, Thea tried again to edge around Lord Tremayne. The bite of his fingers stayed the impulse.

What should she do?

The slight blonde fixed her with a decidedly inquisitive stare.

Under ordinary circumstances, Thea was confident she could hold her own. But this was anything but ordinary. Associating with Sarah and Lord Penry and others of the demimonde ilk was one thing. But a man did *not* mingle his mistress with his—

His *what?*

Who were these people to Lord Tremayne? His friends?

Strangling the strings of her reticule so tightly it was a wonder they didn't snap, she gave a fast, modest curtsy to both the lord and his lady (as competently a curtsy as one can make when their waist is shackled). "Pardon us for the interruption," she said since no one else seemed inclined to speak since the initial outbursts. "We'll take ourselves off, let you return to your evening alone. Forgive us."

But though she again pressed into the brick wall that was Lord Tremayne, he refused to waver. And though Thea *knew* they had to leave, the scrutiny on the other couple's faces was growing.

It was as though she dreamed the next few moments when the woman stepped forward, ignoring the indrawn hiss of her companion, to offer a shallow curtsy of her own. Her eyes flicked back and forth between Thea and the man behind her. "Daniel, aren't you going to introduce me?"

"Ellie," Lord Tremayne said again and his breath brushed across the top of Thea's head, sending a wicked shiver racing across her nape.

How could he stand there? Cage her there as well?

They *must* leave! This woman was Quality. Unmistakable breeding shone in her perfect manner, in her exquisitely coiffed hair and extravagant dress, both of which she wore without a speck of the self-consciousness plaguing Thea.

Already, she'd had to stop herself from fiddling with feathers and checking her bountified bosom. Just how secure—

"Mrs-Hur-well."

Thea heard the ragged syllables come from overhead and for a startled second didn't recognize them as her name.

What was he doing?

She spun within his grip, thankful the glossy material allowed the move. "Lord Tremayne," she said through barely moving lips, the words fast and low, "should we not vacate and leave the box to your friends?"

He ignored her. Ignored her words, that was.

Because right there in the dim interior of his box, partitioned off from the adjoining neighbors but fully visible to anyone with exceptional eyesight in the boxes across, he lifted her hand, inclined his head and turned her to face the other couple.

"THEA, Lord Wylde and his wife, my s—"

Good God, man, some remnant of Daniel's conscience railed. *You can't introduce your fancy piece to your sister.* Bloody hell, he couldn't even *acknowledge* her, not in front of a gently bred female.

Gads. What was he thinking?

Losing it, he was. The ability to think. To act. To behave as he ought.

And why in blazes had that sentence flowed like silk when everything else he'd uttered in the last hour faltered forth like dirt-encrusted flies?

The crux of it was he *wanted* the two cherished females in his life to meet, to get on with each other as well as he—

Cherished? Thea?

Aye, so she was, he could admit to himself, and as she was also tugging on his arm to the point he should fear losing it, he really ought to behave with decorum.

So he tightened his hold on Thea's hand and started backing out. "A-p-pologize. We'll go elsewhere—"

"Wait!" Ellie's raised voice surely raised more than one eyebrow in the vicinity. "Don't go. Not yet."

On the verge of crossing the threshold, Daniel paused. He watched an indecipherable look pass from Ellie to her husband.

Tense seconds later, Wylde jerked his head in the most miniscule show of approval—or acceptance.

What was that all about? Were they going to leave instead?

But no, Elizabeth immediately indicated the six chairs furnishing the tight rectangle he leased for an absurd amount of money. "Let it not be said that we routed you from your own box. Stay and join us."

What?

Thea was hauling on his arm, trying her damnedest to back him out of there. Daniel didn't budge. Had he heard aright?

Wylde gestured to the empty seats. "Aye, you must remain and partake of the performance with us. We insist."

Deuced if this night didn't beat all.

Lighting farts and scandalizing the ton by socializing his sister with his tart.

Only Thea wasn't a tart.

She never had been. Not to him.

Which posed the question, what, exactly, was she?

WHILE THE DANCERS PRANCED ABOUT, everyone took their seats. Daniel positioned himself behind Ellie who sat next to Wylde. Thea he tucked securely on his opposite side, behind an empty chair.

Though he had the distinct impression not a one of them saw the ballet, all four heads remained fixed on the stage as though glued. Poor Thea, she'd approached the seat of her chair as if hot coals waited to fry her bum, her wide eyes imploring him not to participate in this farce.

But it wasn't a jest. Not to him. Or to his family.

Wylde and Ellie might be flirting with social disaster, but Daniel knew his sister didn't give a fig for expected behavior —their father had kept her on such a short chain during his lifetime, she was due whatever indulgence came her way. If associating for a single evening with a less-than-respectable female enlivened her life, then what was the harm? And Wylde? He already had a dubious reputation for flouting convention. As for himself, if a marquis couldn't savor the opera with the companion of his choice, then what was the use of a title?

Hoping he conveyed confidence, he reached over to capture Thea's hand. Never taking his gaze from the exiting dancers, he untangled her fingers from the wreckage she'd made of her purse strings and wound his gloved fingers between hers. Giving a light tug, he repositioned their joined hands atop his thigh.

THE SECOND THE dancers disappeared off the stage, men and women exploded from their chairs and boxes to seek refreshment and recreation and, no doubt, urinary relief. The long interval between ballet and opera served several important purposes but its primary one, Daniel was certain, was to see and be seen. The surrounding melee was made more chaotic by the silence and the stillness that characterized the four of them.

No one moved, no one spoke.

Within seconds, the noise level beyond their silent foursome had increased tenfold.

Finally, some moments into the interval, Wylde nodded stiffly and excused himself.

The moment the door shut behind her husband, Ellie took the opportunity to fly into the empty seat next to Daniel.

"Is she the one?" his sister whispered behind her fan.

The one?

When Thea would have pulled away, Daniel tightened his grip on her hand. Keeping her firmly entrenched beside him, he cocked his head toward his sister, his blank look convey-ing, *The one what?*

Ellie leaned ever closer, flapped that fancy fan of hers ever faster. "The one who put the smile on your face," she said so softly he had to piece together the sentence. "The gouges... your neck."

A grin he couldn't stop gave her all the answer she needed.

She beamed back. Then her expression turned sardonic. Wafts from her fan brushed past his forehead as she inquired lightly, "Any chance she also revels in pounding your face? It looks rather atrocious, brother dear."

"Cream. More?"

"You need another jar of that latest batch? The one with the honeysuckle and cloves? Of course!" His sister's delight knew no bounds.

He wondered what she'd say if she knew he'd given all of his to Thea.

"I'll have it to you as soon as I gather some more and crush the blossoms. It's growing in the conservatory at the estate but it's too early for it to bloom outside— But you don't care about that." Her fan slowed to a crawl as she gave him a measuring glance. "I do believe this is the first time you've ever *asked* for more of a batch."

He shrugged, that was all.

"Bad night?" Ellie deduced. "Your voice?"

"The worst," he strained out.

"She's very elegant." Daniel nodded his agreement. "Refined too." Daniel nodded again. "Are you sure she's a lightskirt?"

He laughed outright. Then took a deep, cleansing breath and laughed again, just for the hell of it. Wonder of wonders, talking might seize him up like a fist clamped round his windpipe but laughter actually felt good.

His mirth drew Thea's gaze. Though her fingers trembled uncertainly within his, she gave him a sweet, almost demure smile, rendering him very, very glad they'd stayed.

To Thea's dismay, Lord Tremayne was called from their box a short time later, leaving her alone with the other woman, vastly curious what they'd just been whispering about.

Unsure where to look, after that too-brief, reassuring clasp of his hand to her shoulder, Thea flashed an uncertain glance past the empty chair between them. When she found the woman staring at her intently, Thea decided she found the stage below worthy of her complete fascination.

Pity nothing much was occurring on it.

Desperately, she looked into the orchestra pit. The musicians were pausing there as well, abandoning chairs and instruments in a bid to stretch their legs.

"Botheration! This will never do," the woman exclaimed, sliding over to sit directly beside Thea. "I know it's not done but I should like to meet you. I'm Elizabeth, Daniel's sister." She gave a light laugh. "Lady Wylde, if I'm to do it right, but I've never been one to stand on ceremony, so please do call me Elizabeth. Neither have I ever seen him so happy. My brother, that is. Thank you for that."

His sister. So much more than simply friends, then.

Despite the invitation, Thea could not bring herself to regard Lord Tremayne's relative so informally, but her genuine warmth loosened Thea's tongue. "Happy? Pray, you must have your men confused."

"As though I have so many!" Lady Elizabeth smiled sincerely. "You're such a wit."

Not hardly. "As to that, why thank me? I've done nothing—"

"Oh, but you have. Tell me, what has he shared about himself?"

"Ah..." Very little, she was shamed to realize. Casting about for a response that might satisfy, Thea blurted, "That he disdains poetry and likes orreries."

Heave me to Hertfordshire, is that all I know?

Nay, for you know he's kind and thoughtful and generous. Thea's fingers twitched as though recalling the feel of the sumptuous winter gloves he'd given her. She also knew he was strong and protective and tender when he was with her, and when he touched her body, it sang more notes than any accomplished opera singer.

I know he makes me feel special.

"Fancy that." Her companion's voice trilled with glee. "He told you of his contraptions. Then you aren't a cabbagehead like his last— Pardon me. I should not have said that." Lady Elizabeth's unfashionably tanned face pinkened. Her agitation gave rise to a furious fluttering of her fan. "I do spells, well *gentle blessings* I prefer to think of them, with herbs and such, did you know?" No answer was necessary because the fan kept twitching, the ebullient woman kept talking. "As to his preoccupation with orreries, has he mentioned that fellow who's come to town to give some lecture or other? Daniel so looked forward to attending that. I know he regrets having to miss it."

Feeling adrift at the rapid topic swings, Thea asked, "What fellow? If he's to make a presentation on orreries, there's a chance I know of him."

"Truly? How grand!" Lady Elizabeth went on to explain about a "monstrous" orrery in Lord Tremayne's study and how it wasn't working properly. Upon learning the acclaimed clockwork expert was come to London, Daniel had made plans to hear him speak. "Only now he's doing a favor for my husband and will miss the lecture. And he was so wishing to gain insight on correcting whatever's wrong with it. Over the years, he's collected a number of working models, but this particular one is special, for it belonged to our grandfather."

Amid her flurry of fan and facts, Thea had pieced together enough to realize it must be Mr. Horatio Taft from Manchester, visiting and lecturing. "I do know him, a Mr. Taft, for he consulted with my late husband on a project or two. If you do not think it's overstepping my place, I could attempt to locate him and see whether he will be in town a while and could perhaps meet with Lord Tremayne another time."

Lady Elizabeth's face took on a glow that turned her from pretty to stunning. "Overstepping, pah. The reality of meeting this fellow would give Daniel no end of delight." She leaned in close and the fan finally stilled. "Tell me, though, has he told you anything more? About himself?"

Suddenly Thea felt as though she were walking a tightrope, wavering upon a fine line between passing and failing. What? What else was he supposed to have told her? "Nothing specific comes to mind," she finally said.

Lady Elizabeth's disappointment was palatable and Thea tumbled right off that rope. Crashed into inexplicable sadness.

Compelled to defend him, she offered, "In truth, he doesn't talk that much. Not when we're together, anyway. We seem to, ah, be busy doing-other-things," she finished swiftly, feeling a hot flush flare over her forehead. "But we have been exchanging wonderfully charming letters."

That confession brightened Lady Elizabeth's countenance. "Letters?"

"Aye, sometimes several in a day." Thea couldn't stop the chuckle that emerged. "He's quite entertaining, has a flair for funning me. I've never laughed so much."

"Fun?" Lady Elizabeth mused on the word. "I don't think

I've ever thought of my older brother as such, not since we were children. He's typically far too busy getting his face bashed in to indulge in something as banal as fun."

Thea winced at the disgruntled tone. "On that, I can commiserate. I did notice his propensity for walking into fists. What's a munsons muffler? Do you know?"

"I haven't an inkling. Why?"

"'Tis simply something that was said the first night we met." Thea waved it off. "I keep meaning to ask him and—What?" She lowered her voice guiltily. "Why are you looking at me so?"

"Because you—you..."

"I what?"

"You're nothing at all like I expected. You're so—" Lady Elizabeth pressed her lips together, as though contemplating whether or not to finish her thoughts. She did—astounding Thea with, "Ladylike! You're good for him. I've never seen him smile so much—"

"Smile? He's been dour since he arrived tonight."

"I'm not only talking about tonight," Lady Elizabeth answered evasively. "As to that, I'm sure he's just worried about tomorrow. He's giving a speech. That's the favor to Wylde and speechifying is one talent my brother would rather not indulge in."

"Really? I hadn't noticed," Thea said dryly, and the two shared a brief laugh.

Then this composed female of elevated station, one who Thea never in a thousand years would have imagined actually conversing with, astonished her yet again. "I've had a brilliant idea—you can surprise him. If you're sincere about asking that orrery expert a favor, I'm sure nothing would mean more to my dear brother than to have the man drop by, assuming it works with his schedule, of course. Will you ask him?"

"Certainly. It would be an honor to please Lord Tremayne after all he's done for me," Thea assured, readily agreeing. "Only...well, to confess, I've no notion of his direction—if I'm able to contact him, where do I request Mr. Taft go?"

"That's easily remedied." Lady Elizabeth reached for her reticule with a bright smile. "I'll give you Daniel's address."

The players had taken the stage during the last few seconds. Music from the orchestra sounded and a full-voiced singer loosed the first notes while Thea watched her newest acquaintance retrieve pencil and paper.

Feeling the need to subdue the other woman's growing excitement, Thea cautioned, "Please realize that I've no notion of Mr. Taft's itinerary or whether his habits have changed. I do know where he stayed during prior visits, however, and I'll do my best to reach him tomorrow."

"That's perfect. All anyone can expect, really." Scribbling away, Elizabeth said, almost to herself, "Aye, I like this idea. You'll tell Daniel to stay at home and ask your Mr. Taft to call, while I—"

"*Tell* him to stay home? I think you overstate my influence on your brother."

"Do I?" She paused and turned to Thea, a look of consternation shading her features before they cleared and she flashed a conspiratorial smile. "I'm sure even mistresses become, ah...indisposed at times. If that's what he believes for a short duration and the end result is his happiness, where would be the harm?"

Where indeed?

The men chose that moment to return, their conversation continuing in hushed whispers before Lord Tremayne resumed his seat beside Thea (only after his sister relinquished it with a bright smile).

Lord Wylde, Thea couldn't help but notice, chose to remain standing. During the first lull of the powerful singing, he leaned down. "We'll be going now. Tremayne. Ahh, Mrs. Hurwell, was it?" He straightened and said in a more commanding tone, "Elizabeth?"

Lord Wylde held out his arm as Daniel croaked, "N-now?" evidently as surprised as she that the other couple would leave just as the performance got underway.

"Aye," Wylde said resolutely, encouraging his wife to her feet when she seemed to hesitate. "We only came for the ballet anyway."

BALLOCKS.

Daniel was hard-pressed not to laugh at Wylde's pronouncement. They were here for the ballet? He knew that to be a clanker of the first-order.

They'd only come to indulge Ellie's desire for opera but if Wylde wanted to leave him and Thea alone, who was he to argue?

Actually, to his utter amazement, when the two of them had quit the box during the interval, the only thing his friend said in regard to Daniel's new mistress was that "she appears a fetching little thing" and he hoped they got on well together. That and a cryptic remark that meeting her might be beneficial for Elizabeth and their marriage—of all things.

Not a word on the inappropriateness of it all.

Daniel couldn't decide if he was thankful on Thea's behalf or offended on his sister's. Shouldn't Wylde take more umbrage over the perceived slight to Ellie's reputation?

Shouldn't you be more concerned over your committee commitments tomorrow?

Gads. He'd rather grow horns than think of all the last-minute counsel and wording suggestions Wylde had shoved down his silent throat out in the corridor.

Horns? Pah.

Much, much better to sit here with his sweet Thea, basking in her presence, than to worry about tomorrow.

After the door shut behind the other couple, Thea fiddled again with her purse, tucking something inside. After placing it on an empty chair, she glanced up at him and leaned a few inches closer. "Your sister. She's a lovely woman."

Daniel nodded.

"I... We... What you must think of me." She floundered about, but her gaze never left his.

He reached over and captured her hand, took his time tugging off her dress gloves. Speaking to her elegant fingers, he willed his neck to relax. "Think you're lovely...too."

"But we were *talking* while you were gone." She sounded as though the offense warranted beheading. "I know I shouldn't have behaved so familiarly but—"

A slight squeeze of her fingers and her ramblings stilled. He met her gaze again. "She's...persuasive."

"Aye," Thea breathed out on a sigh. "Very. It was awfully forward, I know, even being here with her. I hope you don't think ill of me."

As if he could. He brought her bare fingers to his lips. "Never."

She blasted him with a smile so bright he jerked back.

God, how he needed that smile.

And not just for tonight, he was starting to realize. Tomorrow. Next week, next year. When he was fifty. A hundred.

He might have a driving need to bed her—and oh how he did—but it was that smile he was plain coming to *need*.

FOR THE NEXT several thousand heartbeats or so, Daniel gave himself over to the unexpected escape. In their private nook, listening to the dramatic levels of feeling being expressed in song, he discovered both bliss and solace.

With his eyes closed, and his senses attuned to the woman at his side, it was an easy thing to forget the strain gripping his neck. An easy thing to relax and simply be.

Without any conscious effort, he allowed the music to wash over him. The sheer pleasure his auditory senses reveled in, thanks to the deeply sung notes—never mind that they were nonsense as he'd never learned Italian—reached through his lugs and somehow touched his soul.

Despite the clash of instruments and the tragic tale being told so woefully, the sounds loosened the tension, softened the muscles, until he was sitting there, staring at the blackness behind his eyelids, seeing brightness everywhere around him, his body suspended somewhere between alert and drowsy, one of the most peaceful, calming things he'd ever experienced.

The mournful, moving voice approached another, more intense, crescendo, bringing the reluctant awareness that the performance approached its end. That realization, in itself, brought sorrow, gathered grief like a shroud into his being. So much anguish, so much euphoria.

To think, he'd missed countless performances such as this, such depths and pinnacles of emotion, all because he avoided people. Avoided possible confrontations, probable conversations.

He'd been doing his spirit a disservice.

As the final notes wound to a stirring, heart-wrenching close, Daniel blinked open heavy lids. As though pulled by a relentless magnet to seek her out, he turned to study Thea. Rapt, she stared at the stage. A single tear left a glistening trail down her exposed cheek. As he watched, she covered her lips with her hand and compressed damp lashes.

Overcome.

Though he felt the same, he couldn't bear witnessing her reaction.

Startled to find he still held her hand, he released it in order to wrap his arm around her and bring her close to his side. She tilted her head until it rested against his shoulder. He felt the breath go out of her on a shudder.

Long minutes later, neither of them had moved a speck. The stage had emptied, the deafening applause finally drifting to nothing but indistinguishable shouts and murmurs as hundreds if not thousands of people clambered for the exits.

Daniel angled his head until it rested against the top of Thea's. He inhaled deeply, drawing her essence deeper into the cracks of his soul. Cracks he hadn't realized existed until unlocked by the phenomenal talent they'd just witnessed.

He thought she'd eventually pull away. Gain her feet, be keen to go. He knew he'd been deplorable company all evening.

But instead of making any move to join the noisy exodus, she only snuggled deeper into his side.

When had her arm curved around his waist? Her other hand come up to rest beneath his neckcloth? How long had her thumb rubbed a tender caress through his linen shirt, over his heart?

"I don't mind if we wait here until the crowds dissipate." Her quiet voice reached his ears. The gentle caress didn't stop. "One time I overheard two ladies in the shop complaining that it took over an hour just to exit and that one of them was, horror of horrors..." Thea pitched her voice to a whispered nasally screech, *"Groped most objectionably in the bargain!"*

He laughed. A bone-deep, belly-shaking chuckle as he hauled Thea sideways onto his lap, cupped her cheeks in both hands, and wiped away the dried remnants of tears. Staring into her soft eyes, his laughter faded.

He should tell her, explain his mood.

The very atmosphere around them made him feel buoyant, as though the evening, and last few somber notes had lifted his spirit, lightened his load. Lessened the ever-present strain to the point where he felt like *talking*. Who knew when he might be so inclined again?

"There's a t-*task*—" Damn. *Take your time, Daniel.* His grandfather's voice, Everson's too. *There's no reason to rush.* "*Task, an onerous one, I must see...to. Weighing on me and—*"

And God, I need to see you smile.

Thea waited so patiently for him to mutter through. Stared at him so solemnly. Left off rubbing his chest to finger his newly shaved jaw with such a sense of discovery.

Had he really kept himself so closed off from her?

"In truth, I nn—" *Need* almost never tripped him up, never. Sod it—why now?

He had to tell her. All of it. "Explain!" burst out. "I like you, Thea, very much, and...because of that, nn—" *Need to tell you why I'm such an ogre sometimes.*

Goddammit. Why now?

As though she sought to interpret his butchered speech, her brow knit. "Are you pleased? Having me as your mistress?"

He gave a brief, wholly inadequate nod.

"Do you, ah, have any inclinations to end or alter our arrangement?"

Hell, no! An abrupt shake of his head had to suffice.

"You're completely justified, I know, if that is your wish."

He shook his head so hard his teeth rattled.

She still looked perplexed, so he tried again. "You d-d—" *Don't understand, damn me, I'm trying to tell you—*

"'Tis all right" She shushed him with a hug. Her words brushed his ears like velvet. "I know speaking of finer emotions is difficult if not impossible for the masculine sex.

Say no more. Your actions speak more clearly than any I've known before. You care about my happiness and that means the world to me. I care about yours too."

After delivering that little, very welcome speech, she leaned back, eyes bright, her expression sweetly expectant. She was so understanding. So clueless. If she had an inkling—

Buxom Betsy bouncily brings brimming buckets of butter to bossy, blighted Bob. My ballocks are boiling for you.

"Been a bear tonight." Hallelujah! "Forgive me?"

"*Pffft*. There's nothing at all to forgive. You may not have been the soul of joviality but neither have you been mean or harsh." She patted his cheek. "Just frowny."

Which made him smile.

"Oh! You have a dimple. I don't believe I've seen it before."

"'Twas hiding."

"It surely was." She leaned forward to kiss the elusive dimple.

Daniel hadn't the fortitude to tell her what he'd meant: *he'd* been hiding.

Still was.

Still intended to if she kept looking at him as she did when she pulled back. "Tell you what," she posed, her eyes glittering emeralds as she stared at him. "For every frown I counted, I shall take a kiss. *Voilà*. They will be erased forevermore."

Then by God, let them get started. "How many?"

"I do believe I counted seventeen frowns, eight scowls and two snarls."

He couldn't help it. Damned if he didn't laugh again. Two *snarls? I've been a grump indeed.* "Seems I have much...to atone."

"Seems I am due many kisses. Now do you simply want to jaw about them all night or start delivering—"

The little minx thought to turn bossy on him? How adorable.

Daniel's mouth swooped to capture hers. He meant to tease, to tread lightly. He meant to nibble and savor. To suck gently upon her lips, entice her tongue out for a flirtation.

He did none of that. Pure want drove him now.

He thrust his tongue past her lips and hers slid forth to meet it. As they rubbed along each other, her fingers pushed through his hair, nails sank into his scalp.

His broad hand smoothed down her back to settle at her waist. His fingers clenched—just above the womanly flare of her arse.

Suddenly he was strangling to draw breath. A lingering swipe of his tongue along the roof of her mouth and he tore his head back. Gulped for air.

"One," she said on an equally loud breath. "Sixteen more to go—"

With powerful motions of his legs, he scooted his chair backward until it thumped against the closed door, hid them deep into shadows. No one would interrupt what he'd needed all night. *Her.* Completely.

"Want you." He sounded like a deuced caveman.

Her lips trembled but her eyes shone clear. "Then take me."

Before he could debate further with his conscience— frisking Thea in public had not been his plan when they'd set out earlier—she took the decision from him. She leaned forward to claim his lips, whispering just before they touched, "And now for two..."

The kiss was voracious, lacking restraint or finesse. Her tongue dueled with his as she murmured deep in her throat. As for Daniel, he couldn't get enough of her, couldn't slow the sensual onslaught. *Overpower and take. Take her and drown yourself,* seemed to be the litany commanding his actions.

He shifted Thea until she was astride him, wrenching that froth of sea blue higher until her thighs were bared atop the stockings. Her pale thighs, silken skin he couldn't wait to touch.

Only he couldn't stop framing her face with his hands, cupping her cheeks, threading his fingers through the elaborate sweep of hair. Couldn't bring himself to relinquish her precious face long enough to explore the tempting dainties below. Her nails scraped over his jaw as she tilted his head to the side, brushed lips and then teeth over his cheek and chin, down his neck.

"Love the scent you wear, always have," she told him just before applying suction to a part of his neck that inflamed his entire body. He stiffened *everywhere*.

Scent bedamned, he had to be in her, seize her against him or go mad trying. Were those her impatient fingers grappling with the fall of his breeches, slipping inside to stroke his length? Her fingers tightening into a fist around his shaft as he gave a ragged groan?

Had to be, he thought distractedly as he became aware of pure decadence, silky hot and sinfully sweet when his intrepid fingers journeyed far, fatalistically far from her head and—to his dismay and delight—met beneath the plump halves of her arse. Met and slid boldly along the seam between.

Where were her drawers? He was touching skin. Hot, humid skin he was so damn hungry for—

Breath labored, Thea's clasp on his cock jerked. Her whimper came soft but unmistakable.

Don't do it, some prudent part of his brain cautioned.

Oh, aye, do it, the flex of her bum encouraged.

Coated with her heat, his hands kneaded the firm flesh of her flanks, delved a bit farther into the crevice.

"May I..." His voice was a croak. He firmed his resolve and

his palms, stretched his fingers just a wee bit more and was rewarded when her constricting anus met the tip of his longest finger. Daniel circled the digit around the puckered ring. *Play here...* "Linger?"

"Ahh. Um... Should I let you?" she breathed hotly against his neck. "Would a..." *Mistress allow it?*

He could just hear her mind asking the questions—*Do mistresses truly do this? Or is it too tawdry? Totally taboo? Will I be no better than a hedge whore or street doxy—*

But then her hold tightened on his shaft and her luscious derrière rotated beneath his finger, answering for her, even before she said in a low whisper, "All right."

He exhaled in relief and spread his grip over her arse cheeks, loving the feel of the warm flesh against his palms. His middle finger? It wasn't going anywhere. Except deeper. When he navigated the perimeter of the impossibly tight ring, exploring both her body and the boundaries of what she might accept, she pulled his penis taut.

Pressure seized his groin. Longing filled his loins.

Longing to tell her what she meant to him, what exploring her like this did to his body, his mind, his heart—

"Is it terribly wicked? For us to do *this* here? Now?" Upon uttering *this*, she angled her body and his, rocking her hips until his stiff and ready prick was nudging along slick folds.

To strum her, *here* of all places. A private box he'd purchased to salve his conscience and his past. A past that receded far into the shadows when she squirmed her creamy center against him again.

Daniel swore. Good God Almighty—he was close to exploding and wasn't even in her yet. Not properly.

The hot cave of her arse threatened to suck him into its depths. He was sweating, drenched in desire.

Do it, he wanted to tell her, *take me inside. No one will interrupt.*

His damn finger—hell, his whole arm—shook with the force he exerted not to plunge it into forbidden territory.

Thea shifted forward, sliding along his shaft until reaching the crown. A slight wiggle of her pelvis and his cock eased into her as though greased.

She gasped, her feminine muscles pulling him deeper yet clinging together so tightly it was a marvel he could gain any friction at all. When she said, "Terribly wicked for you to touch me *there*," and surged up, then back down, her feet on the floor giving her leverage, damned if her nock didn't open and invite his finger in as well.

"T-terribly." He covered the blunder by latching on to the smooth skin just beneath her ear. Deliberately teasing, he stifled the urge to move—he was liable to nail her to the ceiling if he let his body have its way. Speaking against her skin, he mused, "Shall I stop? With...draw and re...turn you home?"

Any answer she might have made changed to a gasp when he sucked harder. But as he eased the suction and plied his tongue over the succulent spot, she painted rainbows in his sky with her response. "Nay. 'Twould be a crime, for I believe I like being wicked with you here and now. Maybe later too.

"And not to belabor the point..." Every orifice he'd entered rippled against him as she spoke, enticed him to move, so he resisted. "But those snarls still need erased, I'll have you know."

When he made a sound in his throat, she consoled. "Not that I'm complaining, my lord..."

He swore her pelvis jerked against him in all the right places. Pulling him inward from both directions. "Not at all," she offered on another gasp, her lips pressed to the newly sensitive skin of his jaw. "In fact, I understand about tonight. Your sister explained your mood."

It wasn't quite being dunked in an icy lake, but it was close. He tried to articulate but only managed a grunt. "Eh?"

"She said you perform a favor for Lord Wylde tomorrow, a troublesome one." Those lithesome legs of hers lifted her up, then sank her loins back to his, gave a tiny hitch that buried him up to his ballocks. The wave of lust that rolled over him at the sinuous motions threatened to swamp him. "So I understand your fit of the sullens. 'Twill be over in mere hours, though, aye?"

Fit of the sullens? And now he sounded like a grouchy lad of eight. "Sulks b-b—" *Be gone,* dammit!

But her lips vanquished the urge to speak. And the lands south of her hips promised heaven if he would but listen. "'Tis more kisses you owe me, my lord. There's the matter of several scowls... Besides, wicked or ruinous, or tawdry beyond reckoning"—she tightened around him and her breath caught when she lifted to slide along his cock again —"I don't care if it is, not tonight."

Daniel thought he heard a shred of guilt—tempered with defiance, perhaps—but he couldn't have held back, not any longer. Not when he was drowning in such taboo sexual bliss with such an outwardly decorous and demure young woman.

Not when—

Her lower body soared and jerked against his groin, directing, if not controlling, his thrusts. Positioned over him as she was, Thea, his sweet, sexually shy Thea took command.

"Harder," she whispered, swinging her pelvis against him in a tempest of need.

One his body echoed. So he canted his groin until her every downward plunge took him to the root.

She started to squeal, then muffled her lips against his cheek. "Don't stop. Don't ever stop," or something similarly needy emerged.

His fingers took the message to heart. The buried one pulled free and snared a mate. Then the two of them poised to enter, circling the entrance to the hot cavern made slippery by her trickling juices. The ring of her anus was open now, the muscles slightly lax. With just a slight push, both fingers slid past that first constriction; with a firmer nudge, and the friction that his back-and-forth motion created, they sank deep.

And his prim mistress turned into a cavewoman—tugging on his hair, pummeling the muscles of her moist, private places against their invaders, clutching and clasping at him as he pumped fingers and cock both. Sweat rolled from his temples onto her desperate countenance as she marauded and plundered his neckcloth until she could kiss and suck— and bite—the skin lining his neck and collar.

"Ah-oh— Ahh!"

In tandem with her breathy cries and tensing muscles, he ground his fingers into her arse, bucked his ballocks against her buttocks and lunged faster and fiercer, more connected with her, on so many levels, than he ever had been with another. Ever could be.

Oh God. Oh gads.

What was wrong with him?

Why ponder *emotional* closeness when his prick was busy prigging? Time to apply himself to taking his pleasure, by damn.

Only, for once, it didn't seem to matter. Because though he'd long forgotten how to breathe, had been seeing stars and spots and dancing little hearts for some time now, and though his wrist ached and fingers had gone numb, he didn't slow or pause or think to stop. Not until Thea screamed —*screamed*, by damn—and melted over his groin. Not until her arse sucked him so far inside, she promised a home to any and every part of him that ever existed.

Not until he'd pleasured her so thoroughly that she went limp did he give serious thought to taking his own satisfaction.

Only he'd already found it.

Oh, not because he'd peaked—he hadn't, not yet (though bridling the urge nearly did him in)—but because he'd found *his* satisfaction by *giving* Thea hers.

Was that a noose he felt tightening around his neck?

Was that why his brain box had succumbed to fevered chills?

Was this love, the deep, abiding kind he'd never sought, never expected? The overpowering, overwhelming emotion that made fools of men? That made his gut churn with nausea, his beleaguered brain with bopping, bobbing B's? Bouncing Betties and beaming Bobs?

His mind overfloweth with nonsense, his heart with peace. Could love truly be that capricious? That fantastically fickle?

Nay, he assured himself, trying to remember how to draw breath. *Nay!*

'Twas simply tupping the delectable Thea that addled his wits. That was all. A good swiving with a fine mistress likely boggled finer men than him.

After his body crested the pinnacle, an explosive event that took mere seconds to reach once he quit battling the urge, instead of offering recriminations or calling him base and screeching obscenities at him for his obscene behavior, his prim and lusty little mistress only blinked at him wearing a dazed smile.

"Well now." She blinked again, smiled a bit brighter. "I must say, *I* certainly did not mind being groped in that wholly *un*-objectionable manner."

Then, lips and body trembling, she shakily eased off him and to her feet and started riffling inside her bodice. "Here."

She produced a wad of padding that left her bosom decidedly uneven. "Have some cotton. I'm afraid I left you all sticky."

While he sat, benumbed and blighted (were Cupid's arrows poison tipped? he wondered), she proceeded to use the stuffing from the other side's enhancement to clean herself.

And a noose had never felt more welcome.

14

A BIT OF PATHETIC POETRY

THE FOLLOWING MORNING, the day of the Dreaded Speech, found Daniel at the desk in his bedchamber, not yet dressed for the day, trying to coax the right attitude from his mind, the right words from his mouth. But all he could do was agonize over the coming hours...

Not because his neck still felt as though a viper had sunk in its fangs—a single night's sleep had restored his muscles to their customary, on-the-edge-of-tense state; thankfully, they felt no worse for all of yesterday's use—but because he knew he should care more about Wylde's cause.

And frankly, he didn't. Despite his efforts, he couldn't seem to foment any excitement.

His thoughts—his easily aroused excitement—remained squarely with his mistress. She'd sent round a note early this morning by way of Swift John. For once, instead of lingering for a reply, the servant had delivered the letter along with a message that reached Daniel via his butler: "I've a number of errands to run for Miss Thea and will return for any response by nuncheon. Better yet, send John later; his lazy legs could use the jaunt."

Though the sibling jibe had lightened his mood, it hadn't helped his concentration. The neatly folded and wax-sealed square beckoned hordes more than his speech notes.

Notes he'd studiously avoided all morning.

He tapped the edge of Thea's letter against his desktop, sorely tempted to tear into it. "Nay. Use it for incentive."

That was it! He'd review his planned phrasing three times more, the last out loud, before reading her note.

How he wished the day's events were done and over. But it was hours still until the damn meeting. Until his part in it was complete and he could visit her again.

"Enthusiasm," he muttered, reluctantly relinquishing her missive, "need t-to garner some."

"Woof!"

He patted Cy's head, scratched the dog's chin. Wiped the drool on his handkerchief and decided to go about it another way. He located the sheet Everson had written. He'd practice two letters aloud (no sense in overdoing), *then* apply himself to the business of reviewing his speech.

Paul was a pea-goose, a pink of the ton, yet his profound penis promised pleasure to every pudding-headed puss and Pocket Venus on the planet.

Willie had a wee little weedle, but when he grew into Walt, the girls were in alt, for what once was wee could now wiggle and wow!

After reciting the pair of ribald selections, instead of studying the compelling reasons Wylde had so passionately set forth, Daniel couldn't stop his pen from doing a little composing of its own:

There once was a pebble in my shoe.
Cows go moooooooooooooooo.

I once knew a cat,
with a sniveling nose,

"What now?" Testing options, he scratched out *hedgerows, pose, close, grows* and *sews,* frowned, and then chose to move on to more colorful pastures.

Roses are red,
Mr. Freshley was a snoacher
then a poacher and

"Deplorable, D-Daniel! Wretched, sodding po-*poetry.*" But then inspiration struck.

Roses are red,
Your name is Dorothea.
It pains me to say it,
so I changed it to Thea.

"Nay. Too pat." Thinking aloud, he rewrote the last line. "...Name is D-Dorothea. It p-pains me to say it, so I chopped it in half."

There. That brought a smile, and at the man's third knock, Daniel finally allowed his valet to enter and begin the task of outfitting him properly. This included a fresh scrape of any whiskers that dared emerge since yesterday's "sculpting" (why Crowley didn't just call it shaving, Daniel didn't know), complaints about the missing jar of Lady Wylde's latest concoction—known officially as The Miraculous Bruise Vanishing Cream (this nomenclature too from his valet)—and a neckcloth arrangement so intricate, it could hold its own in a contest against Brummell's.

A quick glance in the mirror and Daniel was set.

Still rather pleased with himself for his poetic (if pathetic) turn of phrase where Thea was concerned, feeling lighter than he had all morning, he dismissed Crowley and whisked through his speech notes with nary a slip (shouldn't be too surprising as he'd eliminated most anything likely to incite a stammer).

Relieved at the sense of accomplishment, he reached for Thea's letter.

My dear Lord Tremayne,

He really needed to tell her to call him Daniel.

There stands so much I'd like to say but as I know you have commitments today, I shall endeavor to brevity (do stop laughing at me, if you please; I mean it this time—for yours is valuable).

Let me just convey my sincere appreciation for what proved to be a most exceptional evening. (Though I do tend to find myself thinking the same following every incidence of spending time together.)

I confess, when Sarah first suggested our illicit arrangement, I could never have anticipated that I would find such a valued and cherished companion in the bargain.

I knew I'd been lonely and that things were becoming more dire than I wanted to admit (even to myself). But you, why... Well, having you in my life has made what I thought was my last, most reluctantly agreed to (and dare I admit it, desperate) option into one of the most freeing and splendorous experiences of my life. (I blush, but 'tis true, and so I have admitted it. Dear me, where is a fresh breeze when a girl needs to cool her cheeks?)

Your well-pleasured mistress, Thea

PS. Despite your apparent dread last evening pertaining to today's events—

That gave him pause. *Dread.* Had his disinclination been so very obvious? For one used to masking their inner selves, 'twas a sobering revelation.

Or was it just Thea who could read him so?

Eager to escape his thoughts, he turned to the remaining lines.

...apparent dread...today's events, I have every confidence in you. I know you'll succeed in your efforts and look forward to your realization of the same.

PS. Once Again—I have a full day planned as well and a most peculiar appeal: If you'll indulge me, and forgive me for being so impertinent, please stay at your residence tonight. Possibly tomorrow night as well. Something your sister mentioned inclines me to think she's engaged in arranging a surprise for you, one that can only come to successful fruition if you remain home-bound in the evening.

Though "peculiar" didn't begin to describe her last request, it was the paragraph before that commanded his attention: *I have every confidence in you. I know you'll succeed...*

Her blind faith in him pulled the scales from his eyes.

Light so painfully bright shone into his being and illuminated the truth bursting from his heart. He loved her.

He utterly and totally loved her, by damn.

Doubt, nausea and nooses aside, by all that was holy and
hellacious, he'd fallen in love with his mistress.

—◦◦—

LONG BEFORE THE sun rose that morning, Thea had toiled
over two of the three notes she'd sent out by way of Buttons.
Composing the one to Mr. Taft had been as simple as drawing
a dot. Either he'd be reachable or not. Either he'd remember
her or not. Either he'd be inclined to grant her request or...

Or she'd be vastly disappointed.

And Lord Tremayne would forever wonder why she was
so presumptive as to disavow his presence two nights in a row
by having the effrontery to order him to stay home.

As to that, the note to Lord Tremayne proved significantly
more difficult to write than the brief missive to the respected
clockmaker. When one has thousands of thoughts vying to be
heard, how to select only a few to share? She managed well
enough, or so she'd assured herself before superstitiously
kissing the page (a good-luck gesture intended for the man
who'd open it) and folding it shut with crisp, precise edges.

It was the third and last letter that her pen dithered over
the most. The letter she'd composed in more than a cursory
state of shock because when she'd arrived home hours before
and crawled into bed, intending to commit Lord Tremayne's
address to memory, what should her eyes be greeted with
upon pulling from her reticule the card Lady Elizabeth had
surreptitiously given her just before departing the box?

Not a simple address—which it did have.

But the hastily scrawled-upon card also contained an
additional note, one that rendered Thea wide awake into the

night: *Lord W is away most days from 10 until 6, often later. Please call upon me at your earliest convenience. 'Tis urgent.*

Urgent? Something Thea might assist with?

After scant hours of fitful sleep haunted by rampant curiosity, not to mention persistent recollections of the lusty encounter she'd just indulged in, Thea awoke without an answer. How exactly did one respond to such a note?

She debated and deliberated, paused and pondered.

In the end, she sent Buttons to deliver the other two, asking that he come back straightaway, determined to have decided before his swift feet brought him home.

Simply put, invited or not, Thea couldn't bring herself to show up at the woman's house, and she was reluctant to ask Sarah's advice. Thea was positive one *never* contacted the well-born sister of one's titled protector, but assumed, as with tinkering with Mr. Hurwell's cuckoo clocks, 'twould be easier to ask for penance than permission.

And perhaps, Lady Elizabeth enjoyed writing as much as her brother?

Lady Wylde—

Was that the proper address? Once upon a time, Thea's mother had begun teaching Thea all she'd learned from finishing school, manners and etiquette and how to address those with titles, but the lessons had ceased when Mama became ill and crossed over to another existence.

Much worse than an incorrect salutation, what if the note was delivered to Lady Elizabeth's husband first? Mr. Hurwell always insisted upon reading and approving any correspondence Thea sent or received, likely why she'd lost touch with her few remaining friends shortly after her marriage. She'd wondered more than once whether her letters even made it across the threshold.

Best assume prying eyes might, well...*pry*.
All right then...

Lady W—

If it is not overly presumptive, I would request that you visit me at your convenience. Since you indicated this was a matter of some urgency, I will endeavor to remain home for the next three days

Or should that be two days? That trip to Seven Dials Thea kept putting off weighed on her; her rent might be paid through the following weekend, but who knew whether Grimmett would honor it?

the next ~~three~~ *two days (in their entirety) and you may call at your leisure. My household tends to rise early, so do not fear*

"Thea," she gritted out between clenched teeth, shaking her quill over the wordy missive and speckling it with ink, "keep it *brief*."

Ever mindful of the expense, for paper was precious regardless that it was no longer her purse making the purchase, she folded, creased, and then carefully ripped the page free of her ink-blotched blathering.

Lady W—

Please call upon me at your convenience. Any day or time this week is agreeable.

T.H.

"Ma'am?"

As well he might, Buttons looked startled by her request upon his return.

Thea strove to appear calm and in full possession of her faculties. "Aye. This one is intended for Lady Wylde, Lord Tremayne's sister." Buttons just kept staring and Thea's lips kept flapping. "If it helps, I met her last night and she asked *me* to *call* on her. I'm sending this instead." Thea thrust the labored-over note into his safekeeping.

Diffident now, he nodded. "O' course. Know jus' where she's at, not that you need bother explaining your actions to *me*. I'm just your humble servant."

"Of course not," Thea said dryly. "You tell me that *after* I've babbled a defensive explanation."

With a wink, he was off, leaving Thea to debate anew whether she'd made the right decision.

Ah, well.

Time would tell.

Time that moved wretchedly slowly as every second seemed to expand the longer she waited for a reply. Surprisingly, it was that dot-easy missive that caused her the most unease. Would Mr. Taft remember her? Would he be willing to accommodate the unusual request?

And how many more times could she circle her small entry before wearing through the floor and finding herself instantly dropped into the kitchen? Fortunately it was not a question she'd answer today, for at just that moment, not only did her brazen cuckoo clock gong, bong, chime and chirp, but the knocker on the front door sounded. One of her notes bearing fruit, perhaps?

AFTER RECEIVING Lady Elizabeth in her sedate morning room (hoping the woman had turned a blind eye to the decor on the way), pouring tea and exchanging pleasantries, Thea thought she'd be treated to the reason for this most unusual visit.

Only Lady Elizabeth seemed more inclined to relive last night's adventure, speaking vibrantly of the ballet dancers, the opera (which was odd, given how her husband ushered her out shortly after it started), the crowds, her most "prodigiously happy brother", orreries, speeches, more on the ballet dancers...

Even when moneyed females had deigned to step into Mr. Hurwell's shop, Thea had never seen more elegant daytime attire. Clothed in a pale blue walking dress with a double layer of some fancy lacework at the bottom, Lady Elizabeth managed to look both cool and composed.

Though her visitor chattered away and appeared concerned with nothing more than light gossip and fashion (she'd just begun describing the magnificent opera dress worn by some woman Thea had never heard of), Thea couldn't help but notice the dirt smudged into her slippers and the grass stain on the edge of her double-flounced hem—and the sprig of lavender defying Lady Elizabeth's repeated efforts to tuck it neatly away in her reticule.

What secrets lurked behind the dirt-dusted slippers and speedy sentences sallying forth?

When her guest's third monologue (this one enumerating all of her brother's admirable qualities) showed no signs of abating, Thea decided to implement her newfound habit of speaking what was on *her* mind. "Pardon my boldness, but we both know you didn't come over here so expediently to talk solely of last night or your brother."

Granted the woman had been all that was amiable and affable, issuing none of the warnings or dire predictions Thea had secretly feared. *'Tis a passing fancy,* she'd dreaded hearing. *Certainly, he likes you now, but expect naught next week. Naught but him tiring of you.*

Broooohahaha-ha-ha-ha!

Demonic monsters and armor-attired mice had run amok through her dreams. Shaking off the residual trepidation, Thea implored, "Tell me, what is so vital you risk visiting a woman of disrepute?"

"Please, do not put yourself down so. You are the *perfect* person to help me with my little predicament. Well, I confess, 'tis not so little. It's grown to epic proportions over the last few days, becoming a most Dire Dilemma."

"Whatever it is I shall provide whatever assistance I can."

"Oh," Lady Elizabeth exhaled on a gust. "I knew I could depend upon you! 'Tis a simple matter really..."

"Aye?" Thea prompted when no more was forthcoming.

"Teach me how to be a mistress."

As though a flood of mud clogged her hearing, thickened her tongue and sludged her breathing, Thea slowly enunciated, "You...would...like...*me*...to...do...what?"

Lady Wylde didn't fidget, didn't demure. Her feet remained firmly on the floor, hands folded in her lap. She presented a serene, dignified manner that on the surface appeared everything that was proper. And when she spoke, her words were clear as glass. "Mrs. Hurwell. Thea." But her cheeks bloomed like a rose. "I need you to tell me, precisely, how to go about being a mistress. A spectacular one."

Once Thea quit laughing (which took rather awhile) she attempted, as delicately and decisively as possible, to explain this wasn't exactly a position she'd held long, nor one in which she claimed prodigious experience. "Truly, I am muddling through one encounter at a time."

"But you must be doing it right! I've never seen Daniel so relaxed, so buoyant."

"I'm tickled to hear it, but—"

"There must be *someone* we can ask," Lady Elizabeth said earnestly as though discussing how to cultivate loose sexual behavior was as humdrum as hemlines. "Someone you know who can give me lessons. Pointers. Guidelines." Now she was beginning to lose her polish, as her words came faster and more frantic. "Or just a vague indication of how to behave in a sultry and alluring manner. I'm not overly particular but I need assistance, I tell you! Instruction so I can seduce my husband before he wanders!"

And then the whole story spilled out—how Lady Elizabeth's husband expected *her* to be his mistress (else he'd find another, or so Thea gathered, secretly thinking the man's methods seemed rather sweet but keeping her opinion to herself as Lady Elizabeth's agitation grew).

Eventually Thea rose and placed a calming hand on the other woman's shoulder. "Never fear, we'll find someone," she assured with pure bravado because she'd just recalled Sarah was away from London, visiting family. *Think, Thea!*

She straightened and began to pace. Who—

When the lavender spike peeking out from Lady Elizabeth's reticule again caught her attention, she no longer had to feign confidence, a pair of stockings that exact color flashing through her mind. "I have it. I know just the person! She's young but enthusiastic."

At the pronouncement, Lady Elizabeth's face noticeably brightened, then turned a bit puzzled. "Enthusiastic? About…"

"Sex," Thea said plainly, hoping Buttons knew how to direct her new coachman to wherever Anna and, by association she'd learned the night of Sarah's party, Susan resided.

"THAT WAS POORLY DONE, Dan. Poorly done indeed. The way you treated Everson's boy Tom was abominable! *You let me down.*"

Those were Penry's greeting words, delivered like a death knell, when he walked into Daniel's study after Rumsley showed him in.

After his cryptic note and absence, Daniel had expected to hear from him eventually—either an explanation or the requesting of one. But he'd assumed it would come by letter-bearing footman.

Penry had an aversion to dog drool, something he'd admitted after Cy sniveled over and ruined his second pair of buckskins. And since Daniel had an aversion to visiting any abode with six chirping women in residence, the man's friendship was maintained primarily through correspondence, bouts at Jackson's, and the rare meet at their club.

"Braving Cyclops," Daniel mused, as Penry barreled toward him where he sat at his desk. When his visitor reached it, instead of taking a chair, Penry remained standing, breathing fire. Daniel tilted his head to make eye contact. "Damn. Must be important in-d-d-*deed*."

"Right, it's important, you insolent pup," Penry roared. "I would have been here sooner, much sooner, else for those blasted offers. And tears—buckets of them! They cry if they don't call, they cry if too many do and now— But no, let me not quibble about like a nagging woman.

"I can't stay long," Penry grated out, indignation expanding his chest. "Have an appointment with one of the bucks angling after Eliza. Then there's the committee vote this afternoon."

Penry paused and glanced down, took another, evaluating, look at Daniel's face. "That was accommodating of you—I see you let someone do my job for me and throttle you senseless."

"Let?"

"Come now, we both know no one gets in that many jabs against you unless you allow it. Nevertheless, Dan"—his eyes narrowed to slits and it wouldn't have surprised Daniel to see smoke coming from his ears—"that haughty air you cultivate to avoid others sometimes works to your detriment, if you would but see it! Everson thinks you do not like him."

Startled by that, Daniel protested. "I like him fine. B-better than most." Especially now.

"When are these blamed things going to wind down?" Penry gestured toward the rotating mechanisms abounding at the moment. Trying to come to grips with his recent revelation regarding his mistress—and his *feelings* toward said mistress, Daniel had paced his study, winding up and starting every orrery he owned; the functioning models that was, his prime machine still limped along sadly in the center of the room.

After getting them all going, he'd lounged in his chair to enjoy the show.

"Maggots, one and all!" Penry frowned at a sprightly, spinning tabletop unit as though it were responsible for every unwanted gentleman caller he'd suffered that week. "Distracting as hell!"

Daniel remained silent. Let Penry get it all out; he'd obviously stewed himself into a frenzy.

"Fine! Don't answer me but I'll not leave without telling you this—that boy you disillusioned—he near idolizes you. Has since the Dover match back in oh eight. He was eleven, Dan, *eleven* when he saw you then. Think, man! As far back as that, Tom wanted to make your acquaintance and his father put him off. I told Everson to bring him around Jackson's more than once but you know what he said?"

Daniel opened his mouth to explain how he'd already taken care of things but Penry was on a roll that showed no signs of slowing. "Dammit! He said he respected you too much to spring Thomas on you and didn't want to offend you by asking. Offend you, by God, by *asking* you to meet his boy!" Penry shoved Cyclops away when a clear line dribbled from the side of his smiling mouth, causing a dark spot to appear near Penry's knee.

"I was wrong."

Penry hadn't heard him, was too caught up in his own ire. "Damn you, Dan. I know how they wronged you—I saw it, lived through watching it, which was deuced bad enough. I cannot imagine how it tore you to pieces. But they're gone now, Robert and your father. They're gone. And you're turning into them!"

His blow delivered, Penry glared at him in the echo of the ticking orreries. Had Daniel been kindling, he knew he would've ignited.

Cy barked, filling in the silence.

"Now compose your thoughts." Penry took a few agitated steps. "You're not getting rid of me until I hear something sensible from you—and I'm not talking about *how* you talk, but what you say."

"I know." His murmur went unheard because Penry called for Cyclops and tossed a rag to the other side of the room.

Things must be dire indeed if Penry would stoop to playing with his dog. Daniel pushed back from his desk and went to them.

"I know," he said again, louder. "Agree with everything you say. T-Tom—he's worse off than I ever was, but in ways that count, he's b-better. B-because of his family. Because of Everson. I'm jealous."

"Then go tell him that." Penry threw the toy again. Cy bounded after it (as much as his lazy hide could bound), thrilled with his new playmate. "If anyone would understand your need for privacy, it's them."

He started to tell his friend it was all taken care of, but as it was the first time Penry had ever laid into him—outside the ring—Daniel chose to keep silent. Let Penry think he'd changed Daniel's mind, convinced him how to proceed.

Lord knew it was flattering to be taken to task by someone who cared. Someone who did it without cruelly cutting words or slashing canes. "I will. Soon."

Yesterday, in fact, Daniel thought with a secret smile.

Satisfied, Penry nodded. Then he grinned like the devil. "And now to tell you why else I came round—I've arranged a little celebration tonight. It's in your honor though no one else knows."

"Celebration?" For today's upcoming speech? "I haven't d-done anything yet. Who knows if it will b-be successful?"

"As to that, who cares? This is Wylde's cause. I'm just in on it to annoy the hell out of Bolden." Cy barked happily when Penry circled the rag over his head before flinging it to the side. "I swear he cheated that time he won my greys off me. For tonight, I'm celebrating you—this is the first time you've ventured putting yourself on any public stage, no matter how small, and I'm proud of you. It's about damn time you quit hiding behind your desk or these planets." Penry flicked a tiny turquoise Earth that had clicked to a standstill.

When Cy dropped the rag at his feet, Penry bent to toss it again. Straightening, he glanced at his pocket watch. "I really need to— Hell, Eliza's buck can stew," he said, coming over to take one of the seats flanking the desk.

Eyes lit with an unholy light, Penry imparted, "I saw fit to organize another shadow play. Know how much you like them. Donaldson found a new female—some chit over from Germany, I think. Must be, goes by the name *Fräulein* Wunderbar Oberschenkel, if you can believe it."

Rather than correct his friend (it was Louise who'd favored that particular style of entertainment, not Daniel) and relieved the harangue was over, he walked back to his desk, settling in the companion chair. In *front* of the desk, not behind it, though he suspected Penry might still be too worked up to notice—only for altogether different reasons now.

Penry was grinning, almost daring Daniel to try and pronounce that mouthful. Wunderbar Oberschenkel? He knew better. "Which means...?"

"Best I can gather, it's something like Miss Splendid Thighs."

That brought a much-needed laugh. "What? Does she p-perform tricks with them? Like...pick up...grapes?"

"Now wouldn't that be something! I haven't heard any particulars, other than the name is well earned, but I can't wait to find out. Can you imagine what type of show she must put on?"

Envisioning the possibilities, Daniel's loins started to grow heavy—but only for half a heartbeat. How could he expose Thea to something so tawdry? In truth, his own interest wasn't nearly as keen as it would have been a fortnight ago.

He might want to do tawdry things with his pretty mistress, but that didn't mean he wanted others knowing about them. Didn't mean he wanted to debauch her in public.

It was one thing if *he* showed her carnal pleasures beyond the norm; quite another if she learnt them elsewhere. But how to bow out gracefully?

As if he didn't already have enough weighing on him, the memorized lines in front of him, the *lack* of Thea tonight, the—

That was it!

Daniel shook his head with feigned regret. "Cannot. Thea's not available tonight."

"Not available?" Penry looked incredulous. "Don't let that

stop you! She's your mistress, man, put her in her place. As to that, Sarah's off visiting her sister and you can be assured I'll still be there."

"To watch?"

When Cy nudged his knee, Penry pushed him away. "Or participate if *Fräulein* Wunderbar looks as wonderful as her namesake."

Participate? Daniel frowned. "What of Sarah?"

A snort came from Penry's direction. "What of her? She's comely and accommodating and I've rewarded her well for it. But it's not as if she's my wife. Furnishing that new house of hers set me back a coin or two, I tell you, so she's got nothing to complain about."

Cy whined at the loss of his playmate. Daniel snapped his fingers, calling the dog to him.

"I've been with her going on four years now. The old prick's getting peevish..." Penry rubbed his hands together like a lecher. Not an image that sat well with Daniel. "I've got to get my turn on the comely *fräulein*. Just the thought of taking a ride on those splendid thighs..."

Penry kept talking, and with every word, Daniel's inner disquiet grew. *It's not as if she's my wife.*

Penry's wife. A woman he left at home so he could ramble about with Sarah...

Sarah, who'd introduced Daniel to Thea.

Daniel sank his fingers in Cy's slathered-upon jowls, scratched for all he was worth. Loyalty. Shouldn't it be rewarded?

Loyalty. Faithfulness.

Never would he consider attending such a debauched event on his own—without Thea. To watch, much less participate.

So he declined. Suffered through Penry's vocal objections and declined again.

Bother it. Penry refused to listen, had some chaw bacon idea that Daniel had to attend or 'twould all be for naught.

"Will. *Halt*," Daniel thundered, finally gaining the other man's silence with his rarely used given name. "G-go. Enjoy. B-but 'twill be without me."

"Fine," Penry huffed, heading toward the door with a disparaging shake of his head. "'Tis your loss."

Damn. This visit might have begun with Penry announcing his displeasure with Daniel, but it was ending the opposite—with Daniel regarding his longtime friend with new eyes.

Had Penry always been this callous toward the women in his life?

Or was Daniel's relationship with Thea causing him to see things differently?

———⊷∘⊶———

THOUGH BUTTONS HADN'T KNOWN EXACTLY where Lord Harrison stashed his ladybird, he had known who to ask, and so it was a mere forty minutes later that the two women were shown to a sunny little parlor bedecked with flowers and lemon tarts and an effusively smiling Susan.

Anna was out with Lord Harrison, leaving Susan in place as "Mistress of the Manor" she told them with a laugh as they gingerly took seats on the brocade couch she indicated and just as gingerly divulged the purpose of their visit.

"Really now? You two ladies want me to teach you how to be a mistress?" Thea noticed her H's were flowing much more smoothly. "If that don't beat a rug! I was just thinking the other day about writing a pamphlet on that very topic."

As she spoke, Susan very carefully poured tea for all three of them (Thea was still marveling at being called a *lady* and being lumped in the same category with Lady Elizabeth, however erroneous).

"'Course, it would help a heap if I knew my letters and could write." Susan laughed a tad self-consciously. She settled herself upon the remaining chair, with tea in hand and little finger daintily extended.

"I'll teach you," Lady Elizabeth promised quickly. "Or pen the pamphlet for you under your direction if you prefer, only please, tell me everything you can about how to be a mistress, a good one. And quickly. I don't know how much longer his patience will hold out."

"'E's not treating you rough, is 'e?" Susan dropped her effort at gentility and did a remarkable impression of a gnarler, barking an alarm. "I don't 'old with no man treating 'is mistress bad."

"No! Nay!" Thea's companion practically shouted in her determination to defend her mate (a good sign, Thea thought). "Nothing such as that, I promise. Losing patience with me...sexually"—Lady Elizabeth whispered the last word as though to speak it at full volume might tarnish her tongue —"not physically. 'Tis simply that I don't want him turning elsewhere for carnal companionship, not if I can help it."

Reassured, Susan gulped her tea down to porcelain. With a clack, she returned her cup to its saucer; a clatter and the saucer met the tray. "Can't make no guarantees you understand, men will be men, but I believe I can help you out much as anyone could."

"Thank heavens." Lady Elizabeth placed her untouched tea silently on the tray. "Please, share whatever you will."

"To keep him from *wanting* to stray, you must convince him how much you like havin' *carnal* relations with him." Susan latched on to the phrase with a twinkle. "Now some gents are going to ply their plow in multiple pastures no matter how hard you try to lock the gate, but if yours asked *you* to be his mistress, why 'tis obvious that priggin' others ain't in his plans."

"Ah-ah," Thea interjected when she heard Lady Elizabeth choke back a gasp. "Mayhap 'prigging' isn't the best term to use in this situation. Have you another descriptor?"

"His tiller doesn't seek to venture into other pastures, aye? 'E's content with planting fields close to home. 'Ow's that?"

Though she thought perhaps Susan was getting her nautical ships, garden plots and masculine shafts confused, Thea didn't have the heart to correct her, not again. "I think we can all agree that to be a correct assumption."

"But *how* do I prevent pasture straying or his tiller drifting elsewhere?" Lady Elizabeth cried in a frustrated tone. "I've no notion at all. No understanding of what he *expects* of me. Especially when more experienced fields lie *everywhere*."

"Don't let that bother you none. 'Experienced' might just mean more practiced at falsifying whether he's any good at it."

"I don't quite grasp your meaning."

As though it were knowledge *everyone* possessed, Susan explained, "*Pretending*, Lady Wylde. Really good mistresses know how to feign it with conviction."

"Feign what?"

"How much you're enjoying their cock in your cu—"

"Susan!" Thea gave her head a sharp shake, indicating *that* particular language was well beyond the pale.

Nodding sagely, Susan corrected herself. "Enjoying their penis in your privates." She glanced at Thea, gauging the suitability of her substitution.

Thea smiled her approval, barely masking a very unladylike laugh.

This was delightful. Horrible that Lady Elizabeth felt the need for such assistance, but a positive delight that Thea was, remarkably, in a position to provide education, even in a roundabout way.

And if she happened to benefit from today's lesson? Well then, all the better.

"All right then," Lady Elizabeth said decisively. "Teach me how to fake it. I shall endeavor to be the most convincing mistress in all of England!"

"Wait." That plan troubled Thea. "Does this mean you *don't* enjoy, ah...feeling Lord Wylde *there*?" she managed to ask without putting herself to too terrible a blush.

Lady Elizabeth's gaze bounced around the room while she answered. "I thought I did. Enjoyed it, that is. Or at least I believe I was coming to but then— Well..."

When she trailed off and showed no signs of continuing, Susan took over. "Lady Wylde?"

Red as a cherry, Lady Elizabeth looked back at Susan. "Aye?"

"I believe mayhap we're comin' at this from the wrong side."

"How do you mean?"

Susan thought for a moment. Then she toed off her slippers, brought her legs to the chair beneath her voluminous skirts and leaned forward, elbows to her knees. Looking anything but a mistress, she proposed, "Let's start over with *your* expectations, shall we? With how you're approachin' his, ah...er, *plowing*."

At her hesitant nod, Susan continued. "If you like his aspects, that helps."

"His aspects?" Lady Elizabeth seemed as perplexed as Thea.

"Aye. His manly aspects, the ones beneath his breeches." When that brought no response, Susan pierced Lady Elizabeth with a blunt look. "Do you like the way 'e looks naked?"

Oh, yes, Thea couldn't help but think the answer, picturing Lord Tremayne.

"I, ahm...I..." Lady Elizabeth was having more difficulty it seemed.

"You *have* seen him in the buff, haven't you?" Susan persisted.

"I've—I've seen parts of him without clothing."

"Parts, eh? The parts you've seen, then." Susan was starting to sound exasperated. "'E's your husband and all you've seen are *parts*? Never mind, tell me—when you consider his various naked parts, do you find you want to see more?"

Every time we're together.

Lady Elizabeth's answer was to turn scarlet. And not say a word.

"His face," Susan said patiently, trying another tack, "do you like his face?"

Very much.

"Very much so."

Thea smiled.

"That's real good. How about I make it easy," Susan suggested, "give you a short list of things to work on?"

"That sounds grand. Proceed."

Ticking them off on her fingers, Susan began with gusto. "One, you cannot be afraid to show 'im what you like. Two—"

"But how?" Lady Elizabeth interrupted.

"By touchin' yourself while he watches." Susan admirably ignored the strangling sounds coming from the couch. "There's other ways but that's the easiest. Two, if it feels good, 'ave—have—fun with it. You ain't hurting nobody and who cares what the law says?"

The law?

"Three, make sure you..."

IN THE END, the Dreaded Speech was a near disaster but not a total one. Not from Daniel's viewpoint.

Penry never made it. Daniel found out later another marriage proposal for his second eldest, which resulted in jealous sisters and an elated and effusively talkative wife, delayed him. That and an untimely carriage-wheel mishap conspired to keep him far away from the committee meeting. By the time he finally showed, everyone else had gone home.

Wylde, on the other hand, at least put in an appearance. Pity it was half an hour too late.

The votes had already been tallied, the buffoon arses on the other side of the table unwilling to wait or reschedule before moving for a vote, with his brother-in-law's side coming up three short. So even had both men been present, Wylde still would have gone home disappointed. Although "disappointed" wasn't quite how the man looked... Daniel couldn't tell if that was bashfulness or brazenness filling his friend's distracted gaze, but something was definitely off. Given how intently the man had lobbied for a different outcome, his lack of anger over the result made less sense than a goat with two heads.

As for Daniel's mouth, it stammered and muttered through, hampered by the absence of its two promised and most stalwart supporters, but hearkened by his own revelation: he really didn't give a damn what these men thought about him.

In the last couple of days, he'd realized only the opinions of those *he* truly valued meant a whit. Wylde, Penry, Ellie of course. Thea (went without saying). Even Everson and Tom—possibly especially these two—had all conspired to bring the truth home: he couldn't change what was. He couldn't control how others responded or viewed him. But he could choose his friends and how he dealt with them.

He could focus his efforts on spending more time with those he liked and respected, and his energies in the direction of broadening a few more horizons. After the entertaining hours spent with the Eversons yesterday and the surprisingly pleasurable evening at the opera—with mistress *and* family— Daniel was no longer content to squirrel his life away and himself in a dark corner. No longer agreeable to avoiding every possible conversation.

But now, instead of looking forward to Thea's, at turns soothing and scintillating, company, he was expected to remain home tonight—alone? For some deuced surprise Ellie had concocted?

Devil take him!

What was the world coming to when a man had to moderate his blazing passions at the request of his *mistress*?

15

PLANETARY – AND OTHER – BODIES
COLLIDE

———◦◦◦———

"AH, MRS. HURWELL." Mr. Taft greeted Thea with a warm and relieved expression that evening moments after her clock *dinged* ten times. Refusing to remove his raindrop-speckled greatcoat, he addressed her from just inside the door. "I despaired over finding you at home and receiving, but I only now arrived at the hotel and was informed of your letter. Thank goodness you included your direction. I'm leaving for home early tomorrow—it's my grandson's tenth birthday. Can't miss that, now could I?"

"Of course not," she said automatically, glancing at Buttons who'd let in the renowned clockmaker as Mr. and Mrs. Samuels had already retired.

Upon returning from her excursion with Lady Wylde, Thea had indulged in a thorough washing and donned one of the new ensembles Madame V had graciously delivered while Thea was out.

The dressmaker had sent round two simple day dresses,

both cut down from ones she'd brought the day before, along with matching slippers. The message accompanying the package instructed Thea to present herself Monday morning for fittings on several others.

This gown was much more to her liking than the fancy, false-fronted one of last evening. In the Grecian style, caught up beneath her breasts with a jade ribbon, the pastel green cambric trimmed with a single layer of ecru lace pleased her immensely.

In it, she actually *felt* like a real lady for once, which was the only reason she was still up and attired when her late-evening visitor came calling.

But as Mr. Taft finished his smiling greeting—after expressing his pleasure at seeing her again and his regret at needing to leave at first light—he baffled her thoroughly with his next words. "If you're agreeable and think he won't be overly inconvenienced by the hour, don your winter gear and we'll go visit your Lord Tremayne and see if we can fix his orrery right up."

We? "Now?"

"Of course, my dear. You don't expect me to call upon the man without your chaperonage?" He laughed good-naturedly. "A little above my station, wouldn't you say? But I'm pleased as a pickle to see you've picked up such a lofty suitor. Hate to hear Hurwell's gone but glad you've moved on."

He thought Lord Tremayne was courting her?

Well, shear her like a Suffolk sheep!

Couldn't he tell? That in truth she was Lord Tremayne's kept woman? His strumpet?

Her panicked gaze flicked to the nude portraits. But they were gone, replaced by a waterfall on one side and a close-up of songbirds on the other. Knowing she'd just heard clocks chime, she looked for the sinfully suggestive cuckoo, but the wall was blank. The figurines were missing as well, the only thing gracing her crimson table runner was the silver tray and a vase of fresh, peppy flowers.

Startled, she turned to Buttons, who still stood unobtrusively to one side. Noticing what she was about (no doubt aided by her levitating eyebrows), he pointed directly overhead. *Master chamber* he mouthed and her heart rate settled down from its rapid-fire pace.

Courting me? Thea mouthed back because it seemed as good a way to communicate as any. Buttons shrugged, then nodded, as though uncertain how to correct the erroneous assumption but still offering both support and encouragement.

When the clockmaker again urged her toward the door, Thea finally acquiesced.

It looked as though she and Mr. Taft would be paying her protector a call. Thea forbore from calling on the Almighty to deliver her from this mess. She'd made her naughty bed and enjoyed rolling around in it; now wasn't the time to turn squeamish.

IN MOMENTS, they were rolling swiftly through the wet streets, the jagged lightning in the distance protesting her subterfuge. Buttons had squeezed in next to the driver after whispering to Thea that he'd try to make sure "his lordship got the drift of things".

While Mr. Taft reminisced fondly of his past trips to London and Thea answered appropriately if distractedly, one thought kept her seated and not running for the sanctuary of her just-departed townhouse: she'd learned from Lord Tremayne's sister that he wasn't married.

Thank God and chatty relations for that tidbit. It was one

thing to show up on his doorstep; quite another to be confronted with his unsuspecting, betrayed wife.

———————◦○◦———————

BORED WITH EVERYTHING he'd tried (obsessed with his new mistress, more like) Daniel decided to retire at half past ten.

In his shirtsleeves after more tinkering with one of his working orreries, ironically *slowing* the rotation of Uranus on this particular specimen (darn planet put all the others to shame with its snail's crawl of an eighty-plus year orbit of the Sun), he was just leaving his study and approaching the stairs that led up to his bedchamber when the door knocker clanged.

Who would be calling at this hour?

Frowning, he started down the stairs instead. He'd ordered Rumsley to bed when he found out his butler's gout was acting up again. John had stepped out with Ellie's maid a while ago, after seeing whether Daniel needed anything or wanted him to remain on duty. He'd sent his footman off with his blessing. At least one of them could be with their lady tonight.

The door knocker banged again, and he descended the last few treads at a run before his quiet household was further disturbed by the racket.

He swung the heavy door wide and about choked on his own spit. Surprise warred with astonishment.

"Thea!" On his doorstep and with some spry, grey-haired fellow.

Thea, the guilt in her eyes not enough to temper his pleasure at seeing her. Despite the stormy night, she fairly sparkled in the pelisse he'd given her. Thea was right—the sleeves were overly long. She worried one with several bare fingers while her other hand simply trembled, her arm crooked around that of her companion.

"Thea," he said again, dumbly. Numbly. What was she doing here? At his home? And why did the notion, instead of annoying him as it certainly would have with Good-Riddance-Former Mistress, only seem perfect because it was Thea?

"Mrs. Hurwell?" The elderly fellow smiled at them both. "Is this your Lord Tremayne? And answering his own door?"

Mrs. Hurwell?

It sounded all wrong. How he'd started to hate that name. It wasn't right, not at all.

It should be Mrs. Holbrook, Lady Tremayne.

His lady. And he should swell her trim belly with child.

A child they'd both love whether he or she stammered or whistled or came out plaid.

"My lord." She raised one hand as though to ward him off and Daniel shook himself free of the fantasy with a strangled sound. When had all the air evaporated from his entryway?

"Please forgive our late and unannounced arrival," she began, and shot a worried look over her shoulder. A flash of lightning illuminated Swift John hovering protectively behind her. "This is Mr. Taft. I was given to understand you desired to hear him speak but that your favor for Lord Wylde prevented it."

At the introduction, the other man leaned forward and caught sight of Daniel's bruised phiz (Ellie had yet to deliver that requested batch of cream). "My gracious, my lord. I do hope the other fellow looks worse."

"Lord Tremayne is a pugilist," Thea explained to her companion while somehow managing to shoot Daniel a private glare that would have smote a lesser man than he. But still, he heard the pride in her voice as she defended him.

Him! For childishly fighting to avoid the demons of his past.

Was she an angel, perhaps? An angel masquerading as a mistress? One sent to rescue him from all his demons?

Her subdued voice went on, something about timing and birthdays, but all Daniel heard were her lilting tones. All he saw was the woman never far from his thoughts. All he wanted was to snatch her up and escape with her to his chambers.

As the man beside her chimed in, Daniel finally grasped all they were saying.

This was Mr. Taft, famed orrery expert, who had somehow concluded that Daniel was a suitor for the hand of his mistress. Which would be comical if it wasn't so close to the truth.

Which also explained why Thea looked so miserably guilty and kept trying to edge back. (If it wasn't for Taft's fatherly patting of her hand upon his forearm, she might have succeeded.)

Mr. Taft, offering to help fix Daniel's machine. The very machine his grandfather had consulted with Taft about back in the 1770s.

This was Ellie's surprise?

And it brought Thea to his doorstep?

More than a bit in awe of the older man, never mind that he resembled a grinning, grey-tufted elf, Daniel felt his jaw tightening characteristically. Manners bade he recall himself sufficiently to usher them in.

"P-please," he cleared his throat, praying they hadn't noticed the slip, "come in, b-both of you."

Damn! Was it nerves that made it so bad? Taft's presence? Or Thea's? Or was he simply overly tired after the disappointing showing at the committee meeting?

Taft was waiting for Thea to precede him, but like a giant, unmovable oak, she appeared rooted in place.

"Thea?" Daniel stepped outside and forcibly shepherded her across the threshold. She gave him a grateful look. Weighted with more guilt.

Using the excuse of helping her with her pelisse, he whispered in her ear. "'Tis fine, really. I'm—" *Pleased. Delighted. Blighted by your beauty.* "Stay with my—blsng." *Blessing* got smothered against her nape when he took advantage of the situation to press his lips to her soft, sweet skin. To inhale her unique and calming fragrance. Essence of Thea.

When his lips lingered, he swore she gave a silent moan and leaned into him. Then she nodded, straightening as she pulled her arm from the long sleeve, only to reveal a delightful new dress. He smiled his approval, reluctant to release her, but beyond curious about this unforeseen visit.

AFTER LORD TREMAYNE asked a single question about that afternoon's lecture he'd missed, which started Mr. Taft on a whirlwind of excited explanations, the men headed up the staircase.

Buttons nudged Thea.

She left off staring at the opulent chandelier overhead. "Aye?"

"Go on with you," Buttons told her in a low voice. "Look there—" He nodded toward the stairs. "His lordship's waiting for you."

He was, standing stalwart and strong, gaze intense, hand outstretched. And that's when she noticed his attire. Clothed the most casually she'd ever seen him—save for in her bedchamber—his thick hair was finger-tousled, linen shirt billowing and dark breeches thigh-hugging. No tailcoat. No waistcoat. Neckcloth loose, practically cast aside.

Though he stood there, beckoning to her, she had the uncanny feeling the tiled marble floor she stood on was flinging energy spikes through her slippers and straight up her legs, spikes that loudly proclaimed *You don't belong here. You don't belong!*

Lord Tremayne's townhouse put hers to shame. Everything around her exuded tasteful elegance on the grandest of scales. This townhouse could swallow her entire abode several times over—and that was just for the appetizer.

But it was the man himself who created the longing to stay.

The man with the discolored face and charming smile, the broad shoulders subdued by nothing more than quality linen. The man whose quiet but decisively spoken, "Thea?" tamed those condemning floor spikes into ones of *Welcome.*

The motion concealed by her long dress, she stamped her feet. Yet still, it came again: *Welcome.*

Flashing Buttons a grateful smile, she climbed the stairs after them, glad more than ever for her new dress when Lord Tremayne took stock of it and nodded as she came abreast. "Lovely."

That was all he said. But 'twas enough to have her heart galloping in response. She could repent or regret tomorrow; tonight she intended to collect every glimpse of the inner man Lord Tremayne deigned to share.

"'Tis a beauty!" Mr. Taft exclaimed upon entering the study, going unerringly to the largest orrery in the room. Five or six feet across, it was easily higher than her waist. By far the biggest one Thea had encountered, all of her previous experience being with the miniature clock-top models and an occasional tabletop orrery.

"I'd seen the plans on her," Mr. Taft continued, "but not the finished apparatus. She fulfilled her design and then some. What seems to be the problem with her, my lord?"

"Uranus," Lord Tremayne said succinctly, following Mr. Taft over to the piece while she remained just inside the open door, ready for a quick escape should one prove necessary. "Refuses to or...bit."

"Well then, it's our duty to practitioners of astrolatry everywhere to get her running smoothly, is it not?" While Mr. Taft reached the device and started evaluating the individual planets and parts as he might a hotly desired horse at auction, she worked to puzzle out the meaning of the unfamiliar word. *Astro* was easy: celestial or heavenly bodies. *Latry* had her stumped, until with a mental snap she recalled idolatry and quickly deduced Mr. Taft referenced enthusiastic sky-watchers, worshipers of heavenly objects.

After investigating the orrery's perimeter, he bent to peer into the central shaft where all the planetary orbits originated. "Have you trouble with any others? Or do they all run like clockwork, heh?"

Lord Tremayne smiled at his jest. "Just Uranus. B-b—" He coughed into his hand. "Finished in seventy-eight, you see."

"Ah. That explains it."

Explains what? Thea wanted to venture but was hesitant to speak, hesitant to draw attention to herself. No matter what his eyes and actions conveyed, breaching the home of one's protector was ill-advised—if not an outright hanging offense. *The Mistress Code of Expected Behavior* Susan and Lady Wylde planned to pen was surely catching fire at Thea's brazenness.

Seeing a yawning dog emerge from beneath a huge mahogany desk, she relinquished her post to make her way to one of the large chairs near it. She perched on the edge but the leather was so very comfortable, she found herself sinking right in. She held out her hand and was rewarded when the big canine sniffingly advanced.

"You must be Cyclops, hmmm, boy?" she whispered to the ugliest dog she'd ever seen, one eye vacant, muzzle scarred and askew, drool drizzling from one side of his jaw. Nevertheless, there was something endearing in the way he nuzzled her thigh and pushed his head under her hand, not content until she was scratching everywhere she could reach.

When she approached the underside of his chin, she swore the dog purred. She giggled to herself. He angled his head and gave a happy, slobbering bark, and Thea couldn't help but cringe when she noticed they'd unintentionally captured the men's attention.

So she braved speaking up. "What does seventy-eight explain?"

"Uranus was discovered in 1781, a handful of years after this beauty was built," Mr. Taft told her, arms wide as though he'd hug the huge, broken contraption if he could. "Thought it was a comet at first, but the scientists of the day soon put that to rights. I can just imagine after all the effort put into this darling how its creator would be vexed beyond reckoning to miss out on the greatest astronomical discovery in his lifetime."

When she nodded with interest, he continued, his enthusiasm for his topic growing. "The planets through Saturn were discovered back in ancient times, you see. For centuries, nothing so exciting has been identified so conclusively. And now she has us to set her to rights!" Taft fairly glowed at the challenge.

"Aye," Lord Tremayne confirmed, touching a gentle fingertip to the bright blue ball representing Uranus.

A faraway look came into his eyes as he skimmed his fingers over the longest arm. The light touch was at odds with the hardness she glimpsed in his flexing jaw, the growing tension she sensed emanating from him. Perhaps he realized the absurdity of having his mistress occupy his study, and with a witness he so obviously respected?

She shifted, tempted to flee all over again. But just then Cyclops closed his eye and sighed, nestling his head heavily upon her lap.

"WAS ADDED THEN," Daniel forced out. "Worked." His bloody neck was starting to seize up on him. He wanted to howl, or at least curse his blighted mouth. Instead he ungritted his teeth and tried to explain. "Then stored. A-b-bu-*bandoned*."

Son of a bitch!

"Difficulty getting the words out, my lord? Just take your time." Smiling serenely, the man gave Thea an understanding look during this little speech—the speech that threatened to destroy Daniel's composure if not his life. "I'm in no hurry, not when in the company of such a magnificent specimen and people who appreciate her."

While Daniel felt his world tilt on its axis, sensed more than saw the rigidity that came into Thea's posture, the way she quickly turned from stroking Cy to studying them, Taft blithely carried on. "My uncle was the same way. Got tripped up by stubborn letters now and then..."

Goddammit, why now? Just when he'd started to believe *he* could tell her, could admit his weakness and it might not condemn him back to silence, might not mean the immediate end of what they shared.

But he'd thought to tell her *his* way, in his own time. Perhaps next month, after getting her bosky on fine brandy or sauced on wine. Or next year, after getting her with child—

Good God? Where had that come from? On the heels of his earlier thoughts too. Damn him. Twice in one night he thought to impregnate her?

A child wasn't a pawn. Wasn't, in truth, anything he'd ever thought about before, not in relation to *his* fathering one. But he imagined it *now*? When the sun had exploded and blackness crashed in around him?

Nay, he only sought to hold on to the woman he loved, to keep her by his side—and in the dark about his defect—a little (or a lot) longer.

Daniel didn't have to look at Thea to see how still she'd gone. How alert. How her eyes no doubt narrowed with suspicion when all he could do was keep his gaze fixed on the planet he no longer saw and jerk a nod, agreeing with his idol that he was a clodpated ninnyhammer.

His hand slipped. The gears pinched, then severed his skin. "D-damn."

Hah. How the universe mocked and laughed. He couldn't even get that out, a single swearword?

Couldn't even split his finger and drip blood on his precious orrery without becoming a stammering fool?

"Got you, eh?" Taft commiserated as Daniel whipped out a handkerchief and wrapped it around his finger. Taft was already blotting the crimson smear off the brass. "No matter how much I profess to love them, these orrery rascals have a way of biting back, especially the worthwhile ones."

"Aye." It came out a curse.

"It was the same for my uncle," Taft went on, oblivious to the interstellar explosion he'd just set off in Daniel's stomach. "Hated having to talk in public or meet new people."

And that did it. Nailed him in his coffin as surely as an undertaker. But Taft wasn't finished yet. 'Course not. He just wanted to dig those nails in a little deeper. "Probably why he was so good with mechanics. Screws and such don't talk back, eh, my lord?" He followed up this pithy pronouncement with a heartfelt sigh. "He's the one who fostered my interest in clockworks and orreries, you know. Smartest man I ever knew, my uncle. Miss him terribly."

Smartest man he knew?

There was that, at least.

Daniel had two choices: halt their efforts and deal with Thea—assuming she stayed long enough to let him—or carry on with the plaguingly perceptive man who had troubled himself to come lend aid.

What he refused to do was run away. Hide from the truth any longer, no matter how nauseous he felt, now that it was out.

Breathing through his nose with every bit of control he could exert, Daniel told himself this was his house, his study, his broken orrery, his mistress... Oh God, it was his *everything*. In vain he tried to muster courage where none existed. A fruitless effort. It had fled.

But he refused to let his mind do the same. There would be no pretending this wasn't happening, no cloud-hopping escape to avoid the pain of the whip. Nay, it was time he took a stand. Brave whatever censure might come his way without hiding in the corner as he'd been taught by the lash.

Though it took more nerve than stepping into a ring with the beefiest of opponents, Daniel broke free from the coffin and nailed his feet in place. He swallowed twice, still without looking at Thea. "For me, 't-twas my grandfather."

"Your grandfather, eh?"

"Aye. T-teaching me of orreries."

Taft nodded, pulled a magnifying glass from his pocket and bent closer. "Some say they're a waste of money and one's crown office." The man sniffed as though *those* people were the idiots, not smart ones like his uncle. Like Daniel. He nudged Daniel with an elbow. "But we'll show up their ignorant hides, eh? Get this sweetheart running..."

LORD TREMAYNE HAD TROUBLE SPEAKING?

Thea had forgotten to inhale. When her lungs protested, she came to with a slight choke. One she quickly muffled behind her hand, unable to stop staring at the men whose heads were bent over Uranus's arm, inspecting it from bright-blue ball to innermost gear.

After seven-plus long years with Mr. Hurwell, she'd learned to hold her tongue. She did so now, working through what it all meant.

Lord Tremayne had trouble speaking.

Which explained so much, did it not?

Why he tended to arrive later than expected; it minimized talking opportunities if he was always rushing into place at the last second.

Why their flirty letters flowed with an ease, a verbosity she'd noticed on more than one occasion was absent from their in-person interactions.

Why he spoke so very deliberately, unless they were already laughing and the mirth masked the stammer for him.

Why he never came for dinner. Never lingered once they were intimate.

Has he told you anything more? Lady Elizabeth had asked at the opera. *About himself?*

Her mind whirled, remembering stutters and stumbles she'd overlooked or deemed unimportant at the time, given the wondrous topics they'd discussed. Remembering the ticking jaw or gritted teeth, the strained tendons in his neck that usually gave way to a brief word or two. Remembering the bruises he sported, both old and new.

So, this explained his reserve, his inclination toward tardiness. Did it explain the fighting? She'd have to work on that one.

When she didn't feel so slighted.

At the moment Thea struggled with resentment. Waves of

it clogging her throat, knotting her belly. It was a simple enough difficulty to explain. Why hadn't he told her? Did he not trust her?

Oh, he trusted her with his body but not with who he was. And that hurt. Made her feel as though his lack of trust was somehow *her* fault.

But she hadn't missed how his free hand had clutched the table with a white-knuckled grip. Nor had she missed how his spine had gone stiff, his ears slightly red. How his gaze studiously avoided hers.

He knew she'd overheard. Knew his secret was out. And the information affected him mightily.

Thea chose to stay where she was. Hadn't her mother taught her that actions conveyed more of a person's character than what they said?

Thoughtful gifts, joyous letters, a safe home, friendly servants...

Cyclops huffed, upset when she stopped petting, so she applied herself to making it up to him, never mind the growing damp patch on her dress.

Stray twins (thieves, no less), fearsome, drooly dogs (but lovable for all that)...and now her? It appeared Lord Tremayne had a propensity for rescuing those in need. Thea wasn't quite sure what to make of her new philanthropic protector.

Was she just another in a long line of strays?

A few minutes later, after pulling out several intricate-looking tools from a rolled pouch he carried on his person, Mr. Taft called across the room. "Mrs. Hurwell, can you come over here, if you would? This part here needs a woman's delicate touch and smaller fingers."

"Certainly." She transferred Cyclops's muzzle to the chair and stood without meeting Lord Tremayne's gaze. There was too much unsaid between them, too many emotions roiling through her (and she couldn't even begin to fathom what *he* must be feeling). Nay, when she stared into his eyes again, they needed to be alone.

So she walked forward as normally as she could manage, keeping her gaze trained on the stately contraption. Though the room seemed to swirl and spin around her, the walls coming closer, then receding at once, the giant orrery remained a touchstone.

Lord Tremayne blurred as she approached, the floor beneath her feet pitched as though they were at sea. But the orrery stayed in sharp focus. Uranus wasn't a mere blue ball, she realized as she fought the strange sensations and closed the distance. It was a perfectly spherical carving from lapis lazuli.

How beautiful. How...ordinary.

When her entire world just kept whirling. Whirling. Like that dratted planet needed to, in order to please the man who'd given her so much.

When she reached the intimidating apparatus, she skirted round it and came up directly between the two gentlemen.

Where she reached out and found Lord Tremayne's arm. He was no longer hazy; no longer blurry. He was solid strength and quiet, gentle power. Safety *and* seduction.

He was the best thing she'd ever come into contact with, and she wasn't about to give him up.

She slid her fingers down his shirtsleeve until she could slip her hand into his. Without their audience being aware, she gave a light squeeze, mindful of the handkerchief wrapped around the cut finger, telling him without words that *she* wouldn't be the one to abandon what they'd started.

Only when Mr. Taft spoke again did she reluctantly release her hold.

"Right here." Mr. Taft indicated where he needed her assistance. "If you could just..."

———————◦◦———————

An hour later, after they'd finally coaxed Uranus to rotate as it should, in proper concert with the other six planets, and very aware of Thea's gaze boring into his back, Daniel escorted Taft out of his study.

All things considered, it had been a tolerably successful evening.

In addition to his grandfather's orrery, the three of them had also tweaked another one where Jupiter insisted on circling too fast (actually, Thea had nimbly adjusted the mechanism—after she'd wound them all up for Taft's enjoyment—while the two men looked on).

Imagine that—a mechanically minded female.

Imagine that—his childhood idol exposing his secret sins to that very female.

Imagine his surprise when she *hadn't* stared at him with derision or ridicule. No pity or sympathy either.

Just unwavering, silent support. Daniel hadn't—

"Lord Tremayne, you must forgive an old fool usually surrounded by family and used to flapping his jaws at the least provocation."

Barely three steps down the stairway, Taft launched into the most effusive of apologies. "It became apparent to me as the night wore on I'd veritably stepped in it. Oh, she tried to cover it, but 'twas obvious you'd not yet let on to Mrs. Hurwell about the speaking hesitations. Amazing, really, that you mask it so well. To get close enough to court a woman without her knowing—

"But that's neither here nor there." Upon reaching the entry, Taft stopped to draw on his coat, piercing Daniel with a sincere look of regret. "I humbly beg your forgiveness for letting my tongue tread where it had no business."

Before Daniel could grant absolution and proffer his

sincere thanks for all they'd accomplished, the man clamped his hat on his head and clapped his hands together. "Well now, seeing your collection has proved the pinnacle of my London jaunt. That and seeing Mrs. Hurwell so happy. Do please give her a chance, my lord. With the truth I mean. She's both kind and resourceful. Wouldn't have said so in her presence, but I always thought she was wasted on ol' Hurwell. Bit of a curmudgeondy fellow if you ask me."

"I agree," Daniel got out before Taft nodded politely and exited, Swift John overly eager to summon the carriage that would return the clockmaker to his hotel.

That was fast.

Just then his housekeeper bundled by. Catching sight of him, Mrs. Peterson paused with a smile and open look of inquiry. *Is there anything I can do for you?* her kindly face asked.

The woman couldn't hear a lick, which had always suited Daniel just fine. She read lips and gestures remarkably well. So it was easy to retrieve Thea's pelisse, point to a spot on the sleeve, and make a motion with his fingers. With a nod, Mrs. Peterson bustled off, pelisse in hand.

Swift John stomped back in, wiping his wet feet on the rug. "Nice gent," his footman commented, smoothing down the ever-present cowlick with a rain-slicked hand. "Friendly sort."

Daniel grunted.

What now?

Taft was gone. *But Thea isn't.*

The air expelled from his lungs so hard they ached.

"Well?" Swift John damn near clicked his heels together.

Daniel glared.

His servant ignored him and stared up the staircase, gaze fixed in the direction of Daniel's study. "So, your lordship, she's up there, is our Miss Thea…"

Our Miss Thea?

What? It wasn't enough he'd not been alone with her all day; now he was expected to share her with his servants?

Something rather akin to a growl surfaced from the depths of his chest.

The impudent servant only grinned. "Aye, up there. In *your* study. All alone. *Waiting. Fer. You.*"

Swift John couldn't have yelled *Get your cowardly arse up there!* any louder.

Where was a good opera when one needed to escape?

16

WHEREUPON THE MISTRESS BECOMES THE MASTER

Once the mistress masters masterpieces her masterful master masterfully teaches, she manifests these mastered expertises upon his masterful centerpiece with eager reaches!

Kamasutra (as translated by Thomas Edward Everson into *Adoring Arts of Luscious Love*, circa 1830s)

———◆———

THEA WASN'T QUITE sure how Mr. Taft arranged it, but he'd managed to depart—alone. *Without her!*

Oh, he'd clasped his hands to both of hers, eyes twinkling, as he expressed his delight in seeing her again ("and with you looking so radiant!"), and he'd more reservedly shaken Lord Tremayne's hand and glowed over the shared challenge—and its successful outcome...

But then he'd rendered *her* speechless when he'd secured Lord Tremayne's escort downstairs so he could take his leave after giving Thea a silent but emphatic command to stay put and see things made right, this expressed through the most regretful, and thoughtful, of looks.

Well, surprise her to Southampton and back, but she was starting to think the orrery expert was something of a magician as well. How else to explain her presence—after midnight—in the home of her beloved if bullheaded protector?

"That... Wasn't..." Lord Tremayne came through the open doorway already speaking. "Wasn't..." He stopped far away from where she tinkered with another beautiful specimen, this one more of a fantasy, showing comets and nebulae and all sorts of celestial wonders orbiting their double suns, with nary a planet in sight. Straightening, she faced him and waited.

His breath heaved from him like lava bursting from a volcano. "Find...out."

His jaw was granite, eyes like steel. His hands kept flexing into fists at his sides.

He stood there holding her gaze—the self-loathing so evident in his, she thought her heart would crack.

Despite the heaviness centered in her stomach, the fear he'd push her away now that she knew, now that they were alone, her feet suddenly sprouted wings. She rushed to him and only stopped when he put a hand out as though warding her off.

"Just say it, please," she implored, "without taxing yourself so. Whatever you think to express."

DANIEL CLOSED his eyes against the appeal in hers. "I... can...not."

"But you can with me! The difficulty you have doesn't diminish you in my eyes." Her voice grew softer even as it strengthened. She touched his arm. "Don't you see by now? Nothing could."

At that, his eyelids flew open. "I..."

Her fingers tightened on his wrist. "Except perhaps if you persist in fighting to the point your face looks like a field of wildflowers."

She sounded so like Ellie, he tried to smile. "Thea. I... I—" Tension clawed up his neck and sank talons into his throat.

Penry's morning call, the afternoon speech, utter surprise at his late-evening visitors. *Talking* with Taft the last hour. Exposing his affliction to Thea, unable to hide or avoid speaking...

He was hurting now, every bit as much as after Everson's yesterday. Mayhap more. Scraped raw, swollen, ravaged by invisible arrows—Cupid's damn arrow—he knew not which. Likely everything.

The pain was so great, if it hadn't been for all those years inuring himself against his brother's taunts, his father's beatings, Daniel would've broken down and wept.

Not an option!

He swore and broke away from Thea, marched to the first solid surface he saw—the side of a bookcase, and slammed his hand against it.

He needed distance. Needed to escape.

But he didn't *want* to.

His stinging palm hit the bookcase again as he willed his throat and neck to stop clenching. Stop punishing him.

"Stop." Thea echoed his thoughts, feathering her fingers over his jaw, his cheeks. "Stop. You've done enough for one day. I can see the strain in your neck, the fatigue in your eyes. Tomorrow is soon enough. You can explain then, all you want, and I'll gladly listen. Or later still, next week. Next month, even; I care not which. You need to rest."

She wrapped her hands around his abused one and started tugging him toward the door. "Now, Buttons is here and *could* take me home or *you* could take me to your bedchamber— Ah-ah," she admonished when he started to say something. She was making this too easy for him. "Tonight, I talk for the both of us. Personally, I would just as soon stay here. In your bed, of course. But I'm fully aware how vastly inappropriate—"

"There's nn-*no* mirror," exploded unbidden.

Color mantled her cheeks when she smiled. "Silly man," she spoke to his nicked finger, softly touching the injured spot. "I don't need a mirror to love you."

He couldn't contemplate whether she meant it literally, not now. Not when he needed to hold her so damn bad. Needed to bury his lips against the sweet skin of her neck and forget what a buffoon he'd made of himself the last hour.

With a growl loud enough to be heard in the kitchens, Daniel swung her into his arms and barreled through the doorway.

One look and a hovering Buttons was nodding—his bit-upon lips unable to stifle his grin—and running down the stairs, in the opposite direction, saying, "Aye, milord, you have it. I'll see the team gets stabled for the night and get word to Sam and his missus so they don't worry none about Miss Thea. See you in the morning an' not before!"

"HOW GRAND," Thea enthused, tucking her face in the crook of his neck as he turned toward the stairs. Up close, his divine scent could have crumbled her to her knees. Good thing he carried her.

Warming her lips against his fragrant skin, she said, "It appears as though we get to be inappropriate together." She caressed the thick hair at his nape, threading her fingers through the cool, silken strands. She couldn't help but notice the muscles of his neck beneath. "And look, you're so strong, I don't even need to hold on."

Joyfully, she kicked her feet and waved her arms as he ascended the steps. He didn't make so much as a perceptible pause. "No doubt I could roll over and try my hand at archery and you'd still hold tight."

He muttered something that sounded suspiciously like, "God save me."

"Nuh-uh, my lord," she chided gently when he reached the bedroom—not breathing a speck harder than usual—and swung her to her feet. If she entertained him sufficiently by rattling her own jaws, perhaps 'twould keep him from worrying his. "Do you forget so soon? I'm charged with all the talking tonight. You may reciprocate another time."

Not giving him leave to protest—or herself a chance to inspect his chamber, she set about the smile-worthy task of ridding them of their clothes.

A light push to his chest and she backed him to the bed. A single finger to his shoulder and he sat.

"Boots." She pointed. "Off. Now." She giggled. (Giggled? Definitely not something she'd done much of in her past.) "See? I can say a lot in a few words too."

As she stepped back to give him room, he snared her waist and hauled her to him. Slanting her mouth downward with a strong hand to the back of her head, he captured her gasp of surprise and gave her a bruisingly fierce kiss.

The pressure of his mouth upon hers said so much.

With bold sweeps of his tongue and the firm caress of his fingers against her scalp he expressed his longing. Tender nips greeted first her top lip and then the bottom. His harsh exhalation as he scraped his teeth over the sensitive flesh he exposed when he gently sucked on her lower lip told her he'd been waiting for the right moment to devour her. To explain.

His every action shouted that he was sorry, that he cared,

that he wanted her. Needed *this*. This. Whatever it was between them that defied the short amount of time they'd been together.

His hand swept down to center over one breast, to rub the slight swell, tease the nipple into an aching point. The intense pressure lifted her to her toes and into him as she toppled forward against his chest and he pulled her tongue into his mouth, as she told him, *I'm here. I need you back.*

As fast as it began, he gentled the assault. His other hand slid from her head to her spine, a sweeping caress that left tingles in its wake. The devastating kisses turned soft and romantic.

He wooed her lips into sultry surrender and the rest of her followed.

At her moan, he pulled his head back, held her gaze as his kiss-swollen mouth tilted in a not-quite smile and his palm cupped her breast even more firmly and he eased her back to her feet.

"Well now." She spoke through the passionate fog befuddling her senses. "And here you thought that would keep me quiet! Boots, sir, that's a command."

His eyes promised sensual retribution but he did as bade.

"Breeches next. Then shirt and drawers— Oh, wait!" She turned her back and scooted between his knees, thankful hers hadn't failed her—they were quivering like aspic after that swoon-worthy kiss. "Unfasten me, please? The buttons near my neck."

He did, giving her waist a deliberate squeeze before releasing her.

"Aye, I like this," she said as she untied the ribbon cinching her dress around her middle. "Like having the freedom to say whatever comes to mind without fear of being reprimanded. Mr. Hurwell was rather persnickety in that regard. Thought females didn't have the mental acumen to understand lofty topics beyond breakfast menus or starching neckcloths." She whisked away those old concerns when she whisked her dress over her head.

"My stays? If you would, please?" Again Thea came close. "Mrs. Samuels helped me earlier—" She took a breath to give his freshly revealed chest a kiss. Backing away from his warm skin, she turned and flashed him a flirty look from over her shoulder. "I much prefer it when you help. Thank you. Your drawers now—"

When she took a step away and cast an appreciative glance over his form, the part of him protruding through the fine undergarment threatened to steal her chatter. But she was made of sterner stuff; no turning shy now! "I do realize—"

He halted her rampant ramble with an upraised finger.

"Aye?"

"Why?" He spoke without hesitating although his voice had gone completely hoarse. "Why...?"

"Hurw..." The rough syllable sounded like a shovel scraping over stone.

Thea rushed to guess before he could harm himself further. "Why did he think me feebleminded?"

A frown crinkling his brow, Lord Tremayne shook his head.

She hazarded, "Why did I marry him?"

A relieved smile told her she'd hit upon it.

"I'll answer them both. The man had some odd notions. Thought too much contemplation on any subject would bring on a fever—mayhap that's why he was never sick? As to why I married him, my father and Mr. Hurwell were friends of long-standing—I gather he wasn't always so boorish," she confessed, shifting restlessly within her loose stays. "He'd asked me before, but I kept putting him off. When my father fell ill and urged me to accept, desperate to know I was taken care of, it seemed the most expedient way to secure his contentment before he passed."

Those horizontal lines in Lord Tremayne's forehead grew deeper. "Mo-ther?"

"My mama? She was a lovely and warm woman who perished when I was but eleven. From good, genteel stock, or so Papa told me. She'd been to finishing school and taught etiquette and how to trap—er, *secure* a rich and hopefully titled husband. Even a baronet would have sufficed, but she made the unpardonable sin of falling in love with a lowly shipping clerk, forever earning her family's animosity. Disowned, she was. But that was before I was born." Thea grew warm under his penetrating gaze.

"Was that a growl?" When he gave another, she stroked her fingertips down his neck. "Now I know that can't be good for your throat. Truly, Lord Tremayne, my parents were wonderful and my marriage to Mr. Hurwell wasn't *horrid*. Just horridly tedious," she assured him. "I confess, though, I'm having loads more fun with you."

He laughed at that. And gave her stays a pointed glance.

Given how he was completely bare-arsed by now, she really had no choice.

Wiggling her hips and pushing the stays down, she went back to her earlier topic, hoping the twaddle she kept spewing would cover any lingering nerves. After all, it wasn't every day she determined to seduce a gentleman.

Especially in the particular manner she *intended* to seduce him. The manner that first occurred to her after seeing the lewd and laugh-inducing cuckoo clock, the manner that beckoned even more after today's Mistress Lessons...

"I recognize I may pay for my unmitigated impertinence, taking control as I am. But alas, whether I am taken to task tomorrow or not, tonight you may not tell me 'Nay'. Not until morning light."

Fat drops of rain spattered onto the windowpane, and for the first time, she took note of the lit candles around the room, of the huge, ornate bed worthy of a king, the velvet bed hangings in a rich navy hue, the thick coverlet turned down to reveal smooth and inviting sheets. Why, the chamber appeared almost as though his servants had expected, or hoped, she'd stay the night—everything tidied and readied for seduction. Little did they know 'twas to be his!

Their surroundings bolstered her as she stepped from her stays and readied herself to remove her shift—all that remained. Hands on the bottom edge, Thea stopped to offer an apologetic look at the naked man staring at her with shining amber eyes. "One of these days—I mean nights—I do so hope to wear the extravagant night rail you gave me."

"Nnnn—" He closed his eyes as though in great pain and she didn't have the heart to chastise him, seriously or in jest. After a slow exhalation, he looked at her again. She nodded, a tiny movement meant to give encouragement or permission —or forgiveness. Mayhap all three. Whatever he needed. "Not...n-necessary."

She smiled brilliantly. "Something to anticipate, then?" He nodded and she bravely whipped off her shift. "There! Now 'tis to bed with both of us."

"Nay."

Hands to her bare hips, she frowned. "Did I not just give you orders to the contrary of expressing that particular sentiment?"

He stood, unashamed and glorious in his nakedness. Branding her with his open hand at the base of her spine, he steered her to his dresser. Upon which sat two matching boxes, each tied with a bright green ribbon. The boxes were long and slim, and when he flipped them over, she saw folded notes tucked within the ribbons.

Smiling, she reached for the one labeled *For You*. He cuffed her wrist and nudged the other box in front.

Sensation traveled up her arm. "But this one says *For Me*, which I assumed meant you." When he stroked her skin, a blaze of heat landed somewhere south of her belly. "Judging by how you're grinning, would I be correct to hazard it's for both of us?"

Open, he mouthed.

She unfolded the *For Me* note and read aloud. "*Seeing as how the other necklace is for you to wear in public—long overdue, I might add. I cannot believe I haven't sent you jewels sooner—* Really, Lord Tremayne—how you've spoiled me already! And we've only known each other, what? A week?" Thea counted backward, more surprised with every day she didn't encounter. "*Five* days. Gracious, but it seems longer, does it not?"

In answer, he pointed to where she'd left off.

"Very well," she huffed. "But I expect a full accounting of your life until this moment after you've rested." He made such a face that she laughed till her cheeks hurt. "Not exactly a prattlerate?" She nuzzled her lips to the tempting muscles on his upper chest. "I can be very persuasive, you know. Entice you to sing for me, I daresay, if the reward is sufficient."

"Read!" he barked, but his eyes were smiling. "And please, call me D-D-Daniel."

Though she saw his shoulders tense, he didn't frown at the stumble.

"I'd be honored," she answered simply, not wanting to make anything of it. If he'd just continue to open up more, he could take as long as he wanted with every word he thought to utter. "All right. Where was I?"

She scanned the page, shoring up both her spine and her

voice. "All right. Here. *Sent you jewels sooner but I hope the other* *makes up for the recent lack. Now this one, my dear Thea—* I love it when you call me that. *This one reminds me of your beautiful* *n-nipples—* Ack! Now you have me doing it too!" She stared at him aghast. "I cannot believe you wrote that—"

"Thea." It was a rasp that heated her blood. "You wrote...*my* head..." His voice scratched softer and harsher over each syllable. "...*Your* lap."

"Oh. So I did. Now truly, you must rest your neck. It sounds as though you've been in a screaming contest and have drained yourself to a frazzle."

He pointed.

She read, despite the heat flushing her face with every boldly inked word slashed across the page. "*Your beautiful* *nipples, so bright and cherry-tipped...*"

DANIEL WAS hard-pressed not to rip the note from her hand, bend her over his dresser, and plumb her depths until she screamed his name. Until *she* went hoarse.

Primitive instincts aside, it was an easy thing to tame that urge of his. Because, by God, she was in his room, and for once, despite their nude state, despite what she was reading and the perfume of her arousal, *for once* she wasn't trembling.

Nay, she was giving voice to his words with the most dulcet of tones and it was sheer opera to his ears.

"*Cherry-tipped and so tasty I cannot wait to sup on each* *one*"—the rain pounded against the window in earnest and she strengthened her volume—"*with this little bauble swinging* *between. Wear it for me, and only me, the next time I see you. I* *remain, until our next night together, Yours. Daniel.*"

With endearing sentiment, she sighed and pressed his note to her chest. Right where he wanted the ruby to nestle. So he deftly slid the ribbon aside and opened the hinged box.

Overriding her gasped "*Little* bauble?" he spun her around to fasten the linked chain behind her neck.

As he turned her back to face him, he saw he'd judged the length perfectly. The teardrop stone landed exactly between her beaded nipples.

In truth, it was a gaudy specimen, the red rich and the size garish. He knew the naughty side of Thea would love it. Just as he knew she'd love the entwined strands of lustrous pearls that resided in the other box. The necklace he hoped to see her wear the next time he took her out.

And there would be a next time. Even had her reaction to discovering his speech debility not been as understanding as any man could wish for, Daniel knew he would've fought for her. Argued for her, long and loud. He would have exposed his every weakness for her sake because she made him strong.

A crack of thunder punctuated that thought, crashing right on top of the roof. For a change he didn't flinch, the welts on his arse didn't burn.

Because of her. The dark memories of his past had fled under the light she brought into his life.

Though the changes would no doubt take time, he was done with hiding. He had no plans to flagrantly flaunt his troubles, but neither did he want to let life—or love—pass him by.

"It's splendid," Thea said with an awed smile when she finally stopped looking down and met his gaze. "Thank you very much. Will I be thought unaccountably arrogant if I tell you to get in bed now?"

At her take-no-prisoner's tone, his brows flew upward but he was much too interested in what else she might tell him to do to demur. After all, how many lords were lucky enough to be ordered about by their lovely mistresses?

Stifling his grin, Daniel walked to his elaborate bed and

provocatively situated himself in the middle of the huge mattress—never before had he so appreciated the excesses of the prior century.

"You do realize, do you not," she said from her position near his dresser, "that I'm going to have my wicked way with you and there's nothing you can do to stop me?"

And she thought he'd object?

She took a step forward. The ruby pendant swayed. "Although..." she mused during the torturously slow step that followed, "I do expect something in return."

Entranced by the enticing swing of that damned nipple-red ruby, he made some sort of unintelligible grunt.

"What's that?" She just toyed with him, bringing her hand up to caress the stone. Then the vixen licked one finger and leisurely drew circles around each of her breasts. "You'll accede to anything I ask?"

By now she'd reached the foot of his bed.

By now his prick had pokered up stiff and straight.

By now he'd gladly forsake his birthright if only she'd climb over him and—

"I need a tuner posthaste," she said in a sensual voice that had nothing to do with her request. She brought one knee to the mattress and his heart into his loins. "My ears cannot take much more, you see."

Daniel had no idea what she was blathering about, not with her leaning seductively over his feet, trailing that deuced ruby over the tips of his toes, then across both ankles. He'd promise her the throne if only she'd come higher, skim that ruby over parts longer—and lonelier.

"The pianoforte is woefully misaligned." His brain refused to function when she reached up to unbind her hair, allowing it to drape past one shoulder and follow the path of the gem. "I don't think Buttons or Mr. and Mrs. Samuels can survive much longer, not with their hearing intact."

She laughed, dragged that stone up one shin and then the other. The strands of her hair followed, silken tendrils that wrapped around his will and tugged...tightened, rendering it nonexistent.

"I can tell I may need to remind you, when you're not..." She ringed each knee with ruby and hair, and the muscles in his thighs rippled, drawing her gaze to his groin. "Otherwise engaged."

His demure Thea had decamped, leaving a husky-voiced wanton in her stead. His eyes threatened to glaze over when she bent her head, pressed her lips to his skin, and marked a path for the ruby, sliding her mouth hotly over his inner thigh.

Like a man drunk on too much cheap jacky, his stomach clenched, heart hammered.

How quickly his mistress had gone from shy and trembling to bold and steady. From teasing his legs with the necklace to staring at his shaft. To approaching its hard length, the dangling chain forgotten as she climbed higher until poised above the patch of hair surrounding the root.

She licked her lips, a slow swipe of her tongue from one corner of her mouth to the other.

Her mouth—he'd always wondered what she could do with it.

What her plump lower lip would feel like curved around his anatomy.

You don't need to, his gentlemanly side wanted to shout.

Shut the blazes up! his baser side roared.

"I do believe..." she breathed over his erection and damned if he didn't see it give a little jump. "I'm feeling freer than I ever have in my life."

She shifted to rest one bent arm on his thigh, dropping her chin upon her closed fist. Watching his face, she trailed the ends of her hair over his shaft, up and down, up and around.

When a deep gurgling noise came from the direction of his headboard, she smiled and swung her hair back. "Enough torture? Or mayhap not...?"

Playfully, she walked two fingers up the side of his abdomen. "I believe there exists something I've thought of doing," she kept staring right at him, "only since meeting you, mind, but I was hesitant to attempt it previously, unsure whether it was acceptable. But as someone told me recently..." She leaned forward and licked the crown of his penis with the very tip of her tongue. "If it feels right, 'tis no matter what the law says, wouldn't you concur?"

The law? Who the bloody hell had she been conversing with—about sex?

Who the bloody hell cared when she abandoned her relaxed stance and used her opened fist to clasp his cock and her walking fingers to clutch one side of his hips as she raised up and licked him again. Swirled her tongue around the crest of his erection before bringing it fully into her mouth. Before applying a bit of suction and offering up an appreciative *Mmmm.*

A sound which had him strangling on his excitement, forcing his buttocks back to the bed. Couldn't go scaring her off. Not when she gazed up at him and deliberately did it again. "*Mmmmmmm.*"

"God, Thea!" burst from him as his loins started shaking and one of his blunt nails pierced right through his bed sheets.

After a silent but fierce pull that curled his toes, she eased back. Running her thumb over the purpling head, she shot him a mischievous glance. "Appears I can assume you find that rather to your liking." Her fingers tightened around his shaft. "Then aren't you the fortunate one? For I've been practicing."

Practicing?

With a gleeful laugh, she took the crown back inside her mouth. Lips closed firmly around the corona, fingers snug on his staff, Thea answered his unspoken question in the most spectacular way.

"Hmmmmmmmmmmmmmmmmmmmm..."

And Daniel died and went to heaven.

———————◦◦———————

HE WOKE EARLY the next morning, long before the light of dawn met the day, his body sated and heavy, his mind a jumble of so many erotic images it was hard to settle on just one.

Thea loving him with her mouth.

Thea stopping just when he moaned, a ragged sound that told her the end was near.

Thea gliding over him until she kissed his lips, slanting her body until her feminine depths were within reach.

Thea, her hot and moist center enticing him inside, sliding so snugly around him that he'd never felt more at home.

Thea, whispering to him later as she rode above him and his hands tightened on the cheeks of her arse, dipping between a time or two, "We can do it there. If it would please you," and while his cock rejoiced and his heart cracked, she brought her chest to his, kissed beneath his ear and added, "Sometime soon, I'm thinking, but just not tonight."

Thea, the woman whose warm flesh hugged him skin to skin, no barriers—no preventative nor lies—in the way. It felt so natural, so right, being intimate with her without anything between them that Daniel never thought to question the lack. That told him something right there.

Told him he was bewitched. And not by one of Ellie's little spells, but by the sweet siren who uttered his name in a soft, silken voice. "Tonight, strong Daniel, I want to revel in loving you without any cumbersome uncertainties or self-doubts weighing me down. Time enough for another new amorous adventure in the future, hmm?"

Dazed, he nodded. Anything she wanted, anything. He wanted to be the one to provide it. Any—

"But I would like for you to touch me there, deeper. As you did at the opera. Ah...*mmm*." When his finger greeted her anus, she gave a little cry and her loins surged against his just before the hot wash of her release bathed his shaft in wonder.

A huge, replete sigh heaved from him.

Never mind that the orgasm he recalled occurred hours ago, he still felt it in every pore of his being.

Thea, who'd made his dreams—ones he hadn't even been aware of—possible. Fact.

Thea, whom he loved and wanted for his own. It was time to tell her. Out loud.

Shaking off the drugging vestiges of sleep, Daniel blinked and rolled toward her: Thea, his love.

Thea. Who was gone.

17

A FAN – OR TWO – WHIPS UP A FLURRY

<hr/>

A short while earlier...

IT WAS STILL night when she woke. Dark beyond the edges of the curtains in Lord Tremayne's bedchamber.

Apprehension marked this particular occasion—because unlike the previous times she'd dozed and awoke, this time morning approached. She felt it with a foreboding in her bones.

Morning, which brought harsh, unavoidable realities with it.

Morning. Bah.

She'd growl if she could, for once it arrived, 'twould not do for her to be found in the master's bed. Nay, not when she was his *mistress*, a female relegated to a small and precise role in his life. One who had no right to be here.

Oh, but Daniel's breathing was steady, his warmth

stretched out alongside hers divine, and Thea wanted nothing more than to linger.

A serene smile curved her lips. At least she'd finally spent the night in his arms. Only she'd never imagined it would be in *his* bed!

A sigh huffed gently from his lips, his breath brushing the top of her head and Thea's smile grew. In the next moment, his sleep-husked, nonsensical murmur met her ears as his arms tightened around her—almost as though, even in sleep, he sensed her intention to depart.

She willed her muscles to unclench, to sink deeper into his embrace and savor every second.

She'd slept in the same bed with Mr. Hurwell over two thousand two hundred nights—she'd calculated the depressing number at some point during the sixth year of their marriage. Yet after little more than a single full night, little less than a week total, she knew more genuine caring from the slumbering man holding her now than she ever had from her spouse.

But she had no time to wonder what dreams might be wandering through his mind, what recollections or regrets from the night. No time to ponder the number of minutes until daybreak. Nay, for before the household brimmed with activity, she intended to be back where she belonged.

THE STUNNING RUBY tucked beneath her bodice, stays laced as best she could manage in near silence—and by herself— Thea slipped out Lord Tremayne's bedroom door. Best she began thinking of him as she ought, save "Daniel" for the bedchamber. "Lord Tremayne", she reminded herself, was her protector—a man who paid for the privilege of using her body.

Paid generously and isn't the privilege all yours? some inner imp taunted.

Wall sconces lit the corridor and guided her toward the stairs. Fresh beeswax candles. What a luxury and how quickly she'd grown used to them herself. Such a departure from the candleless black nights she'd endured in recent months.

Tiptoeing down the massive staircase, she was battling guilt over the thought of rousing Buttons to take her home—she'd learned her lesson about roaming London alone—when the servant emerged from the shadows to meet her at the bottom of the stairs.

"He'll not like you sneaking off," Buttons told her with a frown.

"Sneaking!" she whispered back, ignoring the prickle of her conscience. "I'm doing nothing of the sort. I'm returning to my townhouse—where I belong."

Buttons crossed his arms over his chest, looking remarkably intimidating for all his youth. "He'd want you to stay."

"But it's nearly morning."

"Makes no matter."

Irritable because Buttons was only enticing her toward what she already wanted—and knew she shouldn't—Thea walked around him.

"Have it your way, Miss Thea." He sounded aggrieved but turned to follow.

"Don't you ever sleep?" she grumped at him, ashamed of herself when she heard the complaint emerge. "And where's my pelisse, do you know?"

"John will get it from Petie and bring it over later."

That stalled her determined exodus. "Who?"

"Mrs. Peterson, the housekeeper," he explained. "She hemmed the sleeves last night and I don't dare barge in asking for it at this hour."

Hemmed the sleeves? That marvelous man!

They were at the door. Buttons was big enough he could stop her if he chose.

"Please?" Thea said starkly, her gaze unwillingly drawn overhead to the ornate chandelier that graced the ceiling.

That fancy, expensive alliance of metal and glass only illustrated the difference in their stations. Her former ceiling, and the room she'd rented for months, had been water stained, smoke stained, and stained with the taint of the wretched hopelessness that had surrounded her on a daily basis.

She looked back at Buttons. "It's not my place to be here when the household arises. Take me home before everyone in Lord Tremayne's employ knows what I've done. Please?"

After a moment's consideration, he nodded once. "Before we go, I need to tell John that we're off. He had the first watch —that's when I slept. I spelled him a while ago, figurin' you'd try to sneak—er, *leave* early this morning."

He turned to go but immediately swung back. "And you're wrong, if I can say so without gettin' my lugs boxed. Ever'one here likes you jus' fine. Better than fine, I be thinkin'— because his lordship *really* likes you.

"There's fewer servants here than what you'd figure for a house this size, but we've been with him for years, those of us there are. Long before he got the title. An' we're all fiercely loyal to him. Not jus' because he pays us but because we choose to be. We care 'bout him."

At this point during his startling and informative revelation, Buttons gave a light shrug. "He cared about most of us first. Petie? She worked the tavern near the Tremayne Estate, serving and cleaning and motherin' all the local lads in Aylsham. Got turned out when she couldn't hear no more, an' after decades of hard work. When his lordship found out, he rode up to Norfolk and brought her here. I speak for ever'one when I say that you haven't got any censure to fear, not from us."

"No censure to fear..." Thea numbly repeated. It was easier to latch on to that particular phrase than the entire sentiment so eloquently and earnestly just expressed.

"Been workin' on elongating an' expanding my vocabulary," Buttons said with a wink. "It impresses Sally Ann."

DURING THE WEE hours of the night, the quiet, still times between energetic lovings when Thea had slept cradled in his arms, Daniel had remained awake, thoughts brimming, plans forming, words being chosen. Decisions made.

He'd lived for years with his father's harsh disapproval. Some of his choices had been made to flaunt his defiance of the man's authority; more had been made to hide his difficulty.

Well, no longer. He was a man in love with his mistress, and he was man enough to do something about it. But before he tracked down his missing woman, and gave her a lecture on absconding with nary a word—with her person *and* his heart—he had first a relative and then a shopkeeper to see.

Dawn found him approaching Ellie and Wylde's townhouse from the mews, carefully picking his way through the rain-dampened ground. And not disappointed.

"Good," he greeted his sister who was hunkered down in the garden picking through a patch of something. "You're up."

Elizabeth flew to her feet with a startled cry, hand going to her neck. "Daniel! Since when do you rise with the chickens?"

Since he awoke without Thea.

He felt his lips curve at the picture his sister made, wearing old, mud-smeared clothes, intent on bringing life up from the cold and dormant soil. "Always reminds me of Mama, seeing you thus."

The fright left her gaze to be replaced with a flattered flush. "I love hearing you say so. I wish I could remember her."

Laden with her gardening tools, Ellie took a slow step forward and blinked at him in the gloom. "I cannot fathom what brought you here—and so early!"

"Can we t-talk?"

His odd request had her stripping off gloves and setting down the trowel. "Certainly. Come in. I doubt breakfast is ready but I'll have some tea brought— No? Why are you shaking your head?"

"I've ad-di-ditional errands," he told her, taking her arm to steer them toward a bench he'd noticed beneath a leafy tree. "D-don't want to run into Wylde. Just you this morning."

"You're here to take me to task for the opera, aren't you?"

"Nothing of the sort." Daniel had the sense they were being watched and craned his neck around.

"Trust me. He's never up at this hour. I didn't think you ever were either. Come, tell me what brings you here."

They settled on the stone bench, Daniel's gaze going to where he'd originally spotted his sister.

The smell of damp earth was strong. The growing cacophony of chirpy, whistling birds uplifting. As though they too wanted to sing in celebration of what he'd decided. Either that or they celebrated the cessation of rain.

"Daniel." Chastisement was in her tone. "That's the second time you've consulted your timepiece, and you here less than three minutes. I hardly ever see you do so. What has you acting so strangely?"

"I sent John round to Morrison's..." He mentioned the emporium he tended to frequent whenever needing to purchase a gift; a gift he typically let the proprietor choose and send with his name. But not this time. "To inquire whether he'd let me in early. I want to buy a fan for Thea. I noticed she d-didn't have one at the opera."

"A parting gift?" Elizabeth sounded aghast. Her fisted hands rose—as though she wanted to smack him!—before she brought them, shaking, back to her lap. "You should be ashamed! A fan—"

Daniel halted the tirade, placing his large gloved hand over both of hers. "Nn-*nay*. It rankles you should think me so cheap. A fan? As a *congé*? Pah. You're completely off the mark. I want her t-to have one I p-pick out, 'tis all."

"But a fan!" Her irritation over his choice of gift seemed completely over-the-top. Daniel let it slide when she changed the subject with, "You're unusually verbose today. Perhaps I should always schedule my visits at five minutes after sunrise?"

"When I'm usually snoring," he snorted on a smile. He squeezed her bare fingers. "Ellie. I would never d-do anything to harm you. But I find I must. You are my one regret in this, how you will p-p-*pay* for my—"

She snatched her hand free and turned fully toward him. "You're frightening me. You aren't leaving England, are you? Are you sick? Injured? Where? What—"

Touched by her concern, he put one arm around her shoulders and pulled her close. "Nn-*nay*. Nothing of the sort. But I am hoping to be married—"

"Married!" Alarm made her pull back. Her eyes narrowed at him, steely glints in the slowly increasing light. "Now? But what about Thea? I mean Mrs. Hurwell?"

Not the reaction he'd expected. "What about her?"

"Ah...um. I have a confession to make—about your mistress. About Thea."

Why did Ellie look guilty?

"I went to see her yesterday and—"

"You..." He hadn't expected that. "What about?"

"My difficulties with Wylde, if you must know. I needed the advice of someone with more experience. Ah, in the bedroom."

She'd gone to Thea for sexual advice? Daniel was hard-pressed not to laugh.

For his unsuccessful attempt, he got summarily elbowed in the ribs. "Ow! Ellie. They're still sore."

"And I still owe you a jar of cream. But she was wonderfully helpful and, oh, Daniel, I like her very much. And now you're going to get married?" She sounded distraught. "End things with Thea?"

Never would he have expected such disapproval from this quarter. It hadn't escaped him either that Ellie expressed zero interest in his potential future wife; nay, all her concern was for his mistress.

Women!

Ellie sighed. "Thea's not at all what I thought a mistress would be."

Nay, she wasn't. "More like a wife."

"*What?* A wife!" He'd reduced his composed sister to shrieks.

At least they weren't critical shrieks. Nay, given her smile and the clapping and the jumping up and down, given the strangling hug she suffocated him with and the shout in his ear, he'd have to say they were shrieks of approval.

───────◦◦◦───────

"HERE?" Buttons exclaimed after the carriage ride "home" took them across London instead. "*This* is where I'm to let you 'run a quick errand'? His lordship'll flay me alive!"

In the act of getting down, Thea paused. She flashed a

falsely confident smile. "He need never know. I only need one thing from my room—"

Buttons had already jumped to the ground and circled the carriage, as though to bar her from proceeding. At her explanation, he winced. "*Your* room, Miss Thea?"

She saw him look again, more warily this time, at their surroundings. The curve of the sun had just crested the horizon, giving him sufficient light to see the ugly street and uglier building she'd directed them to. Using Hatchards as a starting point, which she'd thought a stroke of brilliance, Thea had given her coachman Jem instructions.

"Aye. Until last week, this is where I lived." The confession was made without inflection.

People were beginning to stir, shutters banging open and the contents of slop jars and chamber pots being tossed into the streets.

Needing to get the distasteful task over with, she stood.

With a shudder, Buttons offered his arm to assist her down. "His lordship will have my head, but I can see sure-like you'll come back on your own later if I order us turned around now." After a severe frown at her, he glanced at the driver. "You see them two men over there, in that alley?" Buttons gestured with the back of his head. "Eyeing the mare, they are. Got your whip handy?"

"Aye, I do."

"Can't tell whether they want to eat her or steal her, but stay sharp." Then to Thea, as if issuing a dare, "Let's see jus' how fast you can be."

As she walked inside after several days' absence, heading down the narrow hallway to her room on the second floor, seeing—and smelling—the bleak accommodations, it struck Thea anew how far she'd sunk.

Was that why she'd insisted they return *this* morning, after she'd basked in the grandeur of her stolen, illicit night?

Why, in spite of her valid desire to retrieve the brush her mother gave her, she felt compelled to remind herself— perhaps to show Buttons—how very much she *didn't* belong in Lord Tremayne's world?

But you don't belong here either, that intrusive inner voice insisted. *You, Thea Jane, were born to gentility. 'Twas shortsighted Hurwell and his selfish cousin who reduced you to these circumstances, condemned you to a future not of your choosing.*

Condemned? Time with Lord Tremayne felt anything but a punishment.

Ascending the rickety stairs, heading deeper into the bowels of the squalid place, especially after all the glitter and gleam she'd fallen into, made her recent past all that more embarrassing.

With every reluctant yet determined step, she was never more grateful for Buttons' solid presence at her heels.

Right before they reached the landing, a sharp double whistle rang out.

"That's Jem—on the carriage," Buttons told her in a low voice. He wavered in place.

"Go." She pointed down the way they'd just come. "We're almost there. I'll retrieve what I came for and meet you outside."

Not waiting for his agreement, she raced to her old room. The door was ajar. "Shouldn't be surprised," she muttered, pushing it wide, amazed to find any possessions remaining. In the grey light of dawn, she stepped to the old trunk that'd doubled as a dresser. Opening the hinged lid to search inside, she heard a tiny cry. Then another.

What was that?

The soft, persistent sounds came again from the corner and quickly bloomed into an all-out baby's wail.

So she had new neighbors on the other side of the wall? The strident cry of a hungry child, something she'd become benumbed to over the months of living in close proximity with so many people, unnerved her.

A baby.

Cherished brush in hand, Thea sat back on her heels and closed the trunk with a *thunk*.

A baby.

Oh Lord, the last two nights she'd forgotten to practice what Sarah had taught her. Nay, Thea realized with a gasp, she'd forgotten it *every* time. Had just assumed it was no longer necessary, not with how Lord Tremayne used the beribboned preventatives.

But at the opera—

And then last night in his bed—more than once!

Last night. The reminder of those precious hours softened the horror of her discovery. The prior eve, she'd been so very concerned for him, intent on showing him how much she cared naught about the stammer; how much she cared *for him*.

Well, blow me to Bedfordshire and back. A baby.

Loving him seemed so instinctive, so perfect, that she'd never thought to question the consequences.

Aye, her sensible side countered, *with a baby and out on your gullible backside—worse off than you were weeks ago if you aren't careful.*

Although that scenario paled in comparison to the idea of Daniel being gone from her life—his witty notes, his hearty laugh, the weight of his hard body coming into hers—

His arms holding her deep into the night.

If she was already enamored this much, after only a few days, what would happen in time, when she was thoroughly entranced by his spell?

Aren't you already?

"Not so bony anymore, are ya, eh?" A menacing voice

hurled the accusation. "Almost didn't recognize that rounded arse on ya. That frilly dress."

Grimmett hauled a dazed Thea to her feet.

She'd been so lost in the fanciful imaginings of rocking Daniel's child, her mind far away from the sickening reality of her time here that it took several seconds to grasp who—and what—she now faced.

"Turned into a short-heeled wench after all. I always knew you were th' sort to fall on your back. Where's he keeping ya? Eh? Answer me, girly!" Grimmett twisted her arm when she remained silent.

Fear rushed in as though it had never left. The past week vanished and she was living on the edge of starvation. The sharp blade of terror.

"So the fancy toff's feedin' you more, I see. Or is it more 'n one that's butterin' yer bun?" Every motion of his cracked lips revealed blackened teeth, blasted rotten breath into her face. "You workin' at Mother Mary's now? Makin' the beast with two backs with any man who gots a shiny coin? 'Sat why ya ain't been around?"

Her heart hammered so hard her chest hurt, limbs tensed so tight they squeaked. The days of meager hope looking for employment, evenings spent trying to block out the neighbors' yelled fights, and the long, rodent-filled nights of despair and hunger squeezed aside her newfound confidence.

Thea all but cowered.

"Don't deny you been whorin'—I kin smell it on ya."

"Nay." It was a whisper, a whimper.

He sniffed her neck, his black teeth snagging her skin as he rooted around like a mole scavaging grubs. "Got the scent of a well-prigged woman..."

She squirmed for freedom.

This couldn't be happening.

It was over! This horrid part of her life. The despicable things she'd eaten, the dirty clothes worn day after day. The tussles with Grimmett. Always watching over her shoulder for him—and others of his ilk. The terror. The *bugs*. Over, by damn!

"Think yer too good for ol' Grimmett, do ya? Always did act like you was above ever'body." He tightened his hold on her wrist and twisted harder. Inches away, his fetid breath assaulted her nose. "I see them fancy, peer-bought duds yer wearing. Can spread your legs for a toff's penny but not Grimmett's?"

She watched in a self-inflicted stupor as his tongue circled narrow lips. His gaze flicked to her chest, eyes gleaming when they caught sight of the chain nestled beneath the bodice.

No! The word got locked in her throat.

God, no!

Fight, Thea!

He reached for it. "What ya hiding here?" He fingered the chain, then gave a yank. When it didn't budge, he slammed her back into the wall and covered one breast. His fingers squeezed cruelly. "Not looking so high and fine, are ya? Just a sniveling street whore is all you are, all ya ever were."

Bile rose in her throat, choked off her air.

He released her wrist and clamped his dirty fingers on her bodice. The material ripped at his downward heave, making way for his insistent fingers to clutch at her bared breast, for his other hand to snatch at the ruby while he pinched and clawed at her nipple.

But his words had unlocked the paralysis imprisoning her limbs. Sniveling street whore, accused Grimmett.

I do have it in my head that he's a snivler, proposed Lord Tremayne in one of his first letters. *Your dear Mr. Freshley...*

Lord Tremayne. *Daniel.*

Her *dear* protector!

In the eyes of God and man, she might be no better than a street whore. And the elevated new status she enjoyed just might come crashing down as soon as Lord Tremayne tired of her, but by all that was good and fun, joyful and right, by God, she wouldn't let anyone take away a single day of her happiness.

Especially not Grimmett.

Unfrozen, Thea kicked and screamed. The brush she'd forgotten she held cracked across his skull.

Her sudden ferocity startled Grimmett. His hold loosened a fraction. Just enough for her to break free. "No, you don't!" she yelled. "You won't touch me ever again!"

She floundered with the drooping bodice, pressing it high across her chest, and wielded the brush again. "Never!" She whacked him again. "You rotten—" Again. "Rotten mouse turd!" *Snap!* The wooden handle split. But her thrashing didn't pause. "You maggoty—"

"Miss Thea!" Buttons charged through the doorway, taking the situation in at a glance. He jerked Grimmett around and planted him a facer.

Incensed at the unexpected interruption, the landlord only spit and came forward for more. While Buttons struggled with the enraged man's flailing arms, Thea dropped the hairbrush, sparing not a thought to its newly broken state, and grabbed up the heaviest thing at hand—an old boot of Mr. Hurwell's. A mateless boot she'd used more than once to scoop up unwanted, multi-legged or whiskered visitors. Grasping it at the top, waiting for the precise moment between the grappling men, she swung. The heavy heel landed solidly against Grimmett's hard head. Finally stunned, he sank against the wall.

She opened her mouth to yell at him some more but Buttons launched himself between them. Assured she was unharmed, he took off his jacket and draped it around her shoulders, ushering her to the carriage after issuing a threat to the older man.

Thea had thought *she'd* learned some ribald slang during her stint in the rough area. Buttons' menacing warning, delivered in colorful and crude terms, actually had her ears stinging more than her abused breast.

Nothing, however, burned more than her pride.

———◦○◦———

UPON RETURNING HOME after the encounter with Grimmett, three unexpected gifts awaited Thea.

One, a lacy ecru fan from Lady Wylde, tied to a note expressing her appreciation for Thea's company and the education she'd helped impart.

The note was read hurriedly—under the guise of pretending that accepting presents from titled ladies for Instruction in Mistressing Arts was nothing out of the ordinary. This farce was enacted given how *Lord Tremayne* looked on.

Aye, Lord Tremayne. Who Thea considered the second— and best—gift of the three.

Whose actual presence, given all that'd gone on since she'd left his abode a scant time earlier was nearly sufficient to reduce her to a watering pot of epic proportions.

Thankfully, that cowardly urge was countered by the lifting of her spirits the moment she saw him waiting in her entry. Once she processed that he'd come after her—and so soon.

He smiled a bit sheepishly when Thea hurried in, still covered in Buttons' coat.

Her instinctive rush toward him was checked with his greeting words.

"Ap-p-pears I'm not your only admirer," he said ruefully,

quickly stashing something behind his back. "I'll let you open that one first, see who it's from."

Though he glanced with interest at the fan, shown to its frilly perfection on the usually empty silver tray, his expression held no accusation, only indulgent curiosity.

Crossing into the sanctuary of her home, taking in everything at a glance and resolved to behave normally, Thea just barely avoided launching herself into his arms.

She sensed Buttons' frowning disapproval at her back. Could she help it if she was loath to explain, to relive the past hour? Better to forget it ever happened. So after quickly refolding the note from Lady Wylde, she used a magnified fascination with the pretty fan as an excuse to avoid looking at Daniel, concerned her expression would certainly convey The Unpleasant Incident.

The incident *already forgotten*.

"A fan! How lovely." Her voice only shook a lot. "I—I've —" She swallowed and tried again. "I've b-been wanting one. It's so nice of—of—" She couldn't very well tell Lord Tremayne that *his sister* had paid her a call. Certainly couldn't meet his eyes when she felt him come up behind her and saw that he, impossibly, held out a fan as well.

Easier to latch on to the incongruous sight of the striking specimen captured gently in his strong, masculine fingers. Easier to keep her neck bent, her head down, her gaze far away from the mirror glaring at her.

Unlike the delicate, lacy one his sister had chosen, the heavier fan he presented would whip up a gale. The screen was thick enough, when he fanned it out to reveal an intricately painted peacock upon the black silk, that she couldn't see the light through it.

"I was looking for something softer, more frilly in d-design, but this one caught my eye and I knew it was p-perf— Thea?"

"It is perfect. L-lovely, in fact." Her face felt uncomfortably warm as she reached to stroke the decisive pleats, to run the pad of one finger over the colorful bird at home within its folds.

Mayhap she could hide behind it? Bring it up in front of her face and sneak upstairs with no one the wiser. "From none to two in one—one m-m-morning—"

It was difficult to speak through the lump swelling her throat. The unshed tears growing dense and hot now that she no longer put on a brave front for Buttons. Now that she was home. Now that *he* was here.

She gave a frantic laugh. "I now have two fans." When only minutes ago she'd been fanless. And accosted. Oh Lord! Another helpless giggle escaped. "T-two *fans!*"

"Thea. Sweetheart." Lord Tremayne stepped closer and curved both hands firmly around her upper arms, pulled her toward him. The line of the folded fan dug into one and she focused on the sensation. "Nnn-*nay!*" he directed over her shoulder, speaking to Buttons, she assumed, "d-don't frown at me again, mouth at me to wait. Her entire body is trembling and— What's this she's wearing...your coat?" And *there* was the accusation she'd expected when he'd noticed the gift from another. "Swift John? T-talk, man!"

"Aye, my lord, 'tis mine." She heard him shuffle in place. "Miss Thea, will you be telling him? Or do I?"

"One of you b-better." The rasp vibrated through her.

She shook her head so hard the coat slid from one shoulder. Nay! She didn't want to tarnish what they had now with her unpleasant past—

"Thea!" Lord Tremayne hissed, his hand following the path of the fallen coat. "Your neck— The chain! It's d-dug into your skin. D-dammit! You're bleeding." Warm fingers caressed across her nape to ease the metal free. Only then did she become aware of the burning where the chain must've sliced into her when Grimmett tried to rip it free.

Shuddering from the reminder, she wiggled from Daniel's gentle touch. "'Tis nothing. Let's forget—"

"Thea." With heavy hands to her shoulders, he shook her once.

She couldn't hide her wince. Neither could she avoid Lord Tremayne's gaze.

Lord Tremayne. Daniel. Lord Tremayne.

She didn't know what to call him anymore. How to think of him. Her past, her present, *their* present, spun her around till she was in knots.

"Daniel." Unbidden, his name, the *right* name, slipped from her lips at the worried concern in his gaze.

"I'm here, sweetheart. Now what..." As his fingers dipped beneath the coat to reveal the shattered state of her dress, his face did an incredulous turn from troubled to livid. He swore, coloring the air with curses that put Buttons' to shame. But when he fingered the torn bodice, when he glided one fingertip over the budding bruises from Grimmett's savagery, his touch was featherlight. "Talk to me, Thea. Who d-did this?"

At the solemn query she dove into his arms, needing to feel them around her, needing his strength, his scent, to obliterate the hateful, hurtful morning. "Please," she implored, her words muffled by his warm body, her eyes shut, frantic heartbeat only now calming. Now that she was with him. "I just want to forget."

She wrapped her arms around his waist and pressed her stinging breast hard against his chest.

Though he held her tight, brushing comforting palms down her back, his posture was steel, breathing choppy. "Swift John? Start t-talking."

"We went to her room, my lord. The one in Seven Di—"

"Seven Dials!" The syllables scratched like blades across boulders. "D-devil take you, you t-t-took her there? *Her?*"

"Don't." Thea wedged her arms against his chest to snare his gaze. "Don't blame him. I insisted. I—"

"Have t-totally ruined my surprise," he said in a doleful tone. He leaned down to kiss her forehead. "But it'll keep. Where else d-d-d—" His eyes squeezed shut, then flashed open, went to her torn bodice and a feral gleam lit their depths. "Hurt you elsewhere?"

"He didn't. Buttons intervened and it's over. Let's just forget this—"

"Go upstairs." He released his hold, his gaze on her torn skin. "T-take care of—"

"Go?" She clutched his arms. "Come with me."

His jaw firmed to granite. "Nn-*nay*." Hands to her waist, he pushed her from him. "Need to see this taken care—"

"This? Grimmett, you mean? Buttons already hit him!" She tried to lace their fingers, to tug him upstairs, but he avoided the maneuver. "Please? 'Tis over and done."

"Miss Thea clobbered him too," Buttons put in. "Don't think he'll trouble her again."

"Of course he won't!" she cried, just wanting it all erased. "I've no reason to go back. Let's just—"

"D-did you flatten him?" Daniel asked Buttons, ignoring her completely.

"Aye. But the bastard's still breathing."

"You can't mean to kill him," she said when some manner of unspoken, masculine accord passed between the men and they headed for the door. "He won't bother me again. I won't go back, I promise! *I've no reason to!*" If the shrill way she screeched after them was any indication, the morning had finally caught up with her.

Daniel returned. He smoothed one hand down the side of

her head, skimmed his thumb over her cheek until he cupped her jaw. "Thea. Why d-did you go?"

"My brush," she replied miserably. "My hairbrush. 'Twas a gift from my mother. But his rotten skull cracked the wood, so it's pointless. Pointless for you to return."

Daniel's thumb dragged over her bottom lip. "D-don't you see? If not you, then another helpless woman—"

"I am not helpless! I walloped him good!"

"With a boot, no less," Buttons supplied. Rather unhelpfully, Thea couldn't help but think now that exhaustion claimed her and she simply wanted to wash off grimy Grimmett's abhorrent touch and sleep for a week.

Daniel meshed their lips for one heart-stopping moment. He spoke to her without words, expressing his frustration, his fears, and his desperate desire to see her unharmed. Without a sound uttered between them, she knew he wouldn't let it go.

When he gentled the pressure and raised his head, she reached for his hand, liberating the fan he still held. She waved it near his temple. "All right. Since I doubt you bought this for me to knock some sense into you, I'll accede. With reservations, mind." She carried his hand to her lips and kissed his fight-hardened knuckles. "No one else should be intimidated by him, you're right on that. But I cannot condone murder." She gave him an arch look.

"How about I rip off his b-ballocks and feed the rats?"

"Well, if you have the peace of mind to jest about it, then I suppose I can allow you to go." Obviously humor and sense had overridden fury and he no longer intended to kill the man. Or so she reasoned. On tiptoe, she kissed his cheek. "I await your return."

Holding up her bodice, she slipped over to Buttons and shrugged off his coat. "Thank you," she told him quietly, transferring it to his hands. "See he comes to no harm."

As the men took their leave, their parting exchange left her gasping.

"No harm?" Buttons laughed. "I'm to protect that pustule from you?"

"Nay. Thea meant pr-protect me, I b-believe," Daniel rejoined, a smile in his voice. "Foolish woman, she thought I was *joking*?"

"So we *are* servin' the sod's stones to the rats? Capital!"

18

PROTECTING HIS OWN BRINGS
THINGS UP TO SCRATCH

JUST OUT OF earshot of the door, Daniel turned to Swift John and grinned. "Think she heard?"

"Clear enough not to go wanderin' in places she oughtn't."

"Good." Waving off the driver, Daniel took the reins. "We have a stop to make. We'll b-b-*be* picking up another."

"Are ye certain, milord?" Jem asked from the ground. "Was a rough place, mighty interested in Callisto here. Don't trouble me none to go back." He patted the whip slung round his neck, then lifted his coat to show he'd armed himself further since their return.

"On second thought, climb on. Think I'll spell Calli, swing b-by and harness Jupit-ter instead."

"Sounds a right idea." Swift John jumped on the seat beside him when Daniel motioned for the footman to join him, the coachman pulling himself up on the back.

"Lord Tremayne," Swift John began formally once they

were off. "I surely regret this morn. Know you'd never forgive me if something had happened to—"

"You're d-damn right I wouldn't have!" Daniel exploded. Then just as quickly calmed himself. No sense getting angry at the wrong person when the right person waited at the end of a carriage ride. "She was d-determined to go. Remember that d-day she got lost? Before I sent you to her?"

"John's complained more than once he's missing out on all the fun. Today was anything but. Scared me, it did, seeing that filthy scourge attack her." He swallowed audibly. "Shouldn't have happened. Not on my watch. Would understand if—if...you sacked my soddin' arse."

"Don't talk nonsense," Daniel barked. They rolled along in silence, his tense grip on the reins conveying his agitation to the mare who picked up speed. "I'm thankful you were with her, Swi..." He trailed off, deciding to try something new. "Glad you were there, B-Buttons."

After mangling the man's preferred name, Daniel glanced over. His footman beamed, noting the change.

Then a haunted look came into his valued servant's eyes. Buttons leaned in, pitched his voice low. "Yer lordship. Godalmighty! You shoulda seen it. 'Twas a tiny hovel in the worst part o' the stews. She was blame near sleeping on rags!"

It took real effort to keep his expression bland, to not let on how much that news affected him.

"Since I d-don't want any of us d-dancing on air with a knot around our n-n-necks, and I'm liable to kill him in truth if I get in more than one rammer—hell, one might d-do it, the way I'm feeling—we're stopping to p-pick up Tom Everson." The long-winded explanation surprised Daniel. He never explained. He never talked, not when he could avoid it.

But still, the words kept gushing forth, the memory of the dried blood on Thea's neck, the torn dress, the way she burrowed into his chest when she finally admitted what happened... It all made him want to rip limbs from the lecher, and damned if talking didn't ease the rage. "He's ab-b-out your age, a fighting enthusiast without much experience. B-but with loads of heart."

"Happy to have another set of fives," Button said, rubbing his together. "'Specially if yours are sitting out."

Daniel's hands flexed upon the reins. "I'm d-det-t-*termined* to teach this Grimmett b-bastard a lesson, though. For Thea and anyone else he's harmed. And...Buttons"—Daniel shot him a grim glance as he pulled around the back of his townhouse, heading to the mews for a fresh horse and a less attractive carriage—"t-tis your and Tom's job t-to make sure I conduct myself in a manner that won't have Thea tearing off *my* b-ballocks for a rat snack."

———————◦∈◦———————

THEY PICKED up more than Jupiter, though, when Daniel's regular driver Roskins learned of their mission.

"I'm from there, milord. Still know my way around. Might just come in handy."

"Jump on."

As he'd hoped, Tom made an eager addition and, once the lanky redhead came aboard, the five of them were soon abandoning the parts of the city they frequented in reluctant favor of the slums.

Where the streets were narrow, the houses crumbling, and the smells atrocious.

"That's it."

"Here 'tis, milord."

Jem and Buttons spotted their destination at the same moment.

Leaving the two coachmen with the carriage and Buttons stationed at the door to prevent an escape should Grimmett think to attempt one, Daniel and Tom went in search of the louse-riddled landlord.

The whiny, grease-faced Grimmett proved easy to find, for he'd made no friends in the area and more than one tenant was eager to give up his location—even before Daniel offered a coin.

All too soon, the wretch sagged to the floor. And with very little effort extended upon either of their parts.

Tom roared forward for another swing, ready to defend the honor of the lovely woman he'd met the night he came looking for Daniel. But he was too late. With a feeble cry, the sorry-arse excuse for a man scrambled drunkenly out the door.

Buttons popped his head in. "Want me to run him down? It'd be a right pleasure."

Daniel considered a moment before answering with a slight shake of his head. On the drive over, he and Roskins had devised a plan whereby his coachman's cousin, who still lived in the area, would keep an eye on the beetle-headed recreant. Satisfyingly, Grimmett was already in half mourning when they'd found him, thanks to the chop Buttons had landed earlier. Or possibly it was Thea's boot swinging that had blackened the bastard's eye (his footman had regaled them with details of the morning's encounter on the way).

"Just m-m-*make* sure he stays gone while we're here."

"Aye, your lordship." As Buttons crossed back into the hall, a ragged cat streaked inside.

Hissing at Daniel and Tom, it raced to a corner and ducked beneath a ratty-looking chest of drawers.

"C-c-c-c-can't believe anyone wwwwould want to-to-to live here that bad." Tom followed the flash of dirty grey. "Hey, b-b-boy, don't you want-t-t to-to come on out?"

Daniel looked around. There wasn't anything worth

salvaging. The brush Thea had come for had cracked, splintered wood snagging on his coat pocket when he tucked the halves inside.

The walls might have been relatively clean, a swipe of his gloved finger across one told him, but no amount of washing could disguise the pallor that permeated the room. The squalidness that surrounded it just steps away. He couldn't believe Thea had been relegated to such dingy and depressing environs. How remarkable that she'd remained so bright and lively—

"He's b-b-bleeding." Tom's voice was muffled. "Come on, k-k-k-itty— Ow!" At the surprised cry, Daniel left off his frowning inspection and walked the mere two paces to the corner.

"Got me, he d-d-d-did." Tiny slashes of red welled from three close-set cuts on the back of Tom's hand. "Sharp claws, that's f-f-f-for sure!"

Another Mr. Freshley?

Daniel knelt to face the growling feline. A smear of dried blood matted several whiskers. The cat hissed and he noticed more blood, redder and wetter, on his chin.

If the blame animal wanted to guard this hovel, he was welcome to it. Daniel tensed his thighs to stand but the plaintive mew the cat gave made him pause. What? Ol' grumpy-puss here wanted attention now? "'Tis all right, Mr. Freshley," Daniel soothed, shifting a fraction closer and keeping his arms tucked safely out of clawing reach. "Let's have a look at you. Find out where that bl-blood—"

"Lookit-it here, D-Dan!" Tom's excited whisper caught his attention.

Seeing where the boy gazed, Daniel peered under the rickety chest.

Only to be confronted with undeniable proof of his mistake.

He turned back to the cat, crossed his arms over his chest. "So, *Mrs.* Freshley, how would you and your rat's nest of kittens like a nice home?"

Moments later, after acknowledging the kittens and their grumpy mama were the only things of value in the room (and theirs dubious), Daniel walked into the hallway and shouted for Buttons.

After he made his request, his footman looked at Daniel as though he'd lost his marbles and the bag they came in. "You want me to *what*?" his servant exclaimed. "Find a padded box for six kittens?"

"Aye, and her too." He pointed to Mrs. Freshley, who'd followed him into the hallway once she realized he didn't intend to harm her brood. "Only b-better make hers a *locked* b-box.

"And get a blanket to wrap her in. Oh, and grab the thickest gloves you can," Daniel added, idly wondering why it was easier to contemplate facing a two-hundred-and-fifty-pound opponent in the ring than a scrawny, fur-covered feline. Something to do with those sharply pointed front teeth, perhaps? "I'd rather not ruin my nice p-pair."

"I'll see what Roskins an' Jem have. Between us, we'll get the little ones and their mama corralled."

The female in question had been rather industrious during their exchange.

When Buttons went off to find suitable cat-catching equipment, Daniel hunkered down to address the newest member of his household. "You'll have one job, Mrs. Freshley —n-nay, make that t-two. Feed those youngsters and b-be *nice* to your new mistress. That's how you'll earn your keep."

The cat just blinked at him, licking her lips and daring Daniel to say a word about the fresh blood on her paw or the mouse tail—suspiciously lacking a mouse body—just behind her.

AFTER DROPPING off an exhilarated Tom and his well-fed servants at their respective lodgings (he'd treated everyone to a thumping good beef steak at a local alehouse Roskins recommended)...

After depositing one very vocal mama cat back with her kittens—"They'll be right fine under my watchful eye, Lord Tremayne," his housekeeper Mrs. Peterson told him quietly and precisely, as she always spoke. "I'll see she has some cream and part of tonight's ham." (Tonight's ham—Daniel's supper? Wondrous. Now *he* was reduced to table scraps?)...

After he washed the stench of the stews off his person and talked (ha!) Crowley out of shaving his jaw (time was precious and hadn't Thea told him she'd come to like his whiskers?)...

After. After. *After.*

Seemed it took an age to arrive at Thea's townhouse, Cyclops in tow. A dreamily dribbling Cy whose constant barking (and resultant drooling) professed his pleasure at the unexpected outing.

Daniel couldn't wait to converse with Thea. Aye, *converse.* To jabber, to jaw. Hell, he wanted to rhapsodize with her. Share his past, convince her to share his future.

But as she'd done from the moment they met, she stumped him once again. Because instead of eagerly awaiting his return, she was upstairs asleep. And softly *snoring*, he realized after he spoke with Mrs. Samuels and showed himself up.

"Said she wanted to know the second ye arrived," the housekeeper had told him downstairs. "Tried to rouse her, I did, when Sam spotted your horse, but the wee thing is done in. Fell into bed the moment we got her washed up."

Here, she'd paused for breath, her gaze drifting to Cy and the puddle he'd left on her entry floor. Least it wasn't piss—

something Daniel would've quipped out loud if Thea, and not the housekeeper, stood before him.

"Yer dog, my lord," Mrs. Samuels said gingerly, bravely venturing a hand to pat Cy's head (and of course prompting that long pink tongue to loll and more drool to fall), "shall I take him to the kitchen? Find a bone..."

Cy whined and leaned into Daniel's leg.

"Ap-pears he wants to see his new mistress. My new marchioness," Daniel said with a straight face, keeping his gaze on Mrs. Samuels.

The woman indulged in a bit of drooling of her own.

To hide his smile, he bent to blot Cy's puddle with his ever-present handkerchief.

"Oh, my lord!" exclaimed Mrs. Samuels once she recovered and saw his actions. "Ye shouldn't be doing that!"

"'T-tis only spit. I can wipe it up as well as anyone." Rising, he pointed up the stairs with his walking stick. "Go." Cy bounded up at the invitation.

"Miss *Thea*?" the housekeeper all but stammered. "Yer new marchioness?"

"If she'll have me." Daniel gave a wink, then sauntered after his dog, tossing over his shoulder, "Please see that we aren't d-dist-t-turbed."

For once, the wretched blunder didn't make him cringe. Far too many more important things lay on his tongue.

"Aye, my lord!"

WATCHING Thea sleep proved an exercise in torture.

It was torture seeing her hair down, long and lustrous, tangled upon the pillow cushioning her head and restraining himself from trying to unknot the strands. Torture seeing that pretty pink mouth part when she groggily rolled over, stopped snoring (which made him smile) and made a tiny *hmmm* in her throat (which made him hard).

Torture watching her fingers seek the black handle of the fan he'd given her, just peeking out from beneath her pillow, until she found it and made another drowsy *hmmm* before drifting back under.

Torture keeping Cy from drowning in his own doggie-style euphoria as his tail thumped and he grinned at the lady occupying the big bed—alone.

Finally, after more than one unsuccessful attempt to gently rouse her, too impatient to wait any longer, Daniel released his hold on Cy's collar and pointed.

After a running start, the lumbering dog cannoned onto the bed.

The echo of his landing likely shook the walls downstairs.

It certainly shook Thea awake.

<hr />

DRIPPY LICKS MET HER CHEEK, an excited bark, her ear.

But it was the husked, "Cy, don't d-drown her," that lured Thea from the depths of slumber.

She wiped at the cool wetness coating her ear and encountered a moist muzzle. "Cyclops?" Heavy eyelids shuttered open to the music of exuberant pants. Only to find the dainty chair painted with trailing roses across her chamber occupied by one very *un*-dainty masculine specimen.

"Lord Tremayne?" Thea jerked upright. Daniel was here?

The opposite of her suddenly tense posture, he lounged —as much as a powerful presence could upon such feminine furniture. By candlelight, she drank him in. His tailcoat was discarded, hanging haphazardly from the arm of the chair. In shirt, simple neckcloth and burgundy waistcoat, thick hair decidedly mussed, shadow of whiskers on his jaw temptingly dark, he devastated her senses.

Kiss *now*. Hold *now*. Love *forever*, was all Thea could think. Notions she had no right to.

You're here for his convenience. His. She reminded herself of one of Susan's less bawdy teachings.

Oh, but he was in her room, looking for all the world as though he had no intention of ever leaving. That made her smile. "I must be dreaming."

She had to be, surely, if she was starting to convince herself *he* belonged here. With her.

His paid whore. That unpalatable reminder made her wince. Self-conscious now, she brought a hand to her cheek. Rubbing back the strands of hair that'd stuck to the side of her face, she felt sleep creases in her skin. "I must look a fright."

"Nay, not now nor the last t-t-two t-times you awoke. Here." He rose and brought her a glass. "And it's D-Daniel, lest you've forgotten."

"Thank you." *Last two times?* Groggily trying to remember, Thea sipped.

"There's a tray t-too, when you're hungry."

The expectant glint sparking from his eyes put the glow of the hearth to shame. Her brow pinched as hazy scenes surfaced. "It's all murky. But I seem to recall you talking, telling me of your grandfather and...and..."

Fresh new memories swirled in her rapidly clearing mind, the fog of sleep blurring some, but she pieced together enough to summon the truth.

He'd told her how, a scant year after his beloved twin fell to his death, both his mother and older brother succumbed to a fever that decimated the townsfolk near their estate. How a young Daniel and even younger Ellie had been left to the "miserable mercy" of a grieving and inconsolable father.

A sire who hired a tutor and forbade Daniel the private school education every other boy of his rank experienced as his due. A sire who blamed a neighboring boy, one who grew to become his brother-in-law Lord Wylde, because he'd brought the fever from the village to the outlying estates.

A sire who punished every misspoken word.

A child who learned 'twas better to keep silent than risk inciting his father's wrath. Wrath that was sometimes visited on his innocent sister as well.

Just when Thea felt the bitter salt of welling tears, she recalled his stories of a loving and aged grandfather, father to his deceased mother, a man confined to a wheeled chair, eventually to a bed. A relative who'd expressed more than once his desire to raise Elizabeth and Daniel but who recognized his own limitations. So he'd done what he could, Daniel had told her, setting aside funds for both of them, encouraging whatever they'd shown an interest in. Inviting them for visits until their father discovered how ill the old man had become and put a stop to it.

A short time later, their treasured grandfather was gone too.

Daniel had shared how fighting—boxing—proved his salvation. The one place he could be surrounded by his peers and feel a part of the camaraderie. When he used his fists, he didn't have to say a word. He'd been liked, respected even, for his prowess. And with every punisher he'd received, he'd considered it deserved—paying the price for daring David to climb up after him...

He'd glossed over his childhood but she'd gleaned enough in the flat telling of what he revealed, in the stark look he couldn't hide, to discern what had been a disheartening existence. She'd learned of a young man escaping his father's restrictive rule the moment he was big enough to fight back, of how he'd set up his own home in London, his only regret the sister he couldn't lure to join him. A sister who by now was their father's caretaker as much as his prisoner.

As though commiserating with his master, Cyclops plopped his woebegone-expressive muzzle on her shoulder. Thea paused her racing thoughts to give a big scratch on his damp chin.

Words. There'd been so many. Hordes of them. Syllables —too many to count. The blessed, cherished sound of Lord Trem—of *Daniel's* voice, telling her so much of what she'd longed to hear.

"I remember now." She placed the empty glass on the night table and reached for his hand. "Tell me I didn't imagine it all."

"'T-tis all true." He nudged Cyclops aside and sat on the edge of her bed. "You fell asleep during the telling of it."

"I would never!" Drat her to Dartmoor, he finally opens up and she goes off to nod?

"You d-*did*."

Avoiding what looked suspiciously like a smirk to her, Thea reached behind her to plump the pillows. "Well. I am wide awake now and quite...um, delighted to have you in my room."

"D-delighted, eh?" The confident wretch laughed at her.

His duty done, Cyclops settled at the foot of the bed, tail occasionally giving a good *thump*.

"Aye! *Delighted*," Thea fairly snarled, plucking the fan from where the handle persisted in poking her posterior. She moved the latch and spread the spokes. Flicking her wrist, she attempted a flirty move. It came off agitated.

A blunt fingertip drew the fan away from her face. "Thea?"

Mayhap one in revealing nightwear was meant to entice, not avoid.

And that was another thing—she *finally* dons the night rail he gave her on the very night he wants only to *talk*?

"Oh, very well." She snapped it shut and met his gaze. "If you must know, I'm humiliated. How could I drift off when *you* finally turn up verbose? It's very poorly done of me!"

He pried the fan from her tense grip and brought her hand to his mouth where he bestowed several gentle kisses upon her knuckles. Only once the tension drained from her arm did he stop. "No more of that now. I d-did not mind. So you shall not either."

"But I—"

He bent his head and slipped her index finger into his mouth. And *suckled* it.

She felt the pull all the way down to her toes. His tongue swirled around the digit as the heat in his eyes became unbearable.

"All right!" Thea conceded with ill grace as her arm melted to cinders. "I'm allowed to fall asleep on you without *ever* feeling remorse. Now do please leave off before I turn to ash!"

Wearing a self-satisfied smile, he pulled her finger free, then carefully, thoroughly, dried it on his tight-fitting pantaloons.

"Wicked, are you," she breathed as she felt the hard muscles of his thigh flexing beneath her finger. "And even *more* wicked," she accused after he finished his task and pressed her fingers to his groin before relocating her hand to the mattress—inches away from his leg.

He only smiled, making no mention of his aroused state. Mayhap talking wasn't *all* he intended.

"Have you anything to ask me, b-b-before I proceed?"

"Proceed?"

"With what I came to tell you."

That sounded ominous. It also put to bed thoughts of things other than talking. "There's *more*?"

"Quite."

"Ummm," Thea stalled. The tingling from her arm had affected her tongue. "How long have you been in my room? Watching me sleep? Or should I say waiting for me to wake?"

He grinned, a boyish, carefree curve of lips that brought the laughter into his eyes, that dimple to his cheek. "Counted eleven whistles from that illustrious cuckoo clock d-down the hall."

She smiled back. "You've restored my faith in clocks."

"Me?"

"You and that particular design. No mean feat, I assure you. I'd quite come to hate the wretched things. But now I only find them *inspiring*."

"As well I know." Daniel inclined his head, what else he wanted—*needed*—to say burning a hole in his gut. "Anything else?"

If so, she'd better ask now because once he started with the rest, he doubted he could stop. His throat was as sore as a goose's golden-egg-laying arse. Knew he'd pay for it tomorrow, but he wouldn't be able to stop until the rest was out.

"Thea?" She looked so much more alert now, still sleep-flushed and inviting but more aware than she'd been the last time they'd spoken.

He shouldn't have been surprised, really. She'd been viciously attacked that morning and wide awake most of last night, vigorously making love. With her doing creative things and taking command of all the conversation; with him simply lying back and loving every second. By all accounts, he should be dead on his feet too, ready to climb under those covers with her and doze until daybreak but he was too worked up to relax.

"Is Grimmett still breathing?" Even as she asked, he saw her rub the finger he'd just bathed.

"Was the last time I saw him." *Crawling away like the coward he is.* "More's the pity."

In the hours he'd been there, rehearsing what was to come, Daniel reasoned against telling her the likely fate of her royally named rodents. That, thanks to Mrs. Freshley's appetite, in all probability he'd brought them over to his household as well. Parts of them, at least.

"After you left, I considered what you said." She left off staring at her finger to fix a worried gaze on him. "How can we be sure he won't assault others?"

"He won't."

"But you don't *know* that," Thea persisted.

"Oh, but I d-d-do." And because she kept looking at him, so trustingly yet quizzically, he explained what he'd intended to keep to himself. "Roskins' cousin is going to keep an eye on Grimmett."

"Why would he do that?" She sounded baffled.

"B-be-be*cause* he's a good man."

"And...?"

Daniel heaved a big sigh. Mouse tails aside, mayhap 'twas best not to keep any more secrets from Thea. "I offered to fund ap-p-prenticeships for his three boys and t-two girls. He works the docks—or did until his arm got crushed."

She grasped the ramifications immediately. "And now he's having trouble providing for his family?"

Daniel nodded. "B-but he's an intimidating hulk who can still use the left one to p-pound away if Grimmett crosses the line."

The admiration in her expressive eyes nearly brought Daniel to the blush. By the devil!

"Your brush," he blurted without any finesse, "was splintered ab-b-bominably."

Admiration faltered to dismay. "I know." She curved her arm through his and leaned into him until she rested along his side, head on his shoulder. "But it was sacrificed for a good cause. Mama would be pleased it cracked smashing such a sap-filled, rotten skull."

Despite the smile her words wrought, Daniel felt her loss. He pressed a soothing kiss to the top of her beautifully mussed hair. "I know I cannot simply buy you another to replace so special a keepsake from your mother. Jem and I think the halves can be glued together sufficiently for you to d-display it or tuck it away for safekeeping. They're clamped now and d-drying—"

She raised her head and stared at him with shining eyes. "You are the most marvelous man."

His face heated all over again. "Such p-praise."

"Well deserved."

And if they continued on this path, he'd have her frothy night rail banished to the floor and his body covering hers in seconds.

Though he was loath to put any distance between them, Daniel disengaged their arms and scooted down a foot. "Have you anything else to ask of me?"

His tone was brusque. He hoped she didn't take offense. Didn't—

"What's a munsons muffler?"

Of all the things she might have said... "Pardon?"

"Munsons muffler," she repeated as though he was *supposed* to know. "I heard it at Sarah's party when the men greeted you. The night we met."

Daniel cast about his brain. "Lord Munson? He and I sparred the d-day b-before. He got in a good punisher, a *muffler*, when he was faster than me." He shrugged. "That's the b-best I can figure."

"You really should learn how to hunker and block. Don't you have a Tremayne coat of arms? Painted on a shield you could use—?"

At the image of bringing a medieval shield into the ring, there he went, laughing again. Which was good. He had important things to say and laughing with Thea always seemed to loosen his throat.

Reluctantly, he stood. "Now p-pull on your wrapper and join me downstairs. If I have to see you in that b-bed one more minute, I'm liable to fall on you like a rabid d-dog and never get the rest out."

19

STARS & SCANDALS ~ MORE POETIC
THAN HE THOUGHT

---◆◇◆---

THE HOUSE WAS SETTLED and silent when Thea made her way toward the drawing room. While he'd lit a surprisingly large number of candles (judging by the glow that reached her well into the hallway), she'd tidied her appearance and done her best to suppress nervously flapping butterflies. What was so important he had to tell her in a more formal setting?

When she entered, Cyclops appeared enthralled with the scraps of beef and bone he noisily gnawed on near the banked hearth, and Daniel—

Her breath sighed out.

For when she glanced his way, Daniel stopped idly rubbing the ivory knob of his walking stick and set it aside. Standing, he waited for her to join him. So big and masculine, casually handsome, *so very appealing*, she feared her hard-won composure would soon crumble.

He'd removed his waistcoat and loosened his cravat. The ends hung loosely, exposing—

"What's that on your neck?" Shutting the door behind her, she went straight to him and peeled back his shirt. Angry red lines slashed across the curve of his shoulder, two and three at a time. She placed her fingers over the worst of the thin welts and met his gaze. "A new style of sparring?"

A rueful grin lifted his lips at both corners. "That's why Cyclops is here. We have more company at home. Feline company."

Her brow crinkled at his perplexing explanation. Feline company? What manner—

"Mrs. Freshley and her six kittens had moved in t-to your old room, t-tucked themselves nicely under that falling-over chest."

Mrs. *Freshley*? A mama cat had been in that den of despair? Which explained the soft cries she'd heard. A mama cat he'd named after her silly, childhood poem?

The ragged skin beneath her fingers burned hot. "And you *rescued* her?"

Would this man never cease to amaze her?

"With help." His big body shifted and she let her hand glide lightly over the scratches and fall to her side.

It was impossible to be this close to him and not touch, so she moved back. He'd asked her to come downstairs to tell her something. Something serious.

Something that took precedence over joining her in bed and finishing what his tongue had so flirtatiously started. Best she remembered that.

Oh heavens—she tensed at the unbidden idea—was he here to tell her goodbye?

"They're ensconced in an extra bedchamber until she quits trying t-to t-take a chunk out of everyone." It took Thea a second to realize he was still talking about cats—and not giving her the heave-ho back into the streets. "I'll relocate her Royal Scratchiness to the stab-b-*bles* once her kittens are old enough. Hopefully, she and Cy will come to an accord b-by then."

At his name, Cyclops abandoned the bone and shuffled over to deliver an impressive slobber on her slippers.

Rather bemused, totally befuddled—trying not to borrow trouble and worry over what hadn't occurred—she watched the spreading stain a second, then raised her gaze to Daniel's. The soft expression in his eyes laid her bare.

"I love you." Did that just fly from her lips?

Granted, she'd been thinking it since last night, since Mr. Taft unwittingly revealed the reasons for Daniel's ongoing reticence—in actuality, she'd thought it even before—but she shouldn't have *said* it.

He hasn't been reticent today, has he? Nay, he'd poured out his heart and she could do no less.

She took a single step toward him. "I do." A step back. Then another. Then her eyes fell to her salivated-upon slippers. How could she look at him after confessing such a thing?

Both Sarah and Susan had warned her against it. *Don't let your heart rule your head, it'll hurt more when it ends,* Susan had instructed. *And with the good ones, it* always *ends.*

But Thea couldn't avoid the truth. "Aye, I do. Love you, that is. But I shall..." And she could no longer avoid him, having to glance up as she finished, somehow the words easier to say to his startled gaze than to her spit-riddled shoes. "You're an incredible man, Daniel Tremayne, but let's forget I said that, shall we?"

"Never." The growl came just before he hauled her against him. "I'll never forget and you can nnn"—he exhaled near her ear—"*never* take it back."

"I can't?" *I don't want to.*

Still holding her tight, he whispered, "And it's Holbrook,

sweet Thea. D-Daniel Anthony Holb-b-*brook*. Tremayne's just the title."

Just the title, she thought on a hysterical giggle. "Aye, well, it's a mighty imposing title and a lovely and strong name."

"It should be yours t-too."

What? Stunned, she pulled back and stared at him.

"Holb-b— Dammit, Hol...brook." Though his jaw had clenched, his eyes, his hands bracketing her waist remained tender. "You. Thea *Holbrook*, not Hurwell."

"I— I—" *I ought to be poked in the eye for even remotely thinking you mean that.* "I think you've rescued one too many strays, Lord Tremayne," she said using his title, hoping it would put some distance between them. "We've— *They*'ve marched away with your wits."

His fingers tightened and he gave her a little shake, bringing her abdomen into contact with his upper thighs. "Strays?"

"Cyclops, Buttons and John." His deaf housekeeper and who knew how many others of his staff. "Your new batch of kittens. *Me*."

"Ah, but haven't you noticed how I *keep* any strays I care enough to bring home?" He skimmed his hands up from her waist to cup her cheeks, to stroke the sides of her face. "Thea. You...are...*not*..." In between every word, he pressed his lips to hers. "Just...a...passing...fancy...t-to...me."

After finishing that touching statement, he kissed her deeply, wielding his mouth and tongue like a weapon of sensual torment. His hands drifted to her shoulders, her back. They shaped her spine and derrière, lifted her to her toes and coiled her arms around his neck.

As the flames from his kiss licked deeper, lower, weaving throughout her body and sapping caution, her last coherent thought was: *So much for distance. I guess he truly isn't telling me goodbye.*

She grew lighthearted, light-headed at relief and lack of air, his powerful kiss stealing her breath.

Feeling him harden against her stomach, Thea moaned and arched closer.

With a ragged groan, he parted their lips. "Nay. Nnn-not yet." He swore, eased her to her feet, and then released her to step back. Putting unmistakable distance between them. Physical and otherwise.

Why?

"Sarah. Your friend," he said in a rigid tone, and Thea couldn't decipher the look on his face. "How invested is she in P-Penry?"

"Invested?" Disquiet over the feelings she'd just verbalized gave way to concern about Sarah. As she mulled the question, her fingers flew to her lips—damp and sensitive from the pressure of his mouth, it was a moment before she realized Cyclops had rested his muzzle on her slipper again.

Forcing her hand down, she curved it against her belly, hoping to quell the increased fluttering. His kiss—gracious, all of tonight—had knocked her askew. "I don't grasp your meaning."

"Sarah," he said again, jaw flexing. "I may be speaking out of t-turn, so please keep this to yourself for nn-now, but if P-P-*Penry* d-dissolves their association, will she suffer? B-be crushed? Or will she suffice?"

He gave consideration to a paid mistress? One that wasn't his own?

You, he'd said. *Thea Holbrook, not Hurwell.*

Numbness gripped Thea, disbelief still whirling about her brain. *Sarah! He's asking about your friend. Answer him.* "Um. Sarah. She'll be disappointed, of that I have no doubt. But crushed?" Her fist dug harder into her middle as she recalled what Sarah had said in the carriage: *He's paying for your services. It's naught but a business transaction.*

Her fist relaxed and she gave a quick shake of her head. "Nay. Sarah will manage. Though I know you wouldn't ask if there wasn't cause. You'll tell me, then, if you find Lord Penry means to end things? So I can prepare her?"

His sharp nod was decisive.

"Sarah knows she's naught but a paid whore, that we both—"

"Thea!" The snarl rumbled the floor beneath her feet.

"She told me 'twas so!" Thea defended, thinking how she needed the reminder, reality having set in after learning her friend's comfortable situation was likely coming to an end.

This was a temporary life she led; no doubt, she'd mistaken his words earlier.

"Thea. Wo...man!" The floor shook again as he drew out the syllables.

"You look furious."

"As well I should. I nn-never want to hear such a d-d-*derogatory term* cross your lips!" He advanced until he was inches from her face. "N-n-not ab-bout yourself or those you consider friends. D-do you hear me?"

Likely the whole neighborhood heard him.

Fully chastised by the vehemence he didn't attempt to suppress, she nodded. "Quite. A whore nevermore," she quipped, hoping for a smile.

She was rewarded with a twitch of his lips and decided that would serve.

"But now I have more to say." He breathed deeply. Then deeper still, and she had the distinct impression he was preparing himself for battle. "Say t-to you." His words had grown raspier, the planes of his face more chiseled. "May I cont-t-tinue?"

Knowing she'd best not interrupt but let him share what he needed with as few words as possible, she nodded. "Please."

"Yester-d-day at the committee meeting, I spoke in front of p-peers. *Spoke*, to a group of men doing nothing b-but sitting and listening—or staring at the wall. I'm not sure they wanted to b-be there any more than I. But d-don't you see, I'd always thought *that* was my greatest fear."

He paused and she realized he'd just confessed something profound. "Now you know it isn't? That you fear something more?"

Eyes stark but impossibly full of emotion, he said clearly, "'T-tis the thought of losing the chance t-to love you that b-br-brings me to my knees."

That was rather telling. Or was it? Was she only hearing what she wanted to?

You. Thea Holbrook, not Hurwell.

She didn't just feel dizzy and off-balance. Nay, she felt as though she inhabited the body—the life—of a stranger. Magical things didn't happen to her. Not since she was a child and Mama wove stories about fairy princesses and far-off castles. Castles with moats and princes and—

"Thea? D-don't swoon on me now."

He shook her upper arms and her feet landed with a thump, reality coming up hard in the form of the floor. In the form of one rapidly cooling foot thanks to the slavering attentions of Cyclops.

She was mistaken. 'Tis all.

He *wasn't* asking her to marry him. Wasn't—

"Oh, but I am, sweet Thea."

He was? And she'd said that out loud?

"What of your *family*?" It came out nearly screeched and she swallowed, tempered her tone. "Lord Wylde? Lord Penry and—"

She thought he muttered something less than complimentary about Lord Penry. But then louder and clearly, he told her, "Ellie's the only close relative I claim. She's b-beyond thrilled. Has, in fact, already b-b-*begun* planning the wedding."

The *wedding*? Theirs? "Naaaaayyy..."

"Doing horse imitations now, are we?"

Thea sputtered.

"Indeed. As for Wylde, his reputation is so tarnn-nished it's practically rust. D-did you sense d-disapproval from him the other night?"

"Not exactly." Was this her? Calmly discussing *this*? As if it were possible? "But he's quite indecipherable."

"Unlike my sister, eh?" He smiled, stroked his palms from her shoulders to her elbows. "Told me you were fetching. He'll b-be fine. As to anyone else, it matters not. I've learned to live my life in ways that p-pl-*please* me and those I care for. You're part of that small, growing number now."

As his conviction and sincerity started to build, and the magical, moat-surrounded castle receded to be replaced by the truth of what this wondrous man offered, her soggy slipper ceased to matter, toes started to warm...

"I wrote you a p-poem."

"But you hate poetry."

"And I adore you. Planned on t-telling you so when I came over, even b-before your d-declaration sang past my ears."

And there it went, wet toes abounded once again, her heart melting right back into her slipper. "D-Daniel."

His thumb caressed her inner arm as he smiled. "That's my pro-nn-*nun*ciation."

Their shared laughter didn't stop her from thinking she really ought to be the voice of reason. She pulled away. "'Tis a lovely sentiment but who knows if I can conceive?" The reality of that had to be faced. Wishing wouldn't make it so. "Years with Mr. Hurwell yielded naught. And that *is* the sole purpose of a peer's wife."

He was already shaking his head. "Ah, b-but you haven't given years with *me* a chance."

"Daniel!" He was making this so difficult. "The reality is you need a titled lady. *An equal*, to bear your heir and—"

He hushed her with his lips. "What—*who*—I nneed is you. No more blathering about equals. I'm more of a man with you than I ever was without. I trust the future will t-take care of itself—as long as ours is ent-t-twined. Now sit."

Feeling more than a bit out of sorts, she turned to Cyclops. "Do you let him talk to you that way?"

"Woof!"

"Thea."

"You growl more than your dog, do you know that?" The heated glare he sent her had her feet stumbling backward until she felt the edge of the desktop at her posterior. She hitched one side of her bottom on its surface. "There. I'm sitting. Are you sure you didn't fight someone today—other than Mrs. Freshley? Get clobbered on the head? Oh wait— you did!" *Grimmett had been that morning?*

He answered her banter seriously. "I'm d-done with fighting, Thea. I'll train Tom, maybe spar a b-bit a few times a year but no more weekly p-pummelings to prove I'm a man or p-punish myself for living when David didn't. You made me see that.

"Now I've worked on this p-poem and speech just for you. Do you want t-to hear it or not?"

"By all means. I can hardly breathe, I'm so bound with anticipation. But I can hear you going hoarse. I do believe you've talked more in the last hour than in all the time I've known you. Should you not rest? I can be patient." Oh, but 'twould surely send her out to sea.

He came up in front of her, the tendons in his strong neck flexing as he swallowed. "It cannot wait. *I* cannot wait."

The desk beneath her backside was as hard as his

whiskered jaw. She feathered her fingers over the beckoning bristle. "Daniel, what if you hurt yourself?"

"Will hurt more t-to keep quiet. Now hush and listen."

Her hand found its way to his chest, just over his hammering heart. "Rapt silence. I shall endeavor to give it to you until you ask for something else."

"Minx." He cleared his throat. Once. Twice. He backed up several paces and clasped his hands behind him. Then he began to speak with that same measured, purposeful quality she'd always found so appealing. "You asked me several questions once. I would like to answer them now.

"I spend my days thinking of you.

"Matters that concern me include fixing that damn orrery —which is finally done, thanks to you and my meddling sister. Getting a good night's sleep. Seeing Ellie made happy. And now you as well..."

As he spoke, answering all the items Thea had listed in that audacious letter, she realized she no longer noticed the stammer. The sound of his deep, so desired, voice glided past her ears without hesitation and went straight to her heart.

She grabbed the sharp edge of the desk and held on. Because with every word this man uttered, he swept her feet right out from under her.

"What do I like? How you viewed me as a whole man before I did myself. I was lost before you, Thea, like a little boy. But through you, I found my way home.

"Gads, I like so much about you—your patience, your smile. How you laugh at the absurd and have taught me to do the same.

"I adore your beautifully expressive eyes, how gentle and caring they are at times, brimming with inner fire at others. How they recall to mind things best recalled and have returned to me sweet memories of the past I'd forgotten before you came into my life.

"I love how you look at me when I talk to you, how calmly you wait, without ever hurrying me to rush my words.

"I love how you ask me to do naughty things to your bum and blush while saying it." (Which only made her face flame anew.)

"How you've opened my eyes—and lugs—to the pleasures to be found beyond my study.

"I could go on, and I will—another time."

She nodded when he paused, seemingly for her agreement. How much more could she take? Her heart was full to bursting.

"I dream of you. Have, I think, for a long while now, but it took meeting you to make me realize all I've been missing." Fearful of fainting on him, given all he now shared, she scooted back until she sat squarely on the desk, feet dangling, fingers still gripping the edge.

"And I had a devil of a time making this part out, but no, I'm definitely not married and have no children. Save for the ones I pray you'll give me. Or let me give you?" He winked. "It's a task I'm willing to work on with the utmost of diligence."

Thea's loins sweltered at that. Dazed, she tried to nod but only succeeded in wobbling in place.

"I've written you a poem."

The solemn way he spoke, the look in his eyes—and the fact that he'd mentioned it thrice now—told her that, clearly, this seemingly simple event was of no little significance. "Well then..." She unpried her fingers from the desk and extended her hand. "I'd be delighted to read it."

"Nay. Poetry is meant to be recited aloud." He paced forward until poised confidently at her knees. With broad hands to each, he widened them and stepped directly between. His face was stern but his eyes, they sparkled at her.

"Roses are red, my name is Daniel. Come be with me. Let's create a scandal."

"A scandal?" she whispered, flustered.

He jerked a nod, licked his lips and very deliberately said, "Now I *am* asking for something else, other than your silence, so feel at liberty to chatter away."

"What?" The question was a near silent sigh.

"Your hand. Your trust. Your life, meshed with mine. I'm asking you to marry me, Thea."

He really meant it! "And live merrily married forevermore?"

"Aye. Though you make light, I do not. 'Tis serious business, woman, talk of taking a mate. A willing leg shackle. Marry me, Thea," he coaxed, digging his thumbs into the tender flesh above her knees. "Love me. Mother my children."

She opened her mouth to protest again but he overrode her before a single sound emerged. "Before you worry overmuch, know that if we don't have our own, England is bursting with babes in need of loving homes."

"More strays?"

"More love."

A whirlwind of feeling pressed behind her rapidly blinking eyelids. She willed it to recede.

"*Family*, Thea." He said it with such strength, such convincing sincerity. "Ours. If you would but agree."

"I..." She gulped. Could she really do that to him? Condemn him and Lady Elizabeth to be ostracized, cast from the social strata that was their birthright? Just because he offered her the world?

For that's what marriage to a peer was—an impossible dream akin to a trip to the moon. *He loves you, Dorothea Jane. Loves you.* "I..."

"Thea," he leaned forward to breathe in her ear. "You're wavering. I can tell."

He pulled back to catch her gaze. "I know it's incredibly sudden, but I love you to the stars and beyond, and I need you to say yes. I need *you*."

The moon *and* the stars?

He hadn't just promised her the known world but the entire universe.

Her toes curled in slippers that suddenly went from damp to snuggly warm. She released her hold on the desk to loop her arms around his neck. "I will."

"Will...?"

"Marry you!" Thea catapulted off her precarious perch and into the haven of his arms. "Always! Always, you wonderful, marvelous man. It was the stars that did it. I rather fancy being loved to them."

"Not the deuced poem?" Though he tried for cranky, she could tell by the way he hugged her how very pleased she'd made him.

"That too." Then she was kissing him and he her, laughing and—

Thea sniffed.

Then sniffed again.

"Oh, look..." She blinked horridly fast and ran her sleeve across her nose. "You've turned me into a snoaching sniveler."

"And you've turned me into a wretched poet. Fine pair we make."

"Fine pair indeed."

The End

Thanks for reading *Mistress in the Making*. I adored Daniel and Thea from the moment I met them; I hope you did too. :)

These two characters have lived on in my heart more than others who have found their happily-ever-afters. Like Daniel, I sometimes have trouble speaking, only from a musculature standpoint not because of severe stuttering, and for an author who uses dictation software to write, that's frustrating on so many levels. I think I may relate to him more than other characters (so much more, that I think I've developed a crush—shhh! We'll not tell Thea or Mr. Lyons about that, all right?).

If you have a chance to write a review, sharing what you liked (or didn't :-0) it's always appreciated—and helps other readers know if a book might be a good fit for them. Reviews and word-of-mouth are two of the *best* things you can do for authors you enjoy.

Meanwhile, take peace in the quiet moments and speak up when you need to. ;)

And, if you aren't quite ready to leave Daniel and Thea and their world, you can meet *him* three years before the events in *Mistress in the Making* take place. Keep reading…

———◦———

What's Next?

Whoo-hoo! I'm glad you wondered, because I am thrilled to report that my Roaring Rogue Regency Shapeshifters are back! With book one, *Ensnared by Innocence*, available now!

Changing into a lion isn't all fur and games.

Turn the page for the blurb and first chapter, and get ready for some roaring fun times.

BLURB - ENSNARED BY INNOCENCE

Ensnared by Innocence

A Regency lord battles his inner beast while helping an innocent miss, never dreaming how he'll come to care for the chit—nor how being near his world will deliver danger right to her doorstep.

If Darcy had been a shape-shifting lion who thought about frisking—a lot...

Lady Francine Montfort may have led a sheltered life till her parents' untimely demise but that doesn't mean she's ignorant. Neither is she blind to the conniving ways of her persistent aunt, who's determined to marry Francine off for her own selfish gain. Forced to drastic measures to avoid the wretched woman's scheming, Francine concocts her own masterful plan.

She might need to beg a favor from Lord Blakely—the sinfully alluring marquis who inspires all manner of illicit thoughts—but she's determined to help him as well. To ease those mysterious, haunting secrets that torment him so...

When Lady Francine, the epitome of innocence, requests he pose as her betrothed, Blakely knows he should handily refuse. He's baffled when unfamiliar, protective urges make themselves known, tempting him to agree while danger stalks ever closer.

Alas, it's fast approaching the season when Blakely loses all control. Either Francine satisfies his sexual appetites or he'll be forced to reveal his beastly side. And that will never do. Not now that he's come to care for the intrepid miss.

STANDALONE ~ HEA ~ 80,000-WORD NOVEL ~ BOOK 1 - ROARING ROGUES REGENCY SHIFTERS

Note: This love story between two people contains some profanity and a lot of sizzle, including one partial ménage scene that gets rather...growly.

EXCERPT - ENSNARED BY INNOCENCE

Chapter 1
The Preposterous Proposition

———————◦◦———————

I leave this recordation for my beloved sons. Erasmus and Nash. My heirs. Who will one day, pray God, live to manhood and conduct themselves in a manner more gracious, more fitting to their station and responsibilities than I have managed.

My dear offspring who I cannot believe I condemned to such a fate, however unknowingly.

A fate I share but one that was not known to me until after you were both conceived. (And which also no doubt explains the sparsity of children in our family, and siblings for you both.)

The urges for The Change first came upon me in the summer of the year I turned five and twenty. It was not yet the middle of July and yet I sensed the stirrings of what I would eventually learn was my animal blood. My feline side, if you boys will only set aside skepticism and believe. Please, sons, heed my warnings, for you do not want to be caught unaware as I—and irreparably harm the woman you love.

To see the fear in her eyes when she looks upon you and beholds a monster. A beast. Your inner beast. The lion, untamable. Unstoppable.

Deadly?

I pray not. 'Tis why I locked myself away, in this, my 28th year, the third of the curse. Why I place armed guards at the door for the entirety of the month.

As I battle the inner demon once again, my only consolation is knowing that you both are still too young to remark upon my absence.

Too young to question why Papa turns into an ogre toward the end of the hot, sultry summer months.

Too young to recall how severely I injured your mother...

———◦○◦———

LONDON, ENGLAND
MAY 1812

"Lord Blakely, pardon the interruption. Might I beg a word with you?"

Erasmus Hammond, Marquis of Blakely, looked down his long patrician—scarred—nose at the intrepid female who dared interrupt the boisterous group of men he currently conversed with.

Delicate, feminine young ladies such as this one definitely did *not* mix with his oft-beastly ways. Not unless they wanted to be torn asunder.

He didn't recognize her, but judging from the looks his companions aimed her direction, they did. The meaning behind the smirks and elbow jabs was unmistakable, confound it.

Just what he didn't need—another wedding-minded miss setting her cap for him. Every Season he remained unmarried, it seemed his value on the marriage market escalated. Despite the air of libidinous rake he cultivated in public—and indulged in private—his attraction as an eligible mate only increased with each year that passed, as though snaring his dissolute self would be something of a coup. Hardly.

Where was her chaperone?

"Gracious me," he drawled as sarcastically as he could manage, "a bold little muff, are you not?" He gestured to his chortling companions, hoping the crude comment would be enough to send her heels flying. "Approaching *me*? Here?"

Here, at Lady Longford's crush, celebrating the engagement of one of her many offspring, the place teeming with too many people and too much perspiration, offensive odors he chronicled as easily as breathing. Odors he tolerated, along with the boorish twaddle that surrounded him, because unlike some others he could name—ahem, his brother for one—Blakely bore his responsibilities, took them very seriously indeed.

Yet, no sweat-drenched, unpalatable odors emanated from the brash one before him, he couldn't help but note. So she wasn't here to dance and make merry?

Dance and make a marriage, more like. Is that not the ultimate aim of every young chit here?

Blakely grunted at the thought, taking her in.

The very definition of English miss—blonde, blue-eyed and insipid—stood before him. Granted, she was a trifle taller than perfection allowed these days, and her face looked decidedly powdered—smelled powdered too, the pale artifice likely hiding all manner of spots, blemishes and daunting imperfections.

But when she shifted, allowing the shawl curved within the crooks of both arms to slide, he noticed the two-inch expanse of skin between the short, puffy sleeves of her gown and her long gloves. Two inches of implausibly dark skin, which forced his attention back to her face. Caused him to study...to linger. Beneath the powder, 'twas smooth as silk. At least that's how it appeared, making his fingers twitch with the sudden urge to test the observation.

So she wasn't hiding spots? Perchance only an unfashionable liking of the sun? As one who spent more time than he'd like in the dark, that alone piqued his interest.

"Please, my lord?" She scooted further around the column separating his small group from the dance floor. "I promise not to take but a few moments of your time." So earnest. Her voice so very serene, even as he scented her... What was it? Fear? Frustration? Apprehension that her asinine errand— approaching him, of all people—would prove unsuccessful?

Of course it would. It has to.

Trying again to discourage her, he glanced around the ballroom, purposely avoiding her gaze and employed his loftiest voice. "I do not believe we have been introduced and therefore, most regretfully, I cannot begin any manner of discourse with—"

"But we have," she had the audacity to interject. "It was three years ago at the Seftons' ball. We danced, but I have no expectation that you recollect the encounter."

He didn't.

And he knew she was shamming him. If they'd met, if he'd been near her for a dance, he'd remember her scent.

A remarkably fresh yet earthy fragrance that appealed to him on so many levels 'twas dangerous. Dangerous for them both.

She stood her ground and spoke calmly, despite their eavesdropping, snickering audience. Taller than most women, she came nearly to his chin. Hers was tilted at such an angle he suspected she must practice the determined stance in front of a mirror.

More than that, most fresh-faced elegants weren't bold enough to approach him directly, and he couldn't help but admire this one in spite of himself. He almost hated to crush her spirit but dissuade her he must. Innocents were not for him. Especially now.

It was nearing the time of year he had two choices: Either secret himself away and privately battle his demons. Or find the wildest women he could to exorcise away his fiendish tendencies through exhaustive, nightly rounds of intense prigging. Smashing choice, that. No wonder he always chose the second, more sociable option. Something he seriously doubted would appeal to this one.

"By all means, do forgive me," he stated, matching her tranquil tone. "But, alas, you are correct. I do not remember you." There was more jostling from his cohorts. They knew the type of female he preferred—and the kind he avoided at all costs. Though several years beyond the schoolroom, the flaxen-haired miss in front of him definitely fell into the latter category.

Even so, he was surprised how her poise drew him. And if he tipped his head...just so...

Ah, yes, he *could* look straight down the front of her pale blue gown, to furtively gaze at the womanly endowments not quite hidden beneath. Of course, he had no business looking at her dugs, none whatsoever.

"A *word*?" she insisted, angling her chin a fraction higher. "Consider it imperative."

Imperative? Intrigued despite his better judgment, he inclined his head in a show of assent.

'Twas odd, how her voice drew him, all calm assurance instead of the more heated, sultry tones he was used to hearing from his experienced lovers. Would she maintain that cultured, confident manner in the throes of passion?

What of it, man? She's not for you.

True. So very true.

Especially now, with his latest suspicions? With even more danger surrounding London than before...

Had he missed one? Failed to pick up on a potential wrong-side-of-the-blanket Hammond offspring? Had all the sacrifices, the years spent miring himself in the dungeons of the *ton*, seeking out the most dissolute, reckless individuals, praying they were only human—and nothing more sinister—been all for naught?

Shaking off the dread that accompanied him these days like a persistent and bothersome fly, he followed her a short distance further, away from the periphery of the crowded dance floor.

When she reached a secluded corner and stopped, he did as well. And found himself curious, if only remotely so, why she had approached *him* directly—and without a formal introduction. Totally unheard of in the upper realms of the *ton* he inhabited.

"Lord Blakely, I have a proposition I would like to put forth to you." For all her height and assured poise, she seemed dainty, almost fragile, standing before him.

"By all means, please do." His curiosity grew by the second. And so did the reluctant attraction running rampant through his veins. Which would never do.

Never! Do you not have sufficient responsibilities, man? Ferreting out who's destroying—

Blakely shook off the annoying reminder, the one that settled fear and concern heavily on his shoulders; far more pleasant to ponder the diverting package before him. "State your case," he encouraged in as droll a voice as he could culti-vate, "so I may rejoin my crew."

When she hesitated, glancing behind her, he took possession of the gloved hand nearest—which brought her attention swiftly back to him. He then lifted it to his lips and kissed the air over her fingers before releasing them. Instead of scaring her away as he'd intended, a blush flared up her chest and over her face, delighting him, which was patently ridiculous.

Blushes were for maidens; whores were for him.

So why was it that the tinge of pink flushing her cheeks fascinated? The slight color was difficult to discern beneath the powder and her unfashionably dark skin but he saw it clearly nevertheless. Unbidden, curiosity rose regarding the extent of her exposure to sunlight. Where might the golden hue leave off and pale porcelain begin?

And why do you care?

Aye, definitely time to curtail their conversation. "You were saying? A proposition, I believe. I weary of being here," he lied. "Speak in haste."

The pale blonde ringlets surrounding her face swayed as she took a fortifying breath, readying for battle. "I know I presume much, but I would be eternally grateful if you could see your way to posing as my betrothed until—"

He laughed outright at her outrageous request, drawing the attention of several guests. Sobering, Blakely stated, "Completely out of the question. But thank you for asking. I needed some amusement this evening."

When he turned to leave, her hand shot out, latching on to his arm with surprising strength. He halted and peered at her gloved fingers until she removed them. Damn if a bolt of *need* hadn't flashed through him at the contact. Astonishing, for he'd just dallied with the amorous and very accommodating Mistress Rose of the Crown & Cock not twenty-four hours before.

"Lord Blakely, please. Hear me out." She rushed on before

he could say yea or nay. "It would be a pretend betrothal, a farce if you will, lasting only a few weeks. Surely you can find it in your heart to assist me for such a short time? I will pay you handsomely for your trouble and release you publicly from our agreed-upon understanding after you fulfill its terms."

"We have no understanding," he felt compelled to remind her. "But for the sake of argument, your reasoning is faulty. How would this assist you in any way? For upon becoming affianced to me, not to mention later breaking said betrothal, your reputation would be tantamount to ruined."

"That has no consequence," she said rather convincingly. "I only want the *appearance* of a betrothal for the remainder of the Season."

Which only intrigued him further. What manner of eligible miss cared naught for her reputation? 'Twas a young female's only currency, all her real blunt controlled first by her father and then by her spouse. "And why is that?"

"My reasons are my own."

Stubborn chit. He half wished he couldn't see her so clearly in the candlelit ballroom. What was it about her that drew him?

The unspoilt scent of heather and fresh air? The sunshine she exudes? The hint of freedom from the chains that bind you to London as surely as if you were locked in Newgate.

"If you will not explain yourself, why should I even consider your ridiculous proposal?"

That willful chin lifted again. "Because I will pay you."

"Not enough, not for what you ask." She had no *idea* what she was asking, what being near her the next few weeks might cost him. Or her.

She proceeded to name an amount that sent his head spinning.

Good God. He'd just been propositioned by a bloody heiress.

To fight the deceptive allure she represented—because it wasn't called a *leg shackle* for nothing—he shifted his weight, tightened the muscles in his legs. "You are a piece of intriguing baggage, I'll grant you that. Why approach me and not some other titled gent in need of the ready and likely to agree?"

"Your standing as one of the most sought-after libertines in the *ton*," she stated baldly, her face flushing even more. "It suits my purposes quite well. And your title, for another reason. Not every marquis has a character such as yours."

"I do not know whether to be insulted or flattered." The inexplicable urge to touch her cheek stormed through him. Since when did he care about cheeks? He fisted his hands and anchored them firmly at his sides.

"I mean no offense, I assure you, but it is not in me to cavil at the truth. You and I both know that you have no intention of marrying this year, and I need someone of your...*ilk* to best ensure the successful outcome of my plan."

He made a noise in his throat, one that could indicate he was considering her asinine idea, which was absurd—because he wasn't. Neither was he convinced he wanted his *ilk*—well-suited to her asinine plan or not—to be what he was known for. Sought after for.

"I only ask that you show me the same courtesy and give me your honest reply posthaste." Again, she looked over her shoulder, as if expecting a dragon to swoop in and steal her away.

Come to think on it, he was surprised they had been left alone this long. "And what is your next course of action, should I turn down your oh-so-tempting offer?"

"Sarcasm does not become you, Lord Blakely," she admonished him.

"Do not talk down to me," he told her, instantly irritated with himself. With her. Why was he still wasting his breath conversing? Why not simply tell her nay and be done with it? Why did he long to touch so much more than her cheek? To see her hair down, her dress gone and her legs wrapped around his waist?

Damn it, where was his control? It seemed to have abandoned him the very moment *she* abandoned her good sense and approached him.

"Forgive me," she said contritely. "The stress of awaiting your reply has put me quite on edge."

"Which is understandable. Considering you have propositioned a man who has not the faintest clue who you are."

"Lady Francine Montfort, my lord." She sketched the briefest curtsy on record.

"Please continue, Lady Francine Montfort." He committed her name to memory; her scent he'd never forget—even if he tried. "When I refuse to be a part of your outlandish scheme, what will you do?"

"*When* you refuse?" She arched a single, chastising eyebrow.

How the hell an eyebrow lift could make him feel small only strengthened his resolve. *Say nay and be gone!*

"If you persist in claiming you have already decided"— she gave a prim little huff—"then there remains no further need to waste your time. Or mine. Good night."

This time it was his hand that halted her retreat.

She spun silently on slippered feet back to him. "Yes, my lord?" Her tone had turned icy.

Blakely released her at once, the tingles attacking his palm something of a surprise. "Humor me, then. *If*. If I decline. What is your plan?"

"Why, I will speak with the next person on my list. Perhaps *he* will be more agreeable."

Unaccountably, disappointment stirred in his chest. "Oh? So this is not an exclusive offer you make to me alone? I am only one in a long line?" *And no doubt farther down the list than your pride deems acceptable.* "Lady Francine Montfort," he continued, and it was an effort to maintain his droll façade, "I must confess I am crushed by the knowledge. Quite."

She looked over her shoulder again, distracted by whatever it was she sought. "If you must know..." Her gaze swung back to his. "You are my preferred choice and the first man I approached, but as you are determined to thwart my sincere overtures, I must move on. I beg of you, please do not speak of this to anyone. It—"

"I would not dream of it."

"Are you positive I cannot persuade you to at least consider my proposition? You have yet to hear my terms in their entirety and yet you are refusing me outright."

"There is more?" The entreaty in her sky-blue eyes was almost enough to convince him to reconsider. But then he saw past the appeal, to the innocence.

Pity. He didn't deal with innocents. Ever. Only those women already hardened by life's experiences, women who liked having their precious egos petted as much as they liked having their slits stroked. Women whose purses he was not averse to lining and who were willing to overlook his behavior, if, in the midst of things, he got a little rough. Certainly, his carnal appetites were too wild for the virtuous dainty before him.

Somewhat regretfully, he opened his mouth to decline.

"Frannnny!"

The screech interrupted him.

"How *dare* you!" An older woman charged at them from the side, brandishing her fan like a bayonet and casting him a glare as if he were Lucifer come to life. Which perhaps he was—for even considering corrupting her charge.

"Franny! You *evil* child!" Sky-high plum-colored feathers stuck out of a forest-green turban, agitating the air above her mottled face. Ire definitely did not sit pretty on this particular matron. "What *are* you doing, talking to *him*?" the woman hissed. Her voice carried like that of a general commanding his troops. More than one curious head turned toward their secluded corner. "Come away this instant!"

"But, Aunt," Lady Francine protested, casting him a commiserating glance. "Lord Blakely and I are only conver—"

"The Lord Blakelys of this world are most certainly *not* for the likes of you, gel. Now come along." A full head shorter and three times as wide as her niece, the harridan grasped Lady Francine's slim arm and tugged.

Pale-blue eyes gazed at him as she silently succumbed to the forced retreat. Just before she disappeared from view, her mouth formed the words, *The garden?*

And he, purveyor of pleasure and avoider of innocents, found himself nodding in assent.

Damn his hide.

Ensnared by Innocence - Read it today!

ABOUT LARISSA
HUMOR. HEARTFELT EMOTION. & HUNKS.

Larissa writes steamy regencies and sexy contemporaries, blending heartfelt emotion with doses of laugh-out-loud humor. Her heroes are strong men with a weakness for the right woman.

Avoiding housework one word at a time (thanks in part to her super-helpful herd of cats >^..^<), Larissa adores brownies, James Bond, and her husband. She's been a clown, a tax analyst, and a pig castrator(!) but nothing satisfies quite like seeing the entertaining voices in her head come to life on the page.

Writing around some health challenges and computer limitations, it's a while between releases, but stick with her...she's working on the next one.

Learn more at LarissaLyons.com.

- amazon.com/author/larissalyons
- bookbub.com/authors/larissa-lyons
- goodreads.com/larissalyons
- facebook.com/AuthorLarissaLyons
- instagram.com/larissa_lyons_author